Time Terror:
Defending Jesus

PK Mags

NEWMAN SPRINGS PUBLISHING
320 Broad Street
Red Bank, NJ 07701

First originally published by Newman Springs Publishing 2023

ISBN 979-8-88763-319-0 (Paperback)
ISBN 979-8-88763-320-6 (Digital)

Printed in the United States of America

To my mom

CHAPTER 1

Ahmed Faquor held his nine-millimeter Glock against the small of the back of his nephew's girlfriend. Ahmed was a cold-blooded killer and terrorist mastermind. As he threatened the young woman, he thought what a disgrace his nephew was to the family and the faith for living with this infidel. Allah himself probably did not know how many men had slept with this American woman.

"Remember, Kumar, be calm and get me inside the lab, and everything will be fine," Ahmed said to his nephew, who was standing in front of the security camera.

The three individuals stood in the back of a closed auto parts store in Langley Shopping Center in McLean, Virginia. To the outsider, it would be impossible to know fifty feet below this out-of-business retail store, which had specialized in parts for vehicles built before 1990, was the most secretive scientific lab in the world. The US government was hiding it in plain sight. One would think a lab holding this important of a secret would be behind a fifty-foot fence and have fifty armed troops guarding the perimeter 24-7. Instead, this lab was five stories below an old auto parts store, with one guard manning several video feeds and one elevator.

"Hey, Stan. It's me, Kumar. I need you to buzz me in, or I'm screwed," Kumar Faquor said into the security camera.

Kumar was only thinking of his crazed uncle with a gun pressed into his girlfriend's back. Kumar concluded the barrel of the pistol rested just above her lower-back tattoo of an eagle. Julia Martin was the first woman he had ever loved, and she loved him back. Julia was tall, blond, and sexy. She was not a Muslim, but really, neither was he. Except for his father's brother, Ahmed, his family no longer practiced the faith. Kumar was a brilliant physicist. Kumar had received his BS and PhD from MIT just five years ago. He had worked his way into the most important project on earth. He loved his research. The work he and his fellow scientists were performing would change humanity, and now his insane uncle was about to ruin his career and his life.

"Are you kidding me?" Stan Garrett said. Stan's fifty-three-year-old body had seen better days. He was sitting five stories below, behind a metal desk, and eyeing several video monitors. The former DC Metro cop did not want to lose his job or his page in his Tom Clancy novel. Stan could only see Kumar's skinny face and his John Lennon glasses on the monitor. Kumar was sweating and looked like a wreck.

"Stan, please. Be Stan the man. I left my cell phone on my desk. I must finish up a report tonight, and I need my phone to access the revolving passcodes," Kumar was pleading. "Otherwise, I can't retrieve my notes and complete the report. Dr. Stevenson is going to have my ass tomorrow. And you know how she likes to bust balls."

Stan knew firsthand how Dr. Victoria Stevenson could bust balls. He had worked the night shift for over four years since calling it quits as a patrolman for the DC Metro Police Department. He saw her at least five days a week, and she had never learned his name. She would just bitch at him about nonsensical things. She would chastise him if his black tie was too loose or his shirt had a stain. How did those things affect his staring at monitors all night? It was not unheard of for some researchers to return after hours to retrieve a forgotten personal item. Besides, he liked Kumar. He was pleasant, always said "Hello" and "Good night," and at least he knew Stan's name.

"Hold on. I gotta get up," said Stan. The pudgy security officer trudged over to the control panel on the wall and entered the code to open the elevator for the scientist.

Ahmed used the opportunity to force the woman and his naive nephew into the small elevator hidden behind a dusty display of

2

vintage floor mats. Ahmed positioned himself behind the woman, his gun on her back. Kumar stood closest to the elevator door as it descended.

Julia wondered how she had arrived at this point in her life. Kumar was a nice-enough guy, and she did care for him. He worked hard, and he was very serious about life. Besides, the guys she normally dated were pretty boys or married men twenty years her senior. Kumar was skinny and clueless in the bedroom, but he was affectionate and made her laugh at his self-deprecating jokes. Kumar being sweet or not, his crazed uncle had a gun stuck in her back, and that was Kumar's fault. Julia's mind was racing. How was she going to survive this situation? Julia was telling herself, *Think, think, think!*

When the elevator doors slid open, Ahmed could see the clean white walls, the commercial-grade gray carpet, and a chubby security guard with a coffee stain on his wrinkled white shirt. The guard was armed, but his pistol rested in the holster. As the trio exited the elevator, Ahmed noticed the guard's facial expression changed from annoyance to confusion. As he forced Kumar and the woman forward, Ahmed knew this was going to be easy. The guard was only five feet away. Ahmed shifted the gun from the woman's back and pointed it at the guard's face. He pulled the trigger, and the guard's head exploded. The single shot splattered blood and brain matter on the wall. The guard's limp body fell backward. Kumar fell to his knees screaming, and the woman shrieked in horror. Ahmed reached into his pocket, grabbed a walkie-talkie, and began shouting instructions.

"Now! Move now! Go to the back of the store. There is an elevator in the back." Ahmed ended the transmission and smiled. He had just entered the most important scientific lab in the world, and he had killed his first infidel of the night. He was unsure how many more he would kill to complete his mission. But he knew he had at least one more person to kill. That death would change everything.

Behind the store, sitting in a Ford passenger van, were eight jihadists. When Ahmed's voice began barking commands through the walkie-talkie, the men sprang to action. They collected their cache of weapons, gathered their supplies, and ran into the store.

When the eight radical Muslims entered the underground facility, they saw Ahmed's nephew frantically working on a computer, a woman lying flat on her stomach with her hands interlocked behind her head, and a dead body.

"Allahu Akbar!" Ahmed rejoiced when he saw his Muslim brothers.

*****

Miguel Sanchez kicked the sheets and punched his pillow as he wondered if he was making the right decision. Correction. Were they making the right decision? He could not sleep, and it resulted from the choice they had made earlier in the day.

Miguel made life-and-death decisions often. Miguel was a leader of a CIA Special Operations Group (SOG) unit. He commanded a six-man team of elite warriors. Miguel was twenty-seven years old and excelled as a fighter and a leader of men. After graduating from the US Naval Academy, Miguel moved up the ranks and qualified as a SEAL and served two tours in Iraq. At age twenty-five, he was the youngest lieutenant commander on the teams. His exceptionalism in battle and ability to motivate his men drew the attention of the higher-ups. They asked Miguel to serve his country as a CIA special operator. After a lengthy conversation with his wife, Beca; a lot of prayer, mostly by Beca; and a thorough list of the pros and cons, Miguel said yes to the CIA.

That was two years ago, and he never regretted the choice. Beca never regretted it either. She knew it was what God wanted. She had prayed so much when they were trying to decide what he should do. Miguel had prayed with her. However, despite being raised Catholic, he was going through the motions. Beca was the true believer, not him, and she was certain his work for the CIA was for the best. Miguel found his work exciting, fulfilling, and he knew he was helping to defend his country. His work was secretive. Beca and his family knew very little about his role with the CIA. He could never tell them what he did or how he did it. The CIA said keeping secrets was for the best, and deep down inside, he knew it. There were just things the average American was better off not knowing. If Americans could go to church, a temple, or their mosque and as long as they could work and live in freedom, did they need to know how that was accomplished? No. They were better off going about their lives as usual and let warriors like Miguel and his team do what needed to be done in the shadows.

This recent decision he and Beca had made was wreaking havoc with his brain. In Iraq and on the field with his SOG team, he had to make calls that determined if people lived or died. Those decisions had to be made in the blink of an eye. There was no time to weigh all the options. He had to decide.

However, for the first time, he was second-guessing himself. That was bad. Confidence and commitment were key attributes for him to be an effective leader. Was he ready for this? Would he be okay? Could he handle the situation? Miguel was not thinking of himself, but of his six-month-old son, Robert Jesus, RJ.

Beca was the religion teacher at St. Jerome Academy. SJA was a Catholic K–8 school in Hyattsville, Maryland. The school was only a few miles from their home. Beca loved the school. She loved the kids, the staff, and she even loved the parents. Beca loved teaching young people about the faith. She was destined to be a religion teacher. As part of Christmas Eve mass, using the Gospel of Luke, the school-children performed a nativity play that told the story of the birth of Jesus. The school asked Beca if RJ could play the role of baby Jesus. Beca was thrilled and honored. Miguel and Beca had said yes. But now, Miguel was debating if they had made the right call. RJ was active and fidgety. Could the eighth-grade girl playing Mary handle him? What if she dropped him? What if he cried? Christmas Eve was in three days, and Miguel was having second thoughts. Beca was excited about RJ playing baby Jesus and was confident the play would be a success. But that was typical Beca, faithful that everything would be fine.

Six years ago, Beca Sanchez was Beca McCarthy, an Irish Catholic girl from New Jersey, when she met a senior at the United States Naval Academy. Beca was a senior at Loyola of Maryland when she and a group of girlfriends hit the bar scene one Saturday night on

Fells Point in the Inner Harbor of Baltimore. The ladies were dressed to entice and impress any males they met that night, but Beca was not "that type of girl." She had gone to Catholic school her whole life, had conservative parents and four older brothers who all played football. She had never been that type of girl. Still, this theology major and education minor was wearing a tight black skirt, a low-cut red blouse, and heels. She and her group of gal pals made their way into the bar. Beca was not a vain person, but even she would admit that with this outfit, her athletic build, and soft brown hair, she looked great.

The bar had a dance floor, which was dominated by other college women and two very drunk college boys doing their best Q-tip dance moves. After a few quick rounds of hard lemonades, the ladies from Loyola claimed their own spot on the dance floor. Out of the corner of her eye, Beca caught a young man checking her out. That was not unusual. It was the point of them all dancing in the first place. As the night progressed, the young man made his way over to Beca and her friends. The ladies had given up their spot on the dance floor to more drunk college students. Beca and her friends were huddled around a table and enjoying their night out.

"Hi. I'm Miguel. Are you having fun tonight?" the very confident young man asked. Beca thought his looks and poise were attractive. Miguel was about six feet tall and lean. He looked like he could do about a thousand pushups without breaking a sweat. However, he was not a muscle head.

"Sure. My friends and I are having a great time hanging out together." Beca liked her answer. She believed it set the ground rules. Her response said, "I am part of a group, and I am already having fun without some random boy hitting on me."

Miguel was sharp, and he picked up on the ground rules himself. They talked for a while. He was intelligent, interesting, made her laugh, and he was cool to her friends. They made plans to have coffee at Starbucks in a few days. Her parents were enthused when Beca first said she was dating a future naval officer who was Catholic. Her four older brothers were less enthusiastic when they discovered their baby sister's suitor was a trained killer who could take down any of them in under five seconds. However, they were impressed when they learned Miguel played football for Navy and even scored a touchdown against their beloved Fighting Irish. Eventually, the two fell in love, got married, and had a baby.

*****

Seven of the eight jihadists from the van were now preparing the pod for what Kumar called a launch. None of the seven knew how it was all going to happen. They just knew they were going on a mission to destroy Christianity. Ahmed, this devoted group's leader, had promised them they would gain incredible favor with Allah. Allah would welcome them into paradise as martyred heroes. These men hated all nonbelievers, the West, and especially America. So while Ahmed's nephew worked feverishly on a computer and the American woman was prone on the floor, they stored their weapons and gear in the pod. The pod was about ten feet by thirty feet and looked like a plane with no wings.

Outside the pod, Kumar was using all his knowledge, expertise, and intelligence to make sure the coordinates and calculations were correct.

"It is not that simple, Uncle," said Kumar. The pistol was still pointed at him. "If I make a mistake, you end up in Africa in the year 550 or fifty million years ago with dinosaurs or in Cincinnati in 1912. Do you want that?"

"You know what I want! I told you what I want! Now do it right, or you both die!" said Ahmed to his trembling nephew.

Omar laughed when he heard Ahmed's "Or you both die!" Omar knew Ahmed's plan. He was the one to carry out the plan. Omar pointed his Glock at the Western woman on the ground. She was only fifteen feet from Kumar and Ahmed. She must have heard the threat and Omar's laugh. Omar noticed she was no longer crying. She seemed, to Omar, resigned to her fate. Ahmed's instructions to Omar were simple. After Ahmed and his seven Muslim brothers departed on their journey, Omar was to kill the woman first. He was to point Kumar toward Mecca, make him pray, and then execute

Kumar with a bullet to the back of the head. Ahmed hoped by praying that perhaps Allah would spare his nephew if he perished while honoring him.

Omar was the obvious choice to leave behind for this assignment. He was over fifty years old, had no military or technical training, and was obese. He did not eat pork, but the Koran said nothing about Krispy Kreme donuts being dirty. Ahmed knew Omar would be of no value on their mission. But even Omar could shoot two people in the back of the head, set the building on fire, and then drive a van back to Paterson, New Jersey.

However, Omar had his own plans. He was content to shoot infidels, start a fire, and miss the journey with his radical brothers. Omar was a pig, and he knew it. He was poorly educated, abused women, and enjoyed the street credit he got for being considered a radical. Omar would brag to the teenage boys on Derrom Avenue in Paterson about how the FBI had a file on him. Omar enjoyed acting like a tough guy and allowing the rumor to spread that he had connections with al-Qaeda. In truth, the Feds did not know Omar even existed.

The self-proclaimed terrorist had not been in a fight since elementary school. On that day in third grade, a second-grader named Ronnie Washington kicked his ass. Omar had been trying to impress a girl and tried to show off by forcing Ronnie to give up his Hostess cupcakes. Ronnie was not one to be messed with during lunch. After landing a right on Omar's sizable gut, he knocked out two of Omar's teeth with a right cross. So much for being a tough guy. Since then, Omar had relied on talking tough, spreading rumors about himself, and either paying for sex or just trying to grope and molest women when he could. Omar planned on killing the woman and Kumar, and setting the place ablaze, but in his own way. He would shoot Kumar, rape and then kill the woman, and finally set the place on fire before hightailing it back home to New Jersey. Ahmed would never know, and besides, to Omar, this Western woman was asking for it by wearing yoga pants and a tight T-shirt when she was kidnapped.

*****

Father Patrick O'Connor was the youngest professor on the Pontifical Faculty of the Immaculate Conception at the Dominican House of Studies in Washington, DC. For over a hundred years, the House of Studies had been educating seminarians in the tradition of Saint Dominic de Guzman and Saint Thomas Aquinas. Father Patrick was only thirty-three years old. As he tried to fall asleep in his room in the priory, he could not help but be proud of himself. He had come a long way from his working-class home in Worcester, Massachusetts. His loving parents, Richard and Mary O'Connor, raised him in a very stereotypical Irish Catholic family. He was one of seven children, and they were all brought up the same way: they went to Mass on Sunday, were educated at Our Liberty of the Angels Elementary and then St. Paul High School, and they rooted for the Red Sox, Patriots, and Celtics. Life was simple.

Patrick had never thought about becoming a priest and a scholar because he assumed he would be the next Nomar Garciaparra, Tom Brady, or Paul Pierce. He accepted an academic scholarship to Providence College, a Dominican college, in Providence, Rhode Island. Patrick saw his faith grow as a student.

Patrick reflected on his time at Providence College. He loved the awesome times he and his buddies had at the hoops and hockey games while cheering on the Friars. Patrick learned a lot from his short stint in the ROTC program. He took away a respect for the military and the men and women who served our nation. It just was not for him. He had a different calling. Life was about his faith, and of course, he was a theology major, and he loved history and the classics. He was engrossed with the historical facts and significance of the Bible. Patrick decided to become a priest, and after graduation, he entered the seminary.

Patrick took his holy orders and became Father Patrick. He continued his studies and earned his PhD from the Pontifical University of Saint Thomas Aquinas in Rome. Father Patrick was a renowned scholar and academic. He spoke several languages and could read and write in a half a dozen more. He was an expert in the history of the New Testament, and he had traveled throughout the Holy Land. Few people in the Western world knew more about the historical significance of the Bible than he did. To put it simply, Father Patrick was a brilliant man.

Yet in all his wisdom and intelligence, he still longed to serve the Lord. He wondered when his time would come to have an impact on the church and its faithful.

CHAPTER 2

The calculations were perfect. The coordinates were exact. Kumar only had to press the launch key. Ahmed and the seven men were all securely strapped into the pod. The pod rested on the launching pad in the center of the giant room. Kumar, Julia, and Omar were positioned behind a plexiglass guard that shielded them and the computer terminal about fifty feet from the launch area. Kumar had explained the plexiglass was really for show since there was nothing they needed protection from. This was unlike standing too close to a rocket launch or a plane taking off. Julia was down on her knees, fingers locked behind her head, while Omar pointed the pistol at the frightened and nervous Kumar. Finally, as the tension grew, Omar roared.

"Just hit the fucking button!"

Kumar hit the launch key, and for a moment, life stopped. It was silent in the room for just a second or two. Then it started. Slowly it began as a low rumble, and it grew. The noise coming from the pod was the sound of metal rattling. Louder and louder it became until the noise was not just emitting from the pod; it was everywhere. It occupied, controlled, and dominated the entire room. The sound was in each person's head. It was becoming so intense it was as if it were in each person's soul. Kumar was kneeling and crying out in pain. Julia moved her hands from behind her head to cover her ears from the bone-shaking sound. Omar was trying to maintain his grip on his pistol while his body battled the roar that surrounded him. The cacophony was now deafening. It seemed the entire world was shak-

11

ing and then…poof! The pod was gone! The head-splitting sound was over. The launchpad was clear, and the room was silent. At that moment, Kumar, Julia, and Omar had forgotten their roles as hostages and terrorist. They were three people in disbelief. Kumar could not believe he had programmed the pod and successfully launched it by himself. The scientific team orchestrated many launches, but the experience was never this extraordinary. Kumar conducted the entire procedure on his own. It was the first solo operation. Oddly, despite being kidnapped by his uncle and having Julia's life and his life threatened, he was proud of himself. "Take that, Dr. Stevenson," he said.

Julia could not comprehend what just happened. There was a ten-foot-by-thirty-foot vehicle in the room five seconds ago and now it was gone. Where did it go? This made no sense to Julia. Things simply did not disappear. Omar looked bewildered. Was that real? The silence was eerie between the three of them.

Julia broke the quietness. "What just happened? What happened to that thing?"

"They are gone," Kumar said with a sound of achievement in his voice.

"Gone where?"

"Yeah. Gone where?" asked Omar.

Kumar gained a feeling of confidence that was not there before. Despite the betrayal of his father's brother, the terroristic threats, and the chaos of the evening, Kumar felt gratified.

"I sent them back in time," said Kumar. "I sent my uncle and those men back to Bethlehem at the time of Christ's birth. That's right. I did the calculations and set the coordinates. I sent them back to two thousand years ago."

"That's not possible," said Julia.

Kumar was now in his element. He had forgotten about Omar and the threat on his life. He was the smartest person in the room, for sure, and possibly the planet too. Kumar had conducted a solo workup and execution of a launch. Kumar was prepared to show off his brilliance. "It's all physics and the correlation with the stars to determine the exact data that is required. Albert Einstein once said—"

Kumar never finished his sentence. Omar regained his focus, pointed his pistol at Kumar, and blew his head off. *Let's see how smart he is with his brains on the wall,* thought Omar.

Omar quickly retook control of the situation and ordered the infidel woman to her feet and demanded she bend over the nearby computer terminal. "It's party time for us before I burn this place and everything in it!" Omar dropped his pants with his left hand while holding the Glock in his right.

Strangely, a calm came over Julia. In the ninety minutes since she was kidnapped, Julia saw a security guard executed, learned time travel was real, and witnessed her boyfriend get his skull blown apart. Somehow, the threat of being raped did not shock her. Julia did as Omar commanded her as she thought of her next move. Sandra Bullock! Yes, Sandra Bullock! *Miss Congeniality,* the Sandra Bullock movie from 2000, came to her. She saw the movie last year on cable TV. In the movie, Sandra Bullock was an FBI agent posing as a beauty-pageant contestant. Sandra's talent was a self-defense lesson for women. SING! Solar plex. Instep. Nose. Groin. SING! Julia knew what to do, and she would take down this piece of shit herself.

While bent over the desk, Julia made two fists and waited for Omar to approach her. She could sense him moving in behind her. Julia felt his left hand on her left hip. She gathered every ounce of strength she had and put it into her right arm. She blasted her right elbow into Omar's fat stomach! He doubled over in pain, but he grabbed onto her hip even harder. Julia quickly raised her right foot as high as she could and forced it down onto Omar's right ankle. He was now down on his right knee and yelling in pain. Julia mustered her strength again and planted her left elbow into Omar's nose. She heard the crack of bone and blood shoot from the front of his face. Omar was now down on his back. His gun had fallen to his side. Julia fought the urge to dive for the gun, so instead, she recalled her days in recreation-league soccer. She kicked Omar in the groin with everything she had! He screamed in pain as he instinctively reached for his family jewels with both hands. Julia reached over and grabbed the gun. Omar regained some control of himself and finally stopped screaming in pain.

"You bitch!"

Omar steadied himself and looked at Julia. She had both hands on the Glock, and her hands were shaking. Omar was lying on his back and was about five feet away from Julia as she stood over him. Omar gathered himself and slowly moved toward her. Julia had never held a gun before, but she had seen plenty of action movies and cop shows on TV. Besides, she was an American. It was her God-given right to bear arms. She could handle this. Omar looked Julia in her eyes and smiled.

He stood. "What are you going to do now? You little bit—"

Julia emptied the remaining fourteen rounds of the clip into Omar's chest and stomach.

"Nobody calls me that."

CHAPTER 3

She got the phone call and could not believe it. No way this was really happening. Dr. Victoria Stevenson ran the lab hidden beneath the Langley Shopping Center. She was a visionary. Her intellect was unparalleled, and few minds on the planet could match her brilliance in physics and exploratory science. Dr. Stevenson was sixty-two years old. She had never been married to anything other than her pursuit of scientific discovery. Stevenson had PhDs and advanced degrees from Stanford, MIT, and Oxford. After Julia Martin had called 911 from a phone on a desk in the lab and begged for help, the emergency dispatcher sent a Fairfax County Police Department cruiser to the scene. The 911 operator then looked up the emergency contact information on file with the county for Heritage Auto Parts. Stevenson was listed as the emergency contact for the defunct retailer at the local strip mall. Based on the county information, she was the world's best-educated auto parts store manager. At 12:04 a.m., Dr. Stevenson received the call she never dreamed could happen. Her lab was exposed.

As Dr. Stevenson's 2019 BMW 330i was pushing eighty-five miles per hour down Westermoreland Street, she called Ben Wakefield. Wakefield was the deputy director of science and technology for the Central Intelligence Agency. He was a seasoned veteran of the CIA and a no-nonsense guy. Ben had been sleeping on the couch while *The Equalizer* played on TNT. He had immediately jumped off his sectional and answered the phone that should not be ringing at midnight.

"Ben. It's Victoria. The lab is exposed! The police called me. A murder, an attempted rape, and I don't know what else. Some girl called 911 from inside the lab. Inside the lab! That's all I know. I will be there in less than three minutes," stated a frenzied Dr. Stevenson.

"What are you talking about?" he said. "How is that possible?"

"All I know is what I just said. I will see you there." Stevenson ended the call as her speedometer hit ninety miles per hour on a residential street.

"Man, the CIA could use some guys like Denzel Washington," Wakefield said to his empty family room.

Dr. Victoria Stevenson felt like crying and hitting something at that same time. The strip-mall parking lot had multiple police cars in it, and yellow police tape was up and around the entrance to the store. She quickly explained her way past the patrolman at the entrance, and she took the formerly secret elevator down to the lab.

Chaos, confusion, and an ugly crime scene greeted Stevenson when the elevator doors opened. Immediately, she saw the body of the night security guard lying dead on the floor. Most of his face was missing. She thought his name was Stan, or maybe it was Scott. She was not sure. Did it matter anymore? Her eyes surveyed the lab, her lab. She saw police officers milling about, looking at things, touching things with their gloved hands, and taking pictures with a county-issued police camera. She saw a young woman sitting at a desk, visibly shaken, speaking to a detective. Stevenson looked at the launch area and screamed. The pod was gone.

Every person in the large room froze as Dr. Stevenson's shriek pierced the air. Every head turned and stared at the woman in pajamas with her gray hair tied in a bun. Her face was as red as a firecracker, and she was just as volatile. She lost control and was yelling at the top of her lungs.

"Everybody out! Out! Out! None of you are authorized to be here!"

Detective Vince Razetti of the Fairfax County PD stopped talking to Julia, turned, and approached the woman in the pajamas. Razetti was lean, tall, and looked every bit of his Sicilian ancestry. He had served on the force for over ten years and was the lead detective in this new and perplexing case. Razetti had been told the contact person for the auto parts retailer was a woman named Victoria Stevenson and dispatch had called her.

"Ms. Stevenson, I'm Detective Razetti of the Fairfax County PD." Razetti spoke in an even and monotone voice. "May we go into an office to chat?"

"First, it is Dr. Stevenson. You and your people need to vacate this location this second."

Razetti closed his eyes for a moment, took a deep breath, and exhaled. This would not be easy. Razetti had a crime scene with three dead bodies and a woman who was a witness, victim, and maybe even a perpetrator. He had an openly hostile older woman who obviously did not want to explain the reason for a science lab buried fifty feet below a cheesy auto parts store. The detective contemplated his next move. Things got more complicated when a dozen men in suits arrived. The suits were clearly federal agents, and Razetti knew his night just got a lot worse.

Ben Wakefield was a thirty-year veteran of the CIA and had spent the last ten as the deputy director of science and technology. He was not a tall man, and his gray buzz cut never quite fit with the suits he wore. Ben was burly and wide and looked like a guy who could handle himself. He recruited Dr. Victoria Stevenson eight years ago when her research came under the wing of the CIA. Wakefield was not always on the management side of the CIA. Wakefield had been in the field, spent some time on SOG, and was an operative. He had done things in Africa and in Bosnia he was not proud of. But he did what needed to be done to close the assignment and protect the overall good. Wakefield now stood in the middle of a crime scene with a dozen CIA officers at his command.

The Fairfax County detective instantly recognized there was a new alpha dog in the room, and they needed to talk. Razetti made eye contact with Wakefield and, without words, agreed they should speak in private with Dr. Stevenson. The three of them moved into Stevenson's office right after Razetti called out an order to his patrolmen. "Everybody just chill for a few minutes. Stop what you are doing. Julia, please stay seated, and I will be back in a few minutes."

Stevenson's office was just down the hall and was so plain and generic inside it looked like a staged office display at a Staples store. Gray carpeting, off-white-painted walls, and a bland metal desk that had two equally boring chairs in front of it made up the entire office. A few diplomas and certifications of degrees hung on the walls, but there was not one photo of a spouse, family member, friend, or even a pet anywhere to be found. Knowing what Stevenson was like and assuming Razetti was in over his head, Wakefield took control of the private discussion.

"Detective Razetti, I presume." Wakefield shook hands with the local lawman. "I am Ben Wakefield. Let's just say I am from the government. I will be as honest as I can. Time is critical right now."

"That's saying something," Stevenson muttered under her breath. Wakefield shot her a stern look to silence her.

Wakefield continued, "Detective, you are an investigator, and I'm confident you have already surmised this…location is a bit of a secret. I can assure you we are not making chemical weapons, meth, or child porn here. It is important government work and needs to stay a secret. Can we count on your discretion?"

"I know I am just a county detective, but I've got three dead bodies and half a dozen police officers trying to work a crime scene. I'm all for being a team player, but I can't just say 'Nothing to see here' and tell everyone to go home," said Razetti.

Wakefield was screwed, and he knew it. The lab had incredible technology, but even this lab did not have a mind-erasing device. Could he pay each cop $10,000 and have them sign an NDA? No, that would not work. He did not want to do this. But he had to go to the old tried-and-true federal government playbook. He marched back into the main room with Razetti and Stevenson in tow.

"I need everyone's attention! Everyone, please. All the Fairfax County law enforcement officers…thank you. We appreciate your hard work and efforts here this evening. Thank you. This is a federal crime scene, and because of national security concerns, I am going to require you to stay absolutely silent on what you have seen and what transpired here this evening. This vow of silence needs to continue forever. Please vacate the premises. Any questions need to be directed at Detective Razetti. Thank you."

Wakefield turned to Razetti, put his hand on his arm, and pulled him in close. "Detective, I really hate to do this. I really do. Do not screw with us on this. You and your people do not know what you stumbled upon. You. Them. All of you need to forget tonight ever happened. Get back in your cars, and leave. Tell your 911 dispatcher it was a prank or a hoax. If word of this leaks out, I swear on my mother's soul there will be consequences. Single-car auto accidents, house fires, random robberies, and suicides can all happen. You name it, and we can do it. I beg you. Shut up, and go home."

Razetti's mouth fell to the floor, and he started to speak. Wakefield stopped him. "Don't! Just don't. It's not worth it. Make sure your people know it too."

Razetti thought about his six-year-old son, who loved trains and cars. He thought about his curly black hair and his teddy bear named Pizza. Vince thought about the spouses and families of his fellow Fairfax County police officers. He also saw the intensity in Wakefield's eyes. This guy was 100 percent serious.

"Fuck it," said Razetti. "You got it. It's not our headache. You want it? You can take it. We are out of here. Good luck."

Ninety seconds later, the Fairfax County PD had packed up, handed over their notes and camera, took down the yellow tape, and left the Langley Shopping Center. Within the hour, the Fairfax County PD would have their entire computer system hacked. Gone would be any record of the original 911 call. The dispatcher's callout for cruisers to respond would be deleted. Every single tangible shred of evidence would vanish. The CIA hackers would make sure there was no record of this incident anywhere. At best, Razetti and the local police officers would keep their mouths shut. At worst, they would talk, and there would be nothing to support their tall tale. It would just turn into another urban legend.

Ben Wakefield turned off his alpha-dog persona and switched to dad mode as he spoke with and comforted Julia Martin. Ben had four kids, and he was hoping to be a grandpa soon as his oldest daughter had been married for a few years now. He would use the skills he acquired as a parent to help Julia. He would also use his skills as a successful intelligence operator to gather much-needed information.

In a small conference room down the hall, and after having a bottle of water, Julia explained what happened that evening. Her boyfriend, Kumar Faquar, was a government scientist and never talked about his work. At about 10:30 p.m., Kumar's uncle, Ahmed Faquar, showed up at their townhouse, banging on the door. She had met him once at a family event in northern New Jersey a few months ago. Kumar was Muslim, but he was hardly devout. Kumar's family was very secular and welcomed her with open arms. She recalled only Ahmed refused to engage in conversation with her and basically scowled and kept to himself at Kumar's parents' lavish home.

Julia told Wakefield what she knew about Kumar and Ahmed. However, there was so much she did not know. The Faquar family had left Iraq in 1999 to come to the US. Kumar had been born in Iraq and was ten years old when his parents, his two younger sisters, his grandparents, and Uncle Ahmed fled Iraq. Both Kumar's father, Ammar Faquar, and grandfather Hassan Faquar were medical doctors and highly educated. Ammar's brother, Ahmed, was sixteen years younger than him. Ahmed's upbringing differed greatly from his older brother's. The family groomed Ammar to follow in his father's footsteps as a doctor and man of science. Ahmed showed no aptitude for anything other than violence. At a young age, Ahmed was always angry and jealous of his successful older brother. Ammar had gone to the best schools, become a doctor helping others, and married a beautiful woman. He had three intelligent, promising children and was liked by everyone. Everyone except for Ahmed. Ahmed was always getting into fights at school, the playground, the backyard, and wherever he was in contact with others. Ahmed had no genuine interest in learning or studying.

Ahmed was only eight years older than his nephew, Kumar. At age sixteen, while his nephew was playing soccer and being loved by an adoring mother, Ahmed was sent by the family to the Iraqi army. He served for two years and thrived as a soldier. Ahmed trained hard, paid attention, and found something where he excelled.

In 1999, Hassan and his older son, Ammar, had the chance to come to America. They took advantage of the opportunity and came to the United States, taking an upset Ahmed with them. Ahmed was torn. He was pleased with the life he had found in the military. The sense of purpose he felt and the Muslim faith he had rediscovered in the army were important to him. However, could he say goodbye to his mother and never see her again? His mother was the only woman who would truly love him. Reluctantly, Ahmed arrived in the US in 1999 with his family.

Kumar had an odd relationship with his uncle. They were only eight years apart, but Kumar always called him Uncle. Kumar was materially much more successful and popular than Ahmed, yet he was always wanting to impress his older relative. Something about Ahmed made Kumar crave his acceptance. Maybe because Kumar had always been a skinny and weak kid and Ahmed was over six feet and had a solid physique. Maybe it was the intensity of Ahmed's eyes and face that drew Kumar in.

Over the years, Kumar had noticed a change in Ahmed. The entire family had become US citizens, except for Ahmed. Since Ahmed was already eighteen years old when he arrived in the US, he did not automatically become a US citizen when his parents took their oaths of allegiance. Later, Kumar was away at college and then graduate school and beyond, but when he was home, he noticed a change in Ahmed. His uncle went to a mosque with a reputation of being radical. The FBI was believed to be monitoring the mosque, and there were rumors and stories of terrorist sympathizers around the neighborhood. It was hard to determine what was real and what was fiction. Each time Kumar saw his uncle, Ahmed was getting more and more angry and isolated. However, Kumar's desire to impress his uncle Ahmed was always present.

Julia explained to Wakefield she first met Ahmed at Kumar's parents' house. They were hosting a party for family, friends, colleagues, and neighbors. The house was in affluent Totowa, New Jersey, and was as elegant as one would expect from a doctor in the New York metropolitan area. Julia said there were close to a hundred people in attendance. She recalled Kumar drinking way too much at the party. Kumar was very slight and thin and was not physically able of handling several mixed drinks. She lost track of Kumar for a while and found him in a corner, speaking quietly with Ahmed. She had not thought about Ahmed again until tonight, when he burst in their front door, wielding a gun and talking about changing the world.

Julia went on to tell Wakefield about the eight Arab men in the van and the bulky big bags they had with them. She described how Ahmed held a gun to her, killed the security guard, and she had her head down for the remaining time until the pod disappeared. Julia talked about Kumar, explaining something about traveling to when Jesus was born. It was crazy. Then the obese kidnapper killed her boyfriend, and she was in the fight of her life to defend herself. Wakefield was proud of her, and he told her as much. Julia asked when she could call her mother and go home.

"Soon. Very soon," Wakefield said, as he walked away, dialing a number on his phone.

Wakefield had to call his superior, James Davidson, director of the Central Intelligence Agency. James Davidson had been an old-fashioned spy during the Cold War. The sixty-eight-year-old was not a political appointee. Quite the contrary, he had served as CIA director for the past two administrations. Educated at Rutgers University and with forty years of espionage and cloak-and-dagger expertise, Davidson understood the world.

Davidson's phone rang in his breast pocket as he was home and heading upstairs. He was heading up to go to bed alone. Forty-plus years in the CIA did not make for a good marriage. Actually, it did not make for three good marriages. The thrice-divorced Davidson answered his phone on the second ring, with a curt "Yes, Wakefield."

"Sir, we have had a breach at the location below the local strip mall."

"What kind of a breach?"

"A terrible one. We've got a stolen pod."

"Stolen? How is that possible?"

"We are investigating that end of it, but here's what we know…" Wakefield briefed Davidson as thoroughly and quickly as he could. He told Davidson about the man known as Ahmed Faquar and the number of Middle Eastern men with him. The deputy director informed him of the woman who survived the attack and how she seemed credible in her story. Wakefield told him about the presumed destination for the missing pod.

"Good God," the director said. "I will call the president now and head to the White House. We will call you from there, and you can brief the president." Davidson called out for his ever-present assistant to bring his driver and car around up front. His mind was already working on a plan.

As his Lincoln Town Car barreled down the road at speeds surreal for a luxury sedan, Davidson worked his phone and contacts. He had called his counterpart in the FBI to see what they had on an Ahmed Faquar from Paterson, New Jersey. The CIA had never heard of the guy. He prayed the domestic wing on the war on terror had some vital intel. The FBI director promised to bang some heads and kick down some doors to get answers right away. Davidson also called his deputy director in charge of ground branch and ordered her to get a Special Operations Group assembled. He ordered his deputy to have the SOG unit sent directly to the Langley Shopping Center. They needed to be geared up and ready to fight.

Finally, Davidson called a contact on his phone. He was reaching out to an old high school friend he had reconnected with two years earlier at a Don Bosco Prep reunion in Ramsey, New Jersey. Paul Daley had grown up to become Father Paul Daley. Daley oversaw the Dominican House of Studies in Washington, DC. This institution was the think tank of American Catholicism. At the reunion, Daley told his old friend, "Call me anytime." Well, Davidson was calling him right now.

CHAPTER 4

"Hello."

"Father Paul?" said the CIA director when he heard his friend's crackling voice as he picked up.

"Yes?"

"It's James Davidson. I think I need your help."

"When I said to call me anytime, James, I really did not mean anytime," said the Dominican priest.

"At risk of sounding like a cliché, it is about national security. You have a young priest there, a Father Patrick O'Connor, is that right? I read about his brilliance and extensive knowledge in an article six months ago. Is he there?"

"I assume so. It's pretty late."

"Does he really speak and comprehend dead languages like Aramaic? Does he speak and understand Greek, Hebrew, and Latin?"

"I don't have his résumé memorized, but he is a brilliant scholar. Why?"

"He is an expert on the movements and circumstances of Christ's birth, right?"

"James, it's late. I think so. Why?"

"Get Father Patrick up. Tell him the CIA is picking him up within ten minutes. Instruct him to tell no one." Davidson ended the call.

*****

Dr. Stevenson held her stomach and fought the urge to vomit as she stood just a few feet from Kumar's corpse. She had recruited Kumar to join her team. Of course, she could not help but feel responsible as the once-eager and brilliant man now lay cold, motionless, and dead. Why was he dead? What was he doing that got him killed? Why was he back at the lab after-hours? Those questions would have to be answered by someone else. She had to determine what Kumar had been doing on the launch computer.

The secret Wakefield and Stevenson were going to such great lengths to prevent from becoming known was time travel. Time travel was real. Time travel had gone from fantasy to reality under the direction of Dr. Stevenson. Eight years ago, when the program was introduced, the idea of traveling through time had been a dream: Dr. Stevenson's dream and, apparently, the dream of Ben Wakefield. Wakefield read Stevenson's essay in *Sky & Telescope* magazine entitled "Do Stars and Quantum Physics Hold the Key to Time Travel?" Stevenson's work and research into time travel had been her passion. She had dreamed of time travel and developed a rather sound theory on the topic. Her life changed when one of the powers that be at the Central Intelligence Agency saw real potential in her theory.

For centuries, empires and nations had always sought military advantages. It had begun with who could make the sharpest sword and who had the best arrow, who could make the most effective gun, and on and on. The struggle went and continues. The race to have the best and most advanced weapons never ends. The USA had Space Force. Why not Time Force? Wakefield knew announcing a Time Force initiative would be mocked, ridiculed, laughed at, and just plain political suicide. Nonetheless, he sought to create a program under the CIA to research, develop, and ultimately use time travel to protect the United States. George Orwell wrote, "Who controls the past controls the future."

One of the significant aspects of having an enormous and out-of-control federal government is the ability to spend millions and even billions of dollars with no one noticing. Congress passes stimulus packages that are over five thousand pages. It is easy to hide programs and spending. If Congress can spend $600,000 to study why chimpanzees throw their feces and $850,000 to study if zoologists can train lions to walk on a treadmill, then it's pretty easy to spend money to create The Indigenous Migrant Experience (TIME). TIME was just another government acronym getting $10,000,000 for initial funding.

Not knowing how long the charade could be maintained, Wakefield spent the money on talent and equipment. He would cut corners on items like security and a massive building. Besides, watchdog groups and consumer advocates would notice a brand-new massive structure for TIME. However, buying a strip mall and doing some excavating and renovating would draw the attention of no one. So it began. Wakefield recruited Stevenson to head the program and gave her free will to hire top talent, design her lab, and start her research. Each budget year, TIME would receive government funding. Just as the federal government spent money on interoperative dance-theory classes in rural community colleges, TIME would continue to be funded. Years went by, and no watchdog group or right-wing congressman ever asked, "What exactly is The Indigenous Migrant Experience, and what does it do?"

As the years went by, the money kept coming as the federal budget grew. Stevenson and Wakefield did not know if the gravy train would end, so they took full advantage. They kept asking for and receiving more funding for the program. Nobody in Congress or the executive branch ever asked what the money was for or how it was spent. Stevenson and Wakefield were certain to make sure the program had plenty of resources if Congress turned off the financial spigot. They doubled everything. Why build a single one-person time pod when you can build two? Might as well build two transport pods if you are already getting one.

*****

Dr. Stevenson anxiously awaited her staff, the Time Team. Time Team was a moniker they came up with for themselves. They were an odd group of extraordinary minds and individuals. The four Time Explorers or pilots liked to be called TEPs. These four were not like the rest. Unlike their teammates, they did not fully grasp how and why it all worked. They were explorers, adventurers, and the astronauts of this century. The TEPs were all men over thirty-five years old. They could complete repairs on the pod if needed. They knew how to enter the return flight data and pilot the pod. Recently, the TEPs were time-traveling in pairs.

Twenty people comprised the rest of the staff. They all performed various functions, such as calculations and coordinate analysis, launch technicians, lab assistants, pod mechanics, and designers. The Time Team had all received emergency text messages. They were to report to the lab as soon as humanly possible. This was a "Stop what you are doing, and get in here now" notification. It was the first urgent alert.

Before the team members began arriving, the CIA officers removed the bodies of Kumar, Stan, and Omar. Unfortunately, nothing could be done about the bloodstained carpet and walls for now. One by one, the team members arrived. Each was nervous, scared, and confused about the emergency. Stevenson and Wakefield hoped to speak to everyone at once, but that was impossible as personnel arrived at different times, and everyone was asking the same questions. Word quickly spread that terrorists had murdered Kumar and Stan and stole the new self-programming pod. Their primary job was to determine where and when the pod had gone. This was a professional group, and they could function at a high level. They knew there would be time to grieve for Kumar and Stan, but that would have to come later.

Stevenson had taken Kumar's data off the launch computer system, but she needed help in determining exactly where and when the pod had escaped to. As intelligent as she was, she was thankful when her top mathematicians and astronomers arrived.

Stevenson was still in her pajamas while she and Wakefield conferred in her office to develop a plan of action. This was Stevenson's lab, but Wakefield was in charge.

"First, we have to figure out when and where they went. The woman said Kumar said something about sending them back to the birth of Christ. Is that possible? You have never gone back that far,

27

have you?" said Wakefield. "How long would that trip even take, assuming it's true?"

"1066 is the furthest we have gone back, and that took about ninety minutes. It is about forty-five minutes per five hundred years." Stevenson was trying to recall the travel time without the benefits of notes or data.

"Can the pod make it back two thousand years?"

"I would say yes."

"How much time will it take to get the other large pod ready to launch?" asked Wakefield.

"Not much. Why?"

"Victoria, we have a group of eight armed terrorists loose with a time machine. What did you think we were going to do? Nothing. I assume our boss will order a team to go after them and stop them from doing whatever they have planned."

"You can't send out my only other large transport pod. What happens if we have an emergency and need it?" asked Stevenson.

"Jesus, Victoria. Do you hear yourself? This is *the* emergency! Just get the damn pod ready."

Stevenson realized she sounded crazy for her last statement and said, "Okay. I can get Kenny and Hal prepping."

"You decide which one is the superior pilot, because only one of them is making the trip. We have a team coming in," said Wakefield.

"Team? What team? You can't send just one pilot. We always send two in case something goes wrong. Do you remember how Hal barely made it back from Paris in the 1920s?"

"Listen, Victoria. We are sending one pilot, and that's it. Actually, forget about Kenny. Hal Nagle is going. His law-enforcement background may come in handy. Hal Nagle is going."

"Why can't we send two pilots like we have been doing for the past several months?"

"We can't give up a seat to another nonshooter. We need as many shooters as possible on that pod."

"Shooters?"

Wakefield did not respond. He left her office as his phone rang.

CHAPTER 5

The president of the United States stood in the Oval Office and was about to talk on the phone with the deputy director of science and technology for the CIA. The president did not know who the DD of science and technology was or what he did for the CIA. All the president knew was his CIA director had pushed for an immediate meeting in the Oval Office with him and his closest advisors. Davidson entered the president's office, talking on his phone. His stride was purposeful and confident. Davidson handed the phone to the president and said, "Sir, this is Ben Wakefield. He is the deputy director of science and technology. He is on site and will give you a briefing."

It was 1:00 a.m., but the president had not retired for the evening. He had been up when Davidson called and insisted on a top-level meeting ASAP. The president was always up. He had boundless energy. He was only forty-eight years old and was in his first term. Pundits questioned how long his high level of vitality would last. The president had hit the ground running and wasted little time in putting forth his agenda. He was very popular with the American people, but he had the feeling this phone call might change his presidency. Over twenty years ago, one of his predecessors, George W. Bush, had his presidency changed only nine months into the job. Now, the current president's administration was about to be rocked.

The tall (and a little too round in the middle, according to the First Lady) former businessman took in the surrounding people. "I am going to put you on speaker, Mr. Bakefield, so everyone can hear you," said the president.

"Of course, sir." *Bakefield? Wakefield?* Ben Wakefield did not think it really mattered, and he was not about to correct the leader of the free world.

The president made his money in a home improvement retail chain and was twice elected governor of Missouri. He came into office after a tremendous victory, winning forty-one states and 57 percent of the popular vote. The former D-1 baseball player was handsome, good-natured, and liked by the American people. The honeymoon was continuing as his approval rating was almost 70 percent. As he laid the phone on the table, the president took a seat. In his office were five key people. The director of the CIA, James Davidson, had just taken a seat. The national security advisor, former general Tyler Evans, was on the couch. Evans had been a tank commander during Operation Desert Storm. Also sitting on the Oval Office sofas was Chief of Staff Ted Bennett. Ted was a highly skilled tactician and political operative who was also a college buddy and loyal confidante of the president. Special advisor Tom Scott was another college friend who was tough and looked at life from a different perspective. Vice President Elizabeth Kim was there too. Liz, as the president liked to call her, was placed in her role to give the ticket some balance. The former member of Congress was a highly intelligent woman, a minority, and from the northeast. It also helped she was a skilled orator and top-level debater.

Wakefield began the briefing. "First, sir, I know we have purposely kept you and some people in the room there with you at an arm's length so you could maintain plausible deniability. But, sir, this is real. We can send people back in time. Time travel is real."

"What?" asked the president. "What are you saying? Did you just say time travel?"

"We can send people back in time," Wakefield said as calmly as possible.

"How is that possible? Since when do we have this technology? How do we have this technology? Why do we have this technology?" The president searched the faces of his advisors for answers. Excluding Davidson, he found only blank stares and bewildered looks.

"With all due respect, sir, I can have our lead scientist, Dr. Victoria Stevenson, give you a full briefing of the how, but right now, we have a bigger problem. Our trips to the past have always been just observational. Our Time Explorers have gone back to record data and get a firsthand account of events to improve our understanding and knowledge of world history. About ninety minutes ago, eight men, who we believe are Muslim terrorists, stole a time pod."

The president and his advisors just sat there in stunned silence. Their mouths were wide open, and they looked at one another in shocked disbelief, again, except for the CIA chief. Davidson did not look like everything he knew in the world had just been turned upside down. He looked calm, focused, and in control. After thirty seconds of confused stillness, Wakefield asked, "Mr. President, are you there, sir?"

The president paused, shook his head. "So where did they go?"

"And when did they go?" Tom Scott added.

"We should know for certain in a few minutes. Right now, our information indicates they went back to what would have been Bethlehem. Today's West Bank in Israel, sir. We think they went back two thousand years ago to the birth of Christ."

"Jesus Christ," said Evans.

"That's right. Jesus Christ's birth," Wakefield said, not knowing the general meant it more as a figure of speech. "Our team is analyzing the data, the launch computer, and everything imaginable to make sure we know exactly when and where they are heading."

"Why would they go back two thousand years?" said the president.

"We don't know, sir."

"How long will it take to get there?"

"It is about forty-five minutes for every five hundred years, sir. So they should arrive at the destination in about ninety minutes," said the deputy director.

"Can we shoot it down or hit a self-destruct button?" said Tom Scott.

"Negative. That's not possible."

"What about a tracking device or a way to disable the...what did you call it, a pod?" The madame vice president was looking for solutions.

"Negative, ma'am. It does not appear this pod was programmed to return, and there is no way they can come back to our time. This is a one-way trip."

"Who else knows about time travel?" asked the president.

"There are about two dozen team members involved in the program. They have all signed more nondisclosure agreements and secrecy statements than you can imagine. In addition, they must pass a polygraph every two weeks. However, there is a civilian here who witnessed the break-in at the lab and the disappearance of the pod. James Davidson also knows," Wakefield said.

All eyes shifted to the CIA director. The old spy could feel everyone looking at him and wondering what he knew and when he knew it. Davidson had succeeded in the intelligence field because he knew how to keep secrets and compartmentalize. He had been doing this for four decades. He had never really believed this theory of using the alignment of the stars and planets and a secret lab hidden in plain sight would amount to anything. However, within the last eighteen months, he started reading reports of some successful trips back in time. He had never understood the science of it. Who could? It was beyond understanding. Even the technicians and scientists who worked on the Time Team did not understand more than what was within their own specialized field. Dr. Victoria Stevenson, with special input from Kumar Faquar, was the overall mastermind. However, it had been the two of them working together who made it possible.

The program's achievements were stymied until Dr. Stevenson finally grasped the idea that definitive rules existed. Davidson recalled one report that always stuck with him. Stevenson wrote they were finally figuring out the ground rules of time travel. *She wrote it was like they could play a god, but just not the God.* Davidson recalled some of what they had learned. A person could not go forward in time because that would create a never-ending time loop. They used a calculation of the positioning of the planets, stars, and heavenly bodies to determine the actual time. Even though he had read reports on the process and function of the pod, he still did not know how it got from point and time of A to point and time of B.

Davidson spoke. "I saw reports and knew they were making progress. But who really knew? Let's move on. Wakefield notified me of the breach about thirty minutes ago, and I have a plan."

All the eyes turned back to the president to follow his lead.

"So this is real, James? This is not a joke or a hoax or a test to grade our crisis management. We are really looking at this for real?" said the president. The heads on the couches went back and forth between the old spymaster and the new commander-in-chief, like a crowd at a tennis match, watching a long rally.

"This is as real as it gets, Mr. President."

The president turned his attention back to the phone. "Ben. I have a technical question for you. Based on what you know, there is no way to contact, destroy, disengage, or terminate the pod from the lab. Is that correct?"

"Yes, sir."

"Do we have a second pod?" said the commander-in-chief.

"Yes. It requires a pilot. It seats eight people, including the pilot."

"Get the pod ready. We will call you back." The president disconnected the call.

"What do we do?" said the POTUS (president of the United States).

James Davidson spoke first. "As I stated before, Wakefield called me about thirty minutes ago and gave me as much intel as he had available to him. A man named Ahmed Faquar kidnapped one of our scientists and his girlfriend. We are certain of this because the girlfriend identified Ahmed. Ahmed used the girl to force his entry into the lab. The terrorists killed the security guard when they entered the lab. There were eight terrorists on the pod when it launched. An additional terrorist stayed behind to kill the scientist, the woman, and burn down the lab. He killed the scientist. However, the woman subdued the terrorist and killed him. We have identified the terrorist as Omar Rasheed, and he was a known associate of Ahmed Faquar.

Based on the ID of the dead terrorist and knowing the leader is Ahmed Faquar from Paterson, NJ, we have been able to figure out the other seven men. Ahmed Faquar is not on our radar, but the FBI has a file on him. He attends a radical mosque, and his internet activity is very…problematic. We coordinated with the FBI office in Newark, New Jersey, and the Paterson Police Department. Basically, we took the list of Ahmed's known associates and kicked down their doors within the last fifteen minutes. We presume anyone who could not be accounted for back in New Jersey is on the pod. We also have an idea of the weapons and gear they have with them."

Scott asked, "How did this woman know the terrorist, this guy named Ahmed Faquar?"

Davidson answered. "It appears the scientist, Kumar Faquar, is Ahmed's nephew or somehow related. Ahmed kidnapped the scientist and his girlfriend. The terrorists gained access to the lab through threats and coercion."

"So the scientist is on it," Bennett said.

"Well, he is dead now, so we will have to figure that out later," answered Davidson.

The president reasserted his control. "The what and how do not matter. What matters now is what we do next. However, before we can decide what action we take, we need to know why these terrorists are going back two thousand years. What's their goal? I am open to suggestions."

"Perhaps Ahmed Faquar wants to replace Muhammad as Allah's prophet," said the VP. "Maybe his plan is to preemptively claim the role as the prophet before Muhammad."

"Muhammad was born at the end of the sixth century and did not receive his first revelation until he was forty years old. It makes no sense to go back six hundred years before that," said Bennett.

"A prelude to the Holocaust?" Evans asked as he shifted in his seat. "They could go back to kill Jews."

"That's a possibility," said Bennett. "The world population was around two hundred million people back then. There would be fewer Jewish people to eliminate to wipe them from history."

"That's absurd! Eight guys can't kill a few million people with some rifles and shotguns," said Tom Scott.

"Hey, I'm just thinking out loud," Evans replied.

"What if their intention is to kill Jesus Christ?" said the CIA head.

The room fell silent. Davidson's theory had the effect of the f-word being said aloud in church. One could hear a pin hit the carpet.

"The birth of Christ is not an exact date. Trying to prevent His birth is not like trying to stop Pearl Harbor or 9/11 from happening. There is a general idea of when Christ was born, but not a confirmed date. The terrorists could arrive two thousand years in the past, and Jesus may not be born for another few years, or He may already be a kid. We don't know," said Bennett.

Again, silence.

"What if that's their mission?" said the president.

Ideas started flying around the room. Was there a military option? Could the air force send an F-16 fighter through a wormhole? Was Space Force operational? Was Iran or al-Qaeda involved? Should they prepare a retaliation strike? Was there a diplomatic option?

Finally, the president quieted everyone down and said, "Here is what I think and what course of action I believe we should take. We will go around the room and get your thoughts. I believe the terrorists are going back to kill Jesus Christ as an infant and His parents. Their intention is to eliminate the Holy Family and thus end Christianity before it begins. Why else would eight Muslim terrorists go back two thousand years ago to Bethlehem? The consequences are simply unimaginable. I want to send back a team to locate and defend the Holy Family, kill the terrorists, and save Christianity. Thoughts?"

"I agree. My plan is already in motion and can commence on your command, sir. I think your evaluation is correct. Why else would they go back? Sounds solid. I can have a SOG team on-site and mission ready in twenty minutes," said the CIA chief.

"I agree. Take immediate action. The enemy already has an early start on us. We need to move ASAP," said Evans.

The VP joined in support. "I think that's the right call, sir. We need to move quickly and decisively."

The president could sense a feeling of hesitation from Tom Scott. He had known Scott since they were teammates at the University of Missouri together. Scott was a tall lefty power hitter, and now he was more power broker than ballplayer.

"My role is always to look at things a little differently. I have two thoughts. Number 1: where in the Constitution does the president have the power to commit troops to save a religious figure? I would think the ACLU would argue the president deciding to save Jesus would constitute breaking the wall between the separation of church and state," said Scott.

Scott was promptly interrupted.

"You are joking, right?" Ted Bennett could not believe what he was hearing from Scott. "You don't think we should save Jesus and the Christian religion because the fucking ACLU might object?" Bennett had also known Scott for thirty years. What the hell was he talking about?

Before anyone else could respond, Scott continued, "Number 2: if God is all-powerful, why would He need us to defend His son? Why would God not just strike these terrorists dead with lightning bolts or have the pod explode? Why does the US military or CIA have to defend the son of God? Why wouldn't He just do it Himself?"

The president quickly responded. "Maybe God's way of defending His son is by having us do it?"

Scott was quick to say, "I am just pointing out a different point of view. I say send in a SOG team and do what needs to be done."

"James," the president said to his CIA chief. "Get the SOG team in action. However, we need to hear from the lab before we commit."

*****

Dr. Stevenson and several of her gifted mathematicians had been crunching the figures and computing the numbers. Kumar was so brilliant. They were working from what he had left on the computer. It felt odd to the team to be backtracking Kumar's work and confirming what he had done. Stevenson knew they had to be certain. So much was riding on this; they simply could not be wrong.

"It's the triple conjunction from 6 BC. I know it," said Dr. Kenneth Zhang. Zhang had graduated from Cornell with a degree in astrophysics at age fourteen. He received a PhD from Princeton before he could drive.

"Are you sure?" asked Stevenson.

Zhang looked at her as if she had asked him if he was sure two plus two equals four. "Yeah. I'm sure."

Stevenson told Wakefield, and they quickly called Davidson.

Davidson's phone chirped in the Oval Office. Five sets of anxious eyes were glued to him as he took the call on speaker so the entire team could hear for themselves. Wakefield knew better than to go into any details. The people in the Oval Office just wanted the cold, hard truth: when and where did the terrorists go?

"I am afraid to say our preliminary speculation was right. They are going back to the birth of Christ, Bethlehem."

"This is the president speaking. I have some questions. We have a CIA special ops team getting ready to go. Can we send them back to the lab ten minutes before Ahmed broke in and shoot him when he gets off the elevator or, better yet, when the van pulls into the parking lot?"

Wakefield explained the same living being cannot be alive twice at the same time. You are born once, and you die once. You cannot be alive twice. Therefore, they cannot go back and kill Ahmed right before he enters the lab or at another time.

"We know when and where the terrorists are going. Can we send the CIA team back to Judea two hours before the terrorists arrive and blow up their pod before they even get out of it?"

Back at the underground lab in Virginia, Wakefield and Stevenson both heard the president's question. Wakefield looked at Stevenson for an answer. She stared at the floor and shook her head in embarrassment.

"No, Mr. President. We cannot," Wakefield answered for Stevenson.

"Why not? That seems like the logical thing to do. We have a time machine."

Again, Stevenson shook her head in shame and mumbled so low only Wakefield could hear. "We can't, and you know why."

"Sir, we do not have the time to figure it out. The terrorists already have about a three-hour lead on us. It would take several days, maybe even weeks, for us to calculate the new coordinates and schematics. Our numbers must be perfect, and we don't have the time to process the equation correctly. We already know exactly where and when the bad guys are going. The best we can do is follow them."

"How is it the scientist who got shot, Kumar, could do the calculations in about an hour?" The president could not understand why his request could not be done. "But you are telling me it will take days or weeks to figure out a new destination point that would put us there before the terrorists arrive. Why?"

Stevenson heard the president's question through the speaker on Ben's phone. She picked up the metal office chair next to her, slammed it to the ground, and stormed out of the room.

"In all honesty, Mr. President." Wakefield's voice was calm and deliberate. "Kumar Faquar was Albert Einstein and Stephen Hawking rolled into one. He was the smartest person on the planet and could figure it out on his own. Without him, we are looking at days or weeks to process the astronomy, mathematics, and run the computer simulations to figure out the proper coordinates. We can't do it without him."

"So much for an ambush. I guess we have to hunt them down in the past."

CHAPTER 6

Miguel Sanchez and his team got dressed and geared up in the break room of the lab. Miguel, like the other five men on his squad, was wondering what the hell was going on. They had all received emergency calls late at night to be ready to roll within three minutes. They all got picked up in separate typical government-owned sedans with four doors and cloth interiors. Each man was escorted from his home and taken to this strange location. They were gearing up for an operation they knew nothing about. No one had told them what was going on or where they were heading. They were told to get ready for a hunt and a fight. Someone would brief them soon. Even though each man wondered why they were five stories below an auto parts store in McLean, Virginia, in some sort of laboratory or science research facility, none of the men spoke. They just got ready. Getting called in the middle of the night was part of the job, but in the nine months these shooters had been working together, it had never happened before.

Sanchez had been asleep when the call came in. Miguel kissed his wife and his son goodbye. He knew he was risking waking RJ, but in his line of work, you never knew how long you could be gone and if you would make it back home. He said a quick prayer and hoped he would be back in time for RJ's first Christmas. The young husband and father threw his Saint Michael the Archangel chain and medallion around his neck, and he was ready to go. Beca bought him the medallion and required him to wear it on missions. Saint Michael the Archangel was the patron saint of warriors. And Sanchez was certainly a warrior.

Sanchez's Special Operations Group was called Alter Ego Team, and they each had appropriate call signs. Xavier Cole was a twenty-five-year-old thrill seeker from California. Cole was a blond-haired, blue-eyed surfer dude. He jumped out of airplanes for fun and was a rock climber. He had played professional tennis for a bit and even took on Roger Federer at the Indian Wells Open when Cole was only eighteen. Cole had made the tournament as a local wild-card entry. Federer beat him 6–0,6–0 in less time than it takes to watch a sitcom on TBS. A month later, Cole ripped up his shoulder. He could not hit his big forehand effectively anymore, but he could still shoot a gun, and thus began his life in the military. Cole spent time in US Air Force Special Forces before joining the CIA. He was Surfer.

Cam McNally was the oldest member of the team at age forty-one. He had been a paramilitary officer with the CIA for ten of the over twenty years he served his country. McNally was a 6'4" tall Irish Catholic from New Hampshire. He had done some boxing as a teenager, but New Hampshire was not exactly known for producing great heavyweight fighters. McNally was quiet and said very little, but when the shit hit the fan in the field, he was a monster of a fighter and showed no fear or hesitation. He was Fighter.

Elston Jackson was a thirty-two-year-old former US Army Ranger from New York City. He was fast as lightning and was quick and skilled in hand-to-hand combat. He and McNally argued all the time about New York versus Boston sports. His father named him after Elston Howard, the first Black New York Yankee. Jackson had been with SOG for five years. He was Gotham.

The sniper on the team was Clint Bedford. Bedford was thirty-three years old and had built the reputation as being one of the best snipers in service of the nation. He felt confident with any shot within a mile if he had the time. Bedford was from Bedford, Pennsylvania. He said it was just a cool coincidence. Bedford had been a Marine for nine years before joining the CIA three years earlier. He was Hunter.

Edwin Tucker was a hell of a fighter and an equally impressive medic. The son of two doctors, he had an inherent sense in treating injured people. Once on a covert operation in Syria as the team was hauling ass to get to the extraction point, he stopped to help a child who had caught a stray bullet from the gun battle. Jackson and Bedford had wanted to scream at him to get moving, but they understood what motivated Tucker. He wanted to help the innocent. Sometimes it meant killing the bad guys, and sometimes it meant risking your exfil to prevent an eight-year-old girl from bleeding out. Tucker was twenty-eight years old and had been on his way to becoming an army doctor when the CIA recruited him away from his father's dream. He was Doc.

The Alter Ego Team was formed nine months ago. There was much debate as to what Sanchez should be called. The men considered his past life as a football player, his Mexican heritage, and his role as a father and husband. Sanchez was the only non-bachelor in the group and had a child. Finally, the men settled on a call sign. Sanchez was Papi. The men bonded and developed into an effective fighting force. Only having six men meant they could be quick and quiet, but they also had to trust one another. They had completed successful ops in Syria, Libya, Thailand, and Canada.

The Canadian op had been an oddity. A covert CIA SOG team running a mission in the homeland of America's closest ally was unheard of. However, the teenage daughter of a US senator was kidnapped from her class trip in Toronto. She was taken to a farmhouse about an hour outside the city. The US rule of not negotiating with terrorists was a gray area when it came to the teenage daughter of a member on the Armed Services Committee. While the senator from New York was trying to negotiate with the kidnappers via his daughter's cell phone, Alter Ego Team was on its way to rescue the girl. The president was not messing around and wanted the situation handled and resolved ASAP. He understood how the senior senator from the Empire State would do anything to save his own child, but he had to worry about the entire country. The president ordered the CIA into action, and Alter Ego Team landed at a private airfield in a small agency jet. The GPS on her phone pinpointed her exact location. The SOG team headed to the farmhouse in SUVs. The kidnapping had been a basic smash-and-grab. The senator's daughter was under no special security, and while she was entering the CN Tower, a van pulled up alongside the line of prep-school kids waiting to enter the tourist attraction. Two guys jumped out, pushed over the kids next to her, grabbed her, and threw her into the van. The vehicle sped away, and in a few seconds, it was gone.

The authorities knew little about the kidnappers, except they were not very professional. No experienced kidnapper would be foolish enough to negotiate on the victim's phone. The Royal Canadian Police and Toronto Police Department had secured the area near the farmhouse and were all too willing to let the CIA SOG team do the actual dirty work. They were not concerned about jurisdiction and were happy to let the US take the fall if the rescue failed. Sanchez and his men arrived on the scene and developed a quick plan of action. Sanchez's orders had been direct: get the girl and kill everybody. Night was about to fall, and Sanchez knew the president and the director of the CIA would want victory sooner rather than later.

The kidnapping was already making international headlines and was the major story dominating the evening news. The Royal Canadian Police had confirmed the owners of the house were away on holiday and only one student, the senator's daughter, had been taken. The RCP believed six men were holding the girl. Except for one sixteen-year-old girl, standing 5'4" and weighing 120 pounds, with light-brown hair and a beautiful smile, everyone was a hostile.

The operation was over in less than sixty seconds. Bedford eliminated two tangos with his sniper's rifle at the start of the rescue. Cole and McNally entered through the front door, which wasn't even locked. Tucker and Sanchez breached the back door simultaneously, while Jackson waited in reserve. Cole and McNally cleared the foyer and then the living room. In the kitchen, they put down two men with short bursts from their M4 carbines. Sanchez and Tucker entered the mudroom then advanced to a family room. They saw the girl in the corner and the shocked look of two men, one of whom was speaking on a cell phone. The CIA men fired quickly with precision, and both kidnappers were dead. Tucker checked on the girl while Sanchez picked up the phone. The voice on the other end was frantic.

"What just happened? What was that noise? Is my daughter all right? Where do you want the money deposited?"

"Senator? This is CIA officer Miguel Sanchez. Your daughter is safe."

Less than an hour later, they were on the same plane heading back to Washington, DC, with one thankful teenager. The Canadian Royal Police and Toronto Police Department took credit for the six dead terrorists and the successful raid to rescue the young American.

CHAPTER 7

The CIA team continued to check their weapons and equipment and put on the Desert Battle Dress Uniforms (DBDU). They packed water, MREs, and body armor. Each man had a nine-millimeter Sig Sauer P226 in a drop leg holster and an M4A1 Carbine. The team also packed McNally's McMillan Tac-338 sniper rifle, two HK MP5 nine-millimeter submachine guns, two FAB Mossberger pistol-grip shotguns, two extra Glock 19 nine-millimeter pistols and one GL6 forty-millimeter grenade launcher. They also brought enough rounds to take out a small army. While they checked and rechecked their gear, one of the lab technicians walked into the room and handed them tunics, robes, and sandals and just said "You might need these too" and exited as quickly as he had entered.

The CIA paramilitary officers entered the main room of the facility. They saw black metal folding chairs set up in three rows, like a briefing room. James Davidson stood at the front of the chairs. The head of the CIA was someone none of them had ever seen in person. They had only seen him on TV and cable news shows. Ben Wakefield was on Davidson's right. He was the CIA man who greeted them on their arrival and showed them where to gear up. The same older woman who was in the pajamas and whom they saw on the way in stood on Davidson's left. She had been yelling at some people when they saw her ten minutes ago. The three of them stood in front of a big fiberglass tube. Xavier Cole thought it looked like a plane with no wings.

Sanchez and his men were told to grab a seat and pay close attention to the briefing, because time was important. Sanchez noticed this made the older woman laugh, and she stopped herself in mid-chuckle. Jackson, sitting behind Sanchez, hit Sanchez on the shoulder, pointed to a man also sitting and said, "Hey, Papi, is that guy a priest? And who is that guy?" He pointed at another middle-aged man who was in tan cargo pants and had a serious look on his face.

"I don't know, but I think we are about to find out."

Father Patrick O'Connor was talking to God and asking Him a lot of questions. *God, what is this place? Why am I five stories below an auto parts store in a lab, looking at a plane with no wings and sitting next to a bunch of soldiers? Please tell me there is a reason, a divine purpose, for my being here right now.*

Less than an hour ago, Father Patrick had been drifting off to sleep when Father Daley went banging on his door to get up. He dressed quickly. He grabbed his rosary beads, which went everywhere with him, and his small Bible. It was the Bible his mother had given him when he took his holy orders. As he and Father Daley rushed downstairs, Father Daley quickly explained the CIA needed him for national security reasons or something. It was all happening so fast, and life was literally a blur. Father Daley explained the CIA chief was a friend from high school and he had called and asked him about Father Patrick's skill in languages and history. None of this made any sense to the young priest from Massachusetts. After a car ride that seemed like something from a *Fast and Furious* movie across Washington, DC, he sat in this room with strangers. He clutched his rosary beads and paid close attention to the director of the CIA.

Hal Nagle sat listening to the head honcho of the CIA talk. Hal was pissed. He was not quite sure what he was pissed about or whom he was pissed at. Hal just knew he was pissed. He was angry terrorists murdered his friends Kumar and Stan. Nagle was mad at Kumar for somehow allowing his own uncle to kidnap him and steal a freaking pod. He was angry because now he had to babysit a priest and six jarheads back two thousand years in time. The first trip was always the worst; the nausea and the painful sound were very intense. The first time just sucked. The secret was you must hydrate, and he doubted these soldiers and this priest had been on fluids and Gatorade for the last eight hours. Besides, he must pilot the pod and explain what the hell was going on to these people. Hal didn't give a shit what Stevenson said to them. They were going to pound him with questions as soon as they launched.

Hal was a forty-three-year-old ex-Pennsylvania State trooper. He used to race sprint cars and repair them too. He was a skilled driver and an excellent mechanic. These traits had made him an attractive hire for the TIME program. The program desired candidates who had military or law-enforcement backgrounds. TIME also wanted individuals who would push the envelope and were not afraid to risk life and limb for a thrill. It was an odd balance that Wakefield and Stevenson sought…a person who possessed an eagerness to be daring and adventurous, at risk of their own well-being, but also followed orders. They also needed someone who could be trusted to keep top-secret information to himself. Few people would fit the bill.

Hal Nagle had been sitting at home, keeping his left knee elevated, per the instructions of his surgeon. Hal had injured himself racing his red Triple X sprint car with number 72 on the side in Selinsgrove, Pennsylvania. Hal had been pushing his nine-hundred-horsepower engine to the max. He came out of the third turn and was looking to make up ground on the four cars ahead of him. He did not care about the trophy, but he cared about the $2,000 he could win by slipping into third place. His car hit 115 miles per hour and was striving to hit its max speed of 150 miles per hour in the straightaway. The number 63 car also wanted the two grand that Hal coveted and was making a similar move. Hal's right rear tire got bumped and almost pushed him into the rear of the racer he was trying to pass. Hal felt the impact, corrected his steering, and quickly tried to downshift to reduce speed and avoid a wreck. But he couldn't. Number 63 was trying to plow his way through and smacked Hal just behind the right rear side at 120 miles per hour. Hal's sprint car spun out to his left. Another racer T-boned him at full speed. Hal and his Triple X were out of control and flipped three times before crashing into the wooden fencing around the track. Hal was fortunate to be alive and escape serious injury. He felt lucky but was more pissed about the $2,000.

It was during his recovery when Hall stumbled upon an odd employment opportunity on Zip Recruiter. The ad said, "Government agency seeks adventurous thrill seeker with military or law-enforcement experience." Hal was certain his days were numbered with the PA State Police. His captain was upset one of his troopers had injured himself again while racing his sprint car.

The trials had been going on for some time when Nagle joined the program. He was divorced, and his two kids lived with his ex-wife in Indiana, so he was excited to move to the DC area. Hal thought this program was the greatest thing ever. He had loved sci-fi and time-travel stuff his whole life. He had become the Neil Armstrong, Christopher Columbus, and Lewis and Clark of time travel. Except he was not famous. He understood why, but still, it would have been cool if people knew what he had seen and when and where he had been.

Stevenson and her staff had been successful in sending back objects, like a stapler or a rubber ball, a few days into the past. Then gradually, they could send these items further and further back and return them to the present successfully. The pods were small, no bigger than a shoebox. Over time, the pods continued to grow and get larger to accommodate larger items. Stevenson then began experimenting with live animals. A baby chick could not be sent back three days, but the baby chick could go back a month and safely return. Each new success would lead to more trials and then more failures. With each experiment, Stevenson and her team would learn more and then attempt different tests.

TIME was constantly building new and better pods for the trips. Of course, the goal was to send a person back in time and return them without their intestines being outside their body or their brain lobotomized. They sent the objects and small animals back using preprogrammed pods. Pods that would automatically return after the set amount of time. As Stevenson began contemplating how a person could make a round trip, she challenged her team to create a pod that could also be piloted, if need be, and be programmed manually by that pilot in the past. She envisioned a human pilot being able to arrive in the past and then determine when to return to the present. TIME continued to come across the same issue. It was easier to send an animal back several months or even years in time, as opposed to sending the animal back one hour or one day. The members of TIME worked on theories on why the shortest time jumps were unsuccessful. The shortest backward time jump was sending a three-day-old chick seven days into the past.

Stevenson had determined time flowed consistently. For example, if a baby chick went back two weeks ago and stayed there for four hours, four hours would pass here in the present. There was travel time involved, and that was constantly being studied. However, Stevenson surmised one day in the past was a day in the present. This was very helpful because it prevented time loops. An object or living being could not return before they sent it.

Stevenson believed they were ready for human trials. TIME's design and production of pods were remarkable. They had designed and constructed different sizes and styles of pods. Except for the small ones that were originally used to test time travel on rubber balls and coffee mugs, the pods were being built for a pilot and the option of programming a return or having the pilot manually adjust for the return trip from the past. Knowing they were advancing the program at an incredible pace and always afraid of being discovered, Wakefield and Stevenson amped up the intensity of the production of pods. Stevenson had the pod she desired, and she had the pilot she believed in, Hal Nagle.

Wakefield and Stevenson had decided on Nagle because of his personality traits, his background, and his skill set. Plus, he had the oddest reaction out of all the team members when they finally explained to him their actual mission.

"Cool. Do I get to go?" was Nagle's reaction when they told him. TIME had him sign more nondisclosure agreements and documents than those of a big tech company buying the silence of a sexually harassed female worker.

The human trials were underway. Nagle situated himself into the pod as techs strapped him in. As he was being secured and team members were busy punching away on computer keyboards, Nagle wondered how all this was going to work. Stevenson explained they used the alignment of the planets and stars to determine the point in time and how an accelerator combining nuclear energy with fusion technology would generate and harness enough power to launch the pod through time and space. This first attempt was to have Nagle arrive at an abandoned baseball field in Bethesda, Maryland, exactly two days ago. The pod was preprogrammed to return in three minutes. They ordered him to stay inside the pod and wait for the return. If something went wrong for his return, he could program the pod manually to arrive back in the present. He assured himself there was really nothing for him to do. They called him a pilot, but he was not really flying the pod himself. Hal was wearing cargo pants, sneakers, and a long-sleeved T-shirt. A space suit was not required. He asked Dr. Stevenson if he had to go through time naked.

"Why would you have to be naked?" she said.

"Well, Schwarzenegger and Kyle Reese had to go back naked in *Terminator*."

"This is not the movies, and we would prefer if you kept your clothes on. Thank you."

The only thing the scientists could tell him about the trip was it would be loud. That was the only thing they really knew about the experience. They could not interview the chick, the duck, and the goat they had sent back and ask them for their perspective. Hal was on his own. He was nervous. He felt the sweat roll down his forehead and his hands get clammy. It had been years since he had gone to church, but he said the Hail Mary as the countdown began.

Ten, nine, eight, seven, six, five, four, three, two, one.

Nagle braced for it. His body tightened, his face cringed, and nothing happened. Out the small window of the pod, he saw the technicians looking around, befuddled. He could hear nothing from the outside, but he had not traveled through time and space. He was still sitting in this contraption fifty feet below the auto parts store.

Stevenson's voice came into his headset. "We are all good. We think we had a misfire. Nothing to be concerned about. We are going to reset and launch you in a few moments." She came back into Hal's headset about five minutes later. "Okay. Here we go."

Ten, nine, eight, seven, six, five, four, three, two, one.

Nothing. He was still in the same space and the same time. Stevenson came back. "We are going to get you out of there and figure this out. Everything looks fine, but something is not right." "I think I need to be naked," said Hal.

She said nothing, but he could see Stevenson's sneer and feel her contempt.

Days turned into weeks, and the attempts kept failing. Nagle would sit in the pod, and nothing would happen as TIME tried to send him back three days into the past or three years back. Every day, he would sit there while the pod wouldn't launch. The Time Team reviewed their notes and data from all the previous attempts. They had sent a goat back seven hundred years in the past to Africa. The pod's camera had photographed and captured the celestial alignment above the pod, and the latitude and longitude coordinates were verified. They knew the goat was in the Sudan on July 17, 1347. That was a fact.

After many failed attempts to launch the pod, Stevenson theorized a TEP could not go back to a time when they were alive. That explained why the chick could not go back one hour or one day. They already knew that one could not go forward in time because that would create a never-ending time loop. Stevenson now learned a person or chick or duck could not go back in time if they were alive during that time. The same life could not simultaneously occupy the same time and space. A person or animal could not be alive twice at the same time. The objects were not alive, so it did not prevent the rubber ball from duplicating itself. Millions of rubber balls were made exactly alike every day. But each living thing was unique. There were no calculations to adjust or different data to input. The machine simply would not do it. Stevenson thought it was like they could play a god, but just not the God.

Finally, she asked when Hal was born, and they would try something new.

Hal was born in Reading, Pennsylvania, on October 23, 1978. Researchers had to look for an abandoned field or farmland where the pod could land in 1977. The ball field in Bethesda, Maryland, was not an option anymore because in 1977 it was the thriving home of several Little League Baseball teams. They sent Nagle back to the middle of an enormous cornfield in Iowa on August 14, 1977. Getting there had been tough. The sound when the pod launched was so intense, he thought his head was going to split open. The extreme clamor lasted about ninety seconds, and then it was over. His head cleared, and the pain subsided. For a while, there was nothing, just him being inside the pod. The excruciating noise returned as he approached the destination. Then, once again, the sound and agony were gone. When Hal looked out his window, he only saw corn. Nagle was no longer in the lab; he was in a cornfield. He took it all in and then waited to be launched back to the present. After three minutes, like originally programmed, the pod created a horrific sound with an incredible volume, and then, just like that, he was back in the lab.

Hal asked to go back to Montreal, Canada, on September 26, 1976. Stevenson agreed, and they tried it. The aim of every trip was to observe and collect data. TEPs were to keep their interactions with people as limited as possible as to avoid any changes or creating a paradox. It was always about learning and not disrupting the timeline. This trip back in time gave Hal the chance to watch his beloved Philadelphia Phillies clinch the National East title with a 4–1 win over the Montreal Expos. Hal sat in the upper deck and paid $3.50 to get through the gate.

A beer cost him $0.75, and a hot dog cost him $0.50. He was thrilled. That was the fun part of the day. He was lucky enough to land in a secluded spot, and he camouflaged the pod with the cloaking device. The cloaking device was effective and essentially made the vessel unseeable to anyone. However, an unknowing person could walk right into it. Hal enjoyed the Phillies game all by himself. He chatted with a few other fans, but he steered clear of true interaction, and he got himself back home.

Stevenson wanted them to travel in two-man teams to avoid anyone getting stranded in the past alone. Two heads were better than one, and maybe one of them could make it back if something went terribly wrong. Eventually, TIME brought on three more TEPs, and the exploration continued. Each trip back would provide more and more knowledge. Stevenson theorized and developed ground rules based on the experience and reports of the TEPs. The present did not seem to change based on anything they had done in the past.

Two TEPs were sent each trip to observe and record events, chart the sky, and continue to learn about history. They took no weapons, and they dressed like those in the period where they were going. They gathered artifacts and brought them back home. The timeline did not change at all. Everything seemed the same. The memories of the TEPs were the same as everyone else's when they came back. Hal interacted more and more with people, but nothing ever changed. Life was the same when they returned as when they had left. Hal went back and watched Nixon and JFK debate on September 26, 1960. He saw Charles Lindbergh land in Paris on May 21, 1927. He witnessed Martin Luther King Jr's "I Have a Dream" speech from Washington, DC, on August 28, 1963. Hal had gone the furthest back when he journeyed to England on October 14, 1066, to witness the Battle of Hastings. The trip was scary. He and his partner were afraid of getting too close to the warfare or interacting with the natives and being dragged into combat. They stayed a mile away and watched with high-powered binoculars. They could never leave behind anything from this time. The effects on technology could shift the timeline and threaten their own existence.

CHAPTER 8

Nagle refocused his attention away from his thoughts about his past trips and now listened as Davidson, Stevenson, and Wakefield were going to explain time travel, the theft of a time machine, and the mission ahead of them as quickly as possible to seven men who until now had thought time travel was something in books and movies. While Nagle prepared to listen, he also prepared himself to watch the faces of the seven men who were about to have their worlds rocked. He truly enjoyed the look of sheer confusion that possessed the faces of people when they found out. Seeing their looks of utter dismay never got old to him.

"Gentlemen, we are facing a national security crisis on a scale that we are only now understanding. The president was briefed, and he authorized the mission you are about to undertake. Right now, you are sitting in a top-secret government laboratory. For the past several years, this facility has been researching our ability to travel through time. The United States is the only nation with this technology. It is real, and we can travel back to the past. We have traveled back in history. Hal Nagle, who is seated to my left, is the Neil Armstrong of time travel," said the CIA chief. He casually pointed at Hal Nagle. Davidson said without missing a beat, "He has witnessed the signing of the Declaration of Independence. He watched JFK get shot, and he watched Michelangelo paint the Sistine Chapel."

"Actually, that was Kenny who watched Michelangelo paint, not me!" shouted Hal from his chair.

Then there was silence. The six paramilitary officers and the priest just sat there and looked at Davidson, then glanced over at Hal, and then looked at one another for a few moments. Then Cam McNally laughed. He laughed again until Tucker laughed, and then Jackson laughed. Soon, the entire team was howling. Xavier Cole stood up and asked if they were being punked.

"Where's Ashton Kutcher?" Cole was flashing his big smile.

"Is this like a psych test or something?" asked Sanchez with a chuckle. "You are messing with us, right? You want to see how much we will believe. How much can you push us? Is that it?"

"Good one!" Jackson said from his seat. "If we call your bullshit, do we pass the test?"

Father Patrick was not laughing. He was just sitting, listening, and observing. He just kept paying attention and waiting. The priest was waiting for the older CIA gentleman to speak again.

"Gentlemen, this is not a joke or a test or anything other than the truth. This is really happening, and I need you to sit down right now. You need to listen and focus on what I am telling you." Davidson spoke with calmness and a lack of emotion.

McNally and Bedford weren't having it. They continued to joke around, slap one another, and ask, "Where is the camera? Where's Ashton Kutcher? Is this going to be on MTV?" Fighter and Hunter were yukking it up and having fun with what they presumed was a prank. They were also the biggest SOG operators on the team and by far the most intimidating. Even when giving them an order in the field, Sanchez secretly hoped they listened. If they didn't, he wasn't sure what he would do. But they always listened because that was part of their job, and these two were excellent at their jobs.

Davidson had been speaking and carrying himself in a confident and cool manner. He counted to five in his head. "SIT DOWN AND SHUT UP! WE ARE NOT FUCKING AROUND! BE QUIET, AND LISTEN TO WHAT WE HAVE TO SAY! NOW!"

The laughter stopped. The horseplay and goofing around ceased, and everyone, especially McNally and Bedford, sat down quickly and quietly. Sanchez looked around at his men to make sure they were now listening and focused. Their faces had shifted from comedic and

TIME TERROR: DEFENDING JESUS

humorous to stone-cold serious in a matter of seconds. Sanchez was a professional, and his men were pros. They knew what to do.

Davidson was no longer yelling or swearing. He showed all the composure one would expect from a man in his position. "First, *Punk'd* got cancelled in 2007. As I was saying, we can travel back in time. Earlier tonight, this project was compromised. Nine Muslim extremists breached this facility. Eight of them stole a time-traveling pod. They are heading back to Bethlehem over two thousand years ago. Our assumption is their intention is to kill Jesus Christ, Mary, and Joseph and, therefore, prevent Christianity."

"Deus meus," Father Patrick said to himself. Latin for *my God.*

"Your mission, as ordered by the president, is to travel back to Judea two thousand years ago. Find Mary and Joseph. Make sure Jesus is born. Find and eliminate the eight suspects. Destroy or return to the present any present-day objects. We can leave behind nothing from our time. Hal Nagle is your pilot. Once you arrive in Bethlehem, his job will be to reprogram the stolen pod to return to our time or destroy it back there. Father Patrick O'Connor, who is sitting right here and you will meet in a minute, will be your interpreter and biblical guide. Questions?"

"Sir, what type of intel do we have on the terrorists?" said Sanchez.

"Their leader is Ahmed Faquar. He was born in Iraq but has been in the US since the late 1990s. Faquar has military experience with the Iraqi army. He is a radical. We believe the seven men with him are American citizens whom he recruited into his group."

"Are they part of a cell for al-Qaeda or ISIS?"

"It does not appear Ahmed has any contact with al-Qaeda or ISIS. We believe he is operating on his own."

"Do we have photographs or information, names, or descriptions of the men we are hunting?"

"We have compiled as much information as possible in very little time. We have driver-license photos, some pictures from social media, and details about their ages, heights, and weights. The trip will take you about three hours. You will have time to review the dossiers on the pod."

55

"How far behind them are we, sir?"

"We expect they will reach their destination in about thirty minutes. If you can leave ASAP, then they have approximately a three-hour advantage."

"ROE?" *Rules of engagement.*

"Kill them. Strip the bodies of any technology, weapons, and anything present-day. But kill them. Make sure they are all dead. You can take any actions you see fit to accomplish your mission. There are no rules. Terminate the eight hostiles, Jesus will be born, and life as we know it continues."

"Director, can you tell us more about Father Patrick and his role?"

"Father Patrick O'Connor is thirty-three years old. He is an expert in the historical facts surrounding the birth of Jesus. He has visited the area in the past and knows the terrain, and he also speaks Hebrew, Latin, Greek, and Aramaic."

"What is Aramaic, sir?"

"It is the language the Jews and people of Judea spoke during the time of Jesus."

"Father Patrick, you speak these languages, correct?" asked Davidson of the priest, with the perplexed look on his face.

Father Patrick was listening to two strangers speak of him as if he were not even in the room. He was still trying to wrap his head around time travel, and now he was going to lead a group of men to hunt down and kill other men. Could he really do this? Was it the right thing to do? "Thou shall not kill." "Thou shall not murder" was the more accurate interpretation. The church had always allowed for killing in self-defense, and Catholics could serve and fight in the armed forces. These men were not murderers. They were going to defend not only Jesus and the Holy Family but Christianity itself, as well. These men, and with his help, would do God's work.

"Father Patrick, are you okay?" said Davidson.

"What? I am sorry," said the startled Dominican.

"Do you speak those languages? Hebrew, Greek, Latin, and Aramaic?"

"Well. Latin and Aramaic are dead languages. No one speaks them anymore. But I can read and write in those languages."

"Can you talk in Aramaic? If you had to, Father?" said the veteran spy chief.

"I guess. Yes. I could. It is like Arabic, and I know some of that language."

"If your life depended on it, could you? Because it does."

"Yes," with confidence said Father Patrick, "I can do it."

Davidson introduced Dr. Victoria Stevenson as the genius and creator of time travel. He asked her to quickly explain a few rules and principles with time travel. Stevenson expected what their questions would be and attempted to answer them before they were asked. The scientist explained they used known alignments of the stars and planets to determine the time. They use basic latitude and longitude figures to establish the location, and the rest was essentially just too complicated for them to grasp. She said time is like a powerful enormous river, like the Mississippi River. It is always charging forward. People new to the program always asked her about new timelines being created and changing one thing in the past would lead to an entirely new timeline and, therefore, wiping out the timeline that created the time machine in the first place. She told the men not to worry about new timelines being generated with insignificant events. She gave them the example of throwing a stone into the Mississippi River. The act of hurling a stone into the mighty Mississippi would not change the direction of the river. A new rock hitting the surface of America's most famous river would not cause it to change course and end up running through South Carolina or New Mexico. Yes, the stone would affect some drops of water but not enough to change the direction of the river. Davidson explained how Jesus Christ not being born would be the equivalent of detonating a nuclear bomb and building the Hoover Dam in the Mississippi River. Minor events would not impact the overall timeline, but major events being drastically altered or not occurring would change the timeline.

Tucker asked why they couldn't go back and eliminate or capture Ahmed before any of this happened. Stevenson explained the same living being cannot be alive twice at the same time. Therefore, they cannot go back and get Ahmed right before he entered the laboratory or any other time within the last twentysome years. They can't get a newborn baby three hours old to travel back in time and shoot Ahmed. Once the Q-and-A session hit three minutes, Davidson put it to a stop. "That's it. Leave now. Hal can explain things during the trip. It will be like riding on a plane."

"But how does it work?" asked Tucker for the third time.

Davidson answered with his own questions, "Tucker, do you know how your computer works? Do you have a complete understanding of how planes fly? No. But you still find women to hook up with on Tinder, and you still fly to Vegas. Who cares how it works? It just does. Get in the pod, and go kill some bad guys.

"Nagle, get ready to launch. Wakefield, have these men move their gear to the pod and get ready. Sanchez and O'Connor, come with me."

Davidson, Stevenson, the young SOG leader, and the priest moved to a corner to speak in more detail. Davidson formally introduced Sanchez and Father Patrick and then got down to business.

"Sanchez, Father Patrick is an expert on the birth of Christ. He reads, writes, and can communicate in the languages of the time. He has been to this area previously," said Davidson.

"Mr. Davidson, I was in Bethlehem two years ago. There was a guy selling T-shirts and Mountain Dew at the Church of the Nativity. I think the situation is going to be different," the priest said.

"What's the Church of the Nativity?" asked Sanchez.

"It is a church built on the presumed birthplace of Jesus," said Father Patrick.

"Well, let's get the latitude and longitude of the church, and we will start our search there. We have to assume the terrorists know this, too, and will head there first," said Sanchez.

"I agree that's the most likely place to begin, but there are so many more factors and concerns. Dr. Stevenson, I presume you are using the triple conjunction as the focal point for your planet and star alignments, is that right?" said Father Patrick.

"Yes," Stevenson said.

At the same time, the two CIA men asked, "What's the triple what?"

Father Patrick spoke before the brilliant physicist and said, "The triple conjunction is a unique positioning of Saturn, Mars, and Jupiter that occurs once every nine hundred years. We believe it to be the Christmas star. It appeared in Judea in 6 BC."

"That's correct, Father. We can't actually set our time travel destination to December 25 in the year 0," said Stevenson.

"We could get there, and the Holy Family won't arrive for another six months. Or we could get there, and Jesus is a year old. We just don't know," said Father Patrick.

"That's correct, but it does not matter," said Davidson. "Your objective is to kill the terrorists before they wipe out Jesus, Mary, and Joseph. You probably will not witness the actual birth. All that matters is that you hunt down the terrorists and eliminate them before they kill Jesus. Based on the calculations, you will arrive a few hours after the terrorists."

Sanchez was trying to develop a plan, a course of action. "Father, let's think this through. Where would you go if you were trying to find an unborn child in Bethlehem two thousand years ago?"

"Okay. As we said, we should start at the presumed location of the child's birth, the Church of the Nativity. It is probably a cave or part of someone's house, but I would start there. Also, you would have to be discreet. The Jews are a close-knit group. They will not take kindly to strangers showing up and asking a lot of questions about their kin. The Romans are big into law and order. The terrorists can't just start killing pregnant women or anyone with infants. The Romans would put an end to that at once."

"So what do we do?"

"I think we watch and wait. We try to observe anyone new to the community. We are looking for a young couple with no other children and the wife is pregnant or maybe has a newborn child."

"Okay. We start there. We head to the latitude and longitude coordinates of the church, and we look for the terrorists. During the trip, we will review their photos. When we arrive, we get to that location, look for the terrorists, and do our own watching and waiting for the Holy Family."

Sanchez and O'Connor were now on the same page. Davidson was pleased with the initial strategy. He said Nagle would be given the coordinates they needed to locate the future location of the Church of the Nativity. He expressed the need to get moving, as the pod was almost ready to launch.

"Wait," said Father Patrick. "We are going to stand out like sore thumbs."

"Not to worry, Father. We are sending the proper attire for the time period with you," Davidson said.

"That's not what I mean. Remember, the average person only lived to about thirty-five years old back then. Mary and Joseph were young. She was just a teenager. The average man was about 5'5", and they were all Middle Eastern."

"So what's the issue?" asked Sanchez.

"The issue? We are going to look like aliens to these people. We are a group of six white guys, a Latino, and a Black man, and we are all six inches taller than everybody, and that one guy, the giant Irishman, is going to look like Goliath to these people. Plus, we are all old by their standards," said O'Connor.

Sanchez and the priest both looked at Davidson for a response. The old spymaster had faced countless questions in his career. Many of them he could easily predict, but not this one. He was in unchartered waters. He wrinkled his nose, pursed his lips, and gave it some thought.

"Well. You are the only option we have, so you will just have to deal with it. The terrorists have the same problem, well...not the Middle Eastern-looking part. But they, too, will be giants and on the older side of life. That should help you identify them. Besides, you aren't there to make friends. Just find the eight bad guys, and take them out," said Davidson.

CHAPTER 9

The CIA troopers and Father Patrick took their seats in the pod. Father Patrick had changed from his habit and shoes into Desert Battle Dress Uniform and boots. Other than his rosary beads and Bible, he matched the six battle-tested warriors perfectly. The eight seats faced each other, four against one wall and four on the other. Nagle was positioned closest to the control panel. Jackson and Bedford finished securing the team's weapons, explosives, and supplies. Besides the military equipment, they were also bringing attire that would match what the locals would be wearing. Packed away were tunics, robes, and sandals. Since Father Patrick was the unit's interpreter, he was also the unit's banker. If they were forced to interact with the people of Judea, it occurred to Nagle they would need money. Andrew Jackson's face on a slip of paper would not get you much two thousand years ago. Nagle commandeered pearls and diamonds from the TIME office to use for currency. Father Patrick held the valuable items in one of his many pockets on his DBDUs.

The eight seats fit tightly together, and there was little room for personal space. While members of the Time Team strapped in the rookie time travelers, one of them pointed out an important accessory. "You each have a barf bag under your seat."

"Barf bag?" said Jackson. "Is this going to be rough?"

As Nagle checked and rechecked the controls for the prelaunch process, he explained. "It can be. I ain't gonna bullshit you. The first few minutes are intense. After that, it will calm down, and it will be like flying in a plane. You are all pros, so you will be fine." Nagle winked at Father Patrick and gave him a knowing smile.

"I got $20 that says McNally blows chunk," said Cole.

"I want in on that for sure," agreed Tucker.

"You pussies are on," said the big man. "Sorry, Father. I meant to say, 'You gentlemen have a bet.' Is that better, Father?"

"Gentlemen, I was not born a priest. Trust me, we're good. I agree with my Irish friend. He's not puking."

It thrilled McNally for the support of the clergyman, and he high-fived Father Patrick. Davidson stuck his head into the pod for one last look at the crusaders. "Defend Jesus, Mary, and Joseph, eliminate the terrorists, and do whatever you have to do. Godspeed."

The door was shut and sealed. "Less than sixty seconds to launch. Gentlemen, it's going to be loud. I mean really loud for about ninety seconds after we launch. The volume will not kill you. You are gonna think it will, but it won't."

The calmness of the CIA men amazed Father Patrick. Their world, like his, had just been transformed less than ten minutes ago, but they seemed…over it. Their attitude was, like, "We got this." Father Patrick was apprehensive and unsure. He was about to travel back in time two thousand years to help defend an unborn or maybe recently born Jesus, and he was going to have to be part of a kill squad. When he was nervous, he prayed.

"I would like to lead us in a prayer."

"Do it fast, Father. We got forty-five seconds," announced Nagle.

"In the name of the Father, Son, and the Holy Spirit." Sanchez and McNally blessed themselves. The other men all bowed their heads in silence. "Dear Lord in heaven, please bless us on this mission to serve Your son. Please give us the strength to do Your work. May our courage not falter. May our efforts bring lasting peace. May we return to our loved ones. Saint Michael the Archangel, patron saint of warriors, pray for us. Our Lady of Victory, pray for us. Amen."

"FIVE SECONDS! HERE WE GO!" yelled Nagle over the growing noise.

Wow! Saint Michael the Archangel. That's cool, thought Sanchez as he made the sign of the cross. He was thinking of Beca and the Saint Michael the Archangel medallion he wore around his neck. He said his own silent prayer, and then it felt like his head was about to explode with pain. Sanchez had never felt such intense discomfort inside his head. The sound was everywhere. There was no escaping it. He tried to open his eyes to check on his men, but he couldn't do it. His eyelids stayed shut as he weathered the waves of pain that coursed through his body. How could anything cause this much physical pain? Sanchez could feel his entire body shaking and prayed it would stop. Then it was over. The sound was gone. The piercing sound that had rocketed through his being was now gone. Everything was silent and still.

Nagle checked the control panel, and everything was okay. One could never get used to the launch pain. He had tried earplugs, headphones, etc. None of them worked. One just had to deal with it and know it would eventually end. After checking the controls and the computer, Nagle looked over at the seven newbies. They were all puking their guts out. Thankfully, they all had barf bags in their hands. He laughed.

CHAPTER 10

Thoughts and emotions ripped through Ahmed's mind so fast he wondered if the vehicle he and his seven fellow fighters occupied was moving as briskly as his own internal reflections. Ever since he had celebrated the Twin Towers coming down on 9/11, he had longed for the day when he would strike at the heart of America. His jihad would be so much more profound than killing a few thousand Americans and destroying two skyscrapers. He would extract Christianity from history. He would erase the Christians and their false god from the face of the earth. Allah and Mohammed would be the true rulers of mankind. All he had to do was to kill an infant. Murder a baby, and he would prevent it all. No Jesus means no Christianity, no dominance of the Western world, no ideas of free will, liberty, freedom, and therefore, no America and no Israel.

Ahmed's hatred toward the United States and the West began when he entered the Iraqi army at age sixteen. He joined not out of a sense of purpose or wanting to serve his country, but essentially because his own father could think of nothing else to do with him. So at age sixteen, Ahmed joined the infantry. Saddam Hussein and Iraq had been humbled by the Americans several years earlier during the Persian Gulf War. Ahmed's superiors instilled in him a hatred toward the American invaders and their ever-present ally, Israel. Ahmed trained hard and discovered he did have a purpose. His life had meaning. Finally, he felt like he was part of something bigger than himself. Ahmed never saw combat, but he was effective with his rifle, and he won more bouts than he lost in his hand-to-hand-combat drills. His officers recognized this tall teenager as fierce, aggressive, and smart. He displayed in his fighting a ruthlessness that made him feared and admired by his fellow soldiers.

Ahmed would never back down from a fight. He had quickly gained the reputation as a promising young soldier who was without fear. Word was spreading throughout camp that young Ahmed Faquar was a force. Tired of hearing this talk about some teenage boy, a twenty-nine-year-old veteran named Samir decided to teach the kid a thing or two. Samir had fought in the Persian Gulf War. He claimed he had killed an American soldier in the Battle of Wadi al-Batin. Samir told the tale that he was two hundred yards from the American armored vehicle when he spotted the blue-eyed and blond-haired American through the crosshairs of his AK-47. He fired a quick burst and saw the American lose his life with two shots through his neck.

Samir was not as big as Ahmed, but he had a similar stature, and his shaved head gave him a menacing appearance. Ahmed was sitting at the end of the bench, finishing his kibbe for lunch, when the older Samir approached him. The soldiers were eating outside in the dusty camp, spread out among several wooden tables and chairs.

"I didn't get enough to eat," barked Samir as he reached in to grab the last few bites of Ahmed's kibbe. Samir leaned his head in close to Ahmed's, and he reached for the dish of minced meat and nuts with his right hand. In an instant, Ahmed used his left hand to grab Samir's right wrist, and at the same moment, he shot out his right fist into Samir's Adam's apple. The blow to the throat caused a muscle spasm, and the victim had difficulty breathing. With his challenger gasping for air, Ahmed rose to his feet, pulled Samir's right wrist toward him. This move caused Samir to roll his shoulders away from Ahmed, thus leaving his face wide-open. Ahmed struck again. A short, quick right to Samir's mouth sent blood from his lip and a tooth shooting across the table. Samir was bloodied and beaten in less than three seconds. Samir was lying with his back on the table and his feet hanging to the ground. Ahmed spit into his lunch plate, picked up the remaining bits of kibbe, and stuffed it into Samir's face.

"You can have the rest." Ahmed strolled away from the lunch table.

The officers did not discipline Ahmed for his mealtime attack. The incident even made him more favorable to them. Captain Abdullah Kazem took a liking to Ahmed. Captain Kazem was in his mid-thirties and believed Ahmed had promise. Kazem had seen action in the war against the US. He did not tell tall tales like the now-battered and bruised Samir. He said, the next time Iraq faces the Americans in battle, "We need to be stronger and mentally tougher than before. Otherwise, we will face the same fate as we did in 1991."

Kazem allowed Ahmed to listen in on his conversations with other officers. Ahmed paid close attention to the talks of tactics and strategies. Kazem gave his young prodigy military books to read and gave him additional training to make him better with his rifle, his knife, and his hands. Ahmed looked forward to the day when he would be tested on the field of battle. Besides the military education from Kazem, Ahmed was learning about Islam. He was studying the Koran with Captain Kazem. Unlike his father, Kazem showed Ahmed where in the Koran it states that Jews and Christians are no friends to the Muslim world and the Christians and Jews can only be allies to each other. Kazem would routinely misinterpret verse 5:51 of the Koran to turn Ahmed against the US and Israel. Verse 5:51 states, "O believers, do not hold Jews and Christians as your allies. They are allies of one another; and anyone who makes them his friends is surely one of them." Kazem spent many hours teaching Ahmed about how to lead men and hate the West.

After two years away, Ahmed was excited to return home on leave from the army. He wanted to see his parents, especially his mother, Aisha, whom he adored. Regardless of creed or color, there is a special bond and love between a mother and a son. Aisha always looked out for her younger son and stood up for him to his father. Ahmed's father, Hassan, was not an abusive man, but he seldom saw the positives in Ahmed. He viewed his younger child as a violent, unintelligent mistake. Ahmed was not planned. No couple planned to have children sixteen years apart. Aisha knew Ahmed was a gift from Allah. For the first time in his memory, Ahmed was proud and confident. He was happy with the direction of his life. He had formed self-worth in the military, had a mentor in Captain Kazem, and a powerful belief in new things he was learning about Islam.

Ahmed's life was about to take a stunning turn when he walked into his parents' home, during his leave for two weeks from the military. He was happy to be back in Al Basrah, the city he grew up in and had lived his whole life in until his departure for the army. He was wearing his dress uniform, and he had expected to be greeted by the pleasing aromas of his favorite foods, kebab, and dolma. Instead of encountering the wonderful smell of grilled lamb, vegetables, and rice, Ahmed's family was hurrying about the house in a hushed panic. His relatives each had a small duffel bag under their arms as they moved about the house, looking through cabinets and drawers.

"Praise Allah! You are home," his mother said as she wrapped her arms around her son's now-broad shoulders. She was a small woman and had to stretch up on her toes to reach him. "Your timing is perfect. I was beginning to worry you were running late."

"Late for what?"

"We knew you would be home today, and we have a two-day window to make our escape," said his mother. "We are leaving Iraq and going to the United States. Your father has made the arrangements. Your father saved the life of a young boy last month on his operating table. This boy's father runs the border checkpoint into Kuwait. He has promised us passage into Kuwait. Once there, we can get to the United States."

"What? Why?"

"Your father and brother are skilled doctors, and we are fleeing a brutal dictator. We will all have a better life."

Ahmed was shocked. He felt betrayed. "But this is our home. Iraq is our country. America is the enemy. Why would we go to the place that wants to destroy us?"

"My darling Ahmed." She took her son's face into her soft hands. Aisha's eyes were calm and filled with love. She knew what was best for her young son. She also knew he would never listen to his father, but he would listen to her. "My son, Iraq is a broken country. This is our homeland, and we will always be proud of our people, but

Saddam is leading our beloved nation to ruin. The sanctions by the US and UN are crippling our economy. Our lives will never be good under his rule. Iraq is headed towards chaos, and we must leave as a family while we can. My son, you know I love you and will always do what is best for you. Haven't I always taken care of you? Protected you? Loved you?"

Ahmed took stock of himself. He was no longer a child. He was eighteen years old. He was a soldier and knew how to fight with a gun, a knife, and his bare hands. They trained him to kill other people, and he knew how to inflict pain on a person. He loved Iraq, and he loathed America and the West. How could he leave his country for the enemy? Yet how could he leave his mother? Isn't it a son's duty to be respectful of his parents? Could he abandon his mother for Iraq? Ahmed looked around his house. He saw the expressions of anxiety and fear on the faces of his father, his brother, and his brother's wife and kids. They looked scared and frightened. He looked back at his mother, and he saw only love. Ahmed knew what he had to do. He had to say yes to his mother's love.

Less than an hour later, Ahmed was out of his military uniform and dressed casually as he sat in a minivan with his parents, his brother, and his family. The irony of driving down the fifty miles on Highway 80 from Al Basrah to the border of Kuwait was not lost on Ahmed. Back in 1991, the Iraqi military had fled Kuwait along this same stretch of highway. The Iraqis had tried to hightail it back to Iraq as the American forces liberated Kuwait in the opening days of the First Persian Gulf War. The US Air Force created a bottleneck along the highway by attacking both the front and the rear of the Iraqi convoy, racing to get back across the border. The allied forces destroyed close to three thousand vehicles and inflicted over one thousand causalities on this paved earth that earned the nickname the Highway of Death. Ahmed was now escaping from Iraq on the same roadway his predecessors had tried to escape to Iraq. He felt shame. Ahmed knew he would never face the Americans on the battlefield, but he vowed he would still fight them in the future.

*****

68

After fifteen minutes of travel time, the unit sent by the US government to defend Jesus started to discuss the mission. Sanchez had passed out photos and hastily prepared bios on the men they would be hunting. The CIA operators, Nagle, and O'Connor traded photos and dossiers back and forth, hoping to memorize each face.

"So this is the big, bad dude in charge of the assholes that we are going to whack?" asked Tucker as he held up the New Jersey driver's license picture of Ahmed Faquar. "He is one ugly dude. No wonder he hates the world. No offense, Father, but I would hate God, too, if He made me this ugly."

"Tucker's right, these guys are really fugly," said Bedford.

"Well, no one can be as pretty as our boy Xavier over there, but these guys are pretty badass," Sanchez said. Cole ran his fingers through his golden locks, smiled, and blew Bedford a kiss just to be funny. Sanchez continued, "The leader, Ahmed Faquar, trained in the Iraqi army, did some boxing when he got to the US and worked as the muscle for a low-level Arab crime boss in Paterson, New Jersey."

"You mean he worked for Muhammad Soprano?" said Bedford.

"Seriously, these guys are nasty. Two of them have fought MMA bouts, two are brothers who went to Afghanistan to fight along the Taliban. How the hell they got back into the US is a mystery. Three others have done real time in prison for assault, kidnapping, arson, weapons charges, and other felonies," said Sanchez.

"Sound like your normal, everyday citizens from New Jersey to me," said Jackson. But nobody laughed. Each man, especially Father Patrick, went back to studying the photos and information. They all wanted to be ready for the challenges that lay ahead.

CHAPTER 11

If she were being honest with herself, and she always tried to be, Dr. Victoria Stevenson knew there was really nothing more she could do at the TIME lab. Her team successfully launched the CIA unit of fighters two thousand years into the past, and now all they could do was wait. They could not contact Hal Nagle. There was no preset return time. There was nothing. The team could return at any moment or never. They just had to wait. The White House called and ordered Davidson and Stevenson to report to 1600 Pennsylvania Avenue. Stevenson was looking forward to it. She only hoped she could stop back at her house, freshen up, and change her clothes. She was still in her pajamas, and her hair was up. Stevenson assumed she would brief the president and his key people on her project. The scientist was really hoping not to do it in pink sleep pants and a purple top.

Davidson told her she would have ten minutes in her house to clean up and change. Stevenson did not waste a second as she bolted up the stairs in her center-hall colonial and raced around her second floor. As she quickly brushed her teeth, washed her face, and threw on a beige skirt and matching blazer, she contemplated what she would say to the leader of the free world. Would he marvel at her brilliance or chastise her for being reckless? She had been to the White House once before. She had been a freshman in high school when she visited the People's House on a class trip. Richard Nixon had been president on that day. She was not sure how her meeting would go, but she knew it would differ from the last time she was there.

Stevenson followed Davidson into the Oval Office. Davidson introduced her to the president, the vice president, the NSA chief, and two other men she had never seen before. She barely caught their names, and she took her seat on the couch. Stevenson tried not to be awestruck in the presence of the president. However, that was a challenge. Stevenson was supremely confident and knew she was the smartest person in the room. Nevertheless, the president was sitting just three feet to her left. He was in the chair in front of the fireplace. She had seen presidents sit in that same spot for decades, and now she was here. Stevenson had not bothered to vote in the last election. Politics was never important to her. She had spent her life focused on science and discovery, but still, this was the president, and she wondered how she would be treated.

The room was quiet, and everyone waited for the president to speak first. "At this moment, I think I understand how Abraham Lincoln felt when he met Harriet Beecher Stowe in 1862. I feel like I must quote our sixteenth president, 'So this is the little lady who made this big war.' Dr. Stevenson, I wish we were meeting under better circumstances. You are obviously brilliant and have created the most incredible...thing... I guess...in human history. I wish I could say congratulations, but I really need to say...WHAT THE HELL HAVE YOU DONE?"

Stevenson's mouth hung open, and the president continued his tirade. "Why? Why? Our existence hangs in the balance here. It truly does. The world as we know it is in peril. Right now, I don't care how it works. I really don't. Hopefully, there will be time for that at some point. Right now, we need to know what will happen if our team fails. What are the effects of time travel on our timeline? Are there multiple timelines? What have you learned?"

Stevenson knew each person had a thousand questions, concerns, and fears. She figured the best way to do this was to just answer each question as they came at her. As calmly and professionally as she could, she replied, "We have learned a great deal through our missions and research. The best we can tell is there is only one timeline, this one."

"How many missions have there been?" said the president.

"If I had my laptop with me, I could tell you exactly, but—"

"Ballpark it for us."

"Over fifty, less than one hundred. I would say about seventy in total."

"Where and when did they go? How far back? What changed after the trip?"

"The missions have been solely observational. Our Time Explorers, we call them TEPs, are instructed not to interact with people in the past, and they do not leave any technology from our time behind. So far, we have seen no changes to our timeline."

"Are there multiple timelines happening at the same time?" asked the VP.

"No. It is not possible."

"Why not?" said the VP.

"It is just not feasible. Think of it this way. If every decision and action that was taken or not taken created a new timeline or parallel universe, the timelines would be infinite and ever changing. Here's an example. I changed into a beige outfit before coming to the White House. If I had chosen a black outfit, would my life be different? Yes. It would be because I am wearing different clothes, then that would have created a new timeline. If you play the theory out, then count-less timelines would be produced for every person on the planet and all occurring simultaneously. It is inconceivable. There is one time-line, but a significant event can alter it."

"Explain," said the president.

"Think of time as an immense and powerful river, like the Nile or the Missouri." Stevenson hoped she could gain some favor from the president by using the Missouri River in her example. "If you throw a rock in the river, it will continue to move forward. Sure, some water molecules will be affected by the rock, but not the river itself. It keeps flowing. That is time."

"What about the butterfly effect?" asked the tall advisor whose name Stevenson had missed when he was introduced.

"You mean the idea that a butterfly flapping its wings will cause a typhoon weeks later? No. That's not a thing. In one of our earliest missions, we had a TEP go back to 1869 to watch the first college football game between Princeton and Rutgers. The TEP watched the game in New Brunswick, New Jersey, and had limited interaction with the people of the time. He had a beer and a bowl of soup at a local inn. When he returned to our time, nothing had changed," she answered.

"But how do you know that? If you play the theory out, the people who did not time-travel would not be aware of a change in the timeline because that is the only timeline they know. Any changes to the past would have already happened to the people who did not travel back. Their lives would be the same. Only the time traveler would know a change. And he can't possibly know if everything is the same."

"Tom is right," pointed out the other advisor Stevenson did not know and whose name she had not caught. "Let's say you sent a Time Explorer back to watch the Battle of Gettysburg. Somehow, he causes the South to win the battle. When the Time Explorer returned to the present, all of us would have the memory that the South had won the battle. We would not know the North was supposed to win."

"We have a safeguard against that," said Stevenson. "Before each mission, we give the TEP a detailed synopsis of historical events he is about to witness. The details of what happened during the event, who was involved, and what were the historical effects of that event. When the TEP returns from the trip, we retrieve the report from the pod and compare it to the known information. So far, we have had no material changes to history."

"What do you mean when you say 'material' changes?" said Tom Scott. Now she remembered. Tom Scott was the really tall one and Ted Bennett was the other guy. Bennett was chief of staff. What role did this tall guy play?

Stevenson replied, "By 'material' I mean significant. We went back to observe central Pennsylvania in July 1863. The North still prevailed, Jeb Stuart still showed up late for the battle, and Pickett's charge failed. However, we can't be sure that every single soldier who was supposed to die, survive, or get wounded actually had the same outcome. But why wouldn't they? We changed nothing, so the outcome should be the same."

"Can we communicate with our CIA team while they are on the ground two thousand years ago? How do we know how they are doing? How do we get a status report?" The president resumed command of the conversation.

"There is no radio contact or communication between us and them," Stevenson said. "It is not possible to communicate with them."

Davidson had been silent for some time and inserted himself into the discussion. "However, we know the terrorists have not succeeded yet in their mission."

"How do we know that?" said Vice President Kim.

"Because we are still here and we all know who Jesus Christ is," said the CIA chief. "As long as we are alive and know who Jesus is, then the mission to stop the terrorists was successful or, at the very worst, still ongoing. Think about it."

"But by your logic, we will not know if they fail," said Bennett.

"We have theorized, if we alter a past event in such a manner that our timeline was to undergo a major shift, we would simply cease to exist. Essentially, we would disappear," said Stevenson. There was a pause in the room as her last statement settled into everyone's mind.

"Like *Avengers: Infinity War*?" asked the president. Like his three kids, he himself was a fan of the superhero genre. "We would just flitter away?"

Stevenson did not get the president's movie reference. With little detail, Tom Scott explained the premise of the plot to the renowned physicist. "I don't know the movie, but I would say...yes. We would just disappear somehow. We would cease to be present."

"Why don't we just send two soldiers back with a rocket launcher to the lab's parking lot ten minutes before the terrorists arrive and then blow them up before any of this happens?" asked Tyler Evans. "There are a ton of actions we can take to wipe them out before any of this happens. Let's do that. Why do we have to chase the terrorist across time?"

"You cannot travel back to a time when you were already alive," said Stevenson. She quickly explained how it had taken them many launch attempts to learn that basic fact. She explained how a person cannot be alive twice at the same time and how time loops were prevented because you could not travel into the future. For the time being, the president had heard what he needed to from Dr. Stevenson. He asked her to return to the TIME lab and monitor the mission from there. Once Stevenson exited the room, the advisors all started talking at once and asking one another questions. During that activity, the president pulled Tom Scott close to him and whispered into his ear.

"Maybe we should have her…you know…permanently retired. I don't know. Just a thought right now. But maybe. Keep this between us." Scott simply nodded and joined in the ongoing discussion.

*****

The pod Kumar had programmed to arrive in Judea two thousand years in the past displayed a countdown to arrival. According to the clock, Ahmed and his men would arrive in the past in twenty-nine minutes and twenty-four seconds. Ahmed called out to his fighters, "We have less than thirty minutes to go. Prepare your gear, and remember our mission. Discipline is key. We must follow our plan to bring glory to Allah."

"Inshallah!" several of the men yelled in unison. *God willing.*

Ahmed felt supremely confident in his strategy. He had done his research and given it a great deal of thought. He knew what to do. The men knew what to do. Patience was going to be vital. They would have plenty of time to search for Jesus and His parents. Omar was going to destroy the lab, and any witnesses left behind would be dead. Nobody would know where and when they had gone. Nobody would be after them. It was perfect. His confidence in the future made him reflect on his past. He thought once again of how he had arrived at this point in his life.

Ahmed's father had been correct. The van carrying his entire family had slipped through the checkpoint into Kuwait without an incident. His father and his brother shamelessly threw themselves at the mercy of the American diplomats at the US Embassy in Kuwait City. The two of them claimed Saddam Hussein had persecuted them and all their lives were at risk. They were just two doctors hoping to make a better life in America. Ahmed knew how to speak English. His parents were both well-educated and had made sure he and his older brother could speak and read English. Ahmed hated the language and had not spoken in the devil's tongue since he had left home for the army. He wished he did not know what his father and his brother were saying to the Americans. It was humiliating to listen to them put down their own homeland.

As the family moved through the diplomatic process, he was getting angrier and angrier as the two of them kept telling the same lies repeatedly to a new set of US State Department officials. His mother could see his temper building, and she assured him it was for the best. She promised him everything would be better once they got to the United States.

"You will see, my son. Once we get to the United States, you will be happy. We will all be happy and safe. Allah is in America. Allah is everywhere. I promise."

*****

Sanchez and his team learned the faces and names of their prey. They knew their objectives, and they had a strategy. Now, they just had to arrive in the past and execute the plan. No pressure, just the fate of life as they knew it was on the line. The team started peppering Nagle with questions about time travel, his experiences, and if the arrival would hurt as much as the departure. Unfortunately for Nagle, what these guys understood from time travel was based on movies.

"I still can't believe we can wear clothes and bring stuff with us," said Jackson. "Kyle Reese and Schwarzenegger had to be buck naked when they went back in time. If you think about it. That's kind of what we are doing. Traveling back to make sure a child is born. But unlike *Terminator*, we get to bring our own weapons."

"You know, Jackson, I said the same thing to Stevenson about being naked when all the early attempts failed. She looked at me like

I was crazy. That's before they understood you can't go back to a time where you were already alive," said Nagle.

"So these movies have been lying to us for all these years?" asked Bedford. "*Back to the Future, Avengers: End Game, Time Cop, About Time*…they are all BS?"

"Basically, yes. Especially *Avengers: End Game.* That one is the worst. It just throws all time-travel logic out the window."

"That's a bummer. I love that movie," said Sanchez. "As a matter of fact, all of us like that movie. Isn't that right, Surfer?"

"Surfer?" said Father Patrick. "Who is Surfer?"

"I'm Surfer, ain't that right, Hunter?" said the tan and blond-haired Cole.

"Hunter? Who is Hunter?" Father Patrick was confused. "Are these nicknames?"

"They are call signs, Father," responded the sniper from Pennsylvania.

"Call signs?" said Father Patrick.

"Father Patrick, I will explain," said Sanchez. "We don't call each other by our names when we are on comms. So we use call signs instead. Each one of us has an alter ego name we use during our ops. I know it may sound juvenile, but it works. I'm Papi because I'm the only one of us married with a kid.

"Cole is Surfer because he's a beach bum from California. McNally is Fighter because he is a big tough guy and was a boxer. Bedford is our sniper, so he is Hunter. Jackson is all about New York City, so he is called Gotham. Tucker is our medic, and his parents wanted him to be a doctor, so we just call him Doc."

"I think Nagle and Father Patrick need call signs too," said Cole.

After much debate among the SOG operators, they decided Nagle would be Fly Boy and Father Patrick would be Preacher. Nagle was concerned with preparing these men for their time travel experience and did not give his new handle much thought. Father Patrick, however, was slightly worried about his call sign.

"Preacher? I am not a great homilist. I am more of a scholar than I am a preacher," said Father Patrick.

"No worries, Father Patrick. I am sure you could deliver a humdinger of a sermon if you had to," Sanchez said with confidence.

"Nagle, can you explain to us what to expect when we arrive and what time-travel rules we need to follow?" asked the SOG leader.

"When we arrive, the high piercing sound will be back, but for whatever reason, it won't last as long. It will be a little disorienting when you first walk around. Sort of like your first few steps in the morning after a rough night of drinking. But eventually, it will feel the same. Going back this far will be really quiet. There will not be the background noise of highways, power lines, or the industrial world around you. It is going to be superquiet. I know Stevenson explained how time is like a massive river and it takes a major event for it to shift course, but that's not entirely true."

"What do you mean? It's not true?"

"Little things can and will make a difference. Think about it. If your great-great-great-great-grandfather dies before he impregnates your great-great-great-great grandmother, then you are never born. That's a problem."

"So what do we do or not do?"

"Do your best not to kill anyone before they are supposed to die. We really do not know the impact because this is the first time we are going back to do more than just observe and watch. We are going back to take action. Try to limit any collateral damage. Granted, going back to this part of the world should not lead to any direct relatives, but you never know. Here is an example. Let's say Bedford is shooting at Ahmed, but he misses—"

"I don't miss," said Bedford with a snarl in his voice and on his face.

"Let's just say you do."

"But I don't. So you can't say that I do."

Bedford's supreme self-confidence unnerved Nagle. The pilot could not tell if Bedford was just messing with him or if he was truly pissed that he insinuated the sniper could miss a shot. Nagle opted for a different analogy. "Okay. Let's say Ahmed kills a citizen of Judea because he needs to steal a donkey."

"Why the hell would anyone steal a donkey?" asked Jackson. "Wouldn't you just steal a horse instead?"

"Horses were very expensive and not very common in Judea back at the time of Jesus," said Father Patrick. "Sorry, Hal, as you were saying."

"Okay. Let's say that citizen was going to father five children but only fathers three because of his premature death. If the child that was never born was going to grow up and have a family but does not…well…we just do not know the ramifications."

The men let the comment sink in and thought about the implications. They exchanged quizzical looks in silence for a few moments.

"Let's make sure we only kill terrorists from 2023. We have eight targets, and let's do our best to only take out those eight," said Sanchez.

"Hey, Fly Boy!" McNally wanted to hear some stories from the experienced time traveler. "How many of these trips have you made, and what's one of the coolest things you have done?"

Nagle answered with a detailed account of the first Super Bowl. As the men asked Nagle more questions and he told more stories, the mood felt more relaxed as the SOG commandos listened to Nagle's tales of adventures in the past. However, Sanchez was not relaxed. Outwardly, he was calm and confident, but internally, he was worried. He was responsible for saving Christianity, and he had to do it without erasing people from the timeline. This was a lot to ask of anyone. At that moment, he wished he had his wife's faith.

CHAPTER 12

Samuel walked through his orchard of olive trees, inspecting and surveying the state of his business. For three generations, his family had harvested olive trees. The trees grew in the rocky and dry soil of Judea. Others thought he grew his trees too far apart. His younger brother, Jacob, would often complain that their father and their grandfather had more trees on the land and Samuel wasted too much space. Jacob was a fool, thought Samuel. Yes, he had fewer trees than the previous generations had, but he produced better-quality olives by having more space in between the trunks. The branches could reach farther and bared more desirable fruit. Better fruit meant a better harvest, a better crop, a better product to sell at the marketplace. It was still months from when it would be time for his family and laborers to gather and pick the fruit, but Samuel never rested. In a few months, the olives would be ripe, and his children and Jacob's children would begin the collection of the fruit. They would lay cloth tarps under the trees. Samuel's oldest son, Jonathan, would hit the trunk or lightly brush the branches to cause the olives to fall onto the tarps for easy collection. Jonathan used an old Roman javelin he had found in the hills one day to strike the trees. Jonathan had discovered the javelin and figured it must have been from an army training exercise. Like most families, Samuel had swords and daggers for protection, but it was rather unique to have an actual Roman javelin. At one point, Samuel and Jacob had been so determined to get every olive off the trees they would climb on ladders to get the olives that just would not fall. However, that practice had ended when Samuel's youngest son, Caleb, fell from a top branch. Twenty-five feet down, he landed on the side of his foot and broke his ankle. The child screamed in pain for days, and now, two years later, he walked with a severe limp.

On this late morning, the sun was not yet overhead and would not be for a while. Samuel was enjoying a walk of solitude among his trees. He strolled just on the outskirts of his orchard, taking in the bitter green scent of the trees. Samuel heard a rumbling in the distance. It was faint at first, but then the rumbling became louder and more pronounced. This strange sound was coming from the clearing not far up the hill to his left. It sounded like a Roman regiment was marching, but he had seen no soldiers. And then he saw it. The brilliance of the light. It was so white and dazzling it blinded him for a moment. He instinctively turned away, fell to one knee, and covered his face with his hands. The illumination had been so intense, his eyes had teared up. Samuel took a moment to gather himself. The rumbling noise had subsided, and the shocking light had faded. Samuel rose again to his feet and stared at something he could not comprehend.

The object was about five hundred paces from him. It looked like an arrow, except it had a roundness to it. Samuel guessed it was about eighteen to twenty cubits long and about six to eight cubits across. But where had it come from? And what was it? Samuel looked around, and he was still alone. He was the only person witnessing this strange event. An opening appeared on the side of the object. Samuel was afraid, and he quickly ducked behind an olive tree. He pressed his entire body against the gnarled and twisted trunk. Samuel peered around the side of the tree to observe the object and what was happening. He saw men exit the object. Even though he was five hundred paces away, he could see these men were very tall and large. Even from this distance, Samuel could see these men were a head or two taller than him. They had olive-colored skin, but their clothing was unlike anything he had ever seen. Instead of tunics or robes, they appeared to have cloth wrapped around each individual leg and arm. These men carried large black arrows that were about a cubit long. They pointed the arrows in each direction as they walked around the object. Samuel was scared but could not move at the same time. Samuel continued to watch as eight men exited the object. Each man was olive-skinned, tall; wore odd clothing; and carried these strange arrows.

Samuel heard movement and a rustling behind him. He turned quickly and saw Jonathan walking up.

"Jonathan, get down on the ground!"

Jonathan did as he was instructed and dropped to the ground. Samuel motioned for his son to stay low and to crawl toward him. Jonathan crawled on his belly and reached for his father. Samuel stood pressed against the tree, and Jonathan lay next to him. Samuel wished the trees were not so far apart. It would be easier to hide if the trees were closer. Damn his desire to produce better olives.

"Father, what is it?"

"Do you see it?"

"See what?"

"To your left. Five hundred paces in the clearing. Do you see it?" Samuel was not sure if he wanted his son to confirm his observation or say he saw nothing, meaning Samuel had lost his mind.

"What is that? Are those men or giants?"

Samuel stuck his head out from behind the tree, and Jonathan rose to his knees as they studied this astonishing object and these mystifying men. The two residents of Judea heard a loud bang, and part of the tree above Samuel's head fell as the tree shook. One giant was pointing the unusual arrow at them. Again, another loud bang, and another piece of the tree fell from above their heads.

"Run!"

He grabbed his son by the shoulders, hoisted him to his feet, and they both ran through the trees and headed back to their home.

"Abdullah! Cease-fire! Are you insane?" screamed Ahmed at the two-time felon.

Abdullah lowered his AR-15 semiautomatic rifle and tried to explain his actions. "But they saw us. We can't let them see us. What if they tell someone?"

"Who are they going to tell? They can't call the police, and who would believe them, anyway?" Ahmed felt his frustration growing.

They had been here less than two minutes, and already he had one of his men acting out. He had to get control and quickly.

"We stick to the plan. Mustafa and Kareem, bring out our supplies and gear from the storage area. Abdullah, you will get your chance to shoot something in a moment."

They had arrived in a remote area in a clearing close to olive trees. It appeared to be an orchard. There were no houses or buildings or structures of any kind as far as they could see. The ground was rocky and mostly dirt. There was some grass, but it was sporadic. The olive trees were tall, close to thirty feet high, and had enormous trunks. Ahmed could not help but notice how quiet it was. There was no background noise from Route 80 or the Garden State Parkway. There was no New Jersey Transit train running in the distance. It was superquiet. The air smelled fresh. Ahmed took a deep breath and filled his lungs with the purest air possible. It was air without the smells from carbon dioxide, pollution, manufacturers, power plants, or sewage treatment plants.

Mustafa and Kareem dragged out their weapons, ammunition, and gear, along with bottles of water and granola bars. Their weapons cache comprised of five AR-15 rifles, three 12-gauge shotguns, and several pistols, which included nine-millimeter Glocks and two revolvers. These were all guns Ahmed had purchased over the years. Two of the semiautomatic rifles had been illegally converted to full automatics. Ahmed knew the weaponry was over-the-top. He really only needed a knife to slit the throat of this woman called Mary and to drive that same knife through her baby. Ahmed only brought the excess to please his men. He had promised them a killing spree once they had achieved their goal. His men then dragged out two ten-gallon containers of gasoline. Ahmed ordered his men to put on the tunics and robes they took with them. The temperature was in the midfifties, so they kept the clothes from 2023 on and simply put the era-appropriate clothing over their jeans, cargo pants, and shirts.

"I am not putting on sandals," said Jabbar when Ahmed handed him a pair. "No way am I walking in those things. My feet will be killing me."

"So you are going to wear a tunic with Nike sneakers. Is that right?" said Ahmed.

"Yeah. Who cares?"

Ahmed was not sure if Jabbar was trying to test his authority or if he was just stupid. Jabbar had spent time in prison for assault, armed robbery, and trying to car jack an off-duty Paterson police officer two blocks from the police substation. Ahmed realized Jabbar was just that stupid.

"Okay. Wear the Nikes, but don't complain when you step in camel shit and ruin them."

In 1519, Hernán Cortés landed in Mexico from Spain. Cortés was a conquistador. His mission had been to conquer Mexico for the Spanish crown. To make sure his men were fully committed to the cause, Cortés scuttled his ships. History is not sure if he sank the ships or burned them, but either way, he eliminated the option of returning to Spain. He and his men had to conquer or die. This action ensured his men were dedicated to the success of the mission. Ahmed was going to follow the example set by Cortés five hundred years ago. Or was it 1,500 years from now?

Ahmed grabbed one of the fully automatic rifles, snapped in a full clip, and handed it to Abdullah.

"Go inside the pod, and go nuts. Shoot the whole place up," said Ahmed to his trigger-happy friend.

Abdullah stepped inside the pod, clutching the AR-15 with its aftermarket magazine that held one hundred rounds. With a giant smile on his face, Abdullah went crazy, blasting the interior of the pod apart. He obliterated the computer, the controls, and the seats. When he was finished, Umar went into the pod and poured the twenty gallons of gasoline all around the interior. Ibrahim, who had spent time in prison for trying to burn down a Methodist church and a Jewish synagogue, was given the honor of torching the vehicle. He tossed in a Molotov cocktail, and the fire was raging in a matter of moments.

"Brothers, there is no turning back. We will accomplish our mission to destroy Christianity and martyr ourselves for Allah," Ahmed stated coldly.

"Inshallah," his men replied.

The eight men from two thousand years in the future walked side by side with their weapons hidden under their tunics and robes. They pulled two utility carts. Ahmed had purchased the carts online. The idea of an internet seemed laughable to Ahmed now, given his current time and location. Each cart was made of steel and could carry over one thousand pounds. The four-foot-long carts rolled along behind them, filled with ammo, camping gear, food, and water. For the umpteenth time, Ahmed reminded his men their primary goal was to find the baby Jesus and His family first. Then, and only then, could the murderous rampage begin.

"Brothers, don't kill or harm anyone until we have eliminated the child. The Roman army maintains law and order. We cannot bring attention to ourselves or cause problems until Jesus is dead. We will have all the time in the world to cause mayhem and death after that."

The men walked in the general direction of 31.7043 degrees north and 35.2075 degrees east. Those are the latitude and longitude figures for the Church of the Nativity. Ahmed's plan was to scope out the area and look for Jesus and His parents. They used a compass to chart their direction and hoped it would get them near where they needed to be. Mustafa, who fought in the light heavyweight division of mixed martial arts, walked closest to Ahmed. He was in his late twenties, with a trim goatee that helped cover a scar that ran from his cheek to his chin. How he got the scar was in question. However, the prevailing theory was it came from a hooker he tried to get too rough with one night. Mustafa was peppering Ahmed with questions, but he was not really listening. Instead, Ahmed was thinking back to his long journey to this exact time and place.

Twenty years ago, when his family arrived in the United States, they settled in northern New Jersey. Paterson, New Jersey, is about twenty miles from New York City. By percentage of population, Paterson was second only to Dearborn, Michigan, for the largest number of Muslims. Of the almost 150,000 residents of Paterson, about 25,000 were Muslims. Ahmed's dad and brother joined the team of doctors at St. Joseph's University Medical Center. Ahmed felt insulted from day one with his father and brother associated with a Christian facility.

Ahmed had to admit he liked Paterson. Neighborhood stores and restaurants had signs and ads in Arabic. There were a dozen mosques in Paterson, and eventually, he found one that suited his radical views. He had joined a boxing gym and could continue his training as a warrior. It was not the same as the Iraqi army, but there was discipline, structure, and commitment. Just as his toughness and fighting style had attracted the attention of the officers in the Iraqi army, the same skills caught the eye of Saeed Aziz. Aziz thought of himself as the Muslim Mafia, but really, he was just a well-organized thug. Aziz was in his early fifties and had become too old, fat, and soft to do his own collections. He was a loan shark, ran a betting book, had a few drug dealers under his wing, and provided some protection for prostitutes who turned tricks out of a local strip club. Ahmed found Aziz completely reprehensible. He was a sinner and would never reach Allah's paradise. To Ahmed, the only people worse than Aziz were the scum and losers who owed Aziz money for their sins. If Aziz wanted to pay Ahmed $500 a week in cash to push around and rough up some infidels, who was he to say no? Ahmed liked his job. It provided him a lot of time to pray, spend time at his mosque, and continue his boxing regimen.

Ahmed had seen a lot and learned a lot during his first few years in America. Ahmed loved his mother more than he loved any person in the world, but she had been wrong. She said Allah was everywhere. He was even in America. However, Ahmed found no evidence Allah was in America. Yes, America had mosques, and some believers prayed five times a day, but this country was full of infidels and non-believers. It was not just the scum he dealt with for Aziz, but it seemed sinners and whores were everywhere in America. They were in the streets, on TV, in the movies, and in advertisements. Women were basically naked as they walked down the street and went shopping in stores and malls. Women practically fornicated on TV and in the movies. Not only did women flaunt their bodies and sell sex, but they also voted, drove cars, and could do as they pleased. This society could not last. It needed to be punished, and it had to be destroyed.

Ahmed viewed the terror attacks on September 11, 2001, as a promising start to America's demise. He did not dance in the streets on that day, but he celebrated internally. The attacks motivated him to do something great, as well. He thought about assembling his own cell. He would recruit and train his own team of jihadists, and one day, they would strike a great blow to the West. September 11, 2001, had motivated Ahmed to bring jihad to America. However, the actual date that changed his life was April 4, 2007.

On April 4, 2007, Levy Cohen was a twenty-two-year-old senior at New York University. Levy was an aspiring actor. He was a drama major and dreamed of following in the footsteps of other NYU alumni like Anne Hathaway, James Franco, and Angelina Jolie. He believed, with his looks, his NYU diploma, and his acting skills, he could write his own ticket, whether it be on the stage of New York City or the silver screen of Los Angeles. Levy had a range in his abilities. He had played Willy Loman and Atticus Finch onstage. He was good-looking, charming, well-connected, and on this Friday night at eleven o'clock, he was also drunk.

Levy had been kicking back at a small house party near mid-town Manhattan with a handful of friends. He had thrown back several Amstel Lights and downed a couple of kamikaze shots. Shots always went right to his head, and he knew it, but what the hell? Why not? He was feeling no pain and was feeling good. His cell phone rang in his pocket. He checked the caller ID, his buddy, Jake.

"'Sup, Jake?"

"Dude, she's here. You gotta get down here."

There was only one "she." She was Tamara Knight. Tamara had been Levy's obsession for the last two years. Tamara Knight should have had the word *sex* written on her forehead. Her body and her attitude exuded sexuality. Tamara was a talented actress, and Levy had first met her in a drama class two years ago. Unfortunately for Levy, Tamara always seemed to have a boyfriend, and she knew Levy desired her. She brushed off his advances, and this ridiculously attractive woman from Chicago just never seemed impressed with Levy's privilege and status. Levy knew by "here" his friend meant

Josie Woods Pub on Waverly Place. Josie Woods Pub was a popular bar for NYU students.

"Tamara is always there. What's different about tonight?"

"Tonight, she is drunk and bitching about how her boyfriend is a prick. And she asked me where you were."

"She asked about me?"

"Dude, if you want to hit that, you gotta get down here. Now!"

"Tell her I will be there in ten minutes. Tonight is the night."

Levy leapt from the couch and headed for the door. He yelled a quick "Thank you" to the host and was racing down the stairs to his car. It was not really his car. It was his dad's. Actually, it was not his dad's car either. It was Israel's car. The 2006 BMW 325i was black, with a leather interior, a kick-ass CD player, and diplomatic plates. Levy's father was Ari Cohen. Ari was the Israeli ambassador to the United Nations. Ari was a dedicated public servant to Israel and had worked his way up the foreign ministry food chain. He had been the UN ambassador for almost five years and used his influence to get his only son, Levy, out of his obligatory military service and into NYU.

Levy had parked in a handicapped spot and had a short distance to cover in the light rain that had been coming down for most of the day. He quickly slid behind the wheel of the German luxury car. The car's diplomatic plates gave it carte blanche to park wherever, speed wherever, and do whatever its driver wanted to do on the road. Levy always carried a diplomatic ID with him. He felt the alcohol rush to his head as he started the car. Levy would cruise down Broadway and bang a left on Eighth Street then park the car, and he would be in the bar in less than ten minutes. He took off and, after a few blocks, realized he was making great time. The road was unusually clear. He was getting every green light, and tonight he would finally sleep with Tamara Knight. Just the thought of her sensuous body made him step harder on the accelerator. Levy did not want to waste time driving when he could get with Tamara Knight.

"Shit!" he yelled. He had almost missed the left on Eighth. He was going close to fifty miles per hour and jerked the wheel hard to the left as not to miss the turn. If he missed the turn, he would have to go around the block and get to Josie Woods Pub three minutes later. That was three minutes less time to seal the deal with Tamara Knight.

Levy turned the wheel hard, and the passenger side front tire caught a slick spot on the roadway. Levy was drunk and reacted poorly when the car lurched on him. He hit the gas pedal instead of the brake.

The car picked up speed and crashed headfirst onto the sidewalk. Levy jumped out of the car to assess the damage and the likelihood he could still get to Tamara. The front grill was bashed in, courtesy of a USPS mailbox, but Levy was pretty sure he could drive it. He hopped back behind the wheel and tried to back up to get out of there. Levy could hear police sirens as people were gathering around the vehicle. He gunned the engine, but something was catching underneath the car. Something was stuck in the undercarriage. He stepped on the accelerator again. Nothing. Now, people were screaming at him, and two guys were pounding on the hood of the BMW. Levy rolled down his window as the police lights now filled the car.

"Hey, asshole! Watch it! Stop beating on the hood! It's a freakin' BMW!"

That was the last thing Levy said at the scene as a NYPD officer dragged him through the window, tossed him to the ground, and cuffed him. With his face pressed against the wet pavement, Levy looked under the car and, for the first time, he saw the two mangled and bloodied bodies.

CHAPTER 13

Ahmed was never close to his brother, Ammar. They were six-teen years apart in age, lived completely different lives, and had very little in common other than having the same parents. Ahmed had almost not picked up when his cell phone trilled, and the caller ID showed it was Ammar. Why was he calling me now? Ahmed thought. He took the call, and sixty seconds later, his world was never the same.

Hassan and Aisha Faquar were dead. They had been walking on a side street in New York after enjoying dessert and coffee at their favorite Turkish restaurant, when a drunk driver lost control and ran them over. The driver was so incapacitated he did not know he had struck two people. Hassan and Aisha were wedged under the car when the drunkard tried to flee the scene and unknowingly ground their bodies up in the wheels and undercarriage. Their deaths had been brutal and painful.

Ammar handled the business of death while Ahmed drowned in his sorrow and anger. Ammar was the one who made the funeral arrangements to make sure they buried their parents within twen-ty-four hours. He was the one who made certain they cleansed the bodies three times. Based on Muslim customs, Ahmed would have three days to mourn the loss of his parents. He intended to mourn for three days, and then he would deal with his anger.

The NYPD and the authorities were not forthcoming with information about the driver and vehicle that killed the Faquars. They cited diplomatic immunity and security concerns to withhold

90

information from the family and the public. However, some members of the NYPD knew who had been driving the car. Saeed Aziz had a sergeant on the NYPD whom he would pay for inside information. It just so happened this police officer worked in the Ninth Precinct. The accident occurred close to the Ninth, and this sergeant had been on duty when the driver was processed. Once it was discovered he was a diplomat, the police released him to the embassy, but the sergeant had learned his name. Sergeant Charles Reynolds sold the information to Aziz for $500. Levy Cohen was a senior at NYU, and anyone could find his photo all over the drama club's website. Aziz would allow Ahmed time to grieve, and then, he would present his enforcer with the name of the man who killed his parents.

Ahmed took the full three days to think about his mother, reflect on her love, and pray for Allah's guidance. On the third day, Saeed Aziz handed him a gift. The gift was a sheet of paper and a photograph. On the piece of paper was the name of the man who had killed his mother and his father. Also included were the man's height, weight, age, and address. Levy Cohen was six feet tall, 175 pounds, twenty-two years old, and lived at 82 West Washington Place. Ahmed spent five days hanging out in Greenwich Village. The Village was an artistic hub in New York City. In the 1960s, Greenwich Village had been at the center of the counterculture. New York City dedicated Washington Square Arch in 1895 to honor the father of our country. The arch sits at the grand front entrance to Washington Square Park. The Village is the home of NYU, Josie Woods Bar, the apartment where Levy Cohen lived, and countless artists, mimes, writers, and freethinkers who expressed themselves daily.

Ahmed spent five days tracking his prey and planning the perfect opportunity to strike. Levy might have been the son of an ambassador, but he had no security detail watching him. This outraged Ahmed even more. The arrogance of the Israelis. They had no respect for Ahmed and his family. The Jewish state did not even consider that the Faquar family would take matters into their own hands. The lack of security proved to Ahmed the Israelis thought Levy was perfectly safe. They shamelessly protected Levy from the justice system, relying on diplomatic immunity. If the American legal system could not bring Levy Cohen to justice, then Ahmed would bring justice to him.

For five days, Ahmed followed Levy. He learned his habits, the routes he took from his apartment to his drama classes at NYU, where he ate, and most importantly, where he drank each night. There were too many cameras and people around at the apartment building for Ahmed to attack there. The one-hundred-plus-year-old building had thirty-five units on six floors and was not the proper place to avenge the deaths of his parents. The academic buildings and small campus of NYU were equally inadequate. Ahmed might take Levy out with a rifle from about one hundred yards, and he was confident he could escape detection from that distance. However, he wanted to kill Levy up close and personal. He wanted Levy to know who was killing him. He wanted to look him in the eye when he killed the drunk driver. Levy needed to know the pain and agony that Ahmed would inflict upon him were for Aisha and Hassan Faquar.

Levy Cohen was unhappy. He hated feeling this way. He should be happy. Levy frustrated himself when he felt depressed. He had so much going for him, and there was no real reason for him to feel lousy. But he had been feeling low all week. It all started with the accident. What a terrible night. He missed his chance to seduce Tamara Knight. He wrecked the embassy's car, and his father freaked out on him. His friends at NYU were avoiding him. How would this accident affect his acting career? Would he always be known as the guy who killed two people because he was drunk? Would people not want to hire him because of this one tragic event? For the last four nights, Levy had gone to the Josie Woods Pub by himself. It was his favorite bar, and he hoped he would run into his friends.

Maybe he would see Tamara too. The bar was an easy ten-minute jaunt from his apartment. He walked right through Washington Square Park on his trek to ease his sadness with beer, shots, and one scotch before he left each night. If only he had been at his apartment and not uptown at that party when Jake had called him last week.

"What is this? Five nights in a row?" said Eddie, the bartender, as Levy settled in at the bar. Eddie was an aspiring painter of landscapes. While he painted in the park each day, Eddie tried to sell his paintings to tourists, businesspeople cutting through the ten-acre park, or anyone willing to give Eddie cash for his work. He doubted he would ever be Claude Monet or Georgia O'Keeffe, but he loved to paint, and he was only twenty-seven years old. Bartending put some spending money in his pocket, but he still needed his monthly allowance from his grandmother to pay his real bills. He was going to give his painting one more year. If he could not support himself by then, he would quit the creative and finally put his psychology degree from Dartmouth to use.

"What can I get you tonight, Levy?"

"Same thing I have been having all week, my friend. A crispy chicken sandwich, waffle fries with cheese, and a pint of Goose Island IPA."

Two hours later, none of Levy's friends had gone into the bar or answered his texts. His only friends had been Eddie and the weird guy who walked into the bar about thirty minutes before. The stranger had entered the bar, looked around like he was searching for someone, and then engaged Levy in a bizarre conversation.

"Have you seen a woman in a pink-hooded sweatshirt, jeans, with really long black hair?" said the unknown tough guy. Levy did not know if he was tough or not, but he certainly looked angry about something.

"Do you mean the color pink or the brand Pink?" asked Levy.

"What? It's pink."

"I know you said it's pink, but do you mean the color or the brand?"

"I don't know what the brand is that you mean, so I guess the color."

Levy thought this guy looked like he was just off the boat from somewhere in the Middle East. He had a large overcoat on, even though it was a pleasant spring night.

"Sorry, bro. I haven't seen anyone like that in here," said Levy.

"Bro? We are not brothers. Why would you call me brother?"

"Dude, chill. It is just a figure of speech. I know we have different mothers," Levy replied with a half laugh.

"Do you know my mother?" asked the powerfully built stranger.

"What? Are you okay? No. I don't know your mom. I was trying to be funny. Sorry, man."

The stranger shook his head to himself. It was like he was having a conversation in his head. The tall Middle Easterner with the broad shoulders looked Levy in the eye.

"Hey. I think I know you. I have seen you before, maybe? Are you an actor? You are, right?"

Levy smiled to himself and then smiled at this very unusual man and said, "Actually, I am an actor. Perhaps you have seen me onstage or on the screen."

"You are Levy, right?"

"Yes. I am. Levy Cohen. Although to be honest"—Levy leaned close as if to tell this man a secret—"I have been thinking of changing my last name to Carter for career reasons."

"I have to leave now. I need to find that girl." And with that, the strange man turned around and exited the bar.

Levy turned back to talk to Eddie. "That was weird and cool at the same time. Did you see that guy? He recognized me as an actor."

"What? No. I did not see anybody. Do you need anything?" Eddie shouted from the other end of the bar.

"I do. Bring me a kamikaze shot, and get everyone sitting at the bar one too. Tonight's going to be a good night, Eddie."

Ahmed was pleased with himself. He had successfully interacted with his target. The conversation had been awkward. Levy had thrown him off when the Jew had said the word *mother* to him. The word surprised and rattled him. But he recovered by pretending to know the Jew as an actor. All actors were vain and self-absorbed. Ahmed would use this to his advantage later. The new sense of familiarity that existed between the Jew and him would help him get close and make it not only easier but also more enjoyable to kill him.

Ahmed was standing in the shadows at the corner of Green Street and Waverly Place. Ahmed wished the temperature were a few degrees cooler. It was a little too warm for the overcoat and gloves he was wearing. However, the extra length concealed his two knives. He carried a Flash hunting knife in his front left pocket, and a Perkins 12.5-inch fixed-blade Bowie knife was hanging from his right hand.

The Flash blade was about four inches long and would only be used as a backup in very close quarters. The Jew had walked home this exact way for the last four nights. He had left the bar each night at eleven o'clock and gone straight home. It was fifteen minutes before midnight, and he had not been by yet. Ahmed wondered, *Could I have missed him? Did he go home another route? Where was he?* Then Ahmed saw the man he would kill in less than ten minutes. The Jew stumbled out of the bar, alone. *Perfect,* thought Ahmed.

Levy walked past Ahmed without noticing him. He was drunk. He was not falling or throwing up drunk, but he was definitely intoxicated. Levy staggered down Waverly Place and entered Washington Square Park. He was about five minutes away from his apartment building. The park was empty except for the homeless man sleeping on a patch of grass and a couple making out on a bench. There were many benches along the walkway, and Ahmed planned on using one of them in a matter of moments.

Ahmed trailed several feet behind Levy. Levy was too drunk to notice his tail, but he heard his name being called.

"Levy? Levy the actor, is that you?" asked Ahmed as he approached. Ahmed held the long Bowie knife in his right hand. He pressed his hand against his chest with the blade pointing up.

Levy smiled and turned backward and to his right to greet the familiar-sounding voice. As Levy turned, Ahmed repositioned his knife to his hip and was ready to thrust the weapon forward. Ahmed moved in close, and as Levy locked eyes with him, Ahmed drove the knife deep into Levy's stomach just near his belly button. The blade tore through the small intestine and almost reached his kidney on the other side of his abdomen. The hilt was almost inside Levy, and Ahmed could feel the warm blood escaping his prey's body onto his own gloved hand. Ahmed twisted the hilt, and the blade cut into more organs. Ahmed was holding Levy up, pushed him across the pathway and onto a bench. Levy and Ahmed never took their eyes off each other. Levy never screamed. He was in so much pain he could not find the strength to cry out. Both men were now sitting on the bench. One was about to die, and the other was about to kill for the first time.

"You killed my parents, and now I am killing you," Ahmed spoke in a hushed voice to avoid drawing any attention. "Allahu Akbar."

Ahmed withdrew the knife from Levy's body. He was dead, and blood oozed from his midsection. Ahmed wiped the blade clean across his victim's chest. He grabbed the dead man's wallet and stuffed it into his front pocket. Ahmed scanned the park. Nobody saw. The park was quiet. Ahmed positioned his own body and Levy's so that it would appear two drunk men were sitting on a bench. Ahmed slipped off a backpack and removed his overcoat. He pulled out another long coat. Ahmed stuffed the bloodied coat into the pack and put on the extra coat. He tucked his now clean blade under the right side of the long coat and put on a ballcap. Levy sat there with his shoulders up, head down, and dead.

Ahmed strolled across the park toward the subway station on West Fourth Street, Washington Square. He pulled the cash from the wallet and stuck the $70 in his right pocket and tossed the wallet in the first garbage can he saw. He removed his bloody gloves and stuffed them in the backpack. Three minutes later, he was sitting on the subway heading to Penn Station. From there, he would grab a New Jersey Transit train to the Paterson station, and he would be home in one hour. He sat in the subway car and smiled. He felt like Azrael, the Islamic angel of death.

After four weeks, Detective Jason Sutton was tired of taking phone calls from the Israeli embassy and everyone else. Sutton understood the implications of the ambassador's son being murdered in a public park in the heart of New York City. His commander was on him. The chief was on him. The mayor's office called him at least every other day. But the truth of the matter was he had nothing to go on. Sutton had been a NYPD detective for eleven years, and he knew how to run an investigation. There was no murder weapon. Only the victim's blood was at the scene. There were no fingerprints. There were no witnesses or video from security or street cameras. The NYPD found the wallet in a trash can thirty feet from the bench where the body had been discovered. The wallet had no cash in it. This looked like a simple robbery. Because of diplomatic immunity, the police had never charged Levy with DUI or any crime, and therefore, Sutton never knew the murder victim had been the drunk driver in a fatal accident that left two pedestrians dead. The powers that be wanted the information to be kept secret. So Sutton never knew about the car crash. He never knew about the fatal wreck, so he never looked at the surviving family members of the dead pedestrians as possible suspects with a motive for revenge. He kept looking for gangbangers, drug addicts in desperate need of a fix, or crazed homeless people with violent pasts. Sutton would never make an arrest.

Unbeknownst to Ahmed, but from a financial standpoint, he had become a rather-well-off individual. Ammar informed him that the two brothers were the recipients of the death benefit from his father's life-insurance policy. Dr. Faquar had a $2,000,000 term life insurance policy with Lincoln Financial Life and considerable assets from his medical practice. The sons split the proceeds equally. Ammar used his half to buy a large home in Totowa, New Jersey, and to pay for his three children to attend the best colleges in the country. The rest he invested in the stock market, mutual funds, bonds, and real estate. Ahmed bought a small row house in Paterson, New Jersey. He used his financial independence to allow himself more time to worship, pray, and fall deeper and deeper into the radical ideology and beliefs of Islam. He used his own money to finance his own plans to attack America. He stockpiled weapons and munitions for a future mission. Without having to earn money by breaking thumbs or smashing knees for Aziz anymore, Ahmed could devote his time to studying, recruiting his own terrorist cell, and planning his own attack.

After a long stretch of time, Ahmed believed he had found the perfect place to hit the Americans. He had a small fighting force, himself and two brothers, Farid and Nabil. They had met at his mosque one evening. The brothers lived together in an upstairs apartment just down the block from Ahmed's house. Like Ahmed, they kept to themselves and talked of bringing death to the streets of America. Ahmed had accumulated firearms and small explosives over the years. He had taught the brothers how to shoot and handle a rifle. Farid and Nabil had never served in the military, been arrested, and as far as Ahmed could tell, they had never even been in a fight. After much research and traveling to locations for an attack, Ahmed had decided the Kings Food Market in Chatham, New Jersey, would be the site of his onslaught.

Chatham, New Jersey, is a small town only thirty miles from Paterson. It is one of the wealthiest areas in the country. The median income is $175,000, and the average home value is $775,000. The town is over 90 percent white, which, to Ahmed, meant it was predominately Christian or Jewish. There are 565 municipalities in New Jersey. Of those 565, Chatham is ranked as the third safest in the Garden State. The police force is not experienced with actual crime. They give out tickets for driving infractions and break up the occasional high school keg party that makes too much noise for an old and grouchy neighbor. Ahmed and his two shooters would not be going up against the LAPD, NYPD, or Chicago's finest. Next door to the popular grocery store were two banks and a preschool. Ahmed told the two brothers that it would be a "target rich" environment.

Main Street in Chatham was busy at noon. People meeting for lunch, moms doing the shopping, kids getting picked up from the morning session of preschool, and people out taking their dog for a quick lunchtime stroll. The plan was simple. They would park the van in front of the grocery store. Ahmed and Farid would enter Kings with guns blazing. Nabil would stay on Main Street. He would hurl homemade explosives at the storefronts and shoot anyone on the street. They would keep gunning down citizens until the police finally killed them. Ahmed figured they would have plenty of time to kill before the police could finally overtake them. Thirty minutes prior to their scheduled departure time, Ahmed's phone rang. It was Nabil.

"Ahmed?"

"Yes, Nabil."

"Farid is sick. I think he has the flu."

"What do you mean?"

"He is throwing up and has a fever. He is sick. We can't do it today."

Ahmed and the brothers were careful not to say too much on the phone. They always discussed their plans in person.

"We will just have to wait until tomorrow when he is feeling better."

"He is really sick. I am not sure he will be better tomorrow." Nabil's voice was anxious, and the words came out of his mouth too quickly. He sounded scared, and Ahmed knew it.

"I want the two of you to rest and get better. Stay home. Do you have medicine?"

"Yes. We have medicine. You do not need to bring us anything."

Ahmed knew they were holed up in their three-room apartment. He could picture Farid and Nabil sitting there scared and trying to decide what to do. Who was going to call Ahmed? What would they say? Should they tell the police? They needed to buy themselves time until they could figure out what to do. Ahmed figured they would call the police and report him within twenty-four hours. He could sense Nabil's fear over the phone.

"You rest up today and tomorrow. I will call you the day after tomorrow, my brother."

"Do not worry, Ahmed. We will get them as soon as Farid is better," Nabil said with no conviction in his voice.

"Inshallah." Ahmed ended the call.

Ahmed knew the men were lying. Farid was not sick. He and his brother were weak and frightened. They were not men, and they certainly were not Islamic warriors ready to fight and die for Allah. Ahmed knew it was just a matter of time, perhaps hours, before the brothers went to the police. A real Muslim would never abandon a fellow believer. Ahmed was convinced Farid and Nabil would betray him and, therefore, betray all of Islam. Ahmed had to eliminate them before they became traitors to Islam. He did not want to kill a fellow Muslim, but were they really Muslim if they would forsake him in this manner? No. They were not Muslim. They were now nonbelievers and their deaths were required for Ahmed to continue to serve Allah.

It was 1:00 a.m., and Ahmed was ready. Ahmed was dressed all in black, with gloves and a balaclava over his head. Years ago, he had purchased a silencer for his Glock. He purchased both the gun and the silencer on the black market. Ahmed had purchased shotguns, rifles, and AR-15s, but handguns were tougher to gain legally in New Jersey. Besides, he would not want to commit a crime, especially murder, with a gun registered in his name if he expected to get away with it. Ahmed had planned on dying that day at the Kings Food Market, but now he had to kill Farid and Nabil and get away with it. He had to kill to live to fight another day. The silencer was not as quiet as they were in the movies, but it would do the trick. Farid and Nabil lived upstairs from an elderly couple from Jordan. Ahmed could probably use a grenade launcher, and the octogenarians would not wake from their slumber, but why risk it?

Ahmed walked two blocks, staying in the shadows. The street was empty, but he played it safe, regardless. Ahmed went around to the back of the two-family house and ascended the fire escape to the small second-floor apartment where the brothers lived. Ahmed had been to their apartment countless times before and knew they kept their spare key in a magnetic hide-a-key box attached underneath the handrail next to the back door. He opened the back door, put the key back in the small container, and slipped it into his front pocket. Ahmed lightly closed the door behind him and entered the tiny kitchen.

Through the doorway, he could see Nabil asleep on the couch in the living room, with ESPN's SportsCenter blasting away. Ahmed knew the one bedroom was off to the left, and that was where Farid had to be. Ahmed gripped his silenced Glock with his right hand. He lifted the remote off the secondhand coffee table and turned off the blaring TV. The immediate absence of sound startled Nabil, and he quickly sat up on the couch. Ahmed wasted no time and squeezed the trigger three times. From less than six feet away, Ahmed put two rounds in his chest and a third in his forehead. Now with the TV off, Ahmed heard a noise coming from the bedroom. He heard low talking and a female moaning. Ahmed nudged open the bedroom door. A naked woman had her back to the door as she straddled Farid. Neither one of them saw Ahmed, as they were too busy grinding their bodies together. The room was dark except for the light coming in from the window and a scented candle burning on the nightstand. Ahmed was not experienced with the fairer sex, but he doubted a lit Yankee Candle in the corner of a dirty bedroom in a cheap apartment with your partner's brother asleep in the next room made sex any more romantic for this woman. While Farid and the woman moaned and groaned, Ahmed lined up his pistol and put one round in the girl's spine and another in the back of her head. She fell off to Farid's side as her blood splattered onto his bare chest. Farid was too shocked to speak and sat up with his eyes wide-open. Ahmed fired twice and put two bullets into his chest. Ahmed took a few steps toward the bed. Farid was still alive and was gurgling blood from his mouth as his body fought for every breath. Ahmed steadied the Glock against Farid's temple and pulled the trigger. On his way out of the apartment, Ahmed slipped the hide-a-key box into a kitchen drawer, locked the back door, and slipped down the fire escape in silence. Once again, Azrael, the angel of death, had successfully left the murder scene without a trace.

Ahmed's hatred for the United States and Israel continued to grow. These two countries were the sources of his pain. The USA had murdered thousands and thousands of Muslims in three invasions in the Middle East. They attacked Iraq twice and invaded Afghanistan. The USA used its wealth and arrogance to buy off other Muslim nations. Only Iran was willing to standup to the great Satan, but they needed help. Ahmed dreamed of striking a blow to both the United States and Israel. They killed innocent Muslims in the name of freedom, liberty, and democracy. An Israeli killed his parents. It did not get more personal than that. Over the years, Ahmed acquired weapons, practiced, and improved his skills as a marksman, continued boxing and working out, and sought recruits. He searched for like-minded males who wanted to destroy Western society and advance the spread of the only one true faith, Islam. Ahmed also wanted men who were violent and not afraid to act. He could have no more followers like Farid and Nabil. No. He needed killers and assassins who would ultimately martyr themselves for Allah.

Ahmed was patient and waited years to find the right men and the right plan to inflict the most death and damage to America. In late November, they would strike. He had planned an assault at Met Life Stadium in East Rutherford, New Jersey, at a New York Giants

NFL game. The National Football League was the crown jewel of American sports. Football had replaced baseball as America's most popular sport. Millions of red-blooded Americans attended NFL games every year. A terrorist attack at an NFL game would send shock waves through American society. Ahmed had assembled a nine-man fire team with enough ammo and explosives to kill hundreds of people, if not a thousand. The attack would occur in the parking lot where people tailgated prior to the game. The fuel in the cars and the propane in the cooking grills would serve as catalysts for explosion after explosion. Ahmed thought, by combining the explosions with their shooting and the ensuing panic, they would slaughter infidels with bullets, shrapnel, and people would be trampled to death by fleeing fans. Ahmed was willing to make some sacrifices to maximize causalities. He had envisioned himself committing jihad in traditional Muslim garb. Jabbar and Mustafa had convinced him, if they dressed like fans, they could murder more people if they blended in better with the crowd. Ahmed agreed, and now he would kill infidels and martyr himself in an Eli Manning jersey.

However, Ahmed's plans all changed a week before the Giants game, because his nephew, Kumar, the brilliant scientist from MIT, got drunk. Ahmed had reluctantly agreed to attend his brother's party at his mansion in Totowa, New Jersey. Ammar's house was filled with neighbors, doctors, and people Ahmed would never look at twice. He had accepted the invitation because Ammar had begged him to go. Twenty minutes into the party, standing on the enormous back patio, which was adorned with white lights and outside heaters that kept the partygoers warm on this crisp fall evening, Ahmed realized he was being set up.

"Ahmed, I want you to meet Gamila," said his brother as he escorted a stunningly attractive Arab woman to shake hands with Ahmed. *Gamila* means "gorgeous woman" in Arabic, and she was. Gamila was in her midthirties and wore a modest dress. She was in the US on a work visa and had just arrived from Jordan. Ahmed and Gamila talked for a bit, and Ammar slipped away to check in with his wife.

"What do you think?" Ammar asked his wife, Iesha. "They seem to be having a pleasant conversation."

"I bet you $10 he blows it like he always does and one of them walks away angry."

"You are on."

"Your brother will never change, and I don't know why you bother. Ahmed wishes it was the tenth century," Iesha said with certainty.

Gamila's eyes grew as big as saucers, and her mouth fell open. "Do you know what century it is?" She stormed off with her heels clacking on the decorative pavers. She approached Iesha, who was already thinking of the Frappuccino and dark-chocolate fudge brownie she would get at Starbucks with Ammar's $10.

"Your brother-in-law is something else, Iesha. He is attractive with an intensity to him, and he's built like a running back. But he is crazy. He does not think I should drive, vote, and I should wear a full burka. I need a glass of wine."

"He is different," said Iesha as Gamila headed for the bar.

Kumar was drunk. Very drunk. He usually got tipsy at the parties his parents hosted. He had proudly introduced people to his new girlfriend, Julia Martin. Julia was the best-looking woman at the party, and Kumar wanted people to know she was with him. His good mood turned into more drinks, and he was just a little too little to handle that much booze. Kumar thought he had it all going for himself. He had a hot girlfriend and a kick-ass job at a supersecret government program. Kumar was making big money, and he was brilliant. He was doing mind-blowing work. Kumar had signed so many nondisclosure forms when he started his job that he thought his wrist was going to snap off. He could go to prison if he told anyone what he really did at work for the government.

Kumar saw his uncle sitting alone on the stone row that outlined the patio. Ahmed always intimidated him. It was not just that Ahmed was eight years older; he had a tension and severity to him that drew Kumar to him. For all his life, Kumar had wanted to impress Ahmed.

"Uncle Ahmed!" exclaimed Kumar as he sat next to his surly relative. "Did I introduce you to my girlfriend? Julia is around her somewhere. She's hot." Kumar was slurring his words.

"Yes. You already introduced me. How is Washington DC? How is your job?"

"It is awesome, Uncle."

"Are you going to a mosque in Washington? Are you praying like you should?"

"No," answered Kumar with a drunken laugh. "I don't do that stuff."

"Why not?"

"Uncle, what I do every day is bigger than God, Allah, whatever you want to call it. What I do can change the world. Change history."

"Really? Can you tell me?"

"Nope. It's top secret. I could go to jail if I told you."

"Then what is it?" pushed Ahmed, hoping to gain some insight he could use.

"I said. I can't tell you."

Ahmed knew the hold he had on his nephew. If he just pushed a little, he knew Kumar would spill his guts to him, assuming he did not vomit his guts up first because of the alcohol.

"Your job is probably nothing. You are just trying to make it sound important. You probably pass out the mail and get coffee all day."

"You are wrong!" proclaimed Kumar. He then looked around and lowered his voice. "You are wrong. I have a big job at the most secretive science lab in the world."

"Is that where you take lunch orders and make coffee?" Ahmed laughed. He had him now.

Kumar looked around the patio to make sure no one was paying attention to them. He pulled Ahmed in close and whispered, "We can control time. Seriously, we can do it. I am the key person to the entire program. It is way too complicated to explain how it all works. Just know that I know. I have sent men back in time fifty years ago, even one thousand years ago. It is crazy."

"Are you serious?"

"Yes. We can do it."

Ahmed doubted Kumar would even remember having this conversation. Kumar would forget what he said in the dense fog of drunkenness. But Ahmed would not forget. Ahmed's mind started racing, and new plots and ideas were flooding into his head.

CHAPTER 14

The CIA men, priest, and pilot had thoroughly gone through the photos and dossiers of the jihadists they were planning to kill. They knew the mission and the plan: locate the Holy Family, kill all the terrorists, bring back any modern-day tech, and don't wreak havoc on the timeline. Davidson made it sound so simple. After outlining the plan of action, Sanchez asked Father Patrick to explain to them what Bethlehem would be like and what to expect.

"According to Matthew, Luke, and John, Bethlehem is a humble town. It was once a city that was fortified with walls, but when we arrive, it will be closer to a large village. Bethlehem will have a population of roughly one thousand people, although it may be more with visitors for the census. You see… Caesar Augustus, the Roman emperor, had ordered a census of the Roman Empire. People had to return to their towns of origin to register and be counted. That's why Joseph and Mary left Nazareth to travel to Joseph's hometown of Bethlehem. Potentially, there may be more people there, but think of Bethlehem as a small town. It should have a town square centered on the water supply, probably a spring or a well. There will be an open-air market, some small shops and places of business, houses, and of course, a temple." The priest spoke as if he were lecturing a class of seminarians.

"So it shouldn't be too hard to ID the terrorists, right, Father?" asked Sanchez.

"I would not think so. They will not blend in very well. But neither will we."

"Men, that's why we gotta wear the tunics, robes, and sandals when we get there. We must try not to stand out as best we can. The more time we can buy ourselves, the better." Sanchez was the one lecturing.

Father Patrick continued with the quick history lesson. "Bethlehem is on the Judean Mountains. Bethlehem is only about ten acres, which is about eight football fields."

"What about the authorities or police or military?" asked Bedford. "Will we have to be concerned about them too?"

"That's another reason we need to blend in as best we can," said Sanchez.

"That's right," said O'Connor. "King Herod is the law of the land. Later, when he learns about the birth of Jesus from the three Wise Men, he orders all males under two years old to be slaughtered. He was afraid of being replaced by a new king of the Jews. At one point, Herod had three legions of Roman soldiers under his command. That's about fifteen thousand troops."

The CIA operators all began exchanging nervous glances. They knew they could eliminate eight bad guys in a few hours and be back home in 2023 before dinnertime, but fighting fifteen thousand men was a different story.

Seeing the change in confidence overtake these fighters, the Dominican quickly resumed talking. "I said 'at one point' he had about fifteen thousand men. Now, his army will be much smaller. Historically, it is unclear what his forces looked like when Jesus was born. I would say maybe he has one legion at his disposal, which is four thousand to six thousand soldiers. However, they will not all be in Bethlehem. The army will spread the troops out over all of Judea. And that's roughly 1,500 square miles. That's a little bigger than Rhode Island."

"Father, how the heck do you know how big Rhode Island is? Seriously, who are you? James Holzhauer?" asked Jackson.

"I went to Providence College. I just know it." Father Patrick smiled.

"All right, this does not sound that hard. We find the other time machine. Nagle, over here," Cole spoke as he pointed at the pilot.

"He sends their time machine back to 2023. We head over to the local inn and find out where they sent Joseph because they have no vacancy. We guard Mary until we take out the bad guys. That sounds easy. Right?"

"Inn does not mean what you think it does, Xavier. There are no Motel 6s or Marriott hotels around. The term *inn* means the guest room of a house. And *manger* does not mean a barn. Back then, people had very simple houses. At night, they would bring their animals into the house to sleep. The extra body heat from the animals helped to keep the house warm and the animals safe. 'No room at the inn' means the guest room was already occupied, so Mary and Joseph would have been welcome to stay with the family, along with the animals within the confines of the house," said Father Patrick.

"Not to pile on you here, Xavier. But it is not like the night clerk at the No-Tell Motel told Joseph to take a hike and his pregnant wife had to go give birth in a barn," added Sanchez.

"One more thing that could make it easier to identify Joseph and Mary is that King David is from Bethlehem, when it was a thriving city. Joseph is a direct descendant of David. The people would see Joseph as part of the royal family, like a celebrity," said Father Patrick.

"So it will be like trying to find a Kardashian in a miniature Los Angeles," Cole said.

"I guess, if Kim Kardashian's descendant showed up one thousand years after she died. You see, King David died in 970 BC."

CHAPTER 15

"How are we keeping a lid on this?" asked the president as he stood behind the Resolute Desk in the Oval Office.

"We have an armed CIA team guarding the lab. Nobody gets in or out," said Davidson. "And besides the people at the lab, the only people who know anything are in this room."

"Good. Now, how do we monitor this situation? How do we check for progress or updates without us all ceasing to exist, as Stevenson theorized would happen if these jihadists are successful? Anyone have any ideas?"

The vice president, the NSA chief, the CIA director, and the president's top two confidants all sat in silence and thought. How did one monitor an event that may or may not have occurred two thousand years ago?

Ted Bennett spoke first. "Okay. We still know that Jesus was born and Christianity is the world's most practiced religion with over two billion followers, right?"

Everyone nodded.

"We need to look for things we never knew." Before the president could cut him off with questions, Ted continued, "Let me explain. We need to search the internet and our databases for anomalies in history."

"What are you talking about?" said the commander in chief.

"We look for events or articles from history that make no sense. The Middle East has been the site of the most archeological digs ever. We look for things that do not belong. For example, if we find out today they found an artifact fifty years ago that dates back two thousand years but the artifact looks like a nine millimeter shell casing, then we know they had a firefight. And if we are still here, then that firefight must have gone well."

"That makes sense," said Kim. "And UFOs too."

"UFOs? My god. Time travel is bad enough for one day. We can't deal with an alien invasion, too," the president joked, and despite him being the most powerful person on the planet, nobody laughed.

"No. I mean UFO sightings from history. When these time-traveling pods arrive and depart, if people witnessed them, they must have told somebody. These pods appear and disappear in the blink of an eye. Even two thousand years ago, there may be unexplained events that were recorded."

"Crazy enough as it is…those are decent ideas and, right now, actually make some sense. I want to keep our inner circle as small as possible. For now, we do it ourselves in the Oval Office, on our laptops. If we need help, then we can bring in our top aides and tell them to look for weird stuff. But do not say *time travel* to anyone."

Not knowing if the crisis would last two hours, two weeks, or forever, the president retreated to the private residence to grab a shower, put on a suit, and head to a luncheon at the Ritz-Carlton. Appearances had to be maintained even when staring the threat of complete elimination in the eye.

CHAPTER 16

The band of jihadists from the Garden State traveled from the east toward the small town of Bethlehem. Ahmed was hoping for a speedy resolution to the mission. If someone truly built the Church of the Nativity where the false savior was born, then he could identify the pregnant woman and slit her throat.

After a walk of about two miles along what Ahmed assumed passed for a road, they entered Bethlehem. They found themselves in an active open-air marketplace with hundreds of people. Makeshift stands were assembled, with locals trying to sell their wares. *This must be the town square*, thought Ahmed. A slight breeze kicked up the dust and rustled the animal-skin tents that passed as retail establishments. Pottery was being sold under one such tent.

Ahmed approached the stand and observed the crudeness of the bowls and dishes on display. It was not Pottery Barn, for sure, but this man in front of him had obviously worked extremely hard to produce these creations. The stand itself, which comprised a few tables covered overhead with an animal-skin roof, was about fifteen feet by fifteen feet. A young boy in the back was working a potter's wheel. He was working on the next piece of pottery. The more Ahmed examined the bowls and jugs, the more impressed he became. Crude may have been too harsh a judgment. He noticed the craftsmanship and the smoothness of the large jugs, and the decorative painting on the vases. These items must have taken considerable time and commitment to make. He was not looking at plastic junk made in China. The cooking jugs were large, made from clay, and the production required them to be heated at incredible temperatures. The proprietor of the tent was in his early to midtwenties and saw Ahmed, despite his unusual height, as a potential customer.

"You like what you see?" the business owner said in Aramaic. "You buy now. We make a deal."

The words were coming too fast for Ahmed to comprehend. Arabic was supposed to be like Aramaic, but he could not decipher a word.

"You like what you see?" he repeated in Aramaic. "You buy now. We make a deal."

Ahmed tried again to listen closely to the local from Bethlehem.

"You like what you see?" A third time. "You buy now. We make a deal."

The third time was a charm because Ahmed understood *buy* and *deal.* Of course, he had no use for these items, but at least he was interacting with a local. He shook his head and retreated from the tent.

Ahmed and his men strolled around the marketplace, taking in the scene. There were several tents offering pottery items, sandals, robes, and cloth. There were also more established retailers that had more permanent structures. These shops were about the same size as that of the pottery stand, but the walls were made of adobe bricks and had stone foundations. The roofs comprised of wood, dried clay, or mud bricks. Ahmed noticed how roofs were being used as living space. People walked on top of the roofs and sat on them. The more strongly structured shops were weavers, carpenters, and blacksmiths. There was a communal well at the center of the town square. It appeared to be the gathering place of the locals. Men and women moved about freely, inspecting goods and haggling over prices. Roads, which were more like footpaths, ran in all four directions but convened in the town square. These streets were the size of an alleyway in a modern US city, but instead of asphalt, they were just beaten-down dirt. Bethlehem was a dry place, and anytime a breeze came through, the dust would kick up for a moment or two. The locals seemed like they hardly even noticed and simply went about their business. To the north and the south of the town center were what Ahmed assumed were residential houses. These houses were built with some stone and a mixture of adobe or dried mud bricks. Farther to the north and closer to the top of the hill, Ahmed could see a temple or synagogue. To his south, down toward the valley, he could see workers toiling in the fields, tending to their crops. Nothing looked formidable, and Ahmed was yet to see a soldier in the marketplace. As he continued to survey his surroundings, he noticed his first cause for alarm.

A Roman soldier occupied a watchtower on the western edge of the town. The watchtower was built of stone and dried mud bricks. It was about thirty feet high and provided a clear view of the town center. The Roman soldier at the top was staring at Ahmed and his men. Ahmed wondered for how long they had been under surveillance. At that moment, he was happy he had left the brothers, Umar and Kareem, outside the town with the utility carts.

"We are being watched. Break up into your two-man teams. Stay in touch with the walkie-talkies. Spread out and just observe and report back to me," said Ahmed. Ahmed and Abdullah took the footpath to the north toward the houses and synagogue. He wanted to keep a close eye on Abdullah since he had fired two pot shots at the olive-orchard farmers. Ibrahim and Jamal headed south. Jabbar, wearing his Nike sneakers, and Mustafa continued to mill about the marketplace.

*****

Nineteen years ago, he was born in a small village outside Jerusalem, and his parents named him Rami. He felt no allegiance to his small town because he knew he was moving on to bigger and better things. When Rami was just six years old, his mother died while giving birth to his little brother. Tragically, the baby also died, and no explanation was given to him other than his father saying "This is the life we lead." His father was an angry man. Angry at the world. Angry at life. Having a father who is always resentful and drinking wine is not a good foundation for a young boy. Following his wife's death, Rami's father spent three years drinking wine and consorting with women of a particular ilk. Rami spent those years wondering when his father would come back home each night. The neighbors were kind enough to give Rami their extra food and always made sure he ate every day. Rami's father would return home each night, smelling of wine and cheap women. He would sleep during the day, and Rami could not remember him ever working.

One night, Rami's father stumbled home into their one-room house and collapsed onto the floor. Rami just lay on his bedroll and continued sleeping. In the morning, he stepped over his dad and went out to find some breakfast. Rami had gotten lucky, and outside a baker's shop, he found some burnt bread, which filled his stomach, and he headed back home. His father was still lying on the dirt floor of their very humble home. He checked on his dad and realized he had stopped breathing. His body was cold and listless. He was dead. Rami packed up a small bag and headed to Jerusalem. For five years, Rami survived on the streets by begging, stealing, and doing what he needed to live. He was way beyond his age in life experience and lessons by the time he was fourteen.

At fourteen, Rami joined the Roman army and told them his name was Linus. Rami was a local name that would get him nowhere. However, Linus was a strong Roman name, and he was going to see the empire. For five years, Linus trained hard, followed orders, and enjoyed being in the Roman army. He was an auxiliary soldier, which meant he was not a Roman citizen. Legionnaires were soldiers who were also Roman citizens. Linus dreamed of proving himself and becoming a legionnaire. Unfortunately, after five years of service, all he had were dreams. He had wished to become a soldier and see the vast empire of Rome. He had seen exactly six miles of the empire. The army stationed Linus in Bethlehem at an outpost camp.

Military life was mundane and boring in Bethlehem. However, Linus enjoyed watchtower duty. He enjoyed watching the activity of the town square and viewing the women. Auxiliaries could not marry, but he could still "know a woman," and manning the watchtower was the best opportunity to view what the female locals offered. As he looked for female companionship from thirty feet in the sky, he observed a group of strange men in the marketplace. They had the same color skin as everyone, but even from this high up, they looked tall. Very tall. And not just one or two of them, but all six of them were significantly above average. They moved differently from everyone else. Linus could not quite explain it, but there was something peculiar about these men. Bethlehem was a small town, and he had never seen them before. Now, people were going to register for the census that Caesar Augustus had decried, so maybe that was why they were in Bethlehem. But Linus had a feeling. For a man who grew up on his own and had survived on the streets since he was a child, a gut instinct meant a lot. He would keep a watchful eye on the men.

CHAPTER 17

"We are fifteen minutes out from arrival! Get ready. The pain and sound in your head will not be as bad as the departure, but it is still going to hurt like hell when we get there," called out Nagle to his new band of cohorts.

"Put your seats back in a straight and upright position, and make sure your tray tables are stowed away properly," said Tucker.

"Hey, Nagle, when we deplane, are you going to thank us for choosing Time Travel Airlines and say 'buh-bye' as we get off?" said Bedford to the pilot. The team chuckled, and the men readied themselves for an excruciating arrival.

"Remember," Sanchez called out. "We are going to arrive, probably within a couple of a hundred yards of the other pod. The terrorists may still be at the pod. They may have left men behind to guard it or have set up base there. We gotta be ready for a fight straightaway. We will have the element of surprise on our side. These assholes do not know we are coming for them. We must take advantage of that."

The SOG commandos were highly skilled, well trained, and knew how to do their jobs. Each man knew he could count on the others and would be ready to roll when the pod door opened.

*****

Sanchez viewed the blaze, using his binoculars from about two hundred yards away. His men had exited the pod with precision and had secured the area. They were standing on the outskirts of

Bethlehem, two thousand years in the past. Sanchez peered through his binoculars, and the young commander could see the terrorist pod was burning. It appeared to Sanchez as the blaze had begun inside the pod. The flames were surging out from the main door. The exterior of the pod was still basically intact. Sanchez knew this was a good thing. It meant this whole exercise had actually worked. Those science geniuses had put them in the right spot at the right time. They had successfully trailed the terrorists through time. Incredible.

"Did it crash?" asked Sanchez as he handed the binoculars to Nagle. Nagle peered through the binoculars and studied what he saw for a few moments.

"No. These things don't crash in the sense you are thinking of," said Nagle. "The pods don't really land as much as they arrive. Besides, there are no bodies or debris scattered around the area."

Sanchez could see no men near the scorching piece of technology. Sanchez was not willing to take any unnecessary risks and ordered his men to approach the other pod with great caution. They had arrived near an orchard of olive trees, and the pod rested in a clearing between the orchard and a copse of smaller trees.

As Alter Ego Team advanced on the hijacked pod in a standard military-attack formation, they could see the pod was abandoned. After making sure the area was clear of hostiles, Sanchez and Nagle inspected the burning pod as best they could. Sanchez ordered Cole, Jackson, McNally, and Bedford to advance out one hundred yards in each direction and to stay in contact using their comms. The men had not yet changed into the clothing of the time and were using their throat mics to communicate.

Sanchez and the former Pennsylvania State trooper saw bullet holes in the pod's fiberglass. "It looks like they shot the pod up pretty good before they set the fire," said Sanchez. "Is any of this salvageable?"

"I don't think so" was Nagle's response. "There is no way to send this thing back to 2023. I gotta blow it to kingdom come to make sure nobody can figure out what the hell it is."

Tucker was scouring the ground for clues or evidence of what had occurred here just a few hours before. Tucker found .223 Remington shell casings in the dust and dirt. He found tracks of several men and tire impressions in the area.

".223 Remingtons, huh? These bastards have at least one AR-15," said Tucker. Sanchez agreed and discussed with Nagle and Father Patrick the next steps they would take as a unit.

"As I said," continued the pilot. "I have to blow this thing to smithereens. It won't destroy all the evidence, but I am not worried about plastic, fiberglass, or advanced metal being found during this time period. However, leaving a circuit broad or microchips intact is a different matter."

"How do we blow it?" said Sanchez.

"The old-fashioned way… C-4." Nagle smiled. "I will set the charges. I have been trained for this very scenario, destroying a pod in the past. I have never actually done it, but I know how."

"Why would they destroy their only way of getting back?" asked Tucker.

"Commitment to cause," answered Father Patrick. "By removing their only way to return, this guy, Ahmed Faquar, is making sure his men are 100 percent committed to the mission. There is no turning back for them. They succeed, or they die trying. Either way, this is it for them."

"You ain't going to blow up our only ride home, are you, Papi?" Tucker had a hint of uneasiness in his voice.

"No. We are completing our mission and going home," replied the young husband with a baby boy back in 2023. "Believe me. We are going home."

Nagle dodged and eluded the flames the terrorists had started and rigged up the C-4 as Sanchez briefed the team on how they were moving forward.

"Tucker spotted tracks heading west into Bethlehem. Here is what we know about them right now. They are extremely committed to their goal. For crying out loud, they destroyed their only ride home. We know they are well armed. We are heading back over to our pod to gear up to do our reconnaissance work. We will wear the tunics, robes, and sandals to better blend in with the locals. Make sure you have your sidearms with you, carry your M4 and extra clips under the tunics. Keep your Kevlar on under the clothing. We are going to use our pod as our base and store our gear on the pod. We are about two miles from Bethlehem. Once we have a better feel for what is going on, we can come back for anything we need. Obviously, this is a unique and fluid op."

Back at their pod, the team covered their modern warfare clothes with robes and tunics, changed footwear, performed a weapons check, and made sure their throat mics were operating properly. Sanchez encouraged Father Patrick to carry a weapon, but he refused. He was confident he would not need one and argued that he had not touched a gun in a decade and a half. However, Sanchez made the priest endure him for a five-minute refresher course on gun safety, and the clergyman even squeezed off a few rounds at a tree.

"How are we going to hide this thing?" said Tucker, as he pointed at the pod.

"It has a cloaking system," explained Nagle. "Once I activate the system, the pod blends in with the surrounding landscape. It is basically invisible. The pod is alarmed, and we get notified if anyone breaches a five-foot perimeter of the pod. Father Patrick and I each have a remote control to deactivate the system. The remote also alerts us if someone violates the perimeter."

"So does the device buzz like at Applebee's when your table is ready?" quipped Tucker.

"It is a little more advanced than that," and Nagle showed them the most technically advanced key fob known to man. "The passcode is Sixers. S-I-X-E-R-S."

"Sixers? As in the Philadelphia 76ers?" cried Jackson. "C'mon, man, they suck," pronounced the adamant fan of all New York sports teams.

"How does this cloaking system work?" said Tucker.

"Holy shit, Tucker! Why do you ask all these tech questions? It works, okay? Who cares how or why? For God's sake, we just traveled back in time two thousand years. Don't you think the scientists can invent a system that disguises fiberglass with the surrounding landscape?" retorted Nagle.

"Okay. We are moving out. Cole, you are on point. Father Patrick, you are with me. Bedford, you bring up our six. Nagle will detonate the C4 once we are clear of the blast zone. He will stay behind to keep watch over our ride home. He has a Glock and is on comms with us. Let's move," ordered Sanchez.

The SOG team moved forward with their weapons under their time period clothing. The fresh air and the quietness of the area helped to heighten their senses. They progressed along a beaten-down road that was about six feet wide. Cole was on point, walking about twenty yards ahead of Sanchez and Father Patrick. Tucker was flanking Cole on the left and Jackson on his right with McNally and Bedford bringing up the rear. Each operator was about twenty yards from the others, forming a well-balanced arrow, if one had an aerial view.

"'Yea, though I walk through the valley of the shadow of death, I will fear no evil: for thou art with me; thy rod and thy staff, they comfort me.' Except instead of a rod and staff, I have my pistol and M4," said Sanchez as he walked with the priest down the dusty pathway.

"Psalm 23:4. Well done, Miguel. I did not know you were a student of the Bible," stated Father Patrick as he strode only a few feet away from Sanchez.

"Well, Father, that's really more of my wife, Beca, than me. You would really like her, Father. She teaches religion at our local Catholic school."

"I did not know."

"Yep. She was a theology major in college. Beca would love to talk with you."

"I am sure I would enjoy the conversation more. Tell me about her, Miguel."

"Beca's the best. She is smart, funny, and has a deep faith. She is a great mom too. We have a six-month-old son named Robert Jesus. We call him RJ. It's funny because he is playing the role of baby Jesus at the school Nativity play in a few days, and well...here we are."

"It must be hard for you to be married and have a child and do this type of job. What is that like?"

"It's my job. It's what I do. It's what all of us do. Some people fix computers for a living, others drive trucks or do a thousand other things. This is what we do…highly dangerous, highly secretive operations that make the world a better place."

"Does having a wife and child change how you do your job?"

"It motivates me, Father. I definitely fight for them. These men we fight. These jihadists differ from any enemy we have ever faced."

"How so?"

"I loved my history classes at the US Naval Academy, and I enjoy reading about American history. al-Qaeda, the Taliban, ISIS, and any other group of crazies you can think of are nothing like America's foes in the past. If you took a typical German soldier in 1942 and dropped him in the middle of Times Square, he would marvel at the lights, sounds, and actions of New York City. He would look for a German pub and try to communicate with New Yorkers. If you took a typical Soviet soldier in 1984 and dropped him in your average American shopping mall, he would be amazed by the quantity and quality of the capitalist's marketplace. He would probably try to ask people questions about the USA. Not these guys, Father. You take a typical ISIS fighter and stick him in any American town, mall, or you name it…do you know what he does?"

"No. What?"

"He kills. He tries to kill as many innocent people as he can with any type of weapon he can use. He shoots, he stabs, he drives people over in his car, or he even blows himself up. He kills as many innocent people as he can."

Sanchez and Father Patrick walked along in silence for a few minutes as Miguel's last comment sunk into the priest's mind. "Is that why you fight, Miguel? To protect the innocent?"

"One hundred percent, Father. Can I ask you a question?" asked the young CIA man.

"Of course."

"I have seen a lot of pain and terrible things in my life. Children in the Middle East with arms and legs blown off. The terrorists brutalize, rape, and kill women and girls. Innocent lives destroyed by evil. If God is good, then why do bad things happen to good people?"

"Wow, Miguel! I was hoping for 'Do I ever forget the words at Mass?' or something like that." The priest smiled and then thought some more about Miguel's query. "That's a tough question. Free will and original sin. Yes, God is all powerful and all-knowing, but He gave man free will. We make our own decisions. Do you agree there is both good and evil in the world?"

"Yes, for sure."

"If evil exists, then evil things will happen. Man can decide for himself if he is good or evil. It is up to each one of us to choose our own path."

"Then why doesn't God intervene to prevent pain and sorrow?"

"Who said He does not?"

"When you see some of the horrific things that I have seen, you wonder…where's God?"

"Miguel, you just said a moment ago you and your men make the world a better place. Maybe you are God's tool to make the world a better place. I am sure you have saved people's lives during your missions, right?"

"Absolutely."

"Well, maybe that's how God helps people. We just don't know. We must have faith and trust in God. We need to believe our own use of free will leads us down the righteous path."

"All right, Father. That's a solid answer, and I like it, for now. But I want to talk more about this. After we complete our mission, Beca and I would love for you to come over to our house. You can meet Beca and RJ."

"I look forward to it. But first, I think we have God's work to do."

CHAPTER 18

Ahmed had very little to show for over three hours of searching for the parents of Jesus. He and Abdullah had headed for the latitude and longitude coordinates of the Church of the Nativity. Ahmed was hoping against hope the secular version of Christmas would be correct. He was hoping Walmart had been right all along. But it was not. Ahmed's mission would have been so much simpler if there had been a two-thousand-year-old Red Roof Inn, a barn full of animals, or even an animal hospital at 31.7043 N and 35.2075 E degrees. So many Christians believed Mary and Joseph had been shunned by the local motel and had gone next door to deliver a baby in a stable of animals. There was nothing special at 31.7043 N and 35.2075 E degrees. It was just a simple house made of stone and adobe bricks, and the woman of the house had chased Ahmed off with a broom when he kept asking questions. She did not know a man named Joseph or his young pregnant bride, and she had chores to do. Ahmed continued to press her with queries until finally she swung her broom at him and forced him to retreat from her little house. Abdullah had wanted to go back and slit her throat after the incident, but Ahmed calmed him down and moved on to another dwelling.

Ahmed and Abdullah had been knocking on people's doors and asking if they knew a couple named Joseph and Mary. No one had heard of the husband with the pregnant wife. Ahmed was told many times there were a lot of new people in town for the census and they could not help him. Ahmed felt like his language skills were improving. With each conversation, he was getting better at mixing his Arabic with Aramaic to understand the locals. Even though they all looked at him funny, he was at least able to communicate and ask questions.

Just as he was feeling like a door-to-door salesman selling vacuum cleaners or encyclopedias, he got a break from an old woman. And by old he meant almost sixty years old, which in this time would have been very impressive. She did not know a Joseph or a Mary, but when Ahmed said the husband was a descendant of King David, the older woman took notice.

"Oh, ask at the larger house with the pink-colored walls and the sizable courtyard. It is closer to the town square than here. A man who says he is from the House of David lives there. He may know if your friend is in town," said the woman.

Ahmed smiled at the woman and thanked her for her help. Ahmed made a mental note of the woman's face. Her face was wrinkled and worn, but her light-brown eyes had a softness to them, and maybe, just maybe, he would spare her life after he killed Jesus and his men were on their rampage. About thirty minutes prior to his encounter with this woman, via the walkie-talkies, Ahmed had instructed Umar and Kareem to head to the west and set up a camp outside town. He warned them to avoid being too close to homes, people's crops, or any semblance of the Roman army. Ibrahim and Jamal had abandoned their wanderings in the southern section of Bethlehem and were on their way to meet up with Umar and Kareem. Ahmed had gotten his money's worth at Dick's Sporting Goods. The walkie-talkies were working as advertised, and now the tents and camping gear he had purchased at Dick's would be put to good use. He wanted to see the house with the pink walls and an enormous courtyard. Ahmed planned on checking out the house before he made his approach to inquire about a family member named Joseph visiting from Nazareth.

*****

The SOG team trekked across the rocky and hilly terrain as they headed to the town of Bethlehem. The air was crisp and clean, and a light breeze helped to keep them comfortable as they wore tunics and robes over their normal DBDUs. Each man had a kaffiyeh or shemagh on his head, a headcloth designed for a desert environment. The shemagh helped to shield their white or black skins from people. Only Sanchez, with his Hispanic heritage, had close to the same coloring as the locals. They encountered a handful of travelers along the route, but they passed without incident. Father Patrick tested his Aramaic with simple greetings of "hello" and "good day." Unfortunately, none of the travelers on the route fit the description of the Holy Family. Father Patrick had explained to the others that Joseph would be in his late twenties and maybe even thirty, while Mary was probably around seventeen years old. Father Patrick was convinced he would recognize Mary when he saw her. She would be graced with the Holy Spirit, and he would sense and feel the purity of Mary. They also did not encounter any of the terrorists from 2023 during their journey into town. The CIA team had seared the images of their faces from the photographs into their brains. They would know those men when they saw them.

The CIA fighters came into Bethlehem in what appeared to be the town square. There was a large marketplace with many merchant shops and stands. It felt like late afternoon, but the marketplace was busy, and people moved about in between the various retailers of pottery, cloths, blacksmiths, and food. Besides the people, animals like donkeys and mules moved about with their masters through the area. The plan was simple. Sanchez, Jackson, and Father Patrick would head for the coordinates of the Church of the Nativity using an old-fashioned compass while Cole, McNally, Tucker, and Bedford would blend into the marketplace, looking for the Holy Family or the terrorists. They were not to engage either if spotted, but to observe and report back to Sanchez.

As they walked, Father Patrick marveled at the sights and sounds around him. He was in Bethlehem in the purest form. There were no Starbucks on the corner or modern-day souvenir shops desecrating the holy importance of this land. While the priest had the look of an eight-year-old at Disney World for the first time, Sanchez and Jackson remained focused and sharp. They constantly looked for threats and stayed on the ready for everything and anything.

The three men arrived at the coordinates and looked at a simple house made of stone and adobe bricks. Father Patrick approached the home and knocked on the front door. An older woman with a broom answered his knock. She was wearing a long cloth that would pass for a dress. Her clothing was the color of almost everything else they had seen so far, light brown or tan. Bright and vivacious colors were not common during this time. It cost money to change the color of fabrics, so most clothes were brown, tan, or gray, with some occasional colors mixed in. The woman was obviously busy and exasperated to deal with these strangers at her house.

"Excuse us, my lady. We are hoping you can help us," said Father Patrick in his first genuine attempt to speak Aramaic. The attempt failed miserably because the woman just looked at him like he had two heads. So he tried again and tweaked the pronunciation. Still nothing from the woman. He tried again, and this try must have been more accurate because he at least got a response from the woman. He did not understand exactly what she said, but he guessed it was something like "What do you want?"

"We are looking for our friend, a man named Joseph, and his wife. She is with child. They are from Nazareth and are here to register for the census." That was the longest sentence he had ever said in this dead language, and he prayed it would translate. He literally prayed she would understand. Again, she stared at him, eyes filled with confusion. He adjusted his pronunciation and attempted the query one more time. She replied in haste, and he gathered she said something like "Who is this Joseph?"

"Joseph? Do you know Joseph?"

"No, but others have asked about him."

"Who asked about Joseph? Was it a man? Was he tall?" Father Patrick held his hand above his own head to emphasize his point. "What did he look like? What did you say? Where did he go? Was he alone?" The questions poured out of Father Patrick like a two-year-old asking his mother why a hundred times.

"Yes." She thought for a moment and asked her own question. "What is wrong with your skin? It is so light," she asked as she tried to peer past his shemagh. She thrust an accusatory finger at Jackson and asked, "Why is his skin so dark? Who are you men?" She reached for her broom.

Father Patrick could understand enough of what she said. He got *skin, light, dark,* and *who.* That was enough for the three men to back away from her simple home. Father Patrick said "Thank you" over and over, and the white guy, African American, and Mexican American quickly departed from her home.

After putting some distance between themselves and the lady with the broom, they continued their search. Father Patrick tightened the covering around his face, and he spoke briefly with other locals. No one knew Joseph or his young wife, named Mary. They asked people outside the synagogue and around some homes. After an hour, their comms crackled to life.

"This is Surfer for Papi, over," stated Cole.

"This is Papi, over."

"We have nothing to report down here. No sightings of either friend or foe, over."

"Same here. However, we think we had a sighting of at least one tango by a local woman we interviewed. We continue to search and will keep you apprised, over."

"Copy that. This is Surfer, out."

Ahmed and Abdullah headed in the direction where the old woman with the light-brown eyes and soft face had pointed. They were on their way to locate the home with the pink walls and large courtyard while Umar, Kareem, Ibrahim, and Jamal were setting up a camp with twenty-first century equipment on the outside of town. Jabbar and Mustafa continued to search the marketplace and town square for their target. Ahmed and Abdullah each had an AR-15 strapped to their backs under their tunics and robes. They passed by a merchant offering baskets woven together with straw and twine. They kept their voices lowered as they moved through one small alleyway after another. For a small town, Bethlehem seemed to have an unlimited number of alleys, footpaths, and side streets that created a maze for its inhabitants. Men selling their wares occupied each part of the maze, with women, children, and animals moving about, carrying water jugs or baskets.

"What will we do when we find this house, brother? Attack it ourselves, or will you call the others to support us?" asked Abdullah in almost a whisper.

"Neither right now," replied Ahmed.

"Why not? Even if we are at the wrong house, they are still Jews who deserve a death not fit for a pig."

"Abdullah, our first attack must be successful in killing the baby Jesus or His pregnant mother. We can't afford to be wrong and then gain the attention of the locals and Roman army. Have you not seen the soldiers I have observed walking through the town?" They had passed two small army patrols during their travels. Each patrol had comprised three or four soldiers with javelins and swords. The two patrols had not taken notice of them and seemed far more concerned with checking out the women and girls of Bethlehem than anything else.

"What threat are they to us? We have guns and bullets, and they are armed with swords and spears."

"Abdullah, there are about five thousand Roman soldiers in this region. Regardless of our technology and weapons, we cannot take on that type of force. We can't have five thousand soldiers looking for us until we are certain we killed the baby and His mother. Trust me, my brother. We have all the time we need. We must be patient."

Abdullah quietly nodded and said nothing further. Ahmed wondered to himself if he was getting through to this violent felon. The two men continued in silence past pottery stands and other ancient retailers until finally they saw it, a home near the town square but set off just enough from the other simpler dwellings to be special. There was a wall that was made of stone and adobe that was indeed pink. It was about seven feet in height and enclosed what looked like several smaller structures. The courtyard in the center of the compound was larger than others. The structures and roofs were solidly built. The two terrorists cased the location in the same manner that Ahmed would check out a house or building back in New Jersey when he knew he would return the next day to break the wrist or elbow of a degenerate gambler who owed his old boss money. Ahmed made mental notes of the comings and goings of the men, women, children, and even animals that always seemed to pass through the front gate of the wall. There was a lot of activity at this place, but Ahmed did not see any pregnant women in the hour that he and Abdullah monitored the home.

*****

Before the SOG team had gone into Bethlehem, McNally had evaded and side-stepped the flames of the stolen time machine to doublecheck Nagle's wiring and setup of the C4. Besides making sure they arrived two thousand years in the past, Nagle's other responsibility was to make sure advanced technology did not fall into the hands of the locals. The consequences could be catastrophic to the timeline and, therefore, their own existence. It was impossible for Nagle to vaporize every bit of the stolen pod to where it would be like it had never been here. However, he needed to destroy enough of the technology that it would be useless to anyone who stumbled upon it. The blaze started by the terrorists and the C4 he would detonate would be enough to do the job. However, the interior was way too hot, and the flames were too intense to set up C4 inside the pod, but he had wired the C4 to the hull and ends of the pod. The explosion would certainly serve its purpose. Nagle was completely alone. The CIA men were in the town, and there was not a local in sight. Nagle took cover behind a large tree at an overly safe distance from the pod. McNally and Jackson had shown him a safe distance to push the detonator from, and he had added twenty yards to that. Nagle looked from behind the tree one more time to make sure the area was still clear, before he pushed the button.

Boom! There was a flash from the explosion, and the pod was torn into countless pieces of debris. The ground shook, and the smoke billowed in all directions. Nagle knew he had been successful. He recoiled the remaining wire as if he was reeling in a trout back at Antietam Lake near his hometown. Nagle felt comfortable moving about now in his time-period attire. He had obliterated any evidence of the future; his own pod was cloaked, and now he could relax and wait for updates from Sanchez. He settled into a great hiding spot in the copse of trees by his pod, kept his comms open, and waited for good news.

CHAPTER 19

"I got something!" shouted Ted Bennett in the Oval Office. After scrolling through obscure websites about archeological discoveries, alien encounters, and historical myths for hours, the chief of staff thought maybe he had found some news. "Check this out."

The president had not returned yet from his fund-raising luncheon, but his top advisors all huddled together around Bennett's laptop to view a five-minute clip from The History Channel's website. *Ancient Aliens* first aired in 2009, but this episode was from 2014 and titled "Aliens and the Bible."

There were tales of alien encounters with Moses and Noah, but this five-minute clip was centered on a story handed down from generation to generation about an olive-tree farmer and his son in Judea. According to the narrator of the segment, at around the time of Jesus's birth, a man and his son witnessed a landing by an alien spaceship. Bennett had viewed the clip twice before sharing it with his peers. Viewing it for the third time convinced him of at least one fact: The History Channel must compensate narrators on this show for every time they say the phrase "according to legend."

The narrator went on.

"According to legend, the spacecraft arrived with a thundering sound and a dazzling white light, which blinded the farmer and his son. Several extraterrestrials, who appeared to be humanlike in form but were much taller than the average man, emerged from the ship. According to legend, one alien spotted the farmer and his son and discharged some sort of booming arrow at them. The blasts landed several feet above their heads and nearly caught a tree on fire. The farmer and his son fled in fear. Thankfully, the aliens did not pursue them.

"Later, according to legend, the farmer and his son returned with other family members. The family saw the spacecraft on fire, and then, according to legend, the ship exploded with an enormous boom that shook the ground beneath them. The farmer tried to recover parts of the ship, but the fragments were too small and were undecipherable. The farmer claimed he only saw the extraterrestrials the one time, and he was not sure if they were inside the ship when it blew up. This account is based on a legend that has been handed down by each generation to the next in Judea.

"Who were these giant aliens? Did their ship explode when it attempted to take off? Are there ancient alien corpses buried among the ancient ruins? Maybe the ship was destroyed while they were exploring, leaving them stranded here on earth two thousand years ago. If so, did they live on earth amongst the common earthlings, or did they form their own colony of extraterrestrials? Maybe today, two thousand years later, we have a race of ancient giant aliens living in our midst."

The video clip stopped playing, and Tyler Evans from the NSA asked, "What does that prove?"

"It proves nothing," said Bennett. "But maybe it is telling us something that we can use as a positive sign. We have been at this online search for over three hours. I have seen stories about aliens parting the Red Sea for Moses and how beings from an unknown dimension teleported two of every animal species onto Noah's ark. I even saw one essay about how Noah's ark was a hovercraft from Mars, which glided over the earth for forty days and nights. But this is the first story I have seen that occurred at the time of Christ's birth."

"Actually, the description of the spacecraft's arrival sounds like what Stevenson told us. She said these things don't really land, but they arrive," stated Tom Scott. "This story did not say the farmer saw the thing in the air and it came down. He heard a loud thunder followed by a dazzling white light. That's how Stevenson explained the experience when the pod returns."

Bennett and Scott went back and forth in agreement that the UFO acted, according to legend, in a manner very similar to a TIME pod. Evans challenged them about the giant alien beings and what they meant.

"I don't know, Tyler. However, considering how our present-day terrorists are much taller than the average person two thousand years ago. They may have looked like giants to a farmer and his kid," Scott theorized.

"And the ship that was burning and eventually exploded. What do you read into that?" asked the skeptical NSA head.

The vice president interjected, "It could mean anything. Maybe a technical malfunction caused a fire, maybe it crashed, maybe our guys found it and destroyed it, or maybe a thousand other things could have happened. Given the limited credible information we have found so far, I think we have to view this story as a bit of a positive development."

"Please explain," demanded Evans.

"Simple. There is an ancient account of something that sounds a hell of a lot like our time-traveling pod showing up in Judea around two thousand years ago. And this is the big thing…we still know who Jesus is and Christianity exists. I would not count this as a win, but I would say, if this were a football game, we at least picked up positive yardage on first down."

Evans liked the football analogy coming from the female vice president, and he smiled at her.

"Remember, Tyler, I went to Boston College, and we play big-time college football. You know who Doug Flutie is, right?"

CHAPTER 20

Bedford saw him first. He cursed himself for not seeing him before. *How could I have missed this guy?* He was about fifty yards to Bedford's right, on the western part of the town square. The man was a tad under six feet tall, and he wore a shemagh tightly across his face. He wore a brown tunic the same color as a deer back in Pennsylvania. The tunic was long and almost entirely covered his feet, but a passing donkey and cart created enough of a stir and, mixed with a faint breeze, caused his tunic to kick up just slightly. And Bedford saw them. Nike Air Max, black, retail for over $100.

"This is Hunter for the team, over."

"This is Papi, Hunter. Go."

"I have eyes on one. Check that, two tangos from 2023. About fifty yards away on the west side of the square, over."

"How do you know they are our targets, over?"

"The one guy is wearing Nike sneakers, and I don't recall passing an outlet on the way into town."

"Did you say Nikes?"

"Yes. I saw the swoosh and everything. His tunic is long, but when it kicked up for a second, I saw them. Black Nike sneakers."

"Are you sure there are only two?"

"So far, that's all I see. Both are fighting-age males. They are only conversing with each other, and both are above average height. The other appears to be wearing sandals. I guess he got the memo on proper dress code."

"Do not engage the tangos. Track and follow them at a safe distance. Hopefully, they will lead us to the rest of them. Do you copy?"

"I copy. Hunter out."

Jabbar and Mustafa continued to walk around, pretending to shop at the basket stand. They would shake their heads and give stern looks that translated in any language to the shopkeepers as they tried to press them into buying their woven products. Each man carried a pistol in his waistband under his long tunic. Each man was also looking forward to getting to the campsite. They were not trained covert operators. They were thugs, plain and simple. Jabbar and Mustafa were tired of pretending to be shopping for two-thousand-year-old pottery products and hand-woven baskets. They wanted something to eat and then to grab a few hours of much-needed sleep.

*****

Nagle saw them coming from a few hundred yards away from the south. Roman soldiers. They looked exactly like they were out of a movie. Nagle counted at least forty of them, plus three or four on horseback. They were not marching or practicing field maneuvers. The troops were clearly searching for something. The men were spread out in a long line across a few hundred yards. The soldiers were heading toward the site of the exploded pod. Nagle hid in the small grouping of trees by his own cloaked pod. He was about two hundred yards from where the Roman troops were headed, but the soldiers were so spread out that the flanks would stumble upon him as they advanced. The closer they traipsed, the better the former police officer could see the soldiers. Each one wore a helmet made of iron, a galea. Some of them, Nagle assumed they were officers or commanders, had red plumes on the top of their helmets. The Romans wore short-sleeved woolen tunics down to their knees. Across their chests they were covered in lorica hamata, chain mail. This type of protection allowed the soldiers to move freely with comfort while still having a moderate level of protection. The chain mail covered their torsos, and some also had small metal scales around their neck and their shoulders. Each man had the standard caligae, leather sandals, to protect their feet. The army expected the average Roman soldier to march close to twenty miles a day. Nagle noticed each man heading in his general direction carried a sword, gladius, on his left side and a dagger on his right. The standard Roman sword was about twenty-eight inches, and the blade was three or more inches wide. The weapon weighed about two pounds. Besides the sword and dagger, each soldier had a spear or javelin, which was six feet long. The killing tool had a wooden shaft and an iron tip. For protection, they carried shields. Shields varied in size and shape, but they were consistently made of several layers of wood. Glue held the wood together, and canvas or leather casing was used to cover it.

Nagle was analyzing his options. If he went south or east, he would rush into the Roman troops. He could head north or west, but there was very little vegetation, brush, or trees to provide him cover. The small group of trees that was currently hiding him did not provide enough coverage for total concealment. Any decent scouting of his immediate surroundings would reveal his presence. He was only about thirty yards from his own pod. He could make a run for it and hide inside. However, he would be exposed out in the open for a good seven or eight seconds if he made a sprint for the pod. Plus, he would have to disengage the security sensors and cloaking system to enter the pod. Then he would have to reengage the system and reset the sensors. That process would take at least five minutes in total. The pod would be completely visible to anyone within several hundred yards. That option was off the table. Nagle figured he had two proper choices—stay partially hidden in his current location and pray he was not discovered or use the trees as cover, withdraw to the north, and run like hell—and hoped he found cover before the Romans spotted him.

The Roman warriors were still searching for something and kept advancing on his position. The right flank of the troops would be on him soon. Oddly, as he studied their movement, he realized the Romans would miss walking into the invisible pod but would still reach his small hiding area. He had to decide and act fast. Nagle was an experienced-enough time traveler to know he had to safeguard his technology from falling into the hands of the locals. Dr. Stevenson had beaten into his head that important concept. Nagle could not risk being captured with a Glock, radio communications system, the pod remote, and his small set of binoculars. He had to hide them. Nagle thought for ten seconds and then decided. However, before he could act, Nagle knew he had to make a call. What was his Alter Ego call signal again?

"This is Fly Boy, for Alter Ego, over."

"This is Papi. Go, Fly Boy."

"I have about forty Roman soldiers advancing on my position. I assume they want to check out the explosion. I am currently in a small group of trees, but I can't hide here. Over."

"Copy that. What are you going to do?"

"I am going to hide my gun and tech under some rocks, and I will retreat to the north and look for a better hiding place. Out."

Knowing he had less than five minutes before the Romans were on him, Nagle tore off his throat mic before Sanchez could even reply. He removed the clip from the Glock and made sure a round was not in the chamber. He began using the gun as a shovel and dug as quickly as he could into the soil. After a minute, he had made a round hole half an inch deep and eight inches in diameter. Nagle placed the pistol, radio, remote control, and binoculars in the hole. He pushed the dirt back into the hole and grabbed several hand-sized stones and placed them over the tech. He took the full clip and thrust it under two other rocks that were a few feet away. It would be bad enough if a Roman scout found a semiautomatic pistol, but it would be even worse with ammo. Nagle looked up, and there were three soldiers about seventy-five yards from his position. He stayed low and backed his way through the trees, monitoring the Romans the entire time. When he got to the end of the trees, he turned and sprinted as fast as he could to the north.

Nagle had never run in a dress before. The tunic was down past his knees, and he had to hold the front of the tunic up with his left hand as he pumped his right arm and raised his knees as high as he could. He was forty-three years old and was never a good sprinter. Hal used the adrenaline rushing through his body to make up for the lack of cardio exercise he had missed for the last twenty years. He raced across the wide-open rocky terrain. His head was on a swivel as he searched for anything he could hide behind. He could feel his heart pumping and hear his own breathing, but he had heard no shouts or calls coming from behind. That must be a good sign. Nagle could feel himself slowing down, but he focused his brain on running. He told himself, *Pump your legs, raise your knees, keep going, or you may die. You can do this. Keep running.*

To his right and about forty yards away was a gigantic pile of rocks and boulders at the edge of a large hill. Nagle thought he would be okay if he could just make it to that spot. There might be a cave at the base of the hill. But those rocks could be enough to protect him for a few hours. He kept going at full tilt and angled his path toward the rocks. Nagle had no time to look over his shoulder. Nagle was too busy concentrating on running as fast as he could in this tunic. He was a few yards away and hoped his footing would hold on the challenging terrain. When he could almost touch the first rock, he launched himself in a full-out dive for cover. Nagle landed hard on his right shoulder, banged his left knee on a rock, and rolled over behind the boulder. He stayed low but scrambled to his feet and stayed in a crouched position. He peered over a boulder and realized he was about two hundred yards from his starting location. For the moment, he could see no advancing Romans. He breathed heavily and tried to catch his breath. His shoulder ached, and his knee was scraped and bloody, but he was okay.

*****

Sanchez, Jackson, and Father Patrick hurried to the square. They pushed themselves past the local citizens. *For a small town, Bethlehem sure seemed to have many people out and about*, thought Sanchez. With good news came bad news. It thrilled Sanchez they had eyes on at least two of the terrorists. Hopefully, they could follow them back to a camp or safe house and end this mission in a few hours. Sanchez did not want to be overconfident, but he knew a group of thugs were no match for his team. He did not care how committed they were to their sick cause. Passion and drive were not enough to overcome skill and experience. His team had the skill and the experience. His men were also dedicated to the mission. They were fighting to defend their families, country, and faith. God, family, country. That is about all the motivation a person needs to do anything. Even if one wasn't the most devoted Christian, everybody loves Christmas. Sanchez and his men knew what was on the line, and they were prepared to do whatever was necessary to achieve a successful outcome. If they could find the terrorists in one place and take them by surprise, heck, this mission would be over, and he might be home for dinner with Beca and RJ.

However, the bad news was the man who would take them home was on the run and hiding from the Roman army. The entire team had heard Nagle's transmission. In the back of their heads was the concern about getting home, but Sanchez knew they had to stay focused on their orders. Defending Jesus and the Holy Family was priority number 1, eliminating the terrorists was priority 1A, and making sure they left no tech behind was number 2. Getting back home was, of course, desired by everyone, but Director Davidson had not put that on his list of orders. Sanchez had to hope Nagle could take care of himself. The guy had been through the Battle of Hastings and who knows what else. He could handle himself for a few hours in Judea. He would have to.

CHAPTER 21

Esther had it rough. She had married poorly and was stuck with a dead-beat husband. Efrayim was a decent man and was never abusive or nasty, but he was cursed with laziness. Efrayim did enough to get by, but he preferred consuming wine and sleeping most of the day as opposed to working. Esther was blessed with five healthy children, all girls. Fortunately, they had all lived to adulthood, which was a rarity during the time. However, with Esther having a loafing and lifeless husband, too many of the household chores and responsibilities fell on her shoulders. Esther and her family lived in a tiny dwelling on the outskirts of Bethlehem. Instead of going to the town well daily, Esther would try to make just two trips per week to save herself time and effort. So twice a week, she would take all her water jugs and place them on her decrepit cart and head down the hill into town for water. Her cart had been used by her father and his father too. The wood was so splintered and sharp she always covered her hands with pieces of leather just to protect herself when she handled the cart. Her mule was pulling the cart as she headed back home with the rickety transport loaded with full water jugs. Unlike the cart, the mule had not been her father's and his father's, but in the world of mules, he was ancient.

The old woman, the old mule, and the old cart were trudging away from the town square when the strain on the fraying twine became too much, and it snapped. The wagon was loose and rolling back into the town square. It was out of control and picking up speed with each foot it traveled. Esther looked back in horror. At first, she was only thinking of her lost water and the demolishment of her containers. Then Esther saw the little girl who was standing in the barrow's destructive path. In just a few seconds, the speeding wagon would crush and kill the small child. Esther screamed.

McNally was moving through the marketplace and tracking the two terrorists. He and Bedford were taking turns watching the two men from a distance. Cole and Tucker were doing the same. McNally saw the cart crashing toward the marketplace. He then heard the desperate scream of a woman, and he saw the young child in the cart's direct path. McNally was about ten yards from the girl, and he reacted.

"Little girl! Look out!" he yelled as he charged toward the impending impact. McNally covered the ten yards in the blink of an eye. He grabbed the girl and pulled her tightly into his chest to shield her from the blow. There was not enough time to avoid the cart, so he pivoted on his left foot and exposed his back to the missile on wheels. The wagon hit him at full force, but he did not go down. He held his ground, and the wooden vehicle exploded against his body. A piece of the shattered cart pierced McNally's right side and stayed there. It impaled McNally against the remains of the cart. The girl screamed. McNally cried out in pain.

Jabbar and Mustafa were still milling about and hoping their walkie-talkies would crackle to life with instructions from Ahmed to head to the camp. From half a football field away, they both heard a woman scream, and then they heard as clear as day, "Little girl! Look out!"

Jabbar and Mustafa looked at each other in astonishment. *English? Is that possible? Did we just hear someone scream out in English?* Jabbar looked toward the screams and crashing boom. He saw people scattering, and then he saw him. A white man. The white man was impaled to a wagon, and he was holding a small child. Not sure what to think or do, Jabbar drew his gun while Mustafa wondered aloud, "Were we followed? Is that another time traveler?"

Cole heard McNally holler out, and then he heard the crash. He instinctively looked to his right at the sound of the commotion. He saw Tucker, the team medic; Bedford; and many of the locals running to McNally's aid. Cole quickly looked back at the two tangos they had identified earlier. One of them had a pistol drawn. In one fluid motion, like he had been doing it his entire life, Cole drew his M4 from underneath his robe and shouldered the weapon. Cole was in a perfect shooting stance within two seconds. He and the armed terrorist locked eyes from forty yards away.

Jabbar had his pistol drawn when he made eye contact with the man, pointing a rifle at him. Once Jabbar saw the blond hair, which was sticking out from underneath the head covering; the blue eyes; and the pale white skin, he knew this man was here to kill him. Jabbar did not know how or when his opponent had arrived two thousand years in the past, but he knew their jihad was now in grave peril. Jabbar fired his pistol.

Cole had his target sighted center mass. The terrorist fired wildly as if he were in a Nicolas Cage action movie from the 1990s. Cole was not concerned about getting hit unless the terrorist just got lucky. Xavier was more concerned with a townsperson getting struck by a stray bullet. Cole wanted to avoid any collateral damage, so he paused, controlled his breathing, and waited for a clean shot. Cole fired a short burst and struck his target three times. One round pierced his right rib, and two more landed in his stomach. The terrorist went down, still alive, but he would not get up.

From his watchtower over the town square, Linus saw it all happen. First, a giant called out in a strange language and blocked a small child from a runaway cart. The wagon had seriously injured the large man, and people were rushing to his aid. The child was safe, and this man had clearly saved her life. Then Linus heard several faint thunderclaps coming from below him. He looked to his right, and a man held a small black object in his hand. It sounded like the thunder was coming from him. Another man Linus had never seen before held a long black object against his shoulder. The strange object was pointed at the man who had just made the thunder sounds. To Linus, the object looked like a short but very thick javelin. The odd-shaped javelin roared three times. The booms were louder than thunder, and lightning came out of the end. The other man fell to the ground with a bloody stomach and was screaming in pain. The marketplace erupted into chaos. It was bedlam. People were now running and yelling in every direction. Some people were trying to hide behind walls, market stands, and anything to protect themselves.

Mustafa dove to the ground when the M4 erupted in his direction. Jabbar was down on his back, clenching his bloody midsection. He was bleeding profusely and was crying out to Mustafa for help.

"Please, brother! Help me!"

Mustafa just looked at him and shook his head. His gun was still in his waistband and he was scrambling to get to his feet. People were rushing past him, and Mustafa was afraid he might get trampled. Mustafa looked back in the direction of the man who had shot Jabbar. He was advancing toward Mustafa with his rifle shouldered. Mustafa knew he would be dead in a matter of moments unless he did something fast. He saw feet running past him, and he reached out and grabbed an ankle. The ankle belonged to a young woman, and she went down face first. Mustafa got his pistol out from under his tunic. He steadied himself and launched his body toward the fallen woman. He landed on her hard and knocked the wind out of her. This gave Mustafa the chance to get to his feet and pull the woman up with his left hand. He held his pistol in his right hand, and both he and the woman were now on their feet. The man from 2023 was still coming at him and closing quickly. Mustafa used the screaming woman as a human shield, and he held her between himself and Jabbar's killer.

Cole advanced toward the second terrorist and reported to his team using his throat mic.

"This is Surfer. I am engaged with tangos. One tango is down and will bleed out soon. Second tango has a hostage and is thirty yards from me at the south end of the square. Over."

"This is Doc. Fighter is seriously injured. He is impaled to a wagon. Hunter and I are with him. Locals are trying to help us, over."

At that moment, Sanchez, Jackson, and Father Patrick entered the square and connected with the rest of the team. A group of locals were all shouting at once and trying to aid McNally, but no one could understand one another. One woman, whom Sanchez assumed was the mother of the child, kept trying to kiss McNally and would not stop crying tears of joy for her child's good fortune. Tucker was working to keep the locals from just ripping the cart away, which could injure McNally even more.

Sanchez said to Father Patrick, "Sort this out with the locals and Tucker, now." Sanchez ordered Bedford, the sniper, to get to high ground anyway possible and get eyes on Cole and the second tango. He told Jackson to check the immediate area for other terrorists and then support Tucker with McNally. Sanchez was going to go for the downed terrorist before he bled out and could no longer provide him with much-needed intel.

Bedford identified a nearby structure with a solid-looking roof. He grabbed a makeshift ladder and hoped it could hold his weight as he climbed up to the roof. The ladder held and Bedford was in position. Bedford was about 250 yards away from Cole's standoff with the terrorist. Bedford did not have his McMillan Tac-338 sniper rifle on him. That weapon was back in the pod. Bedford had used the MK-13 sniper rifle with the Marine Corps, but he switched to the Tac-338 when he joined the CIA. Chris Kyle, America's greatest sniper, had used the Tac-338, and it had become Bedford's rifle of choice. Bedford flipped down the bipod and aimed his M4 rifle. The M4 was accurate from about six hundred meters. The terrorist was well within the weapon's range.

The more Father Patrick spoke and heard the Aramaic language, the better he was getting at being a quality interpreter. Father Patrick had convinced the locals to stand back and let Tucker take charge of the injured man. The handle of the cart was embedded in McNally. Tucker wanted to get the handle off the cart but leave it in the big man until he could get him to a secure location to work on his wound. Tucker used his Bowie knife to cut away the handle from the cart, and McNally was free. McNally was in tremendous pain, but he stayed on his feet and only needed Tucker's support to help him walk. Father Patrick had been conversing with the saved girl's mother, and their home would provide a safe location for Tucker to tend to McNally. The mother, the little girl, and several men led Tucker and McNally to their home. Jackson brought up the rear of this group as they moved to the local house. There was a seven-foot-high wall around the compound. The wall was made of stone and adobe and was pink. It stood out from the other dwellings. The family members and SOG team entered the compound, passed through a large courtyard, and took the injured McNally into the main room of the home.

Ahmed and Abdullah heard the crash and the shouting coming from the marketplace. They had even heard what they thought sounded like gunfire, but that did not make any sense. Their walkie-talkies had not barked to life, and they had heard nothing from the other jihadists. Ahmed had made sure they kept a safe distance from the house with the pink walls. Then they saw a large group of people going toward the home. Four men immediately jumped out to Ahmed as not belonging there. They were big men, three of them were white, one was injured, and the man guarding the rear of the group was Black. It appeared to Ahmed the Black man was holding a pistol down on his side as his head moved back and forth. The group passed through the pink walls and entered the courtyard. The doors closed behind them. Ahmed and Abdullah exchanged shocked looks and wondered what they had just seen.

"Brother, is that a gun? Did you see that? Do you think those men could be looking for us?" said Abdullah.

"I don't know. I just don't. Stay close to me, and let's go back to the marketplace to see what we can find out."

Sanchez ran toward the shot terrorist and barked commands across the comms system. He advised Cole that Bedford had him covered from a rooftop. He instructed Tucker to keep him posted on McNally's condition and he wanted Jackson to stay frosty for other terrorist movements. Bedford had orders to take out the second tango as long as he had a clean shot and the hostage was not in peril of friendly fire.

Cole closed on the terrorist with the human shield. His M4 was at the ready. The jihadist bobbed and moved his head behind the crying woman like Floyd Mayweather Jr., in a title fight, making it difficult for Bedford or Cole to get a clean shot.

"That's close enough! Stop right there!" screamed the disillusioned Muslim from New Jersey.

"Okay. Let the woman go, and we can talk about this. We are both from the same place. Let's talk," Cole said as coolly as he could.

"Who are you? How did you get here?"

"I'm like you, dude. I'm from America, 2023."

"How? Omar destroyed the lab."

"Omar destroyed nothing. We did the same thing you did. We took a ride in some podlike thing. The noise was killing my head, and here we are. Why don't you let the girl go, and we can talk about our trips together?"

"No. You drop your gun, and then we talk. Or I shoot her."

Cole knew he had back up and this guy was rattled and alone. He carefully placed the M4 down on the ground.

"Okay, dude. The gun is down. Let the girl go. What's your name?"

"I am Mustafa, a soldier of Islam," said the terrorist as he kept the barrel of the pistol pressed against the woman's head. Tears streamed down her cheeks. "Put your hands up high. Who are you?"

Cole would never give up important information to an enemy combatant, but he had to keep this guy talking. Besides, Mustafa would be dead in less than sixty seconds. What difference did it make?

"I am Operations Officer Xavier Cole from the CIA. You are from New Jersey, right, dude?"

"How do you know that?"

"Mustafa, we are the CIA. We know everything. We know all about you, Ahmed, and the rest of you guys. Dude, this is over. Put the gun down, and let the girl go. You can't win. There are a ton of us here to get you. We have plenty of room in our pod. You can give up, and we can all go back to 2023 and sort this out. Okay?" Cole was, of course, bluffing about the number of men and Mustafa being able to surrender, but he would say and do anything to save this young woman.

"This is a trick!" shouted Mustafa. "I know you have more guns on you. Take off that robe and tunic. I want to see what you are hiding."

Cole did as Mustafa instructed. He tossed his robe and tunic down to his left and removed his shemagh. He had his arms in the air and did a 360-degree turn to show Mustafa. Mustafa ordered him to drop the hip holster with the nine-millimeter Sig Sauer P226. Cole did. Xavier also tossed his Bowie knife in between him and Mustafa. Cole had a plan, and he was setting the stage to take Mustafa down. He had to create some separation between the woman and the terrorist so Bedford could have a clean shot. Cole made eye contact with the sobbing woman and smiled. Cole stood in his desert DBDUs without a weapon.

"Okay. Mustafa, I have done what you asked. Let her go, and let's talk about this." Cole looked into Mustafa's eyes and saw only hatred and violence. This guy was not giving up. He would martyr himself and take this poor young woman with him. Cole had to make sure that did not happen.

"Get down on your knees! Keep your hands up!" ordered Mustafa.

Cole was an adrenaline junkie from California. He was a live-and-let-live kind of guy, not your typical paramilitary shooter with the CIA. Xavier did not care whom a person loved or what god a person worshiped, but he knew how to get into his opponent's head. He was a professional with mind games, whether it be on the tennis court or on the ocean, battling other surfers for the perfect wave. He had originally joined the military for the rush of action. Now, he could feel his own adrenaline levels escalating as he and Mustafa went back and forth. Cole was ready to roll.

"No! Enough, Mustafa. Let the girl go, now!"

"Get down on your knees!" Mustafa continued to bob and weave behind the terrified young woman.

"Quit hiding behind the girl. Be a man! You and me, Mustafa. Let's do this!" With each threat and taunt, Cole moved a few steps closer to Mustafa.

"Get on your knees, or I kill her!"

"You call yourself a soldier of Islam. I think you are more like a coward of Islam!" screamed Cole as he closed to within thirty feet of his enemy. "Let the girl go, and let's do this. You and me. Man to man. Let's do it!"

"Shut up, and get down on your knees!" cried Mustafa. Cole had him rattled and confused. Cole kept moving closer to him.

"Ditch the girl and the gun. There's the knife. Let's go for it and see who lives and who dies. C'mon! Just you and me!" Cole's adrenaline was at an all-time high. Xavier could feel it raging in his bloodstream. He had his hands up and was eyeing the knife. He was hoping Mustafa would discard the girl and go for the knife. Either way, he would win. Bedford would have a clean shot, or he would kill this guy himself.

Cole was screaming, the young woman was weeping, and Mustafa was losing control.

"C'mon, Mustafa! Let's do this right now! You know you want to put that knife in me. Go for it! Let the girl go, and go for the knife."

"Shut up! Shut up!" Mustafa pleaded as Cole got further and further into his psyche. Finally, Mustafa snapped. He shoved the woman toward Cole and pointed his gun at the CIA operations officer. Mustafa yelled, "Allahu Akbar!" Cole charged at the jihadist. Mustafa squeezed off two shots.

Bedford finally had a chance and fired from 250 yards away.

As Cole charged forward, he caught the woman as she went toward him. The two rounds from Mustafa's pistol landed in her back. Bedford's .223 Remington rifle's shot traveled at 3,200 feet per second. The bullet ripped through Mustafa's neck, and he was dead before his body fell to the ground.

Cole cradled the woman in his arms. He tried to stop the bleeding from her back. She said something to him he did not understand, and then she was dead. Cole had failed to save this woman. He knew nothing about her. He did not know her name or her age or what she liked to do for fun. Did she have a husband or a family? Was she a mother? She was somebody's daughter. Who would mourn her? Who would miss her? Cole then did something he had never done before in the field. He cried.

*****

Linus stood in the watchtower in utter disbelief. The man with the short, thick javelin was now face-to-face with another man, who was hiding behind a shrieking woman. The two men were yelling at each other in a strange and foreign tongue. Then, the man in the open with the short javelin put the magic javelin down and removed his head covering, robe, and tunic. Now, he was dressed like a combination of desert and brush, and his hair was like the sun. *What odd clothing*, thought Linus. The man in the strange clothing had nothing in his hands. The other man shoved the woman at the man dressed like the desert, and Linus heard another booming thunder. The other man's head almost fell off, and he was dead. Linus could not believe such magic and sorcery. How could this man kill another with nothing in his hands? It had to be magic. Linus was terrified. Linus sprinted down the steps of the watchtower. He was in such a panic he forgot his shield and sword and just ran once he hit the ground. He raced as fast as he could to tell his superiors back at camp about the wizardry he had witnessed.

*****

Sanchez moved as quickly as possible against the rush of panicked people. He pressed his way through men, women, and children. After the gunshots, the locals were in a frenzy to get to safety. People were people. Whether it be in East LA, the Southside of Chicago, or Bethlehem, two thousand years in the past, when people heard gunfire, they ran. Sanchez approached the downed tango with his nine-millimeter Sig Sauer P226 out and at the ready. The terrorist was flat on his back and moving very little. Sanchez quickly made sure the injured man was not armed or wearing a suicide vest. He had seen too many men killed by suicide bombers during his tours in the Middle East. Knowing it was safe, he quickly studied the man's face. It was Jabbar Muamod. He knew him right away from his driver's license photograph. Sanchez had graduated from the US Naval Academy with a 3.8 GPA. Some might say he had a photographic memory because he could look at his class notes or read a page and could instantly recall the information. That ability had helped him in school, and now it had allowed him to know the man bleeding to death was Jabbar Muamod from Paterson, New Jersey.

Sanchez knelt, checked Jabbar's vitals, looked at his stomach, and he knew two things right away. First, this guy was in a lot of pain, and second, he would be dead in about ninety seconds.

"Jabbar. Where is Ahmed Faquar?" asked Sanchez as he leaned in close to hear. Jabbar was weak and in pain and would be tough to understand, even if Miguel could get him to talk.

"How do you know my name?"

"I am with CIA. We know everything. Tell me. Where is Ahmed Faquar?"

"You are an American, but how?"

"You are an American too. Where is Ahmed Faquar?"

"I was born in America, but I am a soldier of Islam. I will not tell you a thing," Jabbar said as he coughed up his own blood.

"I know you are hurting, Jabbar. I know it hurts bad. I can make the pain end for you. Just tell me, where is Ahmed Faquar?"

"There is no God but Allah, and Muhammad is his messenger." And with that sentence, Jabbar was gone.

Sanchez collected Jabbar's pistol and searched his body for 2023 technology and any clues that may be helpful to find Ahmed and the other terrorists. Miguel found a small knife, an extra clip of bullets, and a walkie-talkie. It looked like it was from a sporting goods store. Heck, it was enough for these guys to communicate. The walkie-talkie was a potential golden ticket for locating the others. Sanchez shoved the items into his pockets and left the Nike sneakers on the dead man's feet. Phil Knight would be ticked if someone else invented Nike, but he could not concern himself with saving modern-day footwear. He had bad guys to kill. Just then, another shot rang out. It was Bedford's rifle. Sanchez saw the second tango down and Cole was holding a girl.

Sanchez had never seen Cole like this before. He was crying and rocking the girl back and forth as he sat with his arms wrapped around her. Sanchez searched the second terrorist's dead body. Thankfully, Bedford had shot him through the neck, and Miguel could recognize him as Mustafa Bashar. *Two down and six to go*, thought Sanchez.

He grabbed Mustafa's pistol, an extra clip, and walkie-talkie. He had nothing else on him worth saving. Sanchez knelt on one knee next to Cole and talked to him.

"Dude, we gotta go. We can talk about what happened later, but we gotta go."

"I couldn't save her. She was so afraid and confused, and that piece of shit shot her in the back. She died because of me."

"No. She died because of him. We are here to save people, you know that. C'mon, dude, we gotta go. Please."

Sanchez pried Cole away from the girl's dead body just as her family arrived at the scene. The mother was wailing out of control, and Sanchez could only imagine the pain and confusion she was experiencing. He and Cole escaped the converging crowd and headed out to rejoin his team.

Ahmed and Abdullah made their way back to the marketplace, using side alleyways and moving along the adobe walls of homes. Ahmed wanted to stay off the main passageway that he guessed was the main road, but it was hardly a road. In 2023, it would be considered a wide pathway of beaten-down dirt. Moving in secrecy gave Ahmed time to think and theorize about his current predicament. He had clearly seen three white men and a Black man. Caucasians and African Americans were not present in Bethlehem, and the latter had been armed. He and Abdullah saw the pistol.

How could this be? Had Omar failed in his role? How hard was it to kill two unarmed people and start a fire? Maybe his nephew and the woman had overtaken Omar. Did Omar betray his Muslim brothers? Kumar knew where and when they were going. He must have survived and told the authorities of his plan. But who were these men? Army Rangers? Navy SEALs? FBI? CIA? How many were they, and what did they know? Ahmed knew he had to get control of the situation and fast.

As Ahmed and Abdullah entered the square from a side path, they saw groups of people converging at the south end. They approached carefully, not wanting to draw attention to themselves. They hung in the back of a group of about fifty locals. Everyone was looking down and talking. Being taller than most of the men had its advantages, and Ahmed used his height to see the object of everyone's attention, Jabbar's dead body. Someone had clearly shot him in the stomach. His tunic was soaked, almost black, with blood, and the surrounding dirt had turned into a dark crimson. Ahmed needed to know if Jabbar's pistol and radio were still on his person. Forget about blending in with the locals. He pushed his way through the mob. He received dirty looks from several people who were taken aback by his aggressiveness in working through the mass of people. Ahmed bent down and started going through Jabbar's clothes, searching for 2023 tech. The crowd yelled and jeered at him to stop, but he knew he had to continue. There was nothing. No gun. No radio. No extra clips. The only evidence that Jabbar did not belong would be his odd clothing under the bloody tunic and, of course, those stupid Nike sneakers. Whoever had killed Jabbar, be it army, navy or CIA, had taken his weapon and equipment. Based on the crowd's reaction, he knew none of them had stripped Jabbar's body of anything valuable.

Ahmed fought his way through the other side of the rowdy crowd and headed toward the next group of people standing in a circle. Abdullah met him further down the square, and they saw together that Mustafa had also been killed. However, there was also a dead young woman who was being held by a wailing mother and other family members. Ahmed's language skills were limited, but he could make out the "why" in their cries. Mustafa had been shot once through the neck. His head was barely still attached to his body. Ahmed again searched the corpse of a fallen jihadist. Nothing. No weapon. No radio. No ammo. Amid the catcalls and yells from the crowd, Ahmed exited through the people gathered around the bodies.

Ahmed knew their mission was extremely compromised. For the first time, he questioned if they could succeed. He was down two men. His fighting force had been reduced by 25 percent and was facing an unknown enemy force. He quickly grabbed his own walkie-talkie. He knew his opponents would listen, but he could not risk one of his men at the camp giving up their position by mistake.

"Attention. Hold your positions, and stay off the radios. We will see you shortly. I repeat, do not use the walkie-talkies. Out," commanded Ahmed, hoping his men would do exactly as he instructed.

To his surprise and delight, they obeyed. His walkie-talkie did not come to life with a stupid "why" or "what." Ahmed and Abdullah slipped out of the square and headed west to where his men had set up camp. It was getting dark, and the sun was dipping down below the horizon. There would be very little daylight left. He and his men would regroup, and he would devise a new plan to kill Jesus Christ.

*****

The CIA men and group of aiding locals passed through the pink walls and entered a large courtyard. There was a small garden, several short trees, and several mikvahs. A mikvah was a small pool used to collect rainwater to use for cleaning, bathing, and general cleanliness. The openings of several rooms all converged in the courtyard. The scene of the home was chaotic, with a dozen family members moving about, trying to help their injured guest. The little girl's mother was continuing to thank McNally for saving her daughter's life. McNally felt something as he entered the home. Yes, he was in terrible pain, but an odd feeling of familiarity came upon him. He almost felt like he was home. Home at his mother's house in New Hampshire.

When McNally was eleven years old, he nearly lost his leg in a horrific snow-sledding accident. He and his buddies had been sledding for hours down the hill on his parents' property. The track they had created in the snow and ice ran alongside many trees near the beginning of the woods. The boys would always try to build up enough speed to "jump" the track and get some air between themselves and the snow. McNally had done it. He had jumped the track and was flying toward the trees. He hit the first tree head-on. He protected his skull with his left shoulder. His shoulder crashed into the first tree, and he ricocheted off that tree and slid toward another. He smashed into the second tree just as the steel blades of the Radio Flyer tore into his right leg. His tibia was pinned against the tree, and the blade cut him deeply. The snow turned pink when his blood spilled from his leg. His best friend, Jeff, vomited when he first arrived and saw his injury. His four buddies picked him up and carried him home on the sled, which served as a makeshift stretcher. He entered his house, wailing and screaming, but once he saw his mother, he felt a calmness. A feeling of bliss came over him, and he knew he would be fine.

That same feeling of knowing he would be fine came to McNally again. He had not felt that sense of comfort in almost thirty years. Yet two thousand years in the past, he once again had the sensation that he was home.

Tucker needed space to tend to McNally's injury.

"Father, you gotta get these people to back off. They are helping too much. I need a table."

"Please, people. Thank you for your help. Thank you. Do you have a table we can use?" said the priest in Aramaic.

Father Patrick was expecting one of the older men to speak, but they deferred to an older woman, Jessica. Jessica was in her mid-fifties, with soft gray hair but very stern and serious eyes. The plumpness of her physique gave her a jovial appearance, but anyone who assumed that would be wrong. She was anything but jolly. Jessica ran a tight ship in her household. The home had been part of her husband's family for as many generations as anyone could remember. Tobias, the husband, was a quiet man and did not mind his wife running the household. It was less for him to do, and that was fine with him. The house had become very active over the last several days. Family members were arriving from all over Judea to register for the Roman census. The house was overflowing with guests. Jewish culture obliged people to welcome and care for weary travelers and strangers in need. To Jessica and Tobias, their culture mandated they take in these unusual men, and the fact one of them had saved the life of their young niece clinched their commitment.

Jessica gave some quick commands, and two of the men carried a table out to the center of the courtyard. The lighting was better outside, and the cleanup of the blood would be better in the courtyard than inside the house. McNally lay facedown on the table. Tucker opened his medical kit and got to work. He tore off his outer robe and cut away his tunic. He pulled back McNally's Kevlar and shirt as best he could. The residents of the house stared in amazement at the unusual clothing. They had never seen men like these before with the pale skin or the one with the black skin. They were also tall and had the most unusual language and items.

"I need soap and water," Tucker called out. Father Patrick translated, and within moments, Jessica handed a jug of water and a mixture of wood shavings and vegetable ashes to Tucker.

"Borith," said the lady of the house.

"It's soap," explained Father Patrick. "Well, it's what they call soap. It's the best we got."

His injury was on the right side and appeared to be only soft tissue. The piece of the handle stuck in him had not punctured through to the other side. McNally was toughing it out with a four-inch piece of wood sticking out of him. The average man would have passed out long ago from the pain, but not McNally. He wanted to live up to the call signal Fighter. He had walked from the accident site to this house and not complained once. Father Patrick and Jessica were conversing and coordinating Tucker's instructions with the members of the house. Pulling out the broken handle would be a tremendous challenge. The pain McNally would experience would be excruciating. Tucker would have to get as much of the cart's pieces and splinters out of the wound as possible. Father Patrick had to be ready with McNally's discarded robe and tunic to stanch the bleeding. Four men, each holding a limb, secured McNally in place, and they put a wooden block in his mouth for him to bite down on. Tucker was envious of Bedford and Jackson at this moment. Bedford had promptly arrived at the house from his sniper hide. Bedford and Jackson were guarding and patrolling the house while he had to pull off this medical maneuver with the most ill-prepared nursing staff in history.

They were ready. McNally bit down on the object in his mouth while four strangers held his arms and legs in place. Father Patrick prepared himself to jump in fast with the already-bloodied cloth, and Jessica oversaw the entire operation.

"Cam, I am going to count down from three," warned Tucker. "Three...two..." Tucker pulled in one strong, quick motion. McNally's body shook, and the men struggled to hold him down.

The blood started shooting out of the wound, and Father Patrick was on it, jamming the clothing onto the wound.

"Cam, this is going to hurt like a mother, but I gotta stick my fingers in there and clear out any splinters and crap," warned Tucker. McNally just shook his head and readied himself for pain. Tucker told Father Patrick to remove the cloths when he said "Go," and he would put his latex-gloved hand in the wound.

"Go!"

Tucker quickly felt around in the two-inch-wide wound, gripped a large splinter, and slid it out. Father Patrick was back on the wound to stop the bleeding. Tucker used the soap and water to clean the laceration and prepared to staple it shut. Tucker was sure there were more splinters inside his teammate, but he could not get them all without McNally losing more blood. If they were home within the next forty-eight hours, McNally would survive.

"Cam, you gotta hang in for a few more minutes. I got put five staples in you to close it up."

The makeshift medical staff prepared for the last procedure. Tucker opted for the staples over the traditional method of stitches. The staples would be faster and hold longer, given their tenuous setting. Tucker put three staples into McNally and claimed the operation was over.

The men released their hold on McNally. Tucker cleaned the wound a final time and prepared to dress and wrap the wound with gauze. Somehow, McNally could sit up, and he held an instant ice pack on his lower back. Father Patrick and Jessica cleaned up the blood, and Tucker had to admit he was proud of himself. He bet his folks would have been proud too.

"You said you were pulling the thing out of me as you counted down from three, but you pulled at two. What the hell?" asked McNally.

"Yeah, I know. I'm a prick. What do you want me to say?" Tucker smiled.

"You said five staples but only did three. Why?"

"So you would be happy when I didn't do the other two."

CHAPTER 22

Nagle had successfully hidden himself behind a pile of rocks and boulders. He did not want to look to see if he was about to be discovered by the Roman soldiers, but he could not help himself. He peered over the rocks and ducked his head back. Nothing. He would check again in five minutes. He could wait about two minutes, and he checked again for advancing troops. Still nothing. *This might have worked*, thought Nagle. He waited a few more minutes and stuck his head over the rocks again. This time, there was something. Five Roman soldiers were headed right for him with their swords drawn. They were fifty yards out and would be on him soon. It was possible they could walk past him, but that was doubtful, and Nagle knew it. He could not run. They would catch him for sure, and then what would he do? Guilty men run. O. J. Simpson and Scott Peterson both tried to run. It did not matter what century it was; everybody knew that if you ran, you were guilty. Fighting was not a choice. It was five on one, and he had no weapon. He could hold his own in any fair fight, but he was not Bruce Lee or Chuck Norris, and he would just end up with his ass kicked or even dead. The way he saw it, he only had one option, play stupid. His ex-wife had accused him of being a deaf-mute for the last five years of their marriage, so he was confident he could pull it off. The experience of a terrible marriage had allowed him to master the skills of staring into space and pretending not to hear. His wife would ask if her new jeans made her hips look wide or if he could clean out the garage this weekend, and he would just stare straight ahead like his hearing was gone. He had pulled it off during his marriage, and he was confident he could do it again. He told himself, *Pretend you can't hear them and you can't speak. They will realize you are useless and let you go.* He could do this. Hal had done it for years. He leaned against the rocks with his back to the oncoming men and just stared straight ahead. As he saw the first Roman come into his peripheral vision on his left, he thought to himself, *Maybe you aren't as good at this as you think. You are divorced, after all.*

Nagle fully committed to playing it stupid. The five soldiers, who were of all Middle Eastern descent, quickly converged and surrounded him. There was nowhere to go. The soldier with the red plume protruding from the top of his helmet spoke in language Nagle could not understand.

"Who are you? Why are you hiding here?" barked the officer named Cornelius in Aramaic. He had a hardened face and sharp features.

Nagle did not respond. He just sat glassy-eyed and still against the rocks. Cornelius asked again. Still nothing from Nagle. Then the officer did what every non-French-speaking American tourist did at a café in Paris. He just asked the same questions, in his own language, louder and slower.

"Whoooo arrrre youuuu? Whyyyyy arrrre youuuu hidinggggg?" screamed the officer. Just like with a Parisian waiter, this drew no response from Nagle.

The officer nodded at two of his men, and they sprang to action. They grabbed Nagle by the back of the neck and tossed him face-first onto the ground. Still, he lay docile. They searched him for weapons and found nothing. They put his hands behind his back and tied them together with a short piece of rope. The rope was coarse and dug into Nagle's skin. His first real discomfort of the encounter. The rope was not like modern-day thread, smooth. No, this twine cut his wrists right away. The two soldiers picked him up and put him on his feet so he could face the officer. Nagle received his second bit of discomfort when the officer punched him right in the gut, and he doubled over in pain. Nagle remained in character and did not cry out or complain.

"Let's get to camp before it gets too dark. and we will see if you feel like talking then," said Cornelius. With his wrists aching and his stomach hurting, Nagle walked with a circle of soldiers around him and headed back in the direction from which the soldiers had come.

*****

Linus was young and in fantastic shape. However, even he was not physically able of sprinting the entire distance to his Roman military camp. During his four-kilometer run to report what he had seen, he varied between sprinting and jogging back to camp. He approached the camp and could see the classic rectangular shape of an army camp. There was a defensive ditch dug around the walls, and each of the four gates was accompanied by a watchtower. The camp was home to almost a thousand men who lived in goatskin and leather tents. Each tent housed eight men and all their gear. The tents made the camp appear and function like a small city. Paths ran in between groups of tents, and those paths ran both north to south and east to west. Like everything the Romans did, the camps were well organized and run with efficiency. After Linus cleared the security check at the gate, he ran into the camp, looking for his commanding officer, Atticus, his standard bearer.

Atticus was in his midtwenties and commanded the eight men in Linus's unit. Atticus did not live in the same cramped tent as Linus and the other soldiers did. He stayed with three other standard bearers but was in proximity to his men. Atticus was from the town of Aram but had a Roman name, and he claimed he had visited Rome once. Linus assumed Atticus had taken it upon himself, just like he had, to rename himself with a Roman moniker. Atticus would regale his men with tales of adventure and stories about his trip to Rome. He would describe the utter awesomeness of the buildings and, of course, the unrivaled beauty of the Roman women. Atticus would brag about his many encounters of pleasure with the women of Rome and how nothing could compare to their sensuality. To himself, Linus always questioned the truthfulness and accuracy of the stories. The timing of when Atticus was there and how long the journey took never quite added up to Linus. Besides, Atticus bragged about his romantic conquests, yet Linus had never seen Atticus speak to a woman in Bethlehem. Not once in the two years Linus served under Atticus did he ever see him with a woman. Linus dared not question Atticus or challenge the legitimacy of his narratives. He just let Atticus go on and on while the other men sat with eyes wide open and gaping mouths, listening to his exploits.

Linus found Atticus outside his tent, preparing his dinner with several other officers. Atticus was in midsentence about the legs of a particular woman back in Rome when he saw Linus approaching. He halted his tale of erotica and waved Linus over to him.

Linus saluted with his right fist brought to his heart and spoke. He was out of breath and explained he had come right from his post at the watchtower in town to see his standard bearer.

"You came right here to see me, correct?" said Atticus.

"Yes. What I have to report is so incredible that I—"

"Where are your shield and your sword?"

Linus looked down at his arms and, at that moment, realized he must have left them at the watchtower. "I... I... I must have left them at the watchtower. But what I have to tell you is—"

Atticus struck Linus across the face with an open-hand slap. It stung, but Linus had been hit much harder and was unfazed.

"Do you realize what I could do to you for abandoning your post and leaving your weapons behind? They have stoned men to death for less!" yelled Atticus into his face. Linus was not sure if his commander was upset or if he was grandstanding in front of the other officers.

"I am sorry, sir. But what I must report is important and incredible, and I know you would want to know about it as soon as possible. That's why I ran all the way from town and right here to see you."

Linus was playing to Atticus's ego, and he knew he would not get stoned or even a lash after he told Atticus what he had witnessed.

"Very well then. Go on."

Linus recounted the entire set of events, including the injured giant, the strange javelins, the booming thunder, and the odd language they spoke.

Atticus knew Linus was an excellent soldier. He followed orders, always looked sharp, was in great physical condition, and trained hard. But this tale was hard to believe. Atticus knew how to spin a lie or embellish a story, but that was not Linus's style. So he asked questions.

"You say that a man with hair like the sun and pale skin killed another man from ten cubits away with a special javelin. But he held on to the javelin, it roared like thunder, a flash of lightning came out of the end, and then the other man was dead. Did you see an arrow?"

Linus shook his head.

"Then you saw the same man with the golden hair put down the special javelin and take off his robes. Was he naked?"

"No. He had clothes that looked like the desert on his body."

"You said he killed a second man, but without the javelin. He was yelling in a strange language, and then it thundered, and the second man was dead."

"That's right."

Atticus looked at his peers with a look that said "Do you believe this?" The other officers shrugged and waited for Atticus to do something. Atticus could see that Linus was truly rattled and believed what he had reported. Atticus did not know what to do. He could not go to his commanding officer with a tale as far-fetched as this one. He would seem as crazy as Linus.

"Get out of my sight before I give you twenty lashes," barked Atticus. "You better have your sword and shield the next time I see you, or it will be forty lashes."

Linus saluted, bowed his head, and ran before Atticus could change his mind.

*****

The Roman commander had three dead bodies at the south end of the town square. His men had pushed the onlookers back, and he was trying to make sense of what he was seeing. Cato was an experienced officer, respected by his men, and looked upon favorably by his superiors. He was a vigorous leader, competent fighter, and had seen many men injured and die in both battle and in training. The training of the Roman army was infamously known for being brutal and violent. But he had never seen dead people like this before. Two men whom no local would admit to seeing before lay dead with wounds that made no sense. A dead young girl had two similar wounds in her back.

Cato questioned the fifty locals who were gathered around the bodies. He called out questions, and people would shout back answers. He would then shout follow-up questions and get responses from the crowd. It was perhaps the worst method of police questioning, but Cato was not trained to conduct any such investigation. So far, Cato had gathered from the crowd that another man no one had ever seen before performed some sort of magic to kill these people. Several witnesses described him as having pale, almost-white skin, hair that was golden like the sun. He had been wearing a tunic and robe, but then he removed his clothing and was wearing clothes that looked like the desert and trees. Apparently, none of the locals had seen the sun-colored-haired magician leave the town square. One person said he ran toward the west. Another claimed he vanished. A third man said that another stranger led him away to the northern part of the town. The crowd began arguing and shouting different accounts back and forth at one another. Cato was losing control of the situation.

"Enough! Silence! No one is to leave this area until instructed by me," Cato shouted to the people.

Cato called on people one at a time for clarity. The consensus of the crowd was that the two dead men were total strangers. Everyone agreed. They heard thunderclaps before these people died. No arrows were shot, and they saw no swords. Several people claimed to have seen the stranger with the golden hair holding an object that looked like a smaller and thicker javelin. One man said he had seen the two dead men holding small black objects in their hands before they died. The Romans searched the crime scene and found no arrows or spears or swords. A search of the bodies and the area produced no such objects as described by the lone man. Cato allowed the family of the dead Jewish girl to take her body home. Cato was respectful of the

Jewish burial traditions. However, no one claimed the bodies of the two men. The Roman officer ordered his soldiers to commandeer a cart or wagon to take the bodies back to camp. Cato would have the Hippocrates, camp doctor, examine these bodies with the peculiar wounds. Cato dispersed the gathering of locals and ordered his men to haul the dead bodies back to camp.

*****

Sanchez had helped the distraught Cole put his head covering and robe back on over his DBDUs. He wanted to blend in as much as possible as they made their way to reconnect with the unit. After several minutes of walking and some talking, Cole seemed more collected and was getting in a better mental state about the girl. Cole was an experienced professional fighter. Sanchez was confident he would be fine. The walkie-talkies Sanchez had lifted from the corpses crackled to life. "Attention. Hold your positions, and stay off the radios. We will see you shortly. I repeat, do not use the walkie-talkies. Out."

That was Ahmed's voice. It had to be, thought Sanchez. His first instinct was to reply and pretend he was one of Ahmed's men to get more intel. However, he held his tongue and hoped one terrorist lacked the discipline to follow orders and would break radio silence. He waited. Cole looked on anxiously as he, too, waited for the walkie-talkie to chatter. After a few minutes, they realized Ahmed's men were smarter or better trained than they had hoped. Sanchez surmised Ahmed must know they were there hunting them in Bethlehem. Ahmed must have heard the gunfire and gone to the marketplace. He probably saw the dead bodies. Had Sanchez missed an opportunity to see Ahmed for himself? Had the terrorists detected him and Cole? Maybe McNally and the others were exposed in the center of town. Sanchez knew they had lost the element of surprise. What would Ahmed do next? How would he act knowing Sanchez and his unit were here? Sanchez would continue to monitor the captured radio with the hope they would give away their position or plans. At the same time, he would have to alter his own plans, as well.

The two CIA operators knocked on the gate of the house with the pink walls. A serious-looking local man answered their knock. He nodded and let them enter the premises. Sanchez had a strange feeling of déjà vu as he walked into the home. He had an odd look on his face, and Cole noticed.

"What is it?" asked the Californian thrill seeker.

"Nothing. I just had a weird déjà vu. That's all."

"Really? Me too. I felt like I was home for a split second when we came through the door."

"That's what I felt too," replied Sanchez. "Like I said…weird."

CHAPTER 23

The darkness of the night had settled upon Judea as Ahmed and Abdullah made their way to the campsite. Umar and Kareem, the two brothers who had spent almost two years fighting alongside the Taliban, had picked the location about two miles to the west on the outskirts of Bethlehem. The site was well hidden, nestled at the bottom of a hill and next to a small group of trees. Temperatures would get into the forties at night, but a small fire and the twenty-first-century gear would keep the men warm enough. The four terrorists were sitting around the fire, eating Quaker Chewy granola bars and Clif bars for dinner. Ahmed and Abdullah joined them and took spots near the fire and sat down for the first time since they had arrived on the pod.

"Where are Jabbar and Mustafa?" asked Kareem.

Where to begin? thought Ahmed to himself.

"They are in paradise as martyrs. They are dead," answered Ahmed. Before Kareem could get the second half of "what" out of his mouth, Ahmed elaborated, "Men from our time somehow followed us here and killed them."

Ahmed raised his voice and talked over the yelling and questioning coming from the four fighters, who had been setting up the camp when everything went down. Eventually, they settled down, and Ahmed continued, "I am still trying to piece this all together and figure out what happened. Abdullah and I were staking out a house that may be the house of Joseph's family. We heard a crash, and then shortly after, we heard what could have been gunshots."

As the questions began flying at him, Ahmed held up his hand and signaled for them to stop talking and let him continue. "Next, we saw three white men, one was injured, and a Black man. The Black guy had a pistol and was searching for potential threats. Am I right, Abdullah?"

Abdullah confirmed Ahmed's account by nodding.

"These guys could be military, FBI, CIA or something else," continued Ahmed. "I just don't know."

"What do you know?" interjected Jamal.

"I know somebody, and not the four men we saw, killed Jabbar and Mustafa. We saw their bodies. They shot Jabbar three times in the gut, and Mustafa took one through his neck. Whoever shot them was smart enough to strip their bodies of guns, ammo, and walkie-talkies."

"Is that why you said to stay off the radios?" said the convicted arsonist, Ibrahim.

"Yes," replied Ahmed. "The radios are done. Compromised. Our enemy will listen at all times. Changing channels will not help. They will just eventually find our frequency. Stay off the walkie-talkies."

Jamal grabbed his shotgun and rose to his feet. "Let's go kill these mothers. We must make these men suffer for what they did to Jabbar and Mustafa."

Before Ahmed could respond to Jamal's emotional reaction, Umar spoke. "Sit down, Jamal," he barked. "You will just get yourself or all of us killed if you try anything tonight. We must know more about who and what we are up against before we strike. Kareem and I learned a lot fighting in Afghanistan. You cannot take the Americans head-on. The Taliban never attempted a full-frontal attack on a US base. No, we set IEDs. We set up ambushes on US patrols."

"My brother is right," chimed in Kareem.

Ahmed was thankful the two brothers, who were respected by the others, spoke up. Jamal sat back down and took an angry bite out of his Clif bar. There was a part of Ahmed that always doubted the legitimacy of Umar and Kareem's claims about fighting with the Taliban. He knew they had been to Pakistan, but something about their stories of combat and fighting did not ring true to him. They claimed they had been visiting family in Pakistan on a visa. They then slipped across the border into Afghanistan and joined the fight against the Western imperialists. Umar and Kareem told brilliant accounts of heroism and bravery while fighting the Americans. Yet when they would go to the gun range, he was always unimpressed with their marksmanship. Umar and Kareem were not effective with long guns and were even worse with pistols. However, joining Ahmed's terror cell was not the type of thing applicants filled out paperwork for or had their references checked by human resources. Maybe they fought and killed Americans in Afghanistan, and maybe they didn't. But what mattered most to Ahmed right now was that he had two respected allies on his side. He now had to pivot and come up with a new plan to kill Jesus.

"Tomorrow morning, Umar, Kareem, and I will go back to Bethlehem to see what we can discover about the Americans. In the meantime, we will rotate taking watch tonight while we get some rest. Now, it is time for our evening prayers," said Ahmed. The men pulled out their prayer blankets and faced Mecca, or what would be Mecca in about seven hundred years.

CHAPTER 24

When he awoke, his head hurt, and his ribs ached. The head-ache was more of a dull, constant pain as opposed to a throbbing irritation. A few Advil pills would take care of the discomfort in his head, but unfortunately, Nagle did not have any with him. He lay on a dirt floor of an adobe and stone hut that was about eight feet by ten feet. He was alone. Nagle could not remember the dream he was having, but when he woke up, he realized he was indeed in a Roman cell. The nagging headache and the bruised ribs reminded him that the Roman soldiers had kicked the crap out of him just a few hours ago. He had maintained his deaf-mute character successfully during the drubbing. He had not cried out as the punches and kicks rained down on him. Once on a prior mission to witness Charles Lindbergh land in Paris in May 1927, he had taken a solid shellacking.

It was his last solo trip into the past. The CIA deputy direc-tor Ben Wakefield ordered the trip for Nagle to witness Lindbergh's completion of his transatlantic flight. Nagle never saw the purpose of the trip. Lindbergh's arrival in Paris on May 21, 1927, was well documented and witnessed by thousands. Nagle had felt like the trip was a waste of his time. So once in 1927 Paris and with a chip on his shoulder, he pushed his departure time back several hours and went to check out the social scene in Paris following this historic event. He spoke high-school-level French, and so many Parisians wanted to speak English. He knew finding some fun would be easy. The Dingo Bar was home to the Lost Generation. Ernest Hemingway, F. Scott Fitzgerald, and Pablo Picasso were among the legendary patrons of the Dingo Bar. Following the American flyer's triumph, the place was hopping. The jazz band was in full swing, the music was blaring, and there were plenty of attractive French women around. The American, who would not be born for another fifty years, strode into the Dingo Bar with confidence and swagger. His fellow countryman was an international hero, and that had to be good for at least a free drink or two. Nagle cozied up to a beautiful Frenchwoman. She had straight long brown hair and wore a flapper dress. Nagle introduced himself and played up the role as a visiting American.

"My name is Cosette," she said with a sexiness to her voice.

"Like in *Les Misérables*," Nagle offered.

"Oui," she replied with a soft smile. The stylish dress framed her hips and legs to perfection.

"I love that musical. It is my favorite." Nagle was eager to impress the Frenchwoman.

Nagle was not lying just to gain favor with this Parisian beauty. *Les Mis* really was his favorite musical. His ex-wife listened to the soundtrack regularly, and he developed his own affection for the songs. However, Victor Hugo's masterpiece would not be made into a Broadway sensation for another sixty years in this woman's future.

"Musical?"

Before he even realized his mistake, Nagle had a bigger problem. He felt the unfriendly tap of a man's hand on his right shoulder. He turned his head to see who demanded his attention. A hard punch landed squarely on the bridge of his nose. His head snapped back, and eyes watered instantly. The bar prevented him from falling to the floor, which gave his attacker the chance to grab him by his jacket lapels and land another punch to his stomach. Blurry eyed and with his gut screaming in pain, he was clutched by the back of his sports coat and pulled across the dance floor and past the jazz band. A side door opened into an alley, and he was tossed onto the pavement. Nagle got to his knees, when a barrage of kicks to his ribs and midsection sent him back down to the ground. The voices of multiple men rang out in the side alley. Nagle lost count of the voices and the kicks to his body. He kept hearing Cosette's voice crying out.

"Ernie! Stop it before you kill him!"

After a few more hooks and uppercuts landed on his face and his neck, Nagle heard his attacker's voice for the first time. "I will not kill him. Just teach him a lesson. He should know who I am."

An American? Nagle knew he heard the accent right. That was definitely an American named Ernie, who just sucker-punched him and then kicked his ass. The voices left, and Nagle was alone in the alley with a concussion and cracked ribs. Nagle staggered back to the pod, programmed the controls back home, and left 1927. He was convinced he had just lost a fight, albeit a totally unfair fight, to Ernest Hemingway.

The people at TIME were so relieved Nagle had returned after he missed his expected arrival time by almost eight hours that Stevenson completely bought his story about how he had been jumped and robbed. It was a miracle he made it back to the present. They treated him for his injuries and gave him a week off to recoup. Ultimately, Nagle was very disappointed to learn from *Wikipedia* that Ernest Hemingway married his second wife, Pauline Pfeiffer, on May 10, 1927, in Paris. The couple then left for Le Grau-du-Roi in southern France for a three-week honeymoon. Hemingway was not even in Paris when the *Spirit of St. Louis* touched down. Nagle had been brutalized not by a famous sportsman and novelist, but just a guy named Ernie.

The beating Nagle took at the hands of the Romans did not bother him as much as the damage inflicted by Ernie. The soldiers were just doing their jobs. Their hearts were not into the punches and kicks. Nagle felt no passion or feeling behind the crosses and uppercuts that landed on his head. It was just business. No, Ernie's assault was much worse, and the wounds took longer to heal. That attack was filled with passion and anger. The beating was vicious.

As Nagle lay on the dirt floor, he heard the door unlock and open from the outside. Three Roman soldiers entered the small room. Nagle recognized two of them as the ones who had performed their job responsibilities by giving him the beatdown. The third man was younger, and Nagle had never seen him before. The two who had beaten Nagle pulled him to his feet. Once on his feet, the third man gave him a close inspection. He walked around Nagle and gave him a thorough look-over. He shook his head, and then the three soldiers exited the cell. Nagle was alone again.

It was evening in the Roman army camp just a few miles south of Bethlehem. Four officers stood in the largest and most elaborate tent in the camp. The camp prefect's tent was always in the middle of the camp and the biggest. Four officers stood in front of a rather crudely made desk face-to-face with the camp prefect, General Cassius. The chief centurion commander, a nasty man named Lupercal, flanked Cassius. Overlooking the entire scene was an eight-foot-tall wooden sculpture of the Roman eagle. The Roman eagle, or *aquila*, symbolized courage, strength, and immortality. Every Roman legion marched with a symbol of an eagle, but this sculpture was the personal possession of Cassius.

Cassius reported directly to King Herod. He had an audience with Herod twice a month to update the king on military preparedness and the overall state of the army that served him. Cassius was a short, chubby, and unattractive man. Cassius looked utterly ridiculous in his full uniform. He looked as much like a warrior as a donkey looked like a Thoroughbred racehorse. He was in his early fifties and had successfully climbed the army's ladder of command, not by being brave or dauntless, but by being highly organized. Cassius was a highly skilled manager of men and equipment. He was a logistical expert, and his camp ran with great efficiency.

Commander Lupercal was Cassius's right-hand man. His family shared the same name as the Roman pagan festival of Lupercalia. Lupercalia went back hundreds of years to celebrate and promote health and fertility in Rome. Lupercal oversaw the military operations of the army and reported directly to Cassius. Lupercal was roughly the same age as Cassius, different-looking but equally unattractive. He was short and scrawny, with a heavily scarred face. The facial scars resulted from a dagger attack Lupercal had not only survived but won many years ago. Lupercal was ambitious and motivated to advance his career and riches. He desired political power and sought success on the battlefield to gain favor with the ruling class.

Cassius sat at his desk, drinking a cup of red wine. Standing behind his right side was Lupercal. The two senior men eyed the four junior officers standing in front of them. Three relatively young standard bearers named Cato, Cornelius, and Atticus and the camp Hippocrates or doctor, Barnabas, stood at attention in front of the senior leaders. Cassius liked things to be orderly. This day had been anything but. Wild stories were circulating about the camp and the town, of a stranger killing people in broad daylight in the middle of the marketplace, albeit strangers were arriving in the small town to register for the required census, but other unusual men had been seen in town, as well. There had been an explosion and fire just a few miles outside the town. A patrol, under the command of Cornelius, investigated the explosion. There were roughly a thousand men under his control, and Cassius rarely interacted with officers this low down the chain of command. Cassius asked the questions as Lupercal looked on.

"Which one of you looked at the explosion and captured the unknown man?"

Cornelius stepped forward. He was nervous, and his hands were sweating. He had never been in the tent of the camp prefect before. Most men were nervous just to walk past it, and now he was being questioned directly by the general.

"I understand you found some strange materials and the man is a deaf-mute. Is that correct?"

"Yes, sir," stated a visibly anxious Cornelius. He could feel the eyes of Cassius and Lupercal focused on him. He felt like the eagle sculpture was staring at him, as well.

"Tell me more."

"We received a report of an explosion from some locals, and four units went to investigate. We collected many odd pieces of a material that we have never seen before. We gave those pieces to Barnabas to examine."

"Tell me about the man you captured."

"He does not speak or make any sound at all. He does not appear to hear or understand anything we say. When we captured him, he was just sitting behind a pile of rocks, staring straight ahead. He has not spoken or made even a sound since he has been in custody." Cornelius was trying to remember to breathe, so he paused and took a deep breath. Everyone could see how uneasy he felt. "We interrogated him back at camp and still nothing. Our guards punched and kicked him and still got no response."

"I heard he looks very different from us. Describe him to me."

"He has pale skin and light-brown hair. His eyes are green."

"Green? That is strange."

"Yes. It is. He is tall too. Almost four cubits in height. He was wearing a tunic and robe with sandals and a head covering, but underneath, he had peculiar coverings on his body." Cornelius sounded as uneasy as a preschooler trying to get through the alphabet so he could get his name on the classroom wall.

"What do you mean?"

"Under his tunic, he had on clothing that was soft and different colors. It covered his torso and groin area."

"How far away was he from the explosion?"

"We found him only a short distance from the site, maybe two hundred paces."

Cassius was done with Cornelius and moved on to the next junior officer. "Which one of you commands the watchtower guard who saw the killings in the marketplace?"

At first, Atticus had discounted Linus's tale about what he witnessed at the marketplace. However, word spread quickly about the three deaths and the odd way the people were killed. Atticus was compelled to inform his superiors of the report from his watchman.

Atticus stepped forward as Cornelius happily took a step back to fall in line with the others.

"Tell me what he said."

Atticus described in great detail what Linus had reported to him. He spoke about the thunderclaps, the short javelin, lightning bursts from the javelin, and the deaths that were absent of arrows, spears, or swords. Atticus talked of the odd language both men spoke to each other. He described the strange clothing and the golden hair of the man. He was nervous, too, but he was clearly less jumpy than Cornelius. Atticus had hopes of moving up the ranks, and he felt fortunate to speak after Cornelius. The officer who found the stranger had set the bar very low for his fellow officers.

"This golden hair man did not have a sword or a bow, is that correct?"

Atticus nodded.

"There was thunder, and then these people died. Is that correct?"

Atticus nodded again.

"Tell me about this odd clothing."

"According to my watchman, the man removed his robe and tunic and was left wearing a cloth that looked like the desert. The cloth was of many patterns but was the same color as the desert, trees, and brush. It appears to have been made to look like the desert. Like it was part of the sand and dirt."

Cassius was now finished with Atticus and moved on with his inquiry. "Which one of you spoke to the locals and brought the bodies back to camp?"

Cato stepped forward as Atticus took a step back to fall in line with the others. Atticus was pleased with his performance in front of the military leaders.

"When you questioned the locals, were their descriptions similar to that of our watchman?"

Cato nodded and explicated for Cassius. "Yes, they all talked about the odd clothes he wore. He had hair the color of the sun, and his skin was rather pale compared to their own. They heard thunder before the people died. They all said they saw no sword or spear or bow on the man. Just a short black object that looked like a javelin, but he had put the object on the ground when the last two people were killed." Cato noticed Lupercal staring at him, and he wondered what the general with the nasty reputation was thinking about him.

"What about the language he spoke?"

"There was a lot of noise and confusion, but some said the two men were communicating with each other in a foreign language. And there was something else they said…" Cato stopped himself and paused in midsentence.

"What is it?" demanded Cassius.

"Well, some locals said the man with the sunlike hair was very upset when the girl died. He tried to help her and held her in his arms until another man pulled him away."

"Another man?"

Cassius's quick reaction and loud question made Cato second-guess himself. *People said there was another man, didn't they?* "It is unclear. The locals could not give me a straightforward answer. Some said another man took the golden hair man away but were uncertain in which direction they left. Others said the man with the golden hair just vanished. The people were very confused about what happened to the man."

"Did you see any weapons or arrows or anything in the marketplace?"

"No. My soldiers looked and searched the entire area and found nothing."

"Did anyone know the two men who were killed?"

"No. No one claimed their bodies or said they knew them at all."

Cassius was now finished with Cato and moved on with his questioning. He looked at Barnabas and said, "You must be the Hippocrates who examined the bodies and materials from the fire."

Barnabas stepped forward as Cato took a step back to fall in line with the others. Barnabas felt unprepared for this meeting with the brass of the Roman army. Most of the time, no one paid attention to him. He did his own thing and could treat the injured how he saw fit. He was seen as a man of science, so the likes of Lupercal never questioned what he did. But would they now pay attention to what he said and did? Barnabas wanted things to stay the way they were. He longed to return to his tent and treat the sick and injured without being questioned.

"Tell me about the bodies you examined," instructed Cassius.

"Under the robes and tunics, each man had strange clothing. The clothes were not like the desert clothing worn by the other man, but they were different colors and soft. One man had odd-looking coverings over his feet."

"Explain."

"They were not sandals or caligae. They were made of leather and covered the entire foot. A thin piece of rope was intertwined into the foot covering. They had writing and had an emblem on them

174

too." He could feel the beads of sweat coming down his forehead and hoped Cassius and Lupercal would not notice.

"An emblem?"

Barnabas nodded and made a swoosh like motion with his finger to show what the emblem looked like.

"Tell me about these men and the injuries they suffered," stated Cassius.

"Their wounds were very similar. One had three holes in his stomach and chest. The second man had just a singular hole in his neck. The wounds were clean with no jagged marks, as you would see from a sword, javelin, or arrow. From the body of the man with the three wounds, I dug out small pieces of metal. I brought one with me to show you." Barnabas pulled out the washed remnants of a Remington .223 round and handed it to the general.

The camp prefect examined the bullet with great interest, shook his head, and then passed it on to Lupercal for his personal inspection. Lupercal was not sure what to make of the object in his hands, and his confusion showed on his face.

"What do you think it is?" asked Cassius as he looked at the camp doctor.

"I think it is some sort of iron dart or small arrow, but I have seen nothing like it before. I have never seen wounds like this before. The man struck in the neck did not have this metal dart in him. He had holes on both sides of his neck. It was like whatever hit him went right through him. His head was barely on his body. Again, there were no jagged edges or cutting like marks near the wound. The wounds were clean, as if a solo dart just went right through him."

"Tell me about the materials from the fire that were gathered at the scene of the explosion."

"Again, these materials are like nothing I have seen before. They are tiny." Barnabas held his thumb and forefinger about an inch apart to show the size. "The pieces are very hard, but they are not metal or iron. I could not bend them. The pieces are in various colors. Some are white, black, blue, and even red."

Cassius motioned for Barnabas to take a step back. He was done with his questions of the doctor for now.

"Has the watchman seen the deaf-mute? Is the deaf-mute the man from the marketplace?" asked the army leader.

"The watchman went and looked at the man in custody. According to the watchman, he is not the man with the golden hair," answered Atticus.

"The three of us spoke before this meeting," said Atticus as he gestured toward Cato and Cornelius. "The man in the marketplace is not the man in custody. The deaf-mute's hair is not golden like the other man. He was also in custody when the violence erupted in the town square. Cornelius and his men had arrested the deaf-mute before the deaths occurred."

Cassius sat back in his chair and stroked his chubby chin as he thought. He had no further questions for the standard bearers and the doctor. Cassius dismissed them and glanced over his shoulder at Lupercal. He motioned for his confidante to take a seat.

"What do you think, Commander?"

CHAPTER 25

Jewish culture required Tobias and Jessica to provide for the well-being of these men with the strange clothes, strange language, and strange equipment. Not only were they now guests in their home, but one of them had also been seriously injured saving the life of their niece. Providing a bountiful meal and shelter was the least they could do for them. Tobias, Jessica, and Father Patrick had found a method to communicate. They found a combination of Aramaic, Hebrew, Latin, and hand gestures as a successful way to speak. There was a delay of about ten to fifteen seconds after each sentence as the designated interpreters found the right words and motions to convey their thoughts.

Cole took the first watch on the roof as the rest of the SOG team settled in for dinner with this large and extended family. An immense table held the spread of food, but people during this time did not sit around a long dining room table on chairs to enjoy the meal. Instead, everyone would find a spot on the floor to eat, drink, and speak with one another. There were close to twenty people sharing this meal. The CIA men were fortunate to have a proper meal and rest for a bit while Sanchez mentally went through his options of what to do next. The visitors from the twenty-first century enjoyed bread, cheese, and honey to start the meal. Vegetables, beans, and lentils followed along with fish and various nuts, olives, and figs. Father Patrick, Tobias, and Jessica worked hard to translate between everyone. The CIA men wanted to show their appreciation and ate everything presented to them.

"I love this shrimp," stated Jackson as he helped himself to a second small plate. "They are a little saltier than I am used to back home, but they are delicious."

"I hate to spoil this for you, Elston, but those aren't shrimps," explained Father Patrick.

"I don't care what they are. They're awesome."

"Good, because they are locust" the priest grinned. Jackson shrugged and kept on eating.

"Where are you men from?" asked Tobias, and a hush fell over the inhabitants of the house as they waited for an answer.

Father Patrick translated to Sanchez. Sanchez shrugged his shoulders and said to Father Patrick, "That's a good question. What do you think they want to hear?"

Father Patrick faced Tobias and replied, "We are from far away, and we come from a place with different customs, clothes, tools, and speech."

Tobias pressed the issue and wanted to know more. "But where? You men are like no one we have ever seen before, with tools like nothing we have here." He was referring to their weapons, throat mics, and Tucker's medical kit. Father Patrick could feel the sweat forming on his forehead and hands, and he looked nervously at Sanchez for guidance. Jessica mercifully broke the silence and tension in the room.

"Tobias and everyone in our home, what difference does it make? If not for them, then little Rena would be dead. We should celebrate our new friends and be happy they are here."

Father Patrick translated, and Sanchez breathed a tremendous sigh of relief. However, he knew, at some point, some sort of explanation would have to be given. Unfortunately, in the urgency to depart 2023 as quickly as possible to chase Ahmed Faquar and his men, the CIA had not given them any type of cover story.

Jessica turned to Father Patrick and tried to put him at ease. "This is a welcoming house, and we are happy to have you. The last several days have brought an incredible change to this home."

"What kind of change?" asked Father Patrick.

"Oh, ever since Tobias's nephew arrived a few days ago, the feeling inside the house and inside all of us has changed. There is a feeling of love and peace present that was not here before."

"His nephew?"

"Yes. Ever since his nephew and his new wife arrived from their travels, things have been different. Things have been better."

Father Patrick wanted to make sure he was understanding Jessica properly and asked her to repeat herself. He shot Sanchez a quizzical look as the other CIA operators continued to eat, drink, and smile at their hosts.

"Yes," she continued. "They arrived a few days ago for the census."

Nephew. New wife. Love and peace. Father Patrick gathered his thoughts and contemplated what to ask Jessica next.

"Is your husband in the bloodline of the House of David?"

"Yes, but King David's reign was almost a thousand years ago."

"Is your husband's nephew named Joseph?"

"Yes," she answered with a perplexed look on her face.

"Is Joseph an artisan from the town of Nazareth?"

"Yes. How do you know these things?"

Sanchez looked at Father Patrick with a "What's going on?" look. What are you saying? What is she saying?

"Is his wife named Mary?" Father Patrick held his breath and waited for Jessica's reply.

"Yes. How do you know these things?"

"And is Mary carrying their first child?" Father Patrick could feel the sweat pouring off him. He felt like he might vomit at any moment. He had never felt more anxious in his life as he waited breathlessly for this woman to answer.

"No."

Father Patrick's heart sank. He felt his body turn cold in an instant, and now he knew he would be sick. He could feel the bile building in his throat and looked for a place to vomit.

"No. She was carrying their first child when they arrived, but the baby was born three days ago," Jessica said.

Father Patrick asked Jessica to repeat herself just to be sure he had heard her correctly. He felt instantly euphoric when she clearly stated that Mary had given birth three days prior, right here in their home.

"She had a boy, and His name is Jesus, right?" asked Father Patrick.

"Yes. Patrick, how do you know such things?"

The priest could not control his emotions and broke down in tears. He stayed seated on the floor, put his forehead to the ground, and sobbed. Jessica shrugged and looked at her family with confusion and uncertainty. Sanchez and his men stared at Father Patrick, not sure what to do or say. Sanchez, who was sitting next to Father Patrick, leaned in close and asked what was going on.

Father Patrick wiped away his tears and sat up. He whispered to Sanchez, "He is here. Jesus is here. The son of God is here in this house." Father Patrick hugged Sanchez and resumed crying.

The Christian inside Sanchez wanted to rejoice alongside Father Patrick and share in his tears of joy. However, he was a SOG team leader, and they had a mission. Sanchez forced Father Patrick to recount word for word what Jessica had told him. Mary and Joseph had arrived several days ago, and she had given birth to a baby boy named Jesus. The child was born three days ago. Sanchez rose to his feet and pulled Father Patrick up off the ground. A four-way conversation took place with Sanchez asking questions of Jessica and Tobias, with Father Patrick serving as the intermediary.

"Are Joseph, Mary, and Jesus here in the house right now?"

"Of course, she is in no condition to travel," answered Jessica. "They are in a back room, resting. We tried to give them the main room since she was so close to having the baby when they arrived. However, Mary insisted that Tobias's elderly cousin take the room instead. She said she would be fine in a back room. She is so kind and always thinking of others."

"Does anyone know they are here?"

"Just us. Why?"

"We need to speak with them right now," demanded Sanchez as he looked past Jessica and Tobias. He was trying to figure out which room they were in.

"No! Absolutely not!" stated Jessica without hesitation. "Mary is nursing her child. The family is resting, and they need their sleep. You can speak to them in the morning. I will not have strange men disrupting the new mother and her child."

Sanchez tried to make his case and explained it was important for them to speak with Joseph and Mary. Jessica and Tobias would not waver.

"You men are our guests, and you are welcome to stay in our home, but you are not to speak with Joseph or Mary until the morning. Do you understand?" asked Tobias, without really asking.

Sanchez agreed and thanked them for all they had done for him and his men.

Sanchez and his team huddled in the courtyard and reviewed the events of the day. They had killed two of the eight terrorists, McNally was injured, Nagle was missing, they had drawn the attention of the locals with the gunfight in the marketplace, and they did not know the location of the six other terrorists. Sanchez and Father Patrick then dropped the bombshell news that Jesus had been born and He was present, right now, with Mary and Joseph in that same house. The reactions of the men varied from Jackson and Bedford, who both fell to their knees in prayer; to McNally and Tucker, who just stood there in utter disbelief; to Cole, who smiled and said, "That's awesome! Can I see Him?"

"Not until the morning, as ordered by the lady of the house," replied Sanchez. "Take a few minutes to gather your thoughts, collect yourselves, and say a prayer, if you wish, but we have work to do tonight." Five minutes later, the team had their orders and went to work.

*****

Bedford was positioned on top of the roof. People used roofs as living space. They were solidly built and could hold a man of Bedford's size. It was commonplace for people to be seen on rooftops, completing daily tasks or relaxing. However, it was not common for a 6'3" man with an M4 pressed to his shoulder, supported by a bipod to be seen using night vision to scan for hostile targets. Thankfully, other than the people in the house he was defending, no one knew he was there.

McNally was below in the house, trying to catch some sleep in the corner of a room while being careful not to jar the staples in his lower back. McNally took advantage of his exhaustion to fall asleep quickly despite the family's animals inside the home. Father Patrick had explained to the men, during this time, people took their animals into the house for the night. He was not talking about dogs and pets. No, they corralled goats and sheep into the houses each night. The animals being indoors served a multitude of uses. First, it helped keep the houses warm at night. The body temperature of the animals kept the human inhabitants warm by bringing up the overall temperature inside the structure. It also safeguarded the animals from getting lost, eaten by wild animals, or stolen by thieves. The bah, bah, bah of the sheep served as white noise to McNally as he drifted off to sleep. Tucker maintained guard of the lower perimeter. He kept his M4 hidden under his robe, but he still patrolled outside the wall, with the attention and discipline of a seasoned professional.

Father Patrick did not know what to do with himself. He had already said about a dozen rosaries when he learned the Holy Family was in the same house. He would meet Jesus, Mary, and Joseph in the morning. The young friar felt like an eight-year-old boy waiting on Christmas Eve for Santa to deliver an Xbox. He lay on a bedroll, and his eyes were open as he counted the seconds in his head until the sun came up.

Sanchez, Cole, and Jackson had their night-vision goggles on and were moving across the pathway, which served as a road, toward the pod. Jackson wondered if they needed the night vision at all. The sky was extremely bright, given that the sun had set several hours ago. An intensely bright star shone high above them, as if it were directly over Bethlehem.

"Do you think that's what I think it is?" said Jackson as he pointed up at the dazzling star.

"You mean the Christmas star?" said Sanchez as he looked up.

"Yeah. What do you think?"

"I think it is. I really do."

"Me too," said a smiling Jackson.

Their mission tonight was twofold. Sanchez wanted to see if they could get a fix on Nagle. There had been no word from their pilot for several hours. In his last communication, Nagle stated he was heading north from a small group of trees near the pod. He was trying to hide from advancing Roman soldiers. The three CIA operators would search the area for Nagle or at least clues that could, hopefully, tell them something. They would also take their cache of weapons and ammo back to Tobias's house. Each man already carried his M4 carbine rifle and nine-millimeter Sig Sauer P226 pistol. Now, Sanchez would take back Bedford's McMillan Tac-338 sniper rifle, GLG forty-millimeter grenade launcher, three HK MP5 nine-millimeter submachine guns, and the FAB Mossberg shotgun with the pistol grip. Sanchez and his enemy had the same number of fighters now, six versus six. However, he had his foes completely outgunned.

As they advanced to the site of the time-traveling vessel, Sanchez thought of Beca and RJ back at home. He was the only SOG team member who was married and had a kid. The others would be bachelors for eternity. Normally, he did not think of his wife and his child when he was on a mission. *Stay focused on the task at hand,* his trainers at the Farm had told him. *Think of your family just enough for motivation, but think about them too much, and you can become distracted or, worse, afraid.* Sanchez knew you had to be fearless at this job, but there was a fine line between fearless and reckless. Still, Christmas was only a few days away, RJ's first, and the Christmas Eve Mass and play at the parish that had him so worried was approaching. It was odd to think of RJ's first Christmas while here he was at the first Christmas. Beca had gone way over the top for the holiday. The house looked like Buddy the Elf, Will Ferrell's character in the movie *Elf,* had decorated their place. Miguel had almost fallen off the ladder while putting up the outdoor lights and had nearly thrown his back out while carrying the ten-foot-tall tree into the house. Those would have been rough conversations to have with the deputy director. "Sorry, I can't go on the mission to Peru to rescue the hostages. I broke my ankle hanging up blinking lights on my front porch."

Beca's family had gone way overboard too on gifts. Every day, Beca's mom or dad would text them a picture of a new present they had picked up for RJ.

"Your parents are going to have to rent a U-Haul when they come for Christmas," he had told Beca.

"They are just excited. It's their first grandchild's first Christmas," she offered as their defense.

Miguel hoped he would be back in time. He always assumed he would return from each mission. That was the way you had to think when this was your job.

Sanchez, Jackson, and Cole approached the terrorists' blown-apart pod with caution. The C4 had done the trick. The pod was demolished. Nothing bigger than a square inch or two was left. Sanchez wondered how many millions of taxpayer dollars had been spent to build the vehicle, and now it was spread out over dirt and sand two thousand years in the past. No way any of the locals could make heads or tails of the debris. Maybe they could make a necklace out of the small pieces left in the dust but using it to gain a techno-logical advantage or discovery—not happening. The trio continued. Cole spotted the trees where Nagle had been hiding closer to their own pod. This was the location from which Nagle had advised he was heading north to avoid the soldiers. They each fanned out, hop-ing to find Nagle hiding behind rocks or a tree and hoping not to find his dead body. Jackson noticed what looked like a large number of sandal prints in an area that should not have been well traveled.

"I may have something!" exclaimed Jackson as he waved the others over to his position. They converged at a spot about two hun-dred yards from the presumed site from which Nagle had fled. They were at the base of a hill and next to a giant pile of rocks and boulders.

"This would have been a decent place to hide," said the SOG leader.

Jackson showed Sanchez and Cole the prints, which were diffi-cult to see in the dark, even when they used the night vision. There were several sets of prints on the ground. Fortunately, there was no corpse or sign of blood anywhere in the area.

"What do you think of the prints, Papi? Can you track them?" asked Cole.

"Track them? I am Mexican-American. I am not from the Sioux or Apache tribes, and this is not the 1800s. No. I can't track them."

The CIA team continued their search for Nagle or any physical clues he might have left behind. However, it was dark, and they were not forensic investigators, so they came up with nothing. Their search for Nagle's weapon, comms, and tech proved futile in the dark, as well. Sanchez surmised, and Cole and Jackson agreed, the Romans had taken Nagle alive. It was not good news, but it was much better than the alternative.

Sanchez could not believe the incredible effectiveness of the cloaking system. He could not see the pod at all as they made their approach. Sanchez used the device that looked like a key fob to disengage the security system and make the pod visible again. If the team had not been through so much today, he would have ordered Jackson to plug in the code of s-i-x-e-r-s. He did not. In great efficiency, they loaded up the camouflaged pull carts with the weapons, supplies, and gear. Sanchez grabbed the dossiers and photos of the six remaining terrorists and stuck them under his arm. In less than five minutes, they were packed up. The pod was cloaked and basically invisible again, and they headed back to Bethlehem.

CHAPTER 26

Before the crack of dawn, the Roman patrols were on their way out of camp. The commanders instructed the patrols to engage with the locals to find out more about this magical man with the golden hair. Lupercal, ever aggressive and ambitious, had wanted to send soldiers door-to-door to search and find this man. However, he had been overruled by Cassius. Cassius preferred a more subtle approach.

"We do not need to scare people and kick down doors," Cassius had said to Lupercal. "If our patrols ask around and talk to people, we will find out who and what this man is. They cannot keep a secret like this for long, even in a tight-knit group like the Jews."

"We must find out if he is a threat to the town, the army, or even King Herod," stated Lupercal.

"And we will. In due time, we will. Be patient. So far, all he has done is kill two strangers and a Jewish girl. He did not attack a Roman soldier. With the census ongoing, there are many strange people in town. We will sort this out."

Lupercal was not satisfied but held his tongue. For now, he would play the good soldier and bide his time. However, if the opportunity arose for him to advance himself, he would seize it.

*****

Sanchez and Father Patrick were ready and waiting when Jessica came for them in the morning. They were both experiencing a mixture of excitement and apprehension as they approached the small room that housed Jesus, Mary, and Joseph. Jessica pushed aside the cloth curtain that served as a door for the small and simple room. There they were, the Holy Family.

Mary could not have been over eighteen years old. She stood by her husband's side with her brown hair at shoulder length and full of soft curls. Her eyes radiated love and understanding. Not quite brown or blue, but the prettiest hazel eyes either man had ever seen. She was exactly as Father Patrick had imagined her. She greeted the strangers with a smile of both warmth and friendship. Joseph was in his midtwenties and was of average height and a normal build for men. As soon as they saw him, Sanchez and O'Conner recognized him immediately. Joseph had been the man who opened the front door for Sanchez and Cole when they first arrived. Father Patrick knew him as one of the men who had helped control McNally during Tucker's medical procedure. He nodded a hello; his eyes held a strength and confidence. Jesus was just a few feet from His parents. They wrapped Him tightly in a blanket, and He was lying in a makeshift crib of straw. Sanchez could not help but think to himself that He was wrapped in swaddling clothes. It was difficult to see the face of Jesus, other than His chubby cheeks, as He slept. Sanchez and Father Patrick, on instinct, approached the child and dropped to their knees. Looking like they rehearsed it, which they had not, both men made the sign of the cross and prayed silently for several minutes. They fought back emotional tears as Jessica looked at the new parents and shrugged to show her confusion by their reaction to seeing the newborn. Both men again made the sign of the cross and stood.

"Father, you better deliver the homily of your life, because we have to get Joseph and Mary on board with our mission," said Sanchez.

"I know." Father Patrick had spent his sleepless night preparing for this conversation. *How do I convince Joseph and Mary that we know who they are and who their son is without scaring them or freaking them out? What I say must be perfect.* Father Patrick could feel his hands shake as he prepared to speak to Joseph and Mary.

Father Patrick spoke in Aramaic to Joseph and Mary. His language skills improved significantly with each conversation. He made eye contact, first with Joseph and then with Mary, as Sanchez stood in silence behind the priest. Mary now sat on a stool with her husband standing by her side.

"Joseph and Mary, my name is Patrick, and this is Miguel. It is both a pleasure and an honor to speak with you right now. Thank you," began the Dominican priest as he spoke slowly and clearly.

"May I say something first?" said Joseph. O'Connor, of course, nodded and waited, but he was surprised by Joseph's question. Joseph is not credited with a single utterance in the Bible. None of the gospels attribute a quote or any spoken words to Joseph. Joseph is silent throughout the New Testament. "Thank you for saving my niece, Rena. Your man was very brave and sacrificed himself to save a stranger. My family will forever be in his debt."

"Of course. We are strangers to this land, but we are here to help your family. This may sound odd and unusual, but please listen to what I have to say."

Joseph, Mary, and even Jessica exchanged anxious glances at one another before they nodded and listened to Father Patrick.

Sanchez felt a bead of his own sweat roll down across his temple, and he moved his hands to behind his back so the others could not see them trembling. *Please, God, let this go well.*

"We are here to help you, protect you. We know your child is special. We know He is the son of God."

Mary gasped! She reached up and grabbed her husband's hand. He listened intently as Jessica's mouth fell open.

Father Patrick continued, "Don't be afraid. We are here to protect you and Jesus."

"How can you know this?" asked Joseph. Mary was still quiet.

"Mary." The priest got down on one knee and addressed Mary. He looked deep into her eyes, and she held his gaze. "Back in Nazareth, the Lord sent the angel Gabriel to you with a message. Gabriel said." Father Patrick then quoted Luke 1:26–38 to Mary: "Greetings favored one! The Lord is with you. Do not be afraid, Mary, for you have found favor with God. And behold, you will conceive in your womb and give birth to a son, and you shall name him Jesus. He will be great and will be called the Son of the Most High;

and the Lord God will give Him the throne of His father David and He will reign over the house of Jacob forever, and His kingdom will have no end."

Mary gripped Joseph's hand harder as Father Patrick continued, "Mary, you said to the angel, 'How will this be, since I am a virgin?' and the angel said, 'The Holy Spirit will come upon you, and the power of the Most High will overshadow you; for that reason also the holy Child will be called the Son of God. And behold, even your relative Elizabeth herself has conceived a son in her old age, and she who was called infertile is now in her sixth month. For nothing will be impossible with God.'"

Again, Mary gasped. How could this man know this? He must have been sent by God, as well.

"Then Mary, you said, 'Behold, the Lord's bond-servant; may it be done according to your word.' And the angel departed."

"What you have said is true," said a tearful Mary. "How can you know this?" Jessica fainted and would have landed hard on her head if not for Sanchez's quick reaction. As she fell backward in shock, Sanchez reached out and caught her before she struck the floor. He leaned her up against the wall and signaled to Mary and Joseph that she was okay.

Joseph, of course, knew all this from his wife. But how could this strange man know these things and know with such incredible detail? Joseph leaned down low to embrace and comfort Mary as Father Patrick continued. The priest locked eyes with Joseph and said, "'Her husband, Joseph, since he was a righteous man and did not want to disgrace her, planned to send her away secretly. But when he had thought this over, behold, an Angel of the Lord appeared to him in a dream, saying, 'Joseph, son of David, do not be afraid to take Mary as your wife; for the Child who has been conceived in her is of the Holy Spirit. She will give birth to a Son; and you shall name Him Jesus, for He will save His people from their sins.' Now all this took place, so that what was spoken by the Lord through the prophet would be fulfilled: "BEHOLD, THE VIRGIN WILL CONCEIVE AND GIVE BIRTH TO A SON, AND THEY SHALL NAME HIM IMMANUEL," which translated means, "GOD WITH US." And Joseph awoke from his sleep and did as the angel of the Lord commanded him, and took Mary as His wife, but kept her a virgin until she gave birth to a Son; and he named Him Jesus.'" Father Patrick had just quoted Matthew 1 directly to Joseph.

For a few minutes, no one said or did anything. Sanchez nervously looked at Father Patrick but dared not speak. Jessica remained passed out and against the wall. Joseph and Mary held their embrace and comforted each other. Father Patrick stayed on one knee and patiently waited for one of them to say something, anything.

"Were you sent by God? Why do we need protection? Where are you from?" asked Joseph.

O'Connor looked at Sanchez. "How much do I tell him about why and how we are here?"

"Tell him whatever he needs to hear to let us do our jobs. Just don't scare them too much."

"We come from a far-off land. We have a different language, weapons, and clothing. We have things that may appear magical at first, but they are real. Your son, Jesus, is the Savior of the world. We are here to protect Him, Mary, and you from evil men."

"What evil men?" said Joseph as he continued to hold and support Mary. Father Patrick could not tell if she was crying; her head was buried in Joseph's chest. "Why would they want to harm a baby?"

"Jesus is going to save the world, and sadly, some people do not love Him like we do. Some people view Him as a threat. They are wrong. The son of God is here to save the world. Our responsibility is to eliminate these men and defend and protect the three of you."

"What can I do to help?"

*****

The marketplace was busy as the sun hung low in the morning sky. Shopkeepers, tradesmen, and those selling their wares for an honest day's wage were back in operation. The town center was busier than the day before. Maybe it was the growing influx of new travelers into the area, or maybe everyone wanted to talk and gossip about the events from the day before. Men and women alike were telling their own version of the magician with the golden hair. Some claimed they heard the thunderclaps as far as away as the temple in the northern section of Bethlehem. Everyone had a story to tell, and everyone wanted to learn more about yesterday. Who was this man of magic? Was he a demon or an angel? Were there others like him in town? Who were the two men he killed? Nobody in Bethlehem would admit to knowing them. Roman patrols took advantage of the willingness of locals to talk and chat. The soldiers interacted with the merchants and found plenty of people who wanted to tell their stories. The more people shared with the soldiers, the more confused the soldiers became. They were not trained investigators. How could they differentiate between fact and fiction when almost everyone in town claimed to be an eyewitness?

"He killed those three people, and then he just disappeared into the air," said one old man.

"I saw him sprout wings and fly away back over the temple," explained a twelve-year-old boy.

"He is a demon!" shouted an old woman. "I saw another demon lead him away towards a house with pink walls."

"There was a poof of smoke and dust, and he was gone," explained one woman, who was balancing a jug of water on one hip and a two-year-old boy on the other.

"What is being done to protect us?" asked another merchant, who seemed more concerned with his inventory of wicker baskets than the fate of the three deceased people. "What is General Cassius doing to find this wizard?"

"He did not kill that young girl. He tried to help her. The stranger somehow killed that girl with a black object. He pointed it at her and then it made loud noises that hurt my ears," stated a man in his mid-twenties.

Ahmed, Umar, and Kareem worked their way through the busy shops and stands. They watched and listened to what the people were saying and what the soldiers were asking. All three men spoke Arabic and could make out enough words and phrases in the local language to summarize what was happening.

The soldiers were clearly concerned about the golden-haired man and if he had any friends with him. The soldiers viewed him as a threat to themselves and the town. However, the townspeople did not appear to be as scared or as worried as the army was. Clearly, some citizens were afraid, but others were not. They listened to different conversations between the merchants and their customers.

"This wizard did nothing to us. He killed two strangers who had small black objects that had fire come out of them. If you ask me, the dead strangers were the evil ones. They, too, were wizards" was the point made by a chubby man who was trying to sell his inventory of tunics and robes to earn a living.

"Then how do you explain the dead girl? Why did he kill an innocent girl?" countered a woman whom he was losing as a customer the more they talked.

"One stranger killed her, not the Wizard," was his retort.

"How?"

"I am not sure, but the man with the hair like the sun is not a wicked man."

She threw her arms up in disgust and looked around for someone to help her in her debate with the hefty retailer.

"You! Yes, you. What do you say?" She pointed a finger at Kareem. "You must have seen what happened yesterday. What do you say about the man with the golden hair?"

Kareem froze. He did not want to draw attention to himself by trying to answer and butcher their language, which would obviously show that he, too, was a stranger and did not belong.

However, as Kareem paused and before he could mumble a reply, Ahmed spoke.

"We have just arrived this morning. We know nothing of which you speak." Ahmed and his cohorts did not wait for a response. They pivoted away from the woman and her accusatory finger and walked away quickly. The woman waved her arms at their backs in frustration and turned her verbal attack back to the overweight merchant. Ahmed was formulating a plan. He had an idea, and now he would just need to develop the details. If he and his men could pull this off, the Roman army would be his ally by the end of the day.

*****

"You know, they think we are angels," Cole told Sanchez as they stood at the end of the large table in the main room of the house.

"Is that a good thing or a bad thing?"

"I guess we will find out."

Sanchez had his plan in action. Jesus, Mary, and Joseph were stowed away in a back room far from the main room and the entrance to the house. He had a hard perimeter set up around the Holy Family. McNally stood at the ready, always within a few feet of them. McNally was sore and in pain, but he was moving well and not complaining. Bedford remained perched on the roof while Tucker maintained a sentry post outside. It was best to have Jackson and Cole stay inside the compound. Word had probably spread about the magical killer with the golden hair, and Jackson's skin color made him an obvious outsider.

Sanchez needed intel. He needed what they refer to as ground intelligence. His men were not capable of getting the information he needed. That was where Joseph's relatives came into play. Sanchez decided to break every time-travel rule, from the ones Dr. Stevenson laid out to them to the movie rules established by Marty McFly. Sanchez called the family together, and with Father Patrick and Jessica translating for him, he laid it all out or, at least, some of it.

"We have come from far away to protect this family and this new baby from evil men. It is important to everyone these men are stopped and Joseph, Mary, and Jesus live long and healthy lives. Our language is unfamiliar. Our clothes and weapons are different, but we are regular men. We have a responsibility to guard and defend Jesus, and we need your help."

Sanchez passed out the pictures of the six remaining terrorists. The family had no way to even understand the idea of a photograph. But he showed them anyway and hoped they could somehow comprehend these were the men they sought. The house comprised male candidates to fill the roles of spies, guards, and builders of defense structures. The women of the house could also act as spies and look-outs. Enoch, Rena's father, and another male, named Ezekiel (it was unclear if he was a cousin, an uncle, or how they were related), went to the marketplace to gather actionable intelligence. Were the evil men there? What were the Roman soldiers doing and saying? What was the word in the marketplace about Cole? Had anyone noticed the rest of the SOG team? They also tasked two women with listening to the town gossip and reporting back what they had learned. Jessica had warned all of them not to say a word or reveal any information to anyone, no matter who was asking. No one was to know about the birth of Jesus or the strange men in their home.

Tobias oversaw the construction of barricades and bulwarks. For a family of craftsmen, the building was a breeze. Joseph insisted on helping once he heard the woodworking underway. The design was simple: wooden planks nailed together that were about five feet wide and four feet high and several inches thick. They would use them as barriers to protect the Holy Family's room and throughout the house as both obstructions and cover if any foe penetrated the house. The cutting and the nailing created enough noise to wake baby Jesus from His sleep. Jessica scolded the men for making too much noise and helped Mary settle Him back down.

While barriers were being built, Jackson had two teenage boys helping him load spare magazines with rounds of .223 Remingtons. The boys asked no questions and sat on the floor, filling each clip with great precision.

"Is all of this really necessary, Miguel?" Father Patrick said. "Do we have to turn the house into a fortified camp?"

"I am afraid so, Father. We must be prepared for anything and everything. I think the family understands. Hopefully, my spies come back with some solid intel, and we can develop a course of action."

"What do you hope to learn?"

"Where the bad guys are so we can go kill them," said Sanchez with a matter-of-fact conviction.

Father Patrick wished there were a way to avoid killing, but he was a realist and knew there was no arresting the terrorists and bringing them to justice.

"Question for you, Father," stated Sanchez. "Didn't Jesus leave Bethlehem and go to Egypt at some point?"

"Yes. In a dream, an angel comes to Joseph and tells him to flee to Egypt to protect Jesus and Mary. According to the Gospel of Matthew, 2:16–18, when Herod learns the king of the Jews was born, he orders the death of every male child under age two. It was called the Massacre of the Innocents."

"Can you do that?"

"Do what? Tell Joseph to go to Egypt?"

"Sure. Why don't you tell him? Then we will know they are safe while we hunt down the bad guys."

"I can't."

"Why?"

"First, Jesus is older when they make that trip. He is at least a year old, and that journey would be impossible with a newborn and a woman who just gave birth. It's a miracle Mary even survived childbirth. Women died all the time during childbirth. It is not like today where a woman pushes the kid out and the health-insurance company sends her home in two days. And there is another huge reason I can't tell Joseph to leave for Egypt."

"What is that?"

"An angel comes to Joseph in a dream. I am a priest, not an angel."

*****

Enoch's life had always been rather simple. Even in Judea, two thousand years in the past, some would even call his life boring. He was not a handsome man, but he was not ugly either. He was not tall, but he also was not short. There was nothing special about him, good or bad. He just practiced his craft as a carpenter, took care of his very ordinary wife, and prayed his two children would live as long as he did. But something had changed in the last few days. He had lived

195

his whole life in the simple town of Bethlehem, and he would prob-ably die here too. Yet life was different. Life was exciting. As soon as his cousin Joseph arrived with his pregnant wife earlier in the week, things were better. Enoch could not put his finger on it or find the proper words to describe it, but life felt right. He even loved his wife more, and he was just happier the last few days. When Mary gave birth to that baby boy, the feeling in the house was indescribable. It was not just him; the entire family felt it. They felt more alive, more love, and more hopeful about the world.

That new awareness of life was almost destroyed by a runaway wagon. The wagon would have surely killed his younger daughter. If not for the quick action of a strange man, she would be dead. Who were these strange men? They said they were here to protect the baby and the family. They spoke such a strange language and wore bizarre clothing. Enoch had once heard a story of a giant in Jerusalem. People said he was two heads taller than any man and was stronger than anyone else. His shoulders were said to be broader than a horse. Two of these strange men were that big, and the others were a head taller than him. The men had looks of determination and commitment. There was only one God. The Jews worshipped the god of Moses and Abraham, but the Romans worshipped many gods. Enoch did not believe in other gods, but he wondered about these men. Could they be gods? At the very least, they had to be angels sent by God.

Enoch and Ezekiel, his cousin, walked home with a basket full of dates, figs, and olives from the market. They had done as the leader of the strange men had asked. They went to the market and talked and listened and acted as they always did. Enoch was excited about what they had learned. He knew the men would be pleased with their discoveries and they would thank him for doing a great job. First, the unparalleled tangibility of love since the baby had been born, his daughter's life was saved, and now he would gain favor with a group of blessed angels. Enoch's life was anything but boring.

Sanchez and Cole sat listening to the walkie-talkies taken from the dead terrorists. They flipped between channels, hoping their foes would be undisciplined and break radio silence. The CIA men were disappointed. Ahmed and his band of terrorists had not used the radios since Ahmed ordered them off their own communications system the day before. The silence of the walkies gave Cole the chance to bring up an issue that was on all their minds.

"What do we do about our missing pilot?"

"Right now, nothing. Our mission has three objectives. One, defend Jesus, Mary, and Joseph. Two, kill the eight terrorists. Three, don't leave any twenty-first-century tech behind. Davidson said nothing about us being required to make it back."

"Dude, you want to go back home, right?" Cole briefly wondered.

"God, yes! Of course, I want to get back home. For Christ's sake, my kid's first Christmas is in, like, two days." Sanchez grimaced as he realized he had taken the Lord's name in vain with the Lord about thirty feet away in another room. The irony was lost on Cole.

"How are we going to get him back? What's the plan?"

"Our first order of business is the mission. After we take out these last six scumbags and make sure they did not leave an AR-15 lying around, then we find Nagle. And we will find him."

"Thank God."

"If you want to thank God, you can go into the other room. Just make sure you knock first." Sanchez smiled.

CHAPTER 27

It was the fall of 1980. The sixth-grade boy with the curly red hair and pleasant face was not the smartest kid in Mrs. Lalley's class, but he knew the most about the upcoming presidential election. Actually, he knew everything about the national election. He could recite the electoral votes for each state just as easily as some kids could rattle off state capitals. He knew so much about the election that Mrs. Lalley told the eighth-grade teachers about him.

"You have to see this kid," she explained to her teaching peers. "He knows everything."

So the eighth-grade teacher running the school-wide debate decided he wanted to meet this political whiz kid. After ten minutes, Mr. Mason decided Ted Bennett had to be involved in the school-wide mock debate among the eighth-graders posing as Jimmy Carter, Ronald Reagan, and John Anderson. Young Ted served as the debate moderator, and in front of a packed auditorium, he asked the questions, monitored the time, and controlled the debate. That was a week before election day.

The national polls showed the contest between Jimmy Carter and Ronald Reagan was "too close to call." The narrow polls and media coverage were causing his conservative father much angst and nervousness. But not Ted. He knew Reagan would win in a landslide. Ted predicted the margin of victory in the popular vote and the number of states Reagan would win. The kid was officially a political junkie. He was not concerned with being the smartest person in the room or having the highest grades in school, but he always wanted to know the most. Ted wanted to know what was happening before anyone else and what it would mean. Bennett was the top political operative because of his uncanny ability to know what was happening before everyone and what would happen next.

"I got something!" exclaimed the advisor with the once-curly red hair, but still the pleasant face. Bennett had been fixated on his laptop for hours. He had taken two hours off to grab a power nap in his West Wing office, but otherwise, he had stayed up all night, searching obscure websites for any clue of mission success. Bennett wanted to know the most and know it first. The other advisors, including the madame vice president, had gone home for a few hours to rest and change their clothes. However, they were all back bright and early in the Oval Office to continue to handle a situation that was unmanageable.

Sitting in an Under Armour sweat suit and sipping an energy drink, the president asked from behind the Resolute Desk, "What have you got, Ted?"

"I got an old legend from AncientWizards.net. It says here there are several accounts in ancient texts about a wizard with golden hair and a black pointy object. The object shot lightning bolts and boomed like thunder. It says the wizard wore unusual clothing, spoke a peculiar language, and disappeared after killing three people."

"And that's evidence of what?"

"The wizard could be one of our guys. There were not too many blond men roaming around ancient Judea. An object that shoots lightning and booms like thunder. Sounds like an automatic weapon to me."

"Yeah, and it could be the made-up ramblings of a tech geek running a website for nerds in his mother's basement. Ted, I hope you are right. Maybe it is one of our guys and ancient tales are sending us clues about how they are doing, but this won't be over until our SOG team walks off the time-traveling pod and says 'We got 'em all.'"

Bennett nodded at the president. The president was right, but Bennett knew this bit of information from a bizarre website was a good sign. Just like in 1980, he was reading the signs, looking at the data, and he knew what was really happening on the ground.

*****

It was not very often when Sanchez needed an interpreter to get information out of a friendly. Once in Syria, he had required the use of a translator to get the intel out of a local man who desperately wanted to help. Knowing ISIS was not a big proponent of women's rights and fearing for the safety of his three daughters, the local Syrian gave Sanchez and his men everything he knew about the location of ISIS fighters. The information had proved invaluable as an early-morning raid resulted in a dozen ISIS men dead and their leader taken prisoner.

The debriefing of Enoch and Ezekiel was not going smoothly. Sanchez would ask questions, which Father Patrick, Jessica, and Tobias would then translate as a team to the two novice spies. They were all working together to decipher what Enoch and Ezekiel were saying. Ezekiel's mouthful of dates made the task more challenging until Jessica finally yelled at him for talking with his mouth full. Sanchez felt like a CIA case officer working with an informant who was vomiting information. Finally, after much cajoling and coaching, Enoch slowed down and relayed vital information to Sanchez.

Sanchez learned the entire town was abuzz with yesterday's events. Everyone was talking and gossiping, including the Roman soldiers. Sanchez took in everything Enoch and Ezekiel had to report. He was able to separate the useful from the ridiculous. The Roman army was very concerned about the wizard with the golden hair, and the absurd, the wizard sprouted wings and flew away. The army's concern worried Sanchez. Would the army go door-to-door looking for Cole? If they did, how would that compromise Jesus, Mary, and Joseph?

"How many men do the Romans have? How many soldiers are camped near Bethlehem?"

"Maybe one thousand" was the reply from Tobias.

Sanchez also learned no one had claimed the bodies of the two dead men. The bodies had been taken to the Roman camp. According to the soldiers, who were as gossipy as the locals, the bodies had been examined by the camp Hippocrates, and the wounds mystified him. They believed the two dead men to be part of a larger group of strangers. Reports varied on the size of the group, but one local claimed to have seen a fire and tents set up in a secluded area on the western side of Bethlehem.

"If it was secluded, then how did he see it?" said Sanchez to his informants.

"The smoke. When my friend saw the smoke, he went out to see what it was. He saw the men around the fire with shiny tents, and he got scared. He left before they could see him."

Sanchez wished he had more men or a drone or satellite imaging. He needed eyes on the Roman camp and on the hideout of the terrorists. Yet he could not spare to send his operators out on scouting missions. Cole was basically a wanted man. Jackson was Black and stood out worse than an obese man as a Radio City Rockette. McNally was injured. That left him with Bedford and Tucker, but he did not want his sniper or medic wandering too far away.

Enoch's other bit of critical intel was the mystery about the captured deaf-mute. Sanchez learned the average Roman soldier was as chatty as an eighth-grade girl. Enoch had discovered the capture of an unknown man on the eastern edge of the town at the site of a great fire. Enoch explained how, according to the gabby troops, the man would not speak and was found hiding behind rocks to the north of the fire.

"What did the man look like?"

"The soldiers said he had palish skin and light hair, but he never talks or makes a sound. The army locked him away in a small building at the camp. Even when the guards hit and kicked him, he did not say a word."

Tough guy. That must be Nagle. Sanchez now had to plan a course of action based on the new intel from Enoch. Nagle was alive, probably not well, but at least he was alive. The terrorists were set up on the outskirts of town, and the Roman army was afraid of Cole.

Sanchez held a meeting with his men and briefed them on the recent developments. He explained his plan to them. If it all worked according to the strategy, they would all be home in twenty-four hours.

*****

Abdullah's face was pressed up against the tree as he clenched the AR-15. He had been hiding for close to an hour as he and his Muslim brothers waited to strike. He wanted so badly to fire his weapon on the unexpecting Roman patrol. Ahmed had explained his plan, and it made perfect sense. They would ambush a group of Roman soldiers and leave their dead bodies to be discovered. The army would see the wounds of their fellow fighters and blame the wizard with the golden hair. The brutal deaths of their own would incentivize the army to hunt down the other men from the twenty-first century. Ahmed knew he could not take on highly skilled Rangers, SEALs, Delta, or CIA men himself. But if he could get five hundred or more Roman soldiers to fight with him, as allies, then his jihad would succeed. Ahmed and Umar had scouted the area earlier in the day and had determined a patrol would pass through this location in the afternoon. The six attackers were well hidden within a group of trees, rocks, and boulders. Ideally, Ahmed would have positioned his men on both sides of the passway to create a crossfire. However, he was concerned his men might end up shooting each other with inaccurate aim, so he opted to spread them out on the same side. Abdullah was the point man with his AR-15, and Jamal was forty yards farther down with a shotgun to cover the rear of the Roman column. Ahmed expected ten Romans would make up the patrol. Their swords and javelins would be no match for the firepower of his fighting force.

The passway was near the bottom of a hill and was only a half mile south of Ahmed's hideout. The ambush would occur just a few miles from the Roman camp. Ahmed was planning on the noise attracting attention and a quick retreat by him and his men. They positioned Umar on the hill, about seventy-five yards above the passway. Once the entire patrol was within the positions held by

Abdullah and Jamal, Umar would begin the assault by firing the first shot.

"Shoot the officer first," Ahmed had instructed. "He will wear the helmet with the red plume on top. Once Umar takes him out, then the rest of us will open up. There can be no survivors. Listen for my command to call off the attack, and then retreat up the hill to our camp."

Ahmed and Kareem were crouched behind trees only a few yards from Abdullah. Ibrahim and his shotgun were closer to Jamal at the rear. Excitement and adrenaline filled Abdullah. He had gotten a taste of violence earlier when he fired at the olive-tree farmer and his son. All the jihadists were hyped with anticipation of the one-sided skirmish that was imminent. Finally, they could hear the Romans approaching. The distinctive sounds of men trudging along and the obvious commands of a military officer were drawing closer. Umar waited patiently until all ten men entered the kill zone. He took his time and breathed slowly as he eyed his target. Umar fired a single shot.

The Roman officer heard a cracking noise and then felt a whistle just above his head. The Roman leader had thick curly black hair and a thin nose that did not look right on his wide and square face. *What was that?* He used his massive right arm to remove his helmet to inspect it. Part of the red plume was missing. *Odd.* Less than five seconds later, another crack of thunder, and this time, the Roman's head exploded. His thick curly black hair was torn from his head. Then, the gates of hell opened on his men.

Abdullah waited, hidden behind the tree. He heard the pop of Umar's rifle and then nothing. It was like a glitch in life, a pause. He expected to hear shouting, screaming, and chaos. For a few seconds, there was nothing. Another pop came from Umar, and Abdullah glanced around the tree. On the ground lay the top of a man's head. His curly black hair was about a foot away from the rest of his body. Abdullah spun from behind the tree and leveled his AR-15 at the front of the column. He set the rifle on full auto, and Abdullah let loose with one long sustained burst while screaming, "Allahu Akbar!"

Abdullah and his weapon cut the two soldiers at the front of the patrol into pieces. They never knew what hit them. Fingers were separated from hands, hands from arms, and arms were torn from torsos. Their bodies would be unrecognizable, even to their mothers. Abdullah screamed in delight as he watched the bodies disintegrate into mounds of bloody flesh and bone.

Ahmed's assault did not have the timing he desired, as there were delays in his men reacting after Umar began the attack with his opening salvo. Jamal and Ibrahim were slow to fire at the rear of the guard with their shotguns. This gave the Romans time to bring up their shields. The thick wooden shields lessened the impact of the first two shells from the shotguns and added several seconds to their lives. Kareem opened fire on them from behind. Kareem's long burst from his rifle cut them down quickly, and now half the patrol was dead. The remaining five Romans displayed great discipline and strength as they tried to rally for a charge on their attackers. The terrorists fired wildly as the surviving soldiers drew their swords and javelins. One Roman attempted to hurl his javelin at Kareem, who was now exposed and only twenty yards from the patrol. However, Ahmed took aim and delivered three rounds that struck the Roman fighter in the right shoulder and arm. His javelin fell harmlessly to his side as he called out in pain. Kareem fired his AR-15 and put five bullets into the soldier's chest, killing him. Three of the remaining four soldiers charged toward Ahmed and Kareem with their shields up and their swords at their sides. Umar shot one of them from his elevated position. The round traveled through the man's neck and killed him before he fell to the dirt. Ahmed and Kareem cut the last two down before they could even get close to striking with their swords. The rounds from the AR-15 rifles tore their wooden shields to bits. The ammo of the modern world cut through their chain mail and leather armor. Ahmed could not help but to admire their bravery as he unloaded his weapon into their bodies.

Nine men died in about thirty seconds of fighting. One Roman soldier remained alive. As the terrorists advanced to check on their handiwork, they found him cowering under his shield and crying. There was no doubt he was confused and scared beyond his imagination. The soldier pulled himself up to his knees and begged Ahmed for mercy. He was speaking so fast and low Ahmed had no way of knowing what exactly he was saying. However, all men begged and pleaded for the same thing when faced with certain death. Ahmed pulled his Glock from his waistband and put a single round through the Roman's head.

CHAPTER 28

Late in the afternoon, Sanchez and Enoch headed out together to conduct another round of intel gathering. Despite the obvious language barrier, with the help of Tobias and Father Patrick, they had developed a system of hand gestures and nonverbal movements to communicate. Sanchez liked Enoch. He had an easy way about him and was a cheerful man. Sanchez did not know if he had always had this disposition, but he found Enoch wanting to help him and his men. Unlike his relatives, Enoch embraced the chance to interact and spend time with the strangers. While the rest of the family was accommodating to the CIA operators, they lacked the overall enthusiasm displayed by Enoch. Sanchez was happy to have Enoch as his wingman as they entered the town square. Or was he Enoch's wingman?

The marketplace was closing early for the day. People scampered around trying to finish up their day and get back home. Stands selling baskets, pottery, and food were shutting down. The more established locations, like the blacksmith and craftsman, were also ending their days early.

"What is going on? Where is everyone?" asked Enoch to the man who, just several hours ago, had sold him dates and figs.

"Have you not heard?" He continued to load up his wares on his makeshift wooden cart. "The Wizard has struck again."

"Where? When? How?"

"Just a few hours ago. He killed an army patrol. He took out ten men and disappeared again. Everyone is going home to protect themselves."

"Who said it was the Wizard?"

"Everybody! The soldiers were brutally killed with holes covering their bodies. It had to be the work of the Wizard. He is a demon. Sent by the devil himself." He scurried off with his cart.

Enoch talked to a few more locals who all restated the same news. Enoch relayed to Sanchez the need to get back home right away. Hand gestures or not, he needed a translator to convey this news. Back at the house with the pink walls, Sanchez took in the updated news of the day. He was upset, but he had to be impressed with Ahmed Faquar. Ahmed had essentially set up Cole for killing the Roman soldiers. By taking out the patrol to match the killings from yesterday, Ahmed was going to make Cole public enemy number one with the Roman army. The CIA men maintained their positions to defend the house and Jesus, Mary, and Joseph while Sanchez conferred with Tucker and Father Patrick.

"This is a problem," began Sanchez. "If the army looks for Cole…what happens? What do we do? I am wide open for suggestions. Can we send the Holy Family to Egypt while we hunt down the terrorists?"

"No!" was the immediate and simultaneous response from Tucker and Father Patrick.

"Miguel, they can't travel. The baby is a few days old. They got a wagon and a freaking mule, and it's over four hundred miles to Egypt. No way," explained the medic.

"They will eventually travel as part of a large caravan of people. They can't leave for Egypt on their own. It is not like they can hop in the family SUV and drive four hundred miles by themselves. Besides, we would really be messing with history if they left now," added Father Patrick. "The Wise Men need to arrive and see Jesus here, in Bethlehem. An angel warns the Wise Men not to return to see Herod. That all needs to happen here. Historically, religiously, spiritually…they must stay here."

A silence hung in the air as the three men contemplated the best course of action. Sanchez had always just needed to make choices based on military and tactical factors. Many times, those calls were life-and-death decisions, but never historical or religious. This was different.

"What if we moved them to the pod until we take out the terrorists?" queried Tucker.

"No. Can't expose them to that much tech. Besides, once they are inside, there is no way for them to flee if things go sideways. They would be trapped in the pod. In addition, the pod is tough but not indestructible. The pod is not an option."

"How will the Romans hunt for Cole?" asked Sanchez to the biblical historian.

"They will go door-to-door and search every house if need be. Remember, there is no Bill of Rights here. People are not protected by the Fourth Amendment. The army will do whatever they want and do it whenever they want."

"But the army is not looking for a baby boy. They are looking for Cole. So what if they search the house and find Jesus?" said Tucker.

Sanchez was quick to reply. "I don't like it. I don't like the idea of us not being with Jesus while Ahmed and his scum are still out there. Maybe they are trying to draw us out. Maybe Ahmed assumes we will leave to protect Cole."

"But nobody knows Jesus was born yet, but us. Ahmed can't know that Jesus was born," added Tucker.

"I don't like it. Ahmed seems to be a step ahead of us. I can't presume to know what he knows or does not know. We must protect Jesus. That's the mission. We defend Jesus 24-7."

"Copy that."

"Father, could Ahmed speed up the Massacre of the Innocents?" Sanchez wondered. "Could he convince the Romans there is a connection between the Wizard and a newborn king of the Jews?"

"How do you mean?"

"You speak several languages, right? Ahmed speaks Arabic. Arabic is like Aramaic. Could he communicate well enough to convince the Romans to hunt for a baby boy too?"

"But how could he? He would need an audience with King Herod for that. It is not like he can just waltz up to Herod's palace and ask for a meeting."

"But it's possible, right?"

"We traveled two thousand years in the past and are sitting in a room about thirty feet away from Jesus Christ. I would say anything is possible."

*****

Cassius had risen to his rank because of his exceptional ability as a manager and organizer. No one in the Roman army could effectively run a camp like he could. Exercises, maneuvers, and marches were executed with precision. Sentry and guard responsibilities were dutifully maintained. The camp itself was set up like a small city, and everything was run with tremendous efficiency. Patrols went out and returned on time. So when a ten-man patrol did not return to base at the expected time, concern grew. Five minutes turned into ten. Ten became twenty. At thirty minutes past the required arrival time, they dispatched another unit to find the missing patrol. The search party returned with the mutilated bodies of ten fellow soldiers. Word spread quickly through the camp, and Lupercal broke the news to Cassius.

Cassius had just finished his midday meal and a cup of wine when Lupercal reported to him the patrol's ghastly demise. Cassius accompanied Lupercal to the Hippocrates's tent to see the bodies for himself. Upon seeing the dead men, the camp prefect felt the acidy bile build in his throat, jump to his mouth, and he vomited right where he stood. The roasted venison, olives, and wine burned his throat and his nostrils. Barnabas and Lupercal said nothing, for they had done the same when they first saw the deceased. Cassius tried to examine the bodies that were laid out on the ground, but it was difficult to look at the gruesomeness. Arms and legs were severed from the bodies. Their body armor had offered no resistance to the attackers. However, there was one body that perplexed Cassius.

"Why is this man's body intact, except for the single hole through his forehead?"

"I don't know, sir. There is much that I cannot explain. I am sorry, but I have never seen wounds like this before. Except, of course, yesterday, with the two strangers," answered Barnabas.

Cassius and Lupercal walked through camp together as they returned to the camp prefect's tent. The soldiers were eerily quiet. Men sat in stunned silence in front of their tents and ate with very little to say to one another. Never had a thousand men made such little noise.

Back at his tent and away from the eyes and ears of the soldiers, Cassius needed a plan. He paced back and forth as Lupercal simply stood and waited for Cassius to ask for his guidance.

"What should we do? Could all of that carnage have been done by this Wizard?" Cassius asked himself as much as he was asking his confidante. "Is that possible? Those men...my men...were torn apart. Ripped into pieces." Before Lupercal could respond, Cassius continued, "King Herod must know. He has his spies everywhere, and he will know. He is so paranoid and afraid of being challenged... I don't know what he will do."

Lupercal, ever the aggressor, explained the strategy he wanted to implement. However, Cassius was not listening and was developing his own plan of action. Lupercal wanted to take five hundred men and tear the town apart, going house-to-house until they found the Wizard. "Somebody must know something about this Wizard. Eventually, we will find someone who knows, and they will talk. We kick in every door in every house until we find this Wizard or someone who knows how to find him. I don't care if it's a wizard or demons or what. Nothing on this earth can match our men in a straight-up fight."

Lupercal's last sentence struck a chord with Cassius, and he used it to support his own design. "You are right. 'Nothing on this earth can match our men in a straight-up fight.' Head-to-head, we cannot be defeated."

Lupercal was pleased with himself until he heard the actual scheme Cassius was going to utilize.

210

"Herod has his own Praetorian Guard of 150 men, right? Lupercal, you are to take one hundred of our troops to Herod's palace to aid in the king's defense. We will pull back the remaining 900 of our soldiers into the camp. Double our sentries, put more guards and archers on the watchtowers, and wait. We will wait until this wizard or demon or whatever it is comes to us. Then we will take him down."

"But, Cassius—"

"Yes." Cassius was no longer even pretending to listen to Lupercal. His mind was set. "Your presence and one hundred of our finest soldiers will keep Herod in check. He can stay tucked away in his palace, protected by you and his Praetorian Guard. I will write the letter myself to Herod, explaining the situation and everything is under our control. You can deliver the letter for me. I want you to issue my orders to the men. Take one hundred soldiers of your choosing, and leave at once."

CHAPTER 29

"Sadiq!" Friend.

"Zamil!" Mate.

"Rafiq!" Companion.

Ahmed yelled these words repeatedly at the Roman soldiers guarding the walls of the camp. Ahmed, Umar, and Kareem sat on their knees with hands in the air, yelling the same three words at the fort.

"Sadiq!" Friend.

"Zamil!" Mate.

"Rafiq!" Companion.

Arabic was close to Aramaic, and the three jihadists were hoping one soldier would recognize the words as meaning friend. Twenty Roman archers had arrows pointed at them with their bowstrings pulled back and waiting to launch. The three time travelers were easy targets for the archers. They were a mere thirty yards from the wall. The effective range for a Roman archer was up to 150 meters. Despite the nine-millimeter Glocks and AR-15 rifles hidden below their tunics and robes, they would be killed by the arrows if they could not convince the men behind the wall they were friendly. Finally, an officer and fifteen soldiers left the protection of the fort and approached the terrorists with swords drawn and shields up. They quickly surrounded Ahmed, Umar, and Kareem as they continued their chant.

"Sadiq!" Friend.

"Zamil!" Mate.

"Rafiq!" Companion.

Ahmed was banking his entire dream of Christ's death on being able to win the Roman army over as an ally. He had to explain to a commander or general the Wizard was a threat to them, and Ahmed could provide help with killing the foe. The Roman officer, an unattractive man with rotten teeth, jet-black hair, and huge forearms, spoke first.

"Stop talking! You are a friend? A friend to whom?"

Ahmed had struggled the past day and a half with conversing with the locals. His Arabic had been very helpful in speaking with the townspeople. There had been enough similarities to make it work. However, asking a merchant the price of bread or an old woman if she had seen a pregnant woman required fewer language skills than trying to convince people with weapons pointed at you that you were a comrade.

"We are friends to you. To Rome. To King Herod."

"Why?"

"We want to help Rome. Help Herod."

"How do you help?"

"We help you kill the Wizard." Ahmed silently prayed to Allah that his words had been right. *Please, Allah, let him interpret my words correctly so we can serve you.*

The head Roman flashed a smile of missing and crooked teeth. He ordered them to stand and then led them through the entrance of the wall. Once inside the fort, they remained under the watchful eye and drawn swords of the soldiers as they proceeded through the camp. They followed the Roman officer past rows and rows of well-maintained tents and dozens and dozens of hardened men. The men were strong and battle-tested. The average Roman soldier was about 5'7" in height, but his body was lean and muscular…forceful. The Romans had impressed Ahmed with the tenaciousness he saw in the soldiers he had ambushed earlier in the day. While the Romans were being cut apart by technology beyond their understanding, they tried in vain to mount a counterattack. If Ahmed could gain the support of their leaders, these men would serve him well in his jihad.

The officer stopped them in front of a large tent in the center of the camp. He left Ahmed, Umar, and Kareem outside the tent under heavy guard. The three terrorists stood in silence, still with their hands risen, and waited to learn their fate. The ugly officer returned from under the massive canopy.

"Which one of you is the leader?"

Ahmed stepped forward.

"Then you. Follow me."

Ahmed walked into the tent, leaving Umar and Kareem outside with swords pointed at them. By now, close to twenty men held an armed watch over the two underlings. Before he noticed the short and overweight general sitting behind a crude desk and before he paid attention to the dozen soldiers with swords and javelins pointed at him, Ahmed was fixated on the eight-foot-tall wooden sculpture of an eagle. The eagle statue dominated the room.

"So you are a friend. Is that right?" asked the little man, who looked absurd in a military uniform.

"Yes." Ahmed removed his gaze from the eagle and focused on his interrogator.

"I am General Cassius. I am in command of this army. You can help us kill this demon wizard. Is that right?"

Ahmed only nodded.

"Can you tell me how?"

"Our languages are similar but still not the same. I will try my best to explain."

Now, it was the Roman commander's turn to nod, and he allowed Ahmed to continue.

"My name is Ahmed. I have two men outside the tent and three more back at our camp. The man you call the Wizard killed two of my men yesterday. We come from a faraway land. The Wizard is from the same land."

"Where is this land? What is it called?"

Ahmed had decided to tell the Roman commander the truth, except for the time-travel part. He was going to tell the truth, not because he was not a liar, but the truth was easier than making something up. There was no point in saying he was from Persia or another location. Ahmed knew very little about the history of Persia or where he could have claimed they were from. It was just easier to tell the actual story. "We are from a far-off land called America. It is not on your maps, and it is a very long journey. And this man they call the Wizard is not a wizard. He is just a man with incredible weapons. He is not alone and has other men with him."

"How do you know this?"

"This man you call the Wizard and his men were sent here to kill King Herod. In America, we do not call them wizards or demons. They are called Delta, CIA, or Special Forces."

"Delta? CIA?" The words stumbled out of the general's mouth. "Why would they want to kill Herod? Why?"

Ahmed leaned over the crude furniture and spoke softly to Cassius. Cassius sat up in his seat to reciprocate Ahmed's gesture for privacy. Ahmed could smell the meat Cassius had for lunch mixed with an after-vomit scent on his hot breath. The two men were now speaking in hushed voices, like two old high school buddies retelling a story they did not want their wives to hear.

"A new king of the Jews will be born soon in Bethlehem. A male child will be born in the House of David. His name will be Jesus, and His parents are Joseph and Mary. This child, Jesus, will grow up to be the king of the Jews. These men, the CIA, were sent to kill Herod so Jesus can rule all of Judea."

Cassius gasped and sat back in his chair. The soldiers in his tent had not heard Ahmed's warning, but they saw their general was upset and moved on Ahmed. Cassius quickly waved them off, and the soldiers backed away but stayed at the ready.

"Can you say that again, Ahmed? Slowly."

Ahmed quietly repeated himself and allowed Cassius the time he needed to process the information. Cassius knew Herod was a paranoid and insecure man. Cassius believed Herod would become a very dangerous ruler if he learned of this story from the stranger. Herod would take extreme measures to protect his throne and the power that went with it. Cassius was determined Herod must not hear of this plot against him. He had already dispatched Lupercal and one hundred men to support in the defense of Herod. Herod would be safe. Cassius did not want anyone else to know about the coming of the king of the Jews. Besides, who was this strange man who whispered secrets to him and claimed he knew the Wizard? What proof did he have of anything? What was this America he spoke of? Cassius was a man of books and study. He had never heard of such a place. Why should he believe some stranger with a nonsensical tale? King of the Jews? What is this stranger talking about? A plot to kill King Herod? Cassius could feel his own strength and confidence coming back to him.

"What proof do you have of this place called America? What proof do you have of anything you claim?"

Ahmed waited and did not respond right away. This odd-looking Roman general had a point. What proof did he have of America or a plot to kill the king?

"America is very far away. America has weapons that differ greatly from your swords and spears. We have weapons like the Wizard's. I can show you how they work if you like. Do you want to see?"

Cassius rose from his seat and ordered his officer to take two prisoners from the army's cells to his tent. He gestured for Ahmed to continue.

"If I can show you weapons that work like the Wizard's, will you believe me?" questioned Ahmed. "If I can prove myself, will you help us destroy the CIA?"

"Let's see what proof you have first."

*****

It was dusk, and the darkness of the night was still a while away as Sanchez and three CIA shooters made their way through the deserted pathways of Bethlehem. Behind them, they pulled one of Tobias's carts that hid Bedford's McMillan Tac-338 sniper rifle. Sanchez was sure this was the first time the deerskin tarp was being used to conceal a weapon with this type of firepower. Sanchez, Bedford, Jackson, and Tucker were dressed in desert DBDUs with an M4 slung around their backs and a nine-millimeter Sig Sauer P226 on their hips. Large and long robes hung loosely over them to hide their modern gear and weaponry. The plan was simple: follow the directions Enoch had laid out for the terrorist camp, and kill everyone there.

McNally had turned into the personal bodyguard for Jesus. He was still in pain, and he was running a fever as his body fought to stave off an infection. Cam stayed in the house all the time and was never more than thirty feet from Jesus. He had not spoken to Mary or Joseph, not even a hello in English. He simply nodded, smiled, and let them know he was there for their safety. Mary would ask him if he needed a drink of water or food or if he wanted to relax, but he would just decline with a smile and a headshake.

Father Patrick had spent the last few hours with the Holy Family. The language translations were going smoothly, and they talked about the importance of family, and they prayed together. Father Patrick had imagined Joseph would have been like Ward Cleaver of the 1950s TV show *Leave It to Beaver*. Ward was the stereotypical father of American life in the 1950s. Ward probably never changed a diaper or gave a bottle once in his life. But Father Patrick was wrong. Joseph doted on Mary and Jesus and was looking for ways to help his young bride. Father Patrick cherished the time he could spend with Jesus. How could he not? Jesus was only a few days old, and He seemed like a typical baby to Father Patrick. Father Patrick had many nieces and nephews and had performed many baptisms, so he felt comfortable around infants. He could not stop himself from staring at the baby, curly hair, chubby cheeks, and a perfect little nose.

Cole was perched on the roof of the house, using binoculars to scope for any threats. He understood why he could not venture off the premises of the home. Xavier was the most-wanted man in Bethlehem. He had become the Wizard. Still, he loved the action of his career choice, and he longed to be in the fight.

*****

Sanchez spotted the terrorist camp from about two hundred yards away. It was well hidden at the base of a large hill and shielded by some large rocks and a small grouping of trees and brush. Fortunately for him, the jihadists must have been cold or craved an early dinner and had a fire going. The flames and smoke made them easier to see. Sanchez did not want to tip off the terrorists to their presence, so the team stayed in the robes and bunched together. From a distance, they looked like four local men pulling a cart at the end of an honest day's work. Through the binoculars, Sanchez only counted three men at the camp. The terrorists had ditched their robes and tunics and were relaxing around the fire in jeans, cargo pants, and sweatshirts. One appeared to be on watch, as he would occasionally get up from the fire and take a quick stroll around the outer edge of the camp with a rifle. Sanchez and Tucker passed the binoculars back and forth and Bedford shared his sniper's scope with Jackson.

"I only count three men," said Sanchez.

"Copy that," they all replied.

"What do we do? Where can the other three be?" said Jackson.

Sanchez contemplated the question for a moment. "Our mission is to eliminate eight terrorists. We have taken out two. Let's get three more while we can. Let's keep at least one of them alive for questioning. Here's what we are going to do." He explained the plan.

The wooden pull cart no longer hid the sniper rifle. Now, it carried the discarded robes of the CIA operators and was being used by Bedford to support the sniper rifle's bipod. The other three CIA fighters spread out in a skirmish line and advanced on the camp. Each man was crouching with his silenced M4 shouldered and ready. When the attacking men were within fifty yards of the camp, Bedford fired a single shot.

Ibrahim had his rifle slung over his shoulder as he stood next to the fire. He had just finished a casual look around the perimeter of the camp and saw no threats. Abdullah and Jamal were snacking on energy bars and trying to figure out when Ahmed and the others would return.

"Do you think he can convince the Romans to fight with us?" said Jamal.

"He got all of us to hop in a time machine with the promise of killing Jesus and a whole ton of Jews. So I would say...yes. He can convince the Romans to help us," Ibrahim said with half of a laugh. He did not laugh again as a bullet tore through his chest. Jamal and

Abdullah dove to the ground clutching their rifles. As they tried to figure out what was happening, they heard bullets whizzing over their heads.

Bedford put his sniper rifle in the cart and picked up his M4. He started running toward the camp to join in the attack. He covered the ground quickly as his long legs ate up yards with each stride. Sanchez's plan had been to take out one jihadist with Bedford's rifle and then pin the other two down to take at least one of them alive. The terrorists returned fire, but their shots were wildly aimed and out of desperation.

Jamal was too afraid to move and was tucked away against a large rock on the left side of the fire. Abdullah had crawled toward the trees on the right and was now in a kneeling position. He saw movement to his left and fired his AR-15 in that direction.

Jackson hit the ground as he saw the AR-15 rise at him. The bullets sailed over his head, but nonetheless, he was under fire. Bedford saw the flash from the gun by the trees and lay down, suppressing fire as he closed in on the camp. Tucker faced no opposing fire as he moved in on the left flank of the camp. Sanchez lay down additional rounds to provide cover to Tucker as he moved in.

Bedford hit the ground as shots now rang out in his direction. Jackson scrambled to a knee and got into a strong shooting position. He saw the enemy firing wildly at Bedford and sighted him for a short burst. The rounds hit true, and the enemy fell to the ground. Another terrorist was dead. All four CIA men paused. There was no return fire or counterattack, so they advanced into the camp area.

Jamal was curled up in the fetal position, pressed up against a large rock, and clutching his rifle. Sanchez thought of the movie *Saving Private Ryan*. He was reminded of the translator who joined Tom Hanks's unit during the search. The character cowered in the final battle scene and shrunk from his fighting duties. Jackson put a gun to Jamal's temple as Tucker kicked away his rifle. The other two terrorists were dead and out of the fight. Jamal was searched, hands zip-tied behind his back, and propped up for questioning by Sanchez. Tucker, Bedford, and Jackson put fresh clips into their rifles, took watch positions, and waited for the other three terrorists to arrive at the camp. Sanchez took a knee and spoke to Jamal.

"I know who you are… Jamal Salih from Paterson, New Jersey. Do a little MMA fighting, right? And you want to kill Jesus, right?"

"How do you know my name? Who are you?"

"We know everything. We are the CIA. Now, tell me, where is Ahmed Faquar? Where are the Pakistani brothers Kareem and Umar?"

"How do you know who we are?"

"I told you. We are CIA. Where is Ahmed?"

Jamal was thinking about the thick plastic zip cuffs digging into his wrists and barely noticed the pistol in the CIA man's right hand. The CIA man tapped the barrel of the pistol against Jamal's forehead and said, "C'mon, Jamal. Where are they? Think. Think. I know you know."

"What is your name?" challenged the prisoner as the pistol was removed from his head.

"I am a CIA operations officer named Miguel Sanchez. Now stop stalling and talk."

"I will never betray my Muslim brothers. I spit on your mother for being a whore!"

Sanchez was getting ticked off with the act. Sanchez stayed down on one knee, and he stared into Jamal's eyes from twelve inches. The action served two purposes. First, it made Jamal stop talking. Second, it gave Sanchez a few moments to gather his thoughts and determine how he would question this man. Was he going good cop or bad cop? His men were busy looking for the return of the others, so he was the only cop. He holstered the firearm. He was going to try good cop first.

"I don't mean to hurt your feelings, Jamal. But based on your performance during our little shoot-out, I have the feeling you may not be 100 percent on board with being here. Why don't you tell me where your buddies are, and maybe, just maybe, we can squeeze you into our time pod when we go home. Wouldn't you like to go back to 2023?"

Jamal leaned his head back, and there was a hacking in his throat. He launched a large brown chunk of phlegm that struck Sanchez's cheek. So much for the good cop. Sanchez said nothing and just wiped his face with a bandanna from his back pocket. Here came bad cop. Sanchez wanted to punch him across the face, but he did not want to break his hand. He had seen too many guys break their hand or a knuckle while landing a solid punch on someone's head. Besides, this guy fought MMA. He could probably take a punch or two.

"Ya know, Jamal, for a guy who was cowering behind a rock and curled up like a baby, you seem pretty tough now."

Jamal stayed silent.

"Yep, while you were whimpering like a little bitch, your pals, Ibrahim and Abdullah, were getting shot to pieces. How does that feel, Ja…mal?" He emphasized the last symbol of *Jamal*, just to be annoying. "Would Allah be proud of his brave 'Muslim warrior' who cried in the corner while his friends were killed?" Sanchez put *Muslim warrior* in air quotes when he asked. Again, just to be annoying.

Jamal stayed silent.

"Jamal, you will break. Eventually, everyone breaks. It is just a question of time, and right now, I don't have a lot of time. So let's just get to the part when you tell me what I need to know. Save yourself the pain and me the time. Where are they?"

Jamal stayed silent.

After fifteen minutes, Sanchez's attempt at bad cop was not working. Deep down inside, he knew he was not a bad-cop kind of guy. He did not think cutting off a finger, slicing an ear, or threatening to jam a tree branch in him would make him talk. For the last fifteen minutes, Jamal had stayed silent, but Sanchez believed he wanted to talk. Not talk in the sense of saving himself from death or pain but wanting to gloat. To brag. To boast to Sanchez how they would win in the end. Sanchez changed tactics and hoped his hunch was correct.

"It's funny, Jamal. Something tells me you want to talk. Talk trash, that is. Tell me how you are going to win our fight here. Tell me how we are the infidels and we are all going to die. Am I right? You want to tell me how this all ends, don't you?"

The smile that came across Jamal's face made Sanchez want to smash the butt of his M4 in his face. But he didn't. He let that creepy, sickening smile on Jamal's face continue without reprise. It was the smile one saw on every movie villain's face when he thought he had the hero defeated. Except this was no act. Jamal's face showed pure evil. Finally, Jamal spoke.

"You are all going to die such horrible deaths. Your bodies will feel such pain, and the mental anguish will be far worse."

"Mental anguish?"

"The physical pain of your death will only be made worse by knowing you have failed. Failed to protect your God. Failed to protect your families, your country, and everything you know will end."

"Gee, that sounds pretty bad." The over-the-top wiseass in his voice encouraged Jamal even more.

"You big, tough CIA agent, you are no match for what Ahmed has planned."

"Actually, I'm an operations officer, not an agent, but that's okay."

"Whatever. You and your men can't stop what is coming. Even with your rifles and guns and whatever else you have. You cannot defeat a thousand men."

"A thousand? How many time pods did you guys steal?" Sanchez joked.

"Only the eight of us are here. But soon, we will have a thousand Roman soldiers marching with us to kill you, your men, and the king of the Jews. The Romans think you are wizards or demons. After we have killed the baby Jesus, we will kill everybody. Jews. Roman soldiers. Everybody."

Sanchez felt his heart drop as Jamal continued.

"Ahmed and the brothers are meeting right now at the Roman camp. They are telling the Romans all about you and Jesus. You will all be dead soon." Jamal laughed. It was an evil laugh straight out of Hollywood. Except it was real. So was the smash of the M4 into his ear.

*****

Cassius and Ahmed exited the large tent and stood in the middle of the camp. Hundreds of soldiers were there as well. Word had spread that "something" was going on near the camp prefect's tent. The Roman command assigned twenty soldiers to keep a close watch on Ahmed, Umar, and Kareem. The rest were there to see the show. The two prisoners Cassius had called for stood shaking, one more than the other, from several factors. They were barely clothed with only an undergarment covering them. The coolness of the approaching night had settled in. The men were also hungry, dehydrated, beaten, and scared. Roman camps were notorious for violent and decadent "entertainment" for the soldiers. Typically, animals would fight to the death, and even prisoners would fight to stay alive, all for the amusement of the soldiers.

Cassius spoke to the assembly of soldiers. "Attention. Attention. This man, Ahmed, and his two companions"—he motioned to the terrorists—"claim to be our friends. They have incredible weapons that will help us kill the Wizard. We are here to see a demonstration of these weapons."

Linus, the watchtower guard who saw the Wizard in action, pushed his way to the front of the crowd. Could this be true? He had seen what the Wizard had done with a thunderclap and bolt of lightning. Could this man do the same?

The two prisoners just stood out in the open. Their hands were not bound. They were not tied to a stake. The two men just stood there, about ten yards from Ahmed and Cassius. Cassius looked on with great anticipation. Before drawing his AR-15, Ahmed eyed the two men. He guessed the first was a thief of some sort. He looked skinny and hungry. Probably got caught stealing bread or something stupid. Back in America, a criminal could shoplift with no fear of the law. Here, it would cost you your life.

The second man looked different to Ahmed. He was taller and thicker than the assumed thief. He had obviously been beaten and abused within the last twenty-four hours, but his eyes were different. He did not have the same hollowed-out look of the first man. His eyes had spirit and life in them. He also had a Philadelphia Phillies tattoo over his left pectoral muscle. Ahmed locked eyes with the baseball fan and then smiled.

Earlier, Nagle had been sitting in his cell. He was trying to figure out if he had any broken ribs. Bruised ribs? For sure, but maybe cracked. Hopefully, a doctor back in 2023 could patch him up soon. Nagle wondered if Sanchez and the team would attempt a rescue. How could they? They did not even know where he was. Besides, their mission was to protect Jesus and kill the terrorists. After that, then they would go looking for him. He just had to wait this out, keep his mouth shut, and stay alive.

The guards entered the cell and yelled at him in their language, which he could not understand. The two soldiers grabbed him by the elbows and forced him out of the cell. It felt good for Nagle to be out in the cool evening air. He arrived in front of a very large tent, and a crowd of soldiers had gathered around. They acted more like fans or spectators as opposed to troops standing a post. The Romans placed another prisoner at Nagle's side. This man looked scrawny and weak. Nagle assumed the soldiers beat him regularly and gave him little to eat or drink. The air, which at first felt refreshing, was now making Nagle shiver, and he longed for a sweatshirt or a shirt of any kind.

Then Nagle saw him. What the hell? Why was Ahmed Faquar walking with a Roman officer? This was bad. Real bad.

*****

The SOG team knew the Roman camp was to their south. Jackson and Tucker now took up defensive positions in that direction. Bedford retrieved the wagon and was loading up the weapons, ammo, and modern-day supplies. For now, they left the tents up, and the fire continued as dusk had turned into early evening.

Just a few minutes before, Sanchez had explained Ahmed's outreach toward the Romans to Tucker, Jackson, and Bedford.

"Maybe it's a misdirection?" questioned Tucker. "A setup for a bigger play."

"No. This guy, Jamal, is just muscle. He is not smart enough to outmaneuver us. He wants to brag and talk trash," Sanchez replied.

"I know it's real. Ahmed is smart. Let's hope his language skills suck and the Romans either throw him out or kill him themselves."

Bedford pointed a thumb over at Jamal. "What do we do with this guy?"

While Bedford loaded gear into the wagon, Tucker and Jackson maintained their sentry posts, and Sanchez prepared himself to do his job. Sanchez had never executed someone before. He had killed men on the battlefield and on his CIA missions. However, he had never done what he was about to do.

Sanchez thought, *This is your duty. It must be done. There is no other option. This is capital punishment. The person who flips the switch on the electric chair or jabs in the needle for lethal injection is not committing murder. They are defending society from someone so evil and dangerous that they have forfeited their right to live. Take no enjoyment from it. Be merciful. Just do it.*

Sanchez leaned over to speak to Jamal. He was on his knees, and his hands were still zip-tied behind him. He pointed Jamal toward Mecca and told him he had a moment to pray before his life ended.

"You won't feel a thing, Jamal."

"La ilaha illallah," Jamal said repeatedly. *There's no God but God.* The prayer ended with a single bullet to the back of the head.

*****

Ahmed could not believe his good fortune. Allah favored him. The Romans had unknowingly captured a CIA operator or member of Delta Force or whoever these men were. What incredible luck. No. It was not luck. It was fate. It was Allah's will.

Ahmed pulled the AR-15 from underneath his robe. He held it high above his head, showing it for all to see. He flipped off the safety and switched the gun to full automatic. Ahmed wanted to show Cassius and the Romans what this weapon could really do. He shouldered the rifle and aimed at the prisoner. There was nowhere for Nagle to run. Nowhere for him to hide. Nagle was determined to exit this world under his own terms. He held up both middle fingers and shouted.

"Hey, Ahmed! Fuck you!"

Ahmed fired on full auto for five seconds. The AR-15 roared. The Romans had never witnessed a weapon with such ferocity and violence. The rounds tore through the prisoner's chest and cut him wide open.

Nagle winced when he saw Ahmed fire the rifle. He felt nothing. Nothing at all. He felt no pain. No misery. He looked down, and he was fine. He put his hands to his chest...nothing. Nagle looked to his side, and the other prisoner was down on the ground...dead. His upper torso looked like ten pounds of raw hamburger meat chopped up with ketchup poured over it. Ahmed had shot and killed the thief. Ahmed hoisted the AR-15 above his head like it was the NHL's Stanley Cup. The Romans cheered and celebrated like they were drunk hockey fans.

Over the cheering soldiers, Cassius asked Ahmed, "What about the other prisoner? They say he has never spoken before. Are you going to...do what you just did to him?" He motioned to the dead man torn to pieces on the ground.

"No. He is with the one you call the Wizard."

"He is C... I... A? Del...ta?"

"I am not sure what he is. But let me talk to him, and I will find out."

CHAPTER 30

"I feel like I am playing a morbid version of Barbie with my niece," said Bedford to Sanchez.

"We gotta try it. It may actually work."

Sanchez and Bedford were taking the dead bodies of the three jihadis and placing them around the campfire. The CIA operators were staging a scene of Abdullah, Ibrahim, and Jamal sitting in their chairs. It was a challenge. Half of Jamal's head was gone. Abdullah's body was in the best shape. Bedford had taken him out with a single bullet. Ibrahim had taken several rounds from Jackson, and his arm was barely attached to his body.

"Just do the best you can," said Sanchez. "When Ahmed and the others return to camp, our ambush has a better chance for success if they think everything is fine."

The plan was straightforward. The other three terrorists had to return to the camp at some point. Sanchez wanted to stage a scene that would make it look like the three dead jihadis were just hanging around the fire. Sanchez and the other three would hide and wait to attack the three unsuspecting men. Bedford would fire the first shot with his M4, and Sanchez, Jackson, and Tucker would move in on the other two. Five of the eight terrorists were already dead. Sanchez liked the odds of success.

"His head keeps flopping over," Bedford said as he was trying to position Jamal's corpse on a camping chair. "I should say what's left of his head."

"These scumbags will be returning. Just do it…whatever is fine."

*****

Cassius believed it was too dangerous for his new allies to be on their own.

"We saw what they did to our patrol. It will be safer for you and your men to stay within our walls. I will dispatch soldiers to help one of your men return to your camp. My men will help move your equipment and weapons, here, to our base." Cassius insisted, and Ahmed capitulated.

Kareem could not decide if these men were captors or cohorts. Kareem headed back to the terrorist camp with fifty Roman soldiers at his side. Cassius ordered the Romans to escort Kareem back to the camp to retrieve the weapons, gear, and the other three men.

Kareem felt like the silent leader of this expedition. He led the way with a flashlight while the Romans carried torches to see. Yet he also felt like its prisoner. The Romans never took their eyes off him, nor did they take their hands off their swords. They did marvel at the flashlight and how it illuminated the landscape. The Romans also had a horse-drawn wagon to transport the weapons and gear back to their base. The men tentatively advanced out of fear of being the second unit attacked by the Wizard. As they approached the camp and were a hundred yards out, Kareem could make out his three friends sitting around the campfire. He was eager to be back in the company of his fellow time-traveling jihadis. The Romans made him nervous. He could feel their unease about him. Kareem quickened his steps out of excitement to be with Abdullah, Ibrahim, and Jamal again.

The SOG team was perched slightly above the terrorist camp on the hill. Bedford did not need the McMillian sniper rifle from this range. The M4 on its bipod would suit his needs this evening. Bedford was lying on his belly and monitoring the advancing party through the night-vision scope. Sanchez, Jackson, and Tucker were in position to launch an ambush once Bedford identified the tangos. The men communicated in low voices over the throat mics.

"Is this guy using a freakin' flashlight?" Bedford asked.

Sanchez answered. "If he's dumb enough to use a flashlight, I am sure he will fall for our fake campfire scene."

"I only see one of our tangos in this group. The rest are Roman soldiers. Please advise on ROE, over."

Sanchez and the other two operators were using some large rocks and brush for cover and had limited viewing of the enemy. With the campfire blazing, Sanchez was reluctant to look, for fear of exposing himself to the enemy. The flames were giving off a lot of light, and a well-trained combatant would see him. Sanchez had to decide.

"Seventy-five yards and closing, Papi." Bedford was doing the play-by-play.

"Take out our jihadist and him only. Do not fire on the Romans. Kill our tango, and remain hidden. Copy?"

"Copy" was the response from each CIA man.

At fifty yards from the campfire, Kareem waved his arms high above his head and called out for his comrades. Bedford could not have asked for a better target. Aim small. Miss small. Bedford fired. The three rounds from Bedford's suppressed M4 traveled at 3,200 feet per second, almost 2,200 miles per hour. All three rounds were perfectly aimed and pierced Kareem's chest, tearing a hole in him the size of a softball. Kareem was dead and down on the ground before the Romans knew what happened.

Sanchez and the other CIA fighters heard the muffled shots from Bedford's weapon. They dared not move and held their positions, guns at the ready.

The shots from Bedford's suppressed rifle had been so quiet that the Romans never reacted. The horse pulling the wagon remained calm. The unit's commander, Standard Bearer Cornelius, was the first to realize Kareem was down. Cornelius yelled to his men that they were under attack. They quickly dropped to their knees with their shields raised and swords drawn. They waited for the onslaught. Nothing happened. They remained still and silent for thirty seconds.

"Are we being attacked?" called out one soldier.

"Quiet!" commanded Cornelius. "The stranger is down and not moving." Kareem's body was only thirty feet from the officer.

Still, nothing happened. Another thirty seconds passed.

"Stay down. Stay ready," ordered Cornelius. No one argued with the command.

Cornelius rose to his feet with his shield up. He hustled over to Kareem and examined his body. He was dead. His eyes were wide open, and he actually looked happy. He must have been killed while he was waving to his fellow strangers. Cornelius was perplexed. Why hadn't the other men at the camp reacted to the attack? Still with his shield guarding him, Cornelius made his way over to the campfire.

The three men were all dead. Someone had positioned their corpses around the fire. One was missing half his head, and the others had large holes in their bodies. The holes looked like the one in Kareem's chest. Another few minutes passed, and all was still quiet. Cornelius knew there was no second attack coming for him and his men. He ordered his troops to load the dead bodies into the wagon and search the camp for anything of value.

Two soldiers ventured several yards up the hill and were swinging their torches as part of the hunt. The CIA men were well hidden and did not move when they saw the flames only a few feet from their positions. Sanchez and his men did not breathe and stayed completely silent. The Romans saw nothing. After a search, the unit only found the tents with the smooth metal rods and odd fabric. Cornelius left the weird-looking tents and grabbed the flashlight for himself. The soldiers turned back toward their own base and headed home.

"Do you think the Wizard did this, sir?" asked a lanky young soldier who nervously moved his head, searching for threats to his personal safety.

"I would have to think so," answered his commander.

"Why do you think he did not attack us? He only killed the stranger but spared all of us. Why?"

Cornelius shrugged his shoulders. He did not care why they had been spared. He just knew he and his men were the luckiest soldiers in the Roman Empire.

*****

The whip landed hard across Nagle's back. He arched his back in pain but bit his lip so as not to cry out. He was back in his hut of a cell, and Ahmed and Umar were "talking" to him. After the demonstration with the firearm, the Romans had tied him up in his cell. Nagle's hands were tied with a long rope. The rope was looped through a ring that protruded from the wall. He recognized Ahmed and Umar from the photos he had studied earlier with the other team members. Ahmed had not even bothered to ask him a single question yet. As soon as Ahmed walked into the cell, he started with the whip. He could not see it, but Nagle knew his back was bleeding. Hal could feel the warmth of his own blood running down from his upper to lower back. Umar had not used the whip yet, and Nagle guessed it was because Ahmed was a selfish prick and wanted to have all the fun himself. Nagle was searching his mind for a way to make the whipping stop and get the hell out of there. However, in his mind, he could only see his mother.

Martha Nagle was a great mom. The beating was not making him think of his mom. She would never hit him or his sister. It was his Philadelphia Phillies tattoo that caused him to think of her. She had told him not to get it. She told him it was a stupid idea when he said he could get a Phillies tattoo at Welchey's Tattoo and Piercing Shop for only $40.

"Why would you want that? They stink!" she said. "Haven't won a World Series since 1980."

But he was twenty-one years old and a loyal fan. So what if the Phils had just finished the 1999 season with a record of seventy-seven wins and eighty-five losses? If he had listened to her twenty-two years ago, then he would not have had this tattoo, and Ahmed would have shot him. Ahmed would not have known he was from 2023 if it weren't for the tattoo. He was glad he had not listened to his mother's advice. A Philadelphia Phillies tattoo saved his life.

After about a half-dozen lashes, Ahmed finally stopped. The gashes in Nagle's back were screaming, and Nagle struggled to catch his breath. He put his hands on the dirt floor and steadied himself. Hal thought he might vomit from the pain. He spit bile into the corner.

"What was it you said, 'Hey, Ahmed! FUCK YOU!' Yes, that's what you said before. Now, you know who I am, but I don't know who you are. Are you CIA? FBI? Delta? What are you?" Ahmed's tone was calm but forceful.

"I'm a Phillies fan."

The whip cracked his back again.

"You are both clever and stupid at the same time. I like that. Now, tell me who you are."

Nagle had learned years ago as a Pennsylvania State trooper the person asking the questions was in charge of the conversation. The actual power of dialogue was held by the questioner. Nagle wanted to get into Ahmed's head. Any way he could mess with him could be helpful. Make the captor become the prisoner.

"Do you want to know how I got here?" Nagle said.

Ahmed and Umar glanced at each other as if to say "Do we want to know this or not? It can't be good." Before Ahmed could reply, Nagle was talking.

"Poor Kumar. Poor Kumar. He was your nephew, right?"

Ahmed only nodded.

"Kumar was my friend. Good guy. Supersmart too. Definitely the smartest guy in your family, maybe the world, right? Man, he was brilliant. Kumar had that odd sense of humor. He was probably too smart to have a normal sense of humor. Am I right?"

Ahmed just stared at Nagle.

"Back to how we got here. Apparently, the fat guy you left behind screwed up. I assume he screwed up. Your plan was not to have your nephew's girlfriend kick his ass, right?"

Ahmed's blood boiled. He could feel his temporal vein pulsate. He wanted to go back to 2023 and kill Omar for being an incompetent pig, and he wanted to kill this man with the Phillies tattoo.

"Do you want to know what happened in the lab after you left?"

Ahmed's rage was building within him. When he was a boy, his mother would tell him to take deep breaths and count to ten when he became so angry, he wanted to strike someone. He tried to use the technique now as the American continued talking.

"As soon as you and your crew left, the fat guy shot your nephew in the face. Splattered his blood and brain matter all over the place. The shit was still on the wall when I got there. That's not a dignified way to go. I feel bad for Kumar's folks. Having to see your own son… dead…with half his head gone. That's just terrible. Don't you think that's just awful?"

Ahmed kept breathing and counting while his grip tightened on the handle of the lash. Ahmed knew he needed this man for information. He needed him alive to find out more about his enemy. However, his growing desire to whip this man to death was growing with each sarcastic word that came from his mouth.

"How could you do that to your own family? Your brother's son. You had him killed. Why?"

Ahmed continued to stare at Nagle.

"Apparently, after killing your nephew, the fat guy tried to rape the woman. Guess what happened. She goes nuts on him. The woman fights back and somehow gets the fat bastard on the ground. She grabs his gun and unloads a full clip into his chest. Is that crazy or what?"

Ahmed answered with a barrage of the whip. Over and over, he struck. Nagle dropped to the ground and curled up in a ball, trying to weather the storm. His hands…still connected by the long rope, kept him close to the wall as he hoped the bombardment would pass. The pain seared through his body. There was no biting his lip this time, and he screamed. Half the Roman camp heard his cries as Nagle wailed in agony. Finally, Umar emerged from the corner and grabbed Ahmed's arm.

"Brother, stop! You will kill him, and we need to know what he knows!"

Ahmed dropped the whip. He was breathing heavily and spat on Nagle's heaving body. Nagle's back looked like a side of raw beef. He leaned in close to speak, not yell, but to speak to Nagle.

"Listen to me. You had your fun, and you got to be a wiseass for a few moments. When I come back, you are going to tell me what I need to know. If not, I am going to hurt you so bad you will beg me to whip you."

CHAPTER 31

The president had decided the only way to get through this crisis was to go about his normal day. Christmas was in two days. He had presidential holiday responsibilities, and he would not be drawn down into crisis mode. Yes, the stakes were incredibly high, but there was literally nothing he could do about it. He could not huddle up in the situation room with his advisors and military brass and watch live feeds of a commando raid in Syria. The president could not pore over maps and reports with his generals as they waited for updates. He could not sit around watching the major TV networks and every cable news outlet with his political brain trust waiting to see which states fell into his column on election night. Those eight men were on the most important mission in the history of man, and there was nothing for him or anybody to do. He had come to this conclusion while he was grabbing a snack in the residence. He had been biting into a Snickers bar, when it dawned on him. He was helpless. They were all helpless. So he went back to the Oval Office and told his advisors to go home.

"We can't do anything. Go home. Be with your families. Pray. Pray for the men we sent back in time. Pray for baby Jesus, Mary, and Joseph. Pray for our way of life to continue. The lab is being manned every second, and those people aren't going anywhere. We will know something when we know something."

*****

"Do you trust these men?" Joseph asked Father Patrick.

Several minutes before, Sanchez had been in conference with Father Patrick, Joseph, Tobias, and Jessica. After returning from the successful raid of the terrorist camp, Sanchez had to plan their next move. Six of the eight terrorists were dead, but apparently, they had formed some sort of alliance or, at least, cooperation with the Romans. Kareem did not appear to be under any duress when he appeared with the Roman unit back at the camp. Sanchez surmised Ahmed must have at least convinced the Roman command the jihadists were not a danger toward Roman interests. He wondered, *How much had Ahmed told the Romans? Was he able to successfully communicate with them? Did the Romans believe the Wizard was a threat? Did Ahmed tell them about the king of the Jews? What did the Romans believe, and what were they prepared to do? Would they fight alongside Ahmed, or would they just give him the freedom to operate within Bethlehem?*

There was no way for Sanchez to know for sure, but he was going to prepare for every contingency. He was still on track to complete the three objectives of his mission. First, protect Jesus and the Holy Family. Second, eliminate the eight terrorists, and third, prevent twenty-first-century tech from falling into the hands of the locals. The Roman officer had picked up a flashlight, but Sanchez figured the battery would eventually die out, and after that, it would be of no use. His team had taken back to Tobias's house the camping gear, modern food, water bottles, weapons, and ammo from the jihadi camp. Sanchez's biggest concern was an all-out attack by the Roman army on their current position. How would they defend Jesus and His parents? Should he arm Joseph and the other men of the house? He had extra shotguns and machine guns. Could his men properly train them so they would not shoot themselves, one another, or him and his men by mistake?

Sanchez had a plan, and he needed Joseph and Tobias to be on board with it. Father Patrick would carefully explain the strategy to Joseph, Tobias, and Jessica. After learning of Sanchez's intentions but before translating to their hosts, Father Patrick stared at Sanchez.

"Are you really going to do that? Will that work?"

"It has to work," stated Sanchez as the group sat around the large table in the main room of the house. It was late, and Sanchez knew from his world history classes the Romans would often launch attacks just before dawn. The time was now for Father Patrick to convince Joseph the plan would work. Father Patrick translated for several minutes, and based on their facial reactions, Sanchez knew Father Patrick was conveying his thoughts accurately. When Father Patrick was done, Joseph paused. He got up from the table and ducked his head into the room where Mary and Jesus were sleeping. His new bride and the son of God were sound asleep. Joseph returned to the table.

"Do you trust these men?" Joseph asked Father Patrick.

Father Patrick and Joseph had formed a strong bond over the last several hours. They had spoken about their families and their upbringings. They had prayed together and had truly connected and shared a mutual respect and trust. Joseph asked again, "Do you trust these men?"

Father Patrick thought of the mission these CIA men had accepted without question. Without hesitation. McNally had laid out his body to protect a stranger when he saved the little girl from certain death. Cole had been distraught when he could not prevent the murder of an innocent woman. Sanchez had left his wife and his son at home. Bedford, Jackson, and Tucker had dutifully manned their posts and were doing the work of a dozen men themselves. Their ticket home, Hal Nagle, was missing and they could very well be stranded here, two thousand years in the past. Yet they stayed focused on the task at hand. They kept working, kept fighting. Father Patrick had dedicated and committed his life to Jesus Christ. It was easier for him to make sacrifices. But these men had not taken holy orders. They were simply doing their jobs. Complete the mission. Defend America. Get back home, hopefully.

"Yes. I trust them completely."

Joseph nodded. Sanchez put his plan into action.

*****

Umar tossed Nagle a thirty-two-ounce bottle of Dasani water. Nagle eagerly drank the lifesaving fluid. Ahmed knew he had to have this man functioning; otherwise, he would gain no knowledge or intel from him. As soon as Ahmed reentered the cell, he knew the man he had beaten so severely was a broken man. He had whipped the fight out of him. The American clung to the water bottle like it was the favorite toy of a scared three-year-old child during a thunderstorm. Hal was lying on his right side, too beaten to sit up and in too much pain to do anything else but lie there in the dust.

Ahmed began the interrogation right away. Umar paid attention and took mental notes. Ahmed sat on a stool, almost on top of Nagle.

"What is your name?"

Nagle answered without acrimony or sarcasm.

The TEP had held out for as long as he could. He had weathered the attack by the Roman soldiers without speaking. He managed to survive the initial onslaught of Ahmed's whip. However, he was done. No longer could he take the physical abuse and beatings. His entire body ached with pain. He knew if he was not honest with Ahmed that he would die. His death would also mean the demise of his new teammates. The priest and CIA commandos would be stuck in the past if he did not make it out alive. Besides, he knew nothing other than how many men there were and what weapons they carried. Nagle did not know their current location or plans. He felt guilt and self-loathing for speaking honestly with Ahmed. But what choice did he have?

"Are you CIA? FBI? Special Forces?"

"I am not. I am just a Time Explorer sent to program and maneuver the pod."

"The others?"

"CIA."

"Who sent you?"

"The president."

Ahmed smiled. The president. Wow! He had made the big time. POTUS was probably shitting a brick right now because of him.

"And what are your orders from the president of the United States?" Ahmed took great satisfaction in asking the question.

"To kill you and your men."

"Where are your CIA friends now, Hal?"

"I don't know."

Ahmed stood quickly and prepared to send his right foot into the left side of Nagle's face, but before he could unleash, Nagle continued. "We separated right after we arrived. I really do not know where they are."

"Why should I believe you, Hal?"

"After we got here, my job was to blow up the pod you had already set on fire. I stayed behind to detonate the C4. The pod blew sky-high, and they left me to guard our pod to make sure we can go home."

"You are going home?" interjected an excited Umar. Ahmed shot him a look that said "Shut up. I am in command, and I ask the questions."

"Then what happened?"

"I saw a Roman patrol coming, so I ditched my gun, radio, and any gear. I tried to hide, but the Romans found me and brought me here."

"What did you tell the Romans?"

"Nothing. I pretended I was deaf and dumb. After a few kicks and punches, they gave up. Then you showed up."

CHAPTER 32

The CIA men used their night vision goggles to maneuver the pathway to the hill outside town. Enoch and Ezekiel were born and raised in Bethlehem and knew the area like the backs of their hands. They had informed Sanchez, when he asked for an elevated area, about the decent-sized hill to the northeast of the town. It was less than a mile from the house with the pink walls. Sanchez and his men, with the help of Enoch, Ezekiel, and mules and wagons belonging to Tobias, moved the Holy Family and the team's gear to this hill. Any evidence showing the dwelling within the pink walls as the command center for the SOG team was gone. It would be dawn in several hours, and they had little time. The hill was not as big and as steep as Sanchez had hoped. Its incline was about a thirty-degree angle, and the top of the hill was only twenty yards wide and thirty yards deep. They positioned Bedford at the top of the hill with an impressive collection of weaponry. The two-man teams of Sanchez and Cole and Jackson and Tucker took positions on the flanks approaching the hill. At the bottom of the other side of the hill were Jesus, Mary, and Joseph. The Holy Family was guarded by McNally and a security detail that included Father Patrick, Enoch, and Ezekiel. The men from the House of David, including Joseph, were armed with swords and daggers. Father Patrick had reluctantly taken a loaded FAB Defense Mossberg shotgun. He had extra shells in his pockets. When Sanchez handed him the firearm, Father Patrick said, "I pray you and your men are successful and I do not have to use this."

Sanchez looked sternly into his eyes and said, "Will you, if you have to?"

Father Patrick took a moment to ponder the question. "I will be ready."

The wagons and the homemade barricades provided the cover for Jesus, Mary, and Joseph. The vehicles and wooden structures were placed in a tight circle, creating a small fort. Because of the military history he had studied and Father Patrick's *Jeopardy*-like knowledge of just about everything, Sanchez had decided not to make a last stand at the house. He did not want the Holy Family trapped inside a dwelling if the onslaught was too much for his team to withstand. Sanchez wanted some level of flexibility in case they were overrun, and the Holy Family was forced to escape. He knew the Romans would directly attack where they believed the Wizard was located. The Romans would have their archers commence the assault toward the high ground. Therefore, Sanchez did not want Jesus at the top of the hill. Also, having them on the other side of the hill would keep them out of sight and allow them the ability to flee toward the north if necessary. They also figured the likely Roman aggression would begin at daybreak. Father Patrick thought the army would conduct a house-to-house search for Cole. They were counting on this Roman tactic to lead the jihadists and their unknowing allies onto a battle-field chosen by Sanchez.

Sanchez did not know what the Romans knew. What had Ahmed told them? Were they only trying to kill the Wizard, or were they also searching for a newborn baby or a pregnant woman? Ideally, he would avoid unnecessary Roman casualties, but he and his men would do anything to protect Jesus.

*****

Barnabas was quickly growing tired of the bodies piling up in his work tent. Literally, the bodies were piling up on a large table. Four more dead strangers were taken in. According to the unit's commander, the Wizard had killed the one man as they approached the strangers' camp. The other three were already dead when the Romans

240

reached them. Their deceased bodies had been propped up around the fire, like the Wizard had wanted them sitting around the fire... dead.

Barnabas was examining the dead man with the single wound in the back of his head when the strange man, known as Ahmed, stormed into his tent, screaming in a language Barnabas did not understand. The large man pushed Barnabas to the ground and began looking at the four recently killed corpses himself. He screamed in frustration and pain at the top of his lungs. Barnabas stayed on the ground and buried his face in his chest. Barnabas looked up to see another strange man enter the tent. Ahmed quickly grabbed the other man by the shoulders and spoke to him. The other man's face went still, and he walked over to the table. He looked at the one dead body in particular. He did not cry out like Ahmed did. He pounded his fists into the table again and again. The tall stranger smashed his clenched fists into the wood numerous times without uttering a word. Finally, Ahmed put his arm around the man and whispered into his ear. The two men then dropped to their knees and began chanting. Barnabas stayed huddled on the ground and did not dare move until the two strangers vacated his tent.

Ahmed and Umar marched into Cassius's tent without waiting to be escorted in by the guard. The soldier outside the tent had tried to stop them, but the jihadists were not having it. Ahmed put the barrel of his Glock in the soldier's face and then proceeded into the general's tent.

"Now! We go now and kill the family and the baby!" Ahmed screamed. The intrusion startled Cassius, and he wondered what had happened to his guard.

"We go right now! We end this now!"

Cassius arose from his seat and raised his arms to calm his new associate. "Soon, soon...we will begin our search for the Wizard and the baby at dawn. It takes time to organize five hundred men. We have archers, infantrymen, and many parts to our army that require time to be mobilized. We will be ready to move at dawn."

Ahmed breathed deeply and started counting to himself. A moment later, he asked, "Has my special request been done?"

"I do not understand why you want the prisoner. But yes. It is being taken care of for you."

Following the departure of Ahmed and Umar, Cassius thought about his future. He had learned much from Lupercal. Lupercal, always the schemer, was constantly working and developing ways to advance his career. Cassius was now the one looking to manipulate the current crisis to his advantage. The entire town and army knew about the Wizard. However, only three men who were alive knew about the imminent birth of the king of the Jews. He, Cassius, would kill the future king of the Jews and, therefore, gain great favor with Herod. He was still trying to decide what he would want from Herod, but he knew he would use his upcoming success to gain wealth, land, and maybe even political power. Cassius had kept the news of the child's birth to himself. In case he failed or the two strange men from America were unsuccessful in their attempt to do away with the Jewish king, he did not want word of his failure to get back to Herod. The fewer people who knew about the second aim, the better.

*****

It would be light soon, and Sanchez was thinking of so much. The CIA shooters had foregone the charade of wearing tunics, robes, and sandals and were in full modern-day combat uniforms. Father Patrick had assembled everyone together, the entire SOG team, the Holy Family, Enoch, and Ezekiel, to pray before they took their positions. Father Patrick had asked God to watch over them, to protect them, and to give them the strength and courage to do His work. Miguel noticed how calm baby Jesus was during the prayer. His eyes had been opened, and He seemed to smile at His mother. Mary looked at peace as she held her child and rocked Him in her arms. Joseph had been quite intense during the prayer. His head was down. Eyes closed. One hand was resting around Mary, and the other gripped a sword. Sanchez's own thoughts drifted to Rebecca and RJ. What were they doing right now? He was trying to figure out what day and time it was back home. But that proved difficult. Miguel thought of the men under his command. He was proud of his men. They had performed so effectively under such intense and bizarre conditions. Would the plan work? So much hinged on the Romans going house to house in search of Cole and for Tobias and Jessica to do as they were instructed. Where was Nagle being held captive? How could they get him back? First, the mission. Complete the mission, and then get Nagle to get them back home. He cleared his head, checked the magazine in his M4, and waited. That was all any of them could do.

*****

Cato pounded on the big wooden door. The sun was just rising, and there was a coolness in the air. Cassius ordered Cato to thoroughly search the home with the pink walls. Supposedly, the inhabitants of the home were the direct heirs to King David. King David had ruled a thousand years ago, and now his family lived in this nice, but not grand, home. He slammed his fist and his forearm again on the door. Six Roman soldiers waited on each side of the door to enter the courtyard. Their shields were up, and swords were at the ready. Finally, an older man opened the door ajar. Cato, with a hard shove to the chest, quickly pushed him back, and the dozen soldiers poured into the home. They spread out quickly as Cato thrust the man against an adobe wall, creating a small crack. Cato started asking questions.

"Who are you? What is your name, and who is in the house?"

"I am Tobias, and this is my house. Why are you here?" Tobias had a quiver in his voice. He had expected this early-morning raid, but the push against the wall had caught him by surprise. Sanchez and Father Patrick had properly prepared him for this encounter. He just had to play it as they had instructed him.

"Who is in the house?"

"Just my family."

"How many people?"

"About ten. We have relatives here for the census."

The soldiers roused all the inhabitants out of their rooms and took them to the center of the home. The soldiers shoved the men into place as the women comforted one another. Jessica was among the cowering women. Cassius strode into the house with Ahmed and Umar. The general had an AR-15 slung around his back. He had taken the weapon for himself when his men returned from the jihadi camp with Kareem's rifle. The two jihadists openly carried their assault rifles and were in full modern-day clothing and gear. Cassius instructed Cato to release Tobias, and the older man stepped away from the wall and straightened his tunic as the Roman general came within inches of his face.

"Do you know who I am?" said the general.

Tobias remembered what Sanchez had told him to say and how to act. He was to be respectful and concerned but not overly scared. He was to speak for everyone since he was the head of the household. If the Romans began interrogating relatives, Tobias was to step in and state he spoke for all. Father Patrick believed the Romans, not Ahmed, would treat Tobias with a certain level of courtesy. Tobias had to talk; otherwise, the CIA plan would fail.

"Yes, General."

"We have information that the Wizard is here. Is he?"

"No, General. He was here, but he left."

"When was he here? When did he leave?"

"The man that everyone is calling the Wizard showed up here yesterday. He demanded a meal and a place to hide. He was with another man. However, unlike the Wizard's very pale skin and bright-yellow hair, this man had black skin and short black curly hair. We made them a meal, and I could hear them talking to each other. They asked me if there was a hill or mountain where they could take the high ground and set up camp. He wanted to be outside of the town. I told him about a hill over there." He pointed toward the northeast.

"What else did they say?"

"Nothing that I could understand. They spoke to each other in an odd language but spoke our language to me."

"What else did the Wizard say?"

"He warned me not to say anything, or he would be back to kill me and my family."

"But you are telling me now. Why?"

"Because you are here and asking. Now that you know, your army will protect us. I did not go out and tell anyone. I was afraid of the Wizard. I heard what he did to others and wanted to protect my family."

"When did the Wizard and his helper leave your house?"

"I am not sure. They were here last night, and I told them about the hill. They were gone when I woke up this morning.'

Cassius stepped back and tried to take stock of the situation. He confirmed with Cato there was, on the outside of town, a decent-sized hill the Wizard could use. Cassius turned to the huddle of Tobias's family.

"Who else saw the Wizard? Did anyone else speak with him? How about you?" He pointed at Enoch's wife.

"Please, General. My family is frightened. I can assure you I speak for my family. You can understand as the head of the house-hold, I speak for everyone."

Ahmed had grown restless. He did not like the body language of the old man. The patriarch looked like he was holding back. He knew more than he was saying, and Ahmed would make him talk. Without warning, Ahmed drew his knife and launched himself toward Tobias. His arms smashed against Tobias's chest, and he pinned him back against the wall. With the knife pressed against Tobias's throat, he screamed, "Liar! Where is the baby boy? Where is His mother? Tell me or die!"

The Romans and Umar were completely caught by surprise when Ahmed hurled himself across the room. Within several sec-onds, soldiers pulled Ahmed off Tobias. Tobias gasped for air and slumped to the floor. Ahmed now had three soldiers on top of him, and Cassius was screaming.

"Stop! Stop!"

A confused Umar drew his pistol, but within seconds, he had two swords pointed at his neck. Several moments of chaos ensued. Ahmed was physically being held in place by the trio of soldiers. Roman blades guarded Umar; the family was terrified, and Cassius was trying to regain control of the room. After several more seconds, the situation came to a standstill.

"Ahmed, stay down! This is not how we do things." Cassius walked over and took a knee next to a panting Tobias. "Tobias, I am sorry for that. My friend is very…excitable. Tell me, is there a baby in the house?"

"A baby?"

"Yes, a baby."

"Just my grandniece over there." He gestured toward the little girl who had been saved by McNally.

"No. I am looking for a baby boy or His pregnant mother."

"No, General. Just us. I told you where the Wizard is. Please spare us."

"Are you sure? No baby boy?"

"Yes, General. I swear. Please. My family is terrified. We have done what you asked. Please." Tobias was playing his part perfectly, as directed by Sanchez. He had not expected the sudden attack from Ahmed, but he had improvised and used it to sell his desperation to Cassius.

Cassius patted Tobias on the shoulder and stood. "We are done here. This family has been helpful. Everyone outside."

The soldiers released Ahmed but kept their bodies between him and Tobias. Ahmed and Umar left the home with the soldiers. Ahmed was angry with Cassius. He did not believe the story being peddled by Tobias. He had questioned the time-exploring pilot thoroughly. Ahmed knew there were six CIA men and a priest. Why would this old man lie to protect them?

Outside the house, Cassius did not hesitate to get into Ahmed's face and challenge him. The older, much shorter, and chubby general immediately confronted the terrorist leader. They bumped chests, and Cassius warned Ahmed, "Do not do that again! I am in command of this search. I alone decide how to obtain information."

Ahmed, much taller and stronger than 90 percent of the Roman soldiers, did not back down. "Or what? What will you do? You need me to kill the Wizard, his men, and the baby."

"Need you? I have five hundred men with me. Five hundred against a few…what did you call them? C… I… A?"

"You need me and Umar. Otherwise, you would have killed us already." It tempted Ahmed to shove the smaller man down to the ground, but he knew within seconds of Cassius hitting the dirt they would thrust a dozen swords into him. As much as he desired to tear Cassius apart, he wanted to kill Jesus even more. So Ahmed took a step back, slung his AR-15 from his back to his front, and chambered a round. "Let's go." He turned his back toward Cassius and headed for the hill.

Five hundred men marched the mile or so outside of Bethlehem toward the hill. A handful of mounted cavalry, fifty archers and three wagons made up the rest of the fighting force. Two of the wagons carried a surplus of weapons and supplies. The third carried Ahmed's odd request. Cassius wanted his men ready to fight when they arrived at the destination. Therefore, he did not push them too hard. A Roman army could march about two and a half miles in an hour. He wanted his men fresh and primed for combat, so they would arrive at the hill in sixty minutes.

*****

Bedford was set at the top of the hill. He used some brush and a small grouping of trees for cover. He spotted the advancing Romans from a thousand yards out. Sanchez saw them coming too with his binoculars, but since he was positioned at the base of the hill, his vantage point was not as advantageous as Bedford's. Bedford gave the play-by-play over the comms system.

"We have about five hundred tangos, approximately one thousand yards out. They are moving at a leisurely pace. I see several mounted cavalry on our left flank. However, they do not appear to be in any great hurry either. We have roughly fifty archers in the column's rear. I see three horse-drawn wagons, but I do not see any catapults or anything looking like artillery. Infantry is packed together in tight formations. There is no sign of our last two terrorists. What is the effective range of these archers?"

"Roman archers were effective within 150 yards," answered Sanchez. "Hunter, as we talked about, they will probably start their attack with a barrage of arrows aimed at you."

"Copy that. As planned, I will start offensive actions at five hundred yards."

Bedford peered through his scope again and inspected the wagons. "Holy shit!" he called out through his throat mic. "I don't freakin' believe this."

"What is it?" said Sanchez.

"The Romans have a guy on a crucifix in the third wagon."

"What?" Sanchez was confused.

"A crucifix. There is a guy hanging on a crucifix." Bedford studied the figure again. "Jesus Christ! It's freaking Nagle!"

The SOG team all replied at once, "What?"

"Did you say Nagle is on a crucifix?" said Sanchez.

"Affirmative. He is alive. He looks like he is tied to the thing."

"Are you sure it's him?" Sanchez got to his feet and used his binoculars to see for himself.

Bedford saw Nagle's beaten and bloodied face. Hal looked like he had been to hell and back, but it was him. "One hundred percent. It's him, all right."

*****

Nagle's cracked ribs screamed with each painful breath he took. His wrists ached from the coarse rope holding him to the crucifix. The rope around his waist dug deep into the cuts and bruises from the beating and whipping he endured from his captors. The Romans bound his feet at the ankles, and his entire body was in torment.

When the soldiers first pulled him from his cell and he laid eyes on the crucifix, he thought, *This is it. I am going to die right here.* Yet now he was confused. Why was he on a wagon following a Roman army into battle? Was he a mascot? A good-luck charm? A sacrifice?

Ahmed and Umar separated themselves from the army. Ahmed knew Cassius would attack the hill head-on. His plan was to use the fog of combat to allow Umar and him to sneak up along the sides of the Romans and take a wide berth to outflank the CIA operators. Ahmed and Umar would approach from different sides of the battlefield. Five or six men fighting five hundred would create the diversion the terrorists needed to find Jesus or his mother. Ahmed wanted Nagle present at the battle for two of reasons. First, he would be an obvious distraction when the CIA shooters saw him hanging from a crucifix. Second, if he became desperate, maybe the CIA would trade Jesus for Nagle, if their desire to return home was too great. It was about 8:00 a.m., and the sun was just burning through the morning dew. There were not a lot of trees, brush, or ways to conceal themselves, so Ahmed and Umar were relying on their speed, mottled clothing, and the Roman attack to outflank the Americans.

Cassius told his archers to concentrate their arrows at the top of the hill. He assumed their barrage would keep the Wizard and any helpers pinned down while his infantry and cavalry advanced up the hill. Their sheer numbers would overtake the foe. The general was not sure where Ahmed and Kumar had disappeared to, but after their confrontation in town, he was hoping the Wizard will kill them for him. Regardless, after this battle, the strangers would be dead, by his hand or by somebody else's.

At five hundred yards, Bedford launched the first of four concussion grenades from his GL66 forty-millimeter grenade launcher. The grenades landed and exploded among the infantrymen. The magnesium-based pyrotechnic chemicals did as they were designed. They caused temporary blindness, loss of hearing, loss of balance, and panic swept through the army. Fifty Romans were out of the fight for at least the next several minutes. A long burst of automatic gunfire ripped the ground in front of the advancing troops. Dirt and rocks flew in the air as bullets riddled the terrain. Linus, who had seen the Wizard in action from his guard tower, was right there. He stopped dead in his tracks and began backpedaling away from the bullets.

"Get back! Get back!" Linus screamed.

The shots were meant as a warning, and a good number of soldiers heeded the warning. They stopped advancing and turned to run away from the bullets that were tearing the ground apart. The officers screamed and ordered them to continue the advance. Some men did as they were instructed, but others just fled the column. Linus dropped his javelin and shoved a fellow soldier out of his way. Just like he had run from the guard tower, now he was sprinting out of the fray. A long burst of automatic gunfire flew purposely above the heads of the Romans. Troops dove to the ground and scattered on the battlefield. More soldiers left the fight as rounds sailed overhead. The Romans were pinned down in an open field and had not suffered one casualty.

The first few minutes of the fight thrilled Sanchez. He wanted to spare as many Roman lives as he could. These men were not supposed to die here on this field. Dr. Stevenson had talked about changing the past as little as possible. Sanchez knew that ship had sailed days ago, but he wanted to avoid taking unnecessary lives if he could. He estimated 20 percent of the fighting force was taken out by the concussion grenades or deserted from the warning shots. He hoped his hand would not be forced to lay down real death and pain on the Romans.

"Hunter, when you see archers ready to go, wound a few. See if they take the hint. We have to defend ourselves."

"Copy that, Papi." Bedford aimed his McMillan .338 at the unsuspecting group of archers.

From the back of the panicked army, the first set of archers prepared their bows and let fly with a salvo. Bedford unleashed his sniper rifle. Before the second unit could shoot their arrows, an archer's leg erupted into a volcano of blood and flesh. A second archer was struck in the shoulder, and he went down, as well. The remaining masters of the bow hit the ground and crawled away, searching for cover, anything to protect themselves from the Wizard.

The officers of the Roman army were hard and battle-tested men. They rallied their troops, regrouped, and pressed forward. The idea of taking down the Wizard was a motivating factor for the men. The fame and good favor that would come from being the soldier who put the sword in the Wizard was the goal pushing them onward.

Sanchez surveyed the field of battle, and too many Romans were still coming. He and Cole let loose with a long burst several feet in front of the first line of attackers. The Romans kept coming with their shields up and javelins at the ready. Sanchez did not want to order a massacre, but if these men did not stop advancing, he would have no choice. Sanchez directed the other three CIA operators on the ground to throw smoke grenades. After a few moments of a smoke-covered landscape, the Romans kept coming. The horses of the cavalry pierced through the black smoke in a flanking maneuver. Sanchez determined these Romans were not to be deterred. They were now well within one hundred yards of their positions and closing quickly. Sanchez and Cole were on the right flank, and Tucker and Jackson, about fifty yards from them, were on the left flank of the hill. The four men had limited cover and were not in ideal fighting positions. They could allow no one to encroach the hill. The risk of Bedford being overwhelmed was too great. If they lost the hill, then McNally and the Holy Family were doomed.

The thick black smoke from the grenades did not cause the deterrent Sanchez craved but made it more difficult for Bedford to see the archers and the army's movements. The infantry went from a stubborn and disciplined march into a full run toward the hill. They held javelins in attack positions and shields up for defense. Sanchez believed he was looking at something like Pickett's Charge but without the rebel yell. He gave an order he was hoping to avoid, but it was now clear he could not hold back.

"Light 'em up!" Sanchez commanded. "Use of lethal force is authorized."

After sixty seconds of firing, Sanchez felt sick to his stomach. He was praying these men would back down and retreat. It was just awful. M4s on fully automatic versus swords and spears. Three dozen men were not only dead but were also torn apart in half a minute. Sanchez's compassion and mercy would soon change to indifference as the Romans pressed the fight with their overwhelming numerical advantage.

Ahmed and Umar made their ways up the sides, just on the periphery of the battle. Ahmed had assumed the CIA men would want Jesus, if He had been born, and Mary, out of harm's way yet close enough to defend. The terrorist leader heard the start of the fight. Grenades were launched, and gunfire was scattered about the field. Ahmed and Umar were moving in concert along parallel lines. Ahmed could see two CIA men in front of him and on his right. They were engaged with his new allies. Ahmed stayed low and kept about fifty yards between them. While he was tempted to sprint past them and get to the hill, he did not. He kept his discipline and moved quietly. Jesus and Mary had to be close. He just had to find them. Let the other time travelers waste their bullets and time on the Romans. Stay patient. Stay calm. He only needed ten seconds with the baby. Ten seconds to change the fate of humanity.

Sanchez and Cole were firing their M4s in short bursts and scanning for more targets. The Romans just kept coming. Some arrows and javelins landed near their position. They were gunning down the opposing force closer than they had been a few minutes earlier. The two operators could not keep track of how many rounds they fired. Their magazines would click empty, and they would quickly reload and keep shooting. Was Sanchez imagining it, or were the arrows and javelins landing closer?

Bedford launched grenades, not concussion or smoke but the kind that killed men, into the rear of the column. He was hoping to take the spirit out of the reinforcements before they made it to the front line. He also scanned the field for Ahmed and Umar. So far, he had not seen them. Hopefully, they were dead and under a pile of Roman corpses. Jackson and Tucker were feeling the same pressure as Cole and Sanchez. They stood their ground and blazed away. The gunmen had been depleting the thirty-round clips three times every two minutes.

Three Roman troopers, with the aid of two cane corso dogs and a cavalryman, made a decisive counterattack at Jackson and Tucker. The Roman army commonly used this dog breed. The charging beasts were muscular and weighed close to one hundred pounds. The Roman soldiers and animals bull-rushed the Americans while they were aiming and firing at other soldiers. Tucker saw the horse charging at him along with two attack dogs. Before Tucker could react in all the chaos, the horse knocked him over. He lost his grip on the M4 and was down and on his back. The first cane corso launched himself at Tucker. His teeth found a home in the meaty flesh of Tucker's left forearm. The pain shot up his arm, and it felt like this animal might chew his limb off. Tucker grabbed his Sig Sauer from his drop holster and put a single round into the dog's head. The horse and its rider had turned around and were about to trample Tucker. He aimed for the horse's neck and throat latch and fired three times. The horse spun to the side and crashed to the ground, almost landing on Jackson, who had to dive to avoid the bronco. Tucker lost sight of the rider but had to focus on another charging canine and the soldier with the sword coming at his face.

Tucker fired wildly and grazed the soldier's left arm. Despite the injury, the Roman thrust the sword and caught Tucker's left bicep. The combination of the savage dog bite and the piercing from the sword caused the blood to flow freely as the battle waged on. Tucker's human attacker was a foot away and was preparing his sword for another strike. Tucker was assaulted by the second fierce dog. The animal was gnawing on his right calf. Tucker fired straight down and killed the dog. After he fired, he dodged to his right, and the second sword strike landed on the bicep again instead of his chest. Tucker's next shot from his pistol landed in the soldier's forehead, splitting his head in two. Where was Jackson? Was he still down? Where was the cavalry officer? The location of the rider was quickly discovered. The sun hit the blade of the sword at the right moment, and Tucker caught the glare of the steel out of the corner of his eye. As the sword came crashing down toward him, Tucker dove and rolled to his right. The sword missed its target, the top of Tucker's skull, but it caught the back of his left heel. Tucker lost control of his pistol as he scrambled to his knee. He ducked his head in time to evade a death blow that was aimed at his neck. The third Roman grabbed him from behind. Before he knew it, Tucker was trapped in a full Nelson hold, and his pistol was lying in the dirt. The dragoon lined up his sword and prepared to plunge it into Tucker's midsection. The CIA medic leaned back and jammed his left thumb into the left eye socket of the man holding him from behind. He kept pushing his thumb deeper and deeper until he felt a pop and he knew he had dislodged the eye itself. He was free from the Roman's clutch. The man screamed in total agony. A gunshot rang out at close range. Blood poured from the cavalryman's head, and he fell to the ground. Jackson stood behind the cavalryman with his Sig Sauer in his hand. Jackson was back on his feet, and he had just saved his teammate. Jackson leveled his pistol and put the one-eyed man out of his misery.

*****

"Somebody talk to me. What's going on?" said McNally over the comms. McNally was in terrible condition. He was a powerful man with tremendous endurance. But the infection in his back was taking its toll on him. His temperature was spiking, and he was running a high fever. McNally's body temperature rose past 102, and his DBDUs were drenched with sweat. Cam could feel his strength being sucked out of him. Cam worked hard to stay focused and ready. He patrolled the perimeter of their makeshift fortress of wagons and homemade barriers. Inside the mini fort were Jesus, Mary, Joseph, Enoch, and Ezekiel. The men had swords and daggers and were prepared to be the last line of defense. Father Patrick was also on patrol with his shotgun. McNally knew the priest's intentions were good, but he doubted his effectiveness if they got into a firefight.

"These Romans just keep coming. We scared off a few earlier with warning shots and concussion grenades, but the rest of them are tough sons of bitches," answered Bedford. "They show no sign of quitting, and I'm afraid our rifles might overheat. Stay sharp back there. I have not identified our two remaining scumbags on the battlefield. They could be anywhere."

"Copy that."

"What do you think, Miguel? How many men are they down to?" asked Cole, as he took a swig of water and grabbed a grenade from his vest. He chucked the explosive device, and it landed in the center of the Roman column. They could not see the result, but surely, men had just been killed and maimed.

There were always a few moments of calm. This would happen during a gunfight. There would often be a break in the action while the side on the losing end was trying to decide to retreat or counterattack.

They communicated openly over the throat mics. The CIA fighters were still good on ammo, although grenades were running low. They estimated the army was down to about 150 men. The rest were dead, wounded, or had run off. The handful of cavalry had been eliminated. They had been taken out during the battle. Few archers appeared to be active in the fight. They could hear cries for help from the field. No matter the language, desperate men crying out for aid or for mercy ran a chill down one's spine.

Bedford reported from the top of the hill that Nagle was alive but still on the crucifix. There were approximately twenty men staying back over seven hundred yards. Two had eyes on Nagle, but the rest looked like high-ranking commanders and support personnel.

"They can't try to come up the gut again. Watch for them to try to outflank us. It's daylight, and there are not a lot of ways to hide, but be ready for anything desperate," stated Sanchez to the team. "Any eyes on Ahmed or Umar? We should be able to see them."

*****

Cassius talked with his subordinates and contemplated his next move. He had lost almost three quarters of his men in less than an hour of fighting. However, they were making progress. At least one helper, or CIA, was injured. Cassius felt he could rally his troops for one more assault. One more push up the hill. He would send seventy-five men right up the middle for a direct attack on the hill. He would send twenty-five up the right flank and another twenty-five to the left flank. If that failed, then he would try to bargain with the life of the man on the crucifix.

The Romans launched another offensive with three distinct units approaching in different directions. The CIA team sat back and waited. The delay was giving their M4s a chance to cool down, and fighting in close contact would minimize missed shots and, therefore, conserve ammo. At two hundred yards out, the Romans broke into sprints and were moving and weaving to make for harder targets.

Wow! Sanchez thought. *It only took 70 percent casualties for these guys to learn something.* The special operators unloaded on the attacking troops, and again, men fell in every direction. Knowing how far they were from the range of any Roman weapon, Sanchez, Cole, Jackson, and a badly injured Tucker stood out in the open as if they were on a shooting range to maximize their accuracy and efficiency. The field lit up like lightning bolts, and Roman after Roman fell to his death.

Ahmed had slowly made it around the backs of the two Americans and could see the other side of the hill. He could also see what looked like a makeshift defensive position at the base of the hill. Two men with guns were patrolling the site. Ahmed was over a football field away. He used his binoculars to study the two men. One looked like a mountain but sick or ill. He was sweating profusely and kept coughing. The other looked healthy but not very comfortable with the weapon in his hands. Ahmed concluded that was where Jesus and Mary were hiding. They were being protected by a homemade fortress. It was the only thing that made sense. Ahmed had to take out these two guards. Ahmed knew his own limitations as a marksman. He was within range of his AR-15; however, he knew, for him, it would be a very challenging shot. Chances were, he would miss and give up his position. He had to get closer. He could hear the battle raging on, but it was just a matter of time before the Romans realized their futility against men from the twenty-first-century and retreated. Once that happened, once the other CIA men were no longer engaged with the Romans, they would outnumber him. The time was now for him to strike.

Umar missed his opportunity, and he knew it. When the two CIA men were in close hand-to-hand combat with the Roman soldiers, cavalry horse, and dogs, he should have sprinted around them and up the back of the hill. However, he had hesitated, and in a blink of an eye, the chance was gone. He was less than fifty yards from the Americans, but if he fired on them and missed, he would give up his position. He also did not know if Ahmed was successful in his attempt to get around the other flank. If Ahmed failed, then it was up to him to kill Jesus. He held his position, lying on his chest, clutching his AR-15, and watched as the two Americans fired with

TIME TERROR: DEFENDING JESUS

precision at the attacking Romans. After a few tense minutes, Umar made his move. He had always been fast, and he was going to use his speed. Umar rose to his feet and took off in a sprint. He was pumping his legs and focused on bringing his knees to his chest, when he caught his foot in the smallest of gopher holes. He went down hard and landed spread-eagle.

Jackson was replacing his clip on the M4 and, in the few seconds of quiet, heard a crash behind him. He turned his head on a swivel and shouldered his reloaded carbine. About forty yards away was Umar. He had obviously fallen and was trying to get back on his feet. He was alone. Jackson took a deep breath and calmed himself. Umar tried to raise his own rifle, but he was no match for Jackson. Jackson aimed and fired four rounds. The first three bullets tore through Umar's chest, and the fourth ripped his throat apart.

"This is Gotham. Tango is down. I think it's Umar. I repeat, Umar is down and presumed dead. He was trying to outflank us, and I caught him trying to get behind us."

"Fighter, do you copy that last transmission? Watch our right flank. I think Ahmed will come up on our right. Do you copy? Fighter, do you copy?" Sanchez was yelling into his throat mic.

"I got this. Go! Check on McNally and the baby," Cole said to Sanchez. Sanchez nodded and took off in a sprint toward the back of the hill. Cole was left alone with twenty Romans facing him from about forty yards away. These men were some of the last remaining soldiers still on the field and in the fight. They mounted one last assault and charged the Californian thrill seeker.

Cole dodged a thrown javelin with a sidestep to his left. He avoided another with a quick move back to his right. The assaulting combatants were now only thirty yards from Cole. Cole fired four rounds that found their mark, and two more Romans were down. Cole fired again, and his bullet tore through a man's thigh. He may have survived the injury, but he was out of commission and down on the ground. Cole pulled the trigger, and the M4 clicked empty. He instinctively reached for another magazine. He did not have one. He was out of ammo for his rifle. He tossed the carbine to the ground and reached for his sidearm. The Sig Sauer P226 held twelve bullets, and he had one full clip on his belt. Cole could see the intensity of the attacking soldiers. Their eyes were on fire, and he could see the spittle flying from their mouths. Cole did the math in his head. He had twenty-four rounds for about seventeen men.

Cole took out the front row of troops with single precise shots, one after another after another. He eluded the point of another javelin, but the shaft struck his left arm and sent him backpedaling. He fired three more times as he fell backward, striking two more men. He was down on his back and pulled the trigger twice. The Roman, who was now standing over him, was knocked back when the first salvo ripped into his left shoulder. The second bullet never came. The clip was empty. Cole grabbed the knife from his left hip and jumped to his feet. The Roman had regained his stance and was attempting to bring up his sword for a thrust at Cole. Cole repeatedly jammed the knife into his opponent's neck. Blood sprayed from the ancient warrior like a punctured juice box of fruit punch. Cole found himself surrounded by the last five Romans. He had twelve bullets left, but he needed a few seconds to get those deadly rounds from his belt to his gun.

For the first time, the Romans realized they had closed in on the Wizard. At only a distance of a few paces, they now saw his golden locks of hair and pale skin.

"It is the Wizard!" cried out one of the soldiers.

"We have him now!"

"Let's kill him!"

"It is five on one. We can do this," shouted the soldier with a red plume on top of his helmet.

Cole did not understand their language, but he knew they recognized him as the Wizard. He was hoping his reputation preceded him and they would retreat in fear. They did not.

The five Romans formed a circle around Cole. Cole ejected the empty clip and jammed in the new magazine. Before he could fire a shot, the Roman behind him charged forward with his sword. Cole spun to meet him, but he had to parry the strike. He grabbed his attacker by the neck and used the man's momentum to toss him into another Roman. Both men fell to the ground in a mash of tangled

TIME TERROR: DEFENDING JESUS

arms and legs. The other three advanced on Cole. Cole fired and struck the officer in the face. A sword was thrust into Cole's side, hitting his Kevlar vest. The blade did not pierce the modern-day protection, but it caused Cole to lose his balance, and he stumbled into a collision with another soldier. Cole banged off this soldier and landed next to the dead officer. The first attackers had untangled themselves and were back in the fight. It was now four on one. The four Romans attacked Cole at the same moment. The first sword cut Cole's left arm, and the second sliced his left hip. He fired the Sig Sauer, hitting two of his assailants at close range. An excruciating pain filled the left side of his body. He witnessed his blood leaking from his arm and his hip. He saw a blade about to crash down upon him, so he dove headfirst at the man directly in front of him. Cole landed hard on the Roman, knocking the wind out of him, as the sword from the other fighter missed striking a death blow. Cole's pistol was no longer in his hand. He grabbed his knife from its sheath. Cole plunged the knife into the Roman's cheek. The blood splattered on Cole's face, and he rolled to his back, wiping the man's blood from his own eyes as he searched for the final Roman.

Cole was on his back. His pistol had been knocked loose, and his knife was stuck in the face of a dead man. He grabbed the weapon closest to him, the sword of the dead officer. Cole got to his feet. The last Roman was right in front of him and only several feet away. Cole examined his foe closely. This was a real warrior facing him. The Roman was shorter than Cole, but he was jacked. This guy had tree trunks for legs and pythons for arms. He also had a look of crazed delight in his eyes. Cole wondered, was this guy having fun? Cole knew he was no match for this man in a sword fight. He hoped Bedford had a clear shot at this Roman. Cole had just taken out about twenty men on his own. He could use a little help from his friends. Cole was confident he could take this guy if he could get him to lose the sword.

"So what's your name? Maybe we should talk this out. What do you say?" Cole asked with a smile.

The Roman answered with a sword attack that Cole evaded with a jump to his right. Cole swung the sword wildly, and the Roman blocked it easily.

"I am tired of fighting. Aren't you?"

Again, the Roman's reply was an attempt to stab Cole. Cole ducked low and threw himself at the Roman's knees. The Roman fell to the ground, and Cole was on him. Cole had dropped his sword when he went for the knees. Cole landed two hard punches on the man's right temple. He brought his knee up and crashed it into the Roman's groin. The trooper cried out in pain. Cole rolled the man onto his chest and applied a choke hold from behind. He squeezed hard, and the CIA man could feel the Roman kicking and fighting to stay conscious. After ten seconds, the struggle stopped, and the Roman was out.

*****

Ahmed knew he had less than five minutes to live. He would make the most of those three hundred seconds. This was everything. From his vantage point, two men stood in his way of killing Jesus. His adrenaline was flowing through his body. He was ready.

"Allahu Akbar!" Ahmed charged toward the two men near the makeshift barricade. He pressed his finger down on the AR-15's trigger, and his legs were pumping. He was firing wildly on fully automatic. Some bullets sailed high of his intended targets, and others landed low. However, one bullet struck the massive CIA man in the left thigh, and another ripped through his left arm. Ahmed refocused his aim on the target and kept charging.

*****

Cam heard "Allahu Akbar!" and before he could raise his rifle, he felt the first bullet strike his thigh. A second later, another tore through his left arm. McNally spun to his left and saw the jihadist rushing toward him with his gun ablaze. With the M4 only being supported by his right side, he squeezed off two shots that were errant of his attacker. He could hear Sanchez's voice screaming in his earpiece, and another shot obliterated his left collarbone. McNally felt the blood pouring from his leg, and he could not move the left side of his body. On his right, he saw Father Patrick raise and fire his shotgun at his assailant. But the priest was too late. Ahmed kept firing at McNally, and his last volley found its mark. McNally was dead.

Father Patrick heard the gunfire, and he saw McNally's body twisting and turning as he was being shot. He saw the man running and firing his gun at McNally. It was Ahmed Faquar. The killer from Iraq and New Jersey was about forty yards from him and moving from his right to left. Father Patrick never hesitated and fired the Mossberg that Sanchez had given him. He missed. McNally was down on the ground, and Father Patrick knew he would not get back up.

Ahmed stopped running and looked around for an instant. He eyed the priest, pivoted, and took off toward Father Patrick. He fired his AR-15, but it clicked empty. Ahmed threw the carbine to the ground and reached for his knife as he sprinted. It was the same knife he had used to commit murder in New York City. Father Patrick was only several yards from the barricade. He was the only person between his savior and this crazed man. Father Patrick failed to pump the shotgun forcefully enough to chamber another shell. The weapon jammed as he tried to shoot again. He quickly flipped the firearm around and now held the barrel in his hand like a baseball bat. Ahmed was closing fast, and Father Patrick swung the gun and struck a blow to Ahmed's left shoulder.

Ahmed stumbled but did not go down as Father Patrick tried to maintain his balance after his swing connected. Father Patrick sensed and then heard movement to his right. He glanced over his shoulder and saw Joseph charging with a sword in his hands. He was headed right for Ahmed at full speed. Joseph hurled the sword at the jihadist and dove headfirst with his arms outstretched. The flying sword clipped Ahmed's left bicep, drawing blood. The blade landed on the ground as Joseph tackled Ahmed.

Joseph's arms were wrapped around Ahmed's head, and the terrorist's face was pressed against the carpenter's chest. The knife was out of his hand, and Ahmed's right hand frantically searched for the edged weapon. As the two men struggled in the dirt, Ahmed landed two left-handed punches and grabbed Joseph by the hair. Ahmed yanked his head back and landed a right cross on Joseph's left cheek. Joseph was momentarily hurt but responded with a headbutt. He sent the top of his forehead crashing into Ahmed's nose and mouth. The force of the blow caused Ahmed's face to explode with blood. Joseph was still on top of Ahmed and landed a right fist on his face. Still on his back and with Joseph on top of him, Ahmed raised his right knee and caught Joseph in the groin. The blow did not have enough power to subdue Joseph, but it caused enough pain to allow Ahmed to push Joseph off and scramble to his knees. Ahmed saw the knife only a few feet away. He dove for it with his right hand. As he dove, Father Patrick planted the butt of the shotgun on Ahmed's left shoulder, knocking him back down. However, Ahmed grabbed the knife and spun toward Father Patrick. Joseph blindsided Ahmed as he drove the crown of his head into the base of Ahmed's neck. The shock of the hit reverberated through his body. Ahmed was facedown on his stomach with Joseph on top of him. Joseph landed lefts and rights on the back of Ahmed's head. Ahmed was a bigger man than Joseph and could absorb and weather the punches. He used his rage, hatred, and brute strength to get to his knees and knock Joseph off him.

Bloodied and injured but armed with a knife, Ahmed was on his feet. He eyed Father Patrick, who was holding the Mossberg like a Louisville slugger, and Joseph. The three men moved slowly in a close circle, waiting for the other to make a move. Joseph said something under his breath to Father Patrick that the priest translated to mean "I'm going low, you go high."

A second later, Joseph dove for Ahmed's legs and wrapped him like an outsider linebacker bringing down a running back. Father Patrick swung his weapon, and the stock hit Ahmed squarely in the chest.

Behind the barricade of homemade parapets and wagons, Enoch and Ezekiel kept a tight guard over Mary and Jesus.

"Do you hear that? I'm going out there," Ezekiel said as he moved.

"No! We are staying here and protecting Mary and Jesus," Enoch said as he grabbed Ezekiel by the arm. "Joseph made us promise not to leave their side. No matter what. It is our job to protect Mary and the baby."

Outside the barricade, the battle of hand-to-hand combat continued. After being tackled and hit with the gun turned baseball bat, Ahmed was still in the fight. Ahmed's back was facing the barricade, and Joseph was holding on to his legs. Joseph's grip was the only thing stopping him from getting to Mary and Jesus. Ahmed was kicking and struggling to gain a favorable position. He still had the knife and missed twice when he swung wildly at Joseph. The Dominican still had his Mossberg club and was trying to line up another swing. Finally, Ahmed had used his strength and experience as a violent man to break free from Joseph's hold. Ahmed was kicking away from Joseph and had the knife positioned to drive the blade into the back of Joseph's neck. There was a burst of gunfire.

*****

Sanchez had taken off in a sprint from his defensive position on the right flank toward the back of the hill when McNally did not respond to his last radio transmission. He knew Umar had tried to sneak past them on the other flank and assumed Ahmed was trying the same tactic. The cardio he did five times a week was paying off as he was going at full speed with his M4. Sanchez came around the corner of the base of the hill, and from about two hundred yards away, he could see three men engaged in hand-to-hand fighting. As he closed the distance, he could make out the combatants. Father Patrick and Joseph were in a fierce and savage battle with Ahmed. No one was between Ahmed and the rampart protecting Mary and Jesus. Joseph was clinging to Ahmed's legs while Father Patrick was trying to hit Ahmed with the butt of his shotgun. Ahmed had a knife in one hand as he was kicking at Joseph. Sanchez stopped running at hundred yards out. He shouldered his rifle, slowed his breathing, and aimed. For a just a moment, Sanchez lost his self-discipline. In the scope of his weapon, he sighted Ahmed Faquar, the man responsible for the deaths of innocent people. The man trying to destroy Christianity and Western civilization. The man trying to eradicate the current world. Sanchez should have seen just another target and fired a quick burst at the middle of his body. However, Sanchez saw hatred and ugliness. He fired a long-sustained stream of bullets at pure evil.

The first round struck Ahmed in the throat. It tore a hole the size of a golf ball in his trachea. The second round shattered his collarbone, and the third bullet ripped through his left pectoral muscle. The next several rounds were literally overkill as round after round tore through Ahmed's head and chest. He fell back to the ground with his torso a bloody mess of exposed organs, tissue, and muscle.

Ahmed Faquar was dead.

CHAPTER 33

Sanchez ran to check on the fallen McNally. As he approached the body of his friend, he knew McNally was gone. He dropped to his knees to search for a pulse. Sanchez realized his hope for a sign of life was futile. Gunshot wounds to his thigh, arm, shoulder, midsection, and neck were too much for any man, even one as strong as Cam, to survive. Sanchez closed McNally's eyelids and said a silent prayer.

Father Patrick and Joseph stood a few feet from Ahmed's dead body. They both just looked at it. Ahmed's eyes and mouth were wide open. His eyes were open because he died trying to stab Joseph, and his mouth was still open because Sanchez had blown a hole right through it. Sanchez arrived at the scene and made sure both men were okay. Joseph left to be with Mary and the baby on the other side of the barricade.

"Miguel, I am so sorry. I shot at Ahmed but missed, and he was on Cam so fast." The priest's words drifted. "I… I… I shot and missed, and then he was on me…" Again, his speech was fading.

"Father Patrick, you did your best. Thank you. Please go give Cam his last rites. Can you do that for him?"

Father Patrick nodded and took off in a sprint. Sanchez needed to communicate with his team.

"This is Papi. Give me a sit rep. Over."

"Hunter here. Currently, we are clear of tangos on the battlefield. They have retreated about four hundred yards from the base of the hill. We are holding our current positions. I estimate maybe thirty tangos are congregated at the far end of the field. They appear to be just standing around. Honestly, they look completely clueless about what to do."

"Status on Nagle?"

"He is alive. I can see him. Still tied to the crucifix but alive for now."

"Injuries?"

"This is Doc," said Tucker over the comms. "My left arm has seen better days. I got a sword wound, and a dog tried to chew it off me. I got clipped by a sword on my left heel, but I will be fine. I've already bandaged my arm up pretty good."

"This is Surfer," said Cole. "I got sword wounds on my left arm and hip, but I will be fine. It hurts like a mother, but Doc will patch me up."

"Copy that. Ahmed Faquar is dead," Sanchez reported. The men let loose with a collective cheer. It made Sanchez smile for a moment. He knew the smile would be gone from his face in a few seconds, but it felt good.

"That's all of 'em! Let's get Nagle back and get back home," exclaimed a happy Jackson.

"McNally is dead." Sanchez loathed himself for being so matter-of-fact, but they still had work to do. There would be time to mourn and honor McNally, but now was not the time. Sanchez's news was like a smack across the face of each operator. It saddened them but also woke them up. There was still a job to do, and they would have to work together even more to complete the mission.

"Copy that," was the unified response. "What are your orders?"

Sanchez issued his commands, and his men sprang into action.

CHAPTER 34

He was arguably the top advisor to the most powerful man on earth. Yet Tom Scott was a heavy sleeper. He always slept like a log once his head hit the pillow. Much to the chagrin of his wife, Chrissie, he slept through teething babies, screaming kids, and important government phone calls that came at 2:37 a.m. It had been a long time since midnight feedings, but Chrissie never let him forget who had cared for their children 95 percent of the time.

His phone was chirping, and he kept sleeping. Chrissie rolled over and smacked him on the shoulder.

"Are you going to get that?"

No response.

"Are you going to get that?"

Nothing.

"Hey! Answer your freakin' phone!"

Scott blinked himself awake, grabbed the phone from his nightstand, and instinctively checked the caller ID: Ted Bennett.

"Talk to me, Goose." Scott would never miss an opportunity to use a classic movie line when he had the chance, no matter the time or situation.

"Ever hear of a website called UnexplainedTruth.net?" Bennett sounded wide awake.

"No."

"Ever hear the name Gretchen Turnes?"

"No."

"Me neither."

"Good talk, Ted." But before Scott could end the call, Bennett continued.

"I had never heard of either until today. Gretchen Turnes runs a website called UnexplainedTruth.net. The site has a story that it very interesting given our current situation."

"How so?"

"In 1987, an archaeological dig in Israel discovered Roman swords, shields, and javelins dating back two thousand years ago. All normal stuff these Indiana Jones wannabes find when they do this type of work. Except this one dig also found shell casings, metal jackets that are commonly used with modern-day bullets."

"So what? The Israelis probably held training exercises or had a shooting range there in the '70s or '80s. Back then, M-16s would have left casings all over the place."

"No. That's not what I mean. The shell casings were the same age as the swords. The shell casings they found had been in the ground as long as the swords and javelins they unearthed."

"What? How can they know that? What, did they carbon-date them or something?"

"No carbon dating can only be used on organic objects like trees, plants, and animals. This technique uses corrosion to date the age of a nonorganic materials...like metals."

Scott had never been much of a student with the natural sciences. He had also been more of a social-science type, political science, psychology, and economics. However, he paid enough attention to know what metal corrosion was in plain English.

"Do you mean rust?" Scott said.

"Basically, yes. These scientists can use rust to determine the age of metal objects. It is not exact, but they know these shell casings were used at the same time as the swords. And there are hundreds of these casings in this one area outside of Bethlehem."

"So what are you saying? Our SOG team had a firefight with a bunch of Roman soldiers?"

"I think so. But here's the really weird part. I thoroughly reviewed this website like eight hours ago, and there was no mention of this story. None. But I checked it again just for the heck of it, like an hour ago, and the story was on the website."

"That means they just posted it," explained Scott.

"But they didn't just post it. According to the website, the story first ran in 2012. It's been up there this whole time."

"What are you saying, Ted?"

"History is changing. Things are happening back there that are impacting us now."

"It's still Christmas Eve, right?"

"Yes, it's Christmas Eve."

"Well, that's a good sign. Give me an hour. I will meet you in your office."

*****

Mary, Joseph, and Jesus, along with Father Patrick, Enoch, and Ezekiel, were heading back to Tobias's house. Tucker and Cole were providing the escort. The wagons were back to being used as transports and were hitched to the mules. Enoch and Ezekiel were at the reins, and the two CIA men moved alongside the small caravan. It had been an exhausting morning, both physically and emotionally. Joseph kept a steady arm around Mary's shoulder as she clutched Jesus close to her chest. They would all feel better when they were back with Tobias, Jessica, and the extended family.

Jackson had the unfortunate task of taking care of the deceased. Always included in the team's gear was a body bag. With the aid of Tucker and Cole, before they left with the Holy Family, the three of them transferred McNally from the field to a body bag and placed him in one of the modern-day push carts. Sanchez decided that Umar's and Ahmed's bodies would remain where they fell. Time did not allow for Jackson to do more with their remains. The operator from New York City collected all their guns, ammos and twenty-first-century gear. He made an extensive pile and rigged up grenades, C4, and a trigger system to destroy the weapons. Leaving behind twenty-first-century weapons would wreak havoc in the timeline. Jackson placed the cart carrying McNally along their route back to the pod.

He would join Bedford on the hill to blow up the weapons and pro-vide support for Sanchez. The SOG leader was taking on the most dangerous assignment to end the mission.

*****

Sanchez walked alone down the middle of the battlefield. He walked precariously past dead Romans and was careful not to mis-step and plant a foot on a severed limb or deceased soldier. His M4 was locked and loaded and ready to unleash on the Romans if his plan did not work. He and Bedford were in constant contact. The Romans were so utterly beaten and distraught about their losses and causalities, they never noticed Sanchez walking toward them. He was thirty yards from Nagle on the crucifix. Nagle was perched in a wagon. Sanchez observed an ordinary guard and another man close to the time-traveling pilot. The second man had a grand helmet with a giant red plume protruding from the top. Sanchez believed this man had to be the general who commanded the army. He was over-weight, looked nothing like a soldier, and he had an AR-15 slung around his shoulder. Only a selfish general would take a valuable weapon and keep it for himself rather than give it up to a man in the field who could put it to good use. Nagle saw Sanchez before any of the Romans perceived an invader stood within their midst.

Nagle cracked a smile of relief, and Sanchez simply winked. Cassius noticed the change of Nagle's expression and soon saw the cause for his change of attitude. Cassius began yelling and pointing at Sanchez, but Sanchez understood nothing of what he said. Sanchez had picked up several important words in the Arabic language, and he hoped his limited knowledge may allow him to converse, just a little, with the head Roman. The troops closest to Sanchez showed no sign of putting up a resistance to his presence. They were too tired and too defeated. Cassius began yelling at Sanchez and waving his arms. The rifle stayed hanging from his side. Sanchez wondered if he even knew how to use the damn thing. Probably not. The chubby blow-hard seemed like the only man with any fight left in him. Sanchez assumed it was because he had not been in the fight himself and had not seen up close and personal the pain and suffering the Roman troops endured.

Sanchez picked up two words that he could translate come out of the fat general. Sanchez had dealt with enough Middle Eastern merchants over the years to recognize the word *trade*. One had to haggle just to purchase a kebab and a lemonade in this part of the world. The next word he felt he understood was *devil*. The general wanted to trade Nagle for the devil. Sanchez figured the Wizard was the devil. Cassius drew his sword and held it to Nagle's throat. Sanchez still had his hands by his side and had displayed no signs of aggression. He calmly and softly spoke into his throat mic.

"Hunter, do you have eyes on this chubby officer with the big red fluffy thing?"

"You mean the one with the rifle on his back and the sword pointed at our ride home?"

"That's the one."

"Affirmative. I got him."

"You know what to do, both of you. Gotham, do you copy?"

"Copy. Hunter and I are a go."

"On my mark," Sanchez confidently stated into the mic. "Five, four, three, two, one…mark."

Sanchez knelt on his right knee and pulled his M4 to his chest in anticipation. Bedford fired. The round tore Cassius's chest wide-open. The next bullet went through his face, and he was dead as he slumped to the base of the wagon. Three men knew of the birth of the Son of Man. The first two were lying dead behind the hill. The third was now dead in the wagon.

Jackson detonated his rigged explosives. The blast shook the ground. With its fireball, the makeshift bomb of grenades and C4 easily destroyed the AR-15s, ammo, and gear the terrorists had used.

The remaining Roman soldiers were so scared and mentally fried from the day that Sanchez did not even have to fire warning shots or hurl his last smoke grenade. They just all took off running as far from the hill and Sanchez as possible. They abandoned Nagle, their prisoner, and ran to get away. Sanchez jumped into the wagon and cut Nagle down from his crucifix.

"Thank you. Thank you. Can you believe those assholes had me tied up like that?"

"How are you feeling? You ready to get us back home?"

"You know it."

Bedford and Jackson collected Nagle and helped him as they moved toward the site of the pod. Jackson pushed the cart containing McNally, their gear, and the AR-15 taken by Cassius. It was not the most distinguished manner to transport their friend's body, but they had no other options under the circumstances.

Bedford and Nagle limped along together. Nagle did not want to ride in the cart next to McNally's corpse. He insisted he was okay to walk. He reported injuries of cracked ribs, a concussion, and maybe a broken bone in his face to Sanchez when he inquired about Nagle's condition.

"I think I will be on the injured list for a few weeks, but I can get us out of here," Nagle had told Sanchez. Sanchez had left them and hightailed it back to Tobias's house to reconnect with the rest of the team. Now, the two CIA paramilitaries and the Time Explorer were slowly making their way across dirt pathways toward their time-traveling pod. Bedford updated Nagle on everything that had happened since they parted ways less than two days ago.

"Sounds like you guys were seeing a lot of action. All I did was get my ass kicked. First, by the Romans and then by Ahmed," Nagle said rather matter-of-factly. He added, "I am sorry about your friend, Cam."

"Thank you," Bedford and Jackson said at the same time.

"For what it's worth, I am glad you can bring him back home. No man left behind, right?"

Bedford and Jackson just nodded, and the three men continued their trek.

*****

Joseph's family was in a rather-jubilant mood when Sanchez arrived. He found Tucker and Cole doing exactly as he had instructed them. Tucker was on the roof, scanning for any threats, and Cole was a disciplined sentry by the wall. A cheer went up when Sanchez entered the main part of the home. The family was celebrating the safe return of their relatives. Sanchez knew they meant no disrespect to McNally. They were just elated and relieved to be home safely. The effects of what they had done and gone through would hit them after the adrenaline wore off. Sanchez figured Joseph might have to deal with some PTSD after the violent hand-to-hand battle. But for now, the family was safe. The strange men who aimed to do them harm had been eliminated. Mary was smiling and had her arms wrapped around Joseph. Jessica was holding baby Jesus, and Father Patrick was conversing with Tobias. Enoch was bragging to other relatives about Joseph's bravery while Ezekiel was trying to explain the sounds of the battle waged on the other side of the hill. Sanchez pulled Father Patrick aside, and they ducked into a side room for a conversation.

"Father, it is time for us to get out of here. I'm concerned the Romans may come back with more men to take us on. I am confident the Holy Family is fine. Obviously, we messed with the timeline…a lot. However, I think even you would say things are the way they are supposed to be. Right? I mean, Jesus was born in Bethlehem. The Wise Men have not shown up yet. Herod does not yet know about the king of the Jews. We did our job. Mission complete. Let's go."

Father Patrick thought for a moment and said nothing. Then he responded, "Miguel, you and your men have performed magnificently. You have truly done the work of God. I am so sorry for the loss of Cam. I will pray for him every day for the rest of my life. And yes, you are right. You have done a terrific job of maintaining the historically important facts about the birth of our Savior. It is a shame so many Roman soldiers died unnecessarily, but you must know, you did all that you could."

Sanchez was not the type to get all sentimental, especially as he was trying to exfil on an operation. "Thank you, Father. Now, let's get out of here and head back home." Sanchez started to exit the small room.

"I am not going with you, Miguel. I am home"

"What are you talking about? It is time for us to leave."

"It is time for you to leave. Not me. I am staying here. This is my home now."

"What about the timeline? The last time I checked the Bible, there was not a thirty-year-old American priest hanging out with the Holy Family."

"I took holy orders to serve Jesus Christ. What better way to serve the Lord than to be here with Him? This is what I am meant to do."

"Father, our mission is to preserve the timeline as best we can. Leaving you here does not do that."

"Miguel, I am a biblical scholar. I will not disrupt the timeline or jeopardize our world."

"What do I tell the White House and the CIA?"

"You tell them I stayed to serve the Lord. You tell them I stayed home."

"Are you sure, Father?"

After a thoughtful pause, Father Patrick said, "Yes. I am home."

CHAPTER 35

Lupercal returned from Herod's palace with a dozen cavalry. He left the rest of his force to stay and guard the king. He sensed Cassius's expedition was not going well, and he returned to the camp. Lupercal briefly interviewed soldiers as they arrived back from the conflict. One frantic Roman soldier returned to the camp after another. All their stories were the same. The Wizard and his helpers were just too much. Their weapons were magical. Thunderclaps and lightning bolts were everywhere. The Roman arrows and javelins could not reach the enemy, and the army was wiped out with ease. Five hundred men had left to defeat the Wizard, and other than the initial deserters, fewer than thirty came back. They shared the same tales of horror and confusion. How could men fight like that? How could they have weapons that killed and maimed with such ease? Lupercal heard several accounts of Cassius's gruesome and inexplicable death.

Lupercal had always been a man of action, and that was why he was upset with the decision by Cassius to send him to Herod's palace. He was a fighter, not a sentry. Now he was back. He was second in command, and Cassius was dead. This was his army now, and he would take action. However, Cassius's plan to overwhelm the Wizard with an abundance of manpower had obviously failed. He had a strategy of his own. Lupercal planned to go after the Wizard. He wondered to himself, *what was the name of the officer who captured the deaf-mute? What was his name? Cornelius!* Hopefully, Cornelius had not been killed in today's battle with the Wizard. Lupercal ordered for Cornelius to be found and brought to him.

*****

Sanchez was yearning to get back to the pod and return to their own time. The CIA paramilitaries were confident the Holy Family was no longer at risk. After speaking with Tobias and Jessica, Sanchez learned only Cassius had asked about a baby. None of the other soldiers seemed to have a clue about the significance of a baby boy. Sanchez surmised Ahmed only told Cassius about the birth of Jesus, and apparently, Cassius had told no one else. Sanchez thought it through, and it made sense to him. Why tell anyone else about the birth of the king of the Jews? If Cassius did not kill the future king, then nobody would know he had failed. If he succeeded, then he could announce his triumph to everyone. Cassius was dead and, with him, the news about Jesus.

Sanchez, Tucker, and Cole said goodbye to Tobias, Jessica, and the family. Enoch wrapped his arms around Sanchez and lifted him off the ground with a gigantic bear hug. Joseph thanked and embraced each man. Mary gave each one of them a kiss on the cheek and thanked them for their protection. Baby Jesus laughed and smiled. Each of the men, Sanchez, Tucker, and Cole, got to hold Him for a moment.

"I am sorry I won't be getting dinner with you and Beca back in 2023," Father Patrick said to Sanchez.

"Me too."

"Please tell her I regret not getting the chance to meet her and RJ. I know she is a wonderful person, and I am sure RJ will grow up to be like his dad."

"I will."

"Miguel, thank you. Thank you for bringing me here. I will pray for all of you every day."

The two men hugged. Father Patrick whispered a request to Sanchez. He nodded, and the CIA men departed the home and headed toward the pod to meet up with the rest of the team. As they jogged away, Father Patrick called out one last time, "Merry Christmas!"

*****

Lupercal had assembled a ten-man cavalry team and had two horses pulling a wagon for the last twelve archers in the army. He was ready to lead this fast-moving unit and, hopefully, have his first opportunity to take on the Wizard. The only thing delaying his quest from beginning was the inability of Cornelius to mount his horse. The low-level officer kept falling off his steed.

Cornelius could feel Lupercal looking at him with thoughts of annoyance and disgust. Cornelius did not want to admit he had never been on a horse before. He had always served in the infantry, and horses were rare in this part of the world. After several failed attempts to secure his feet in the stirrups, Lupercal finally exploded.

"Just get in the wagon with the archers! I should have you whipped for wasting our time!"

Lupercal wanted to punish Cornelius, but he needed him to guide the unit to the site of the deaf-mute's capture. Lupercal believed the Wizard and his men might rally at that location. Finally, the soldiers were ready to go, and they stormed out of the camp on horseback.

CHAPTER 36

"Nagle, you know what you are doing, right?" Bedford asked the time explorer as he punched in coordinates on the computer. "I don't want to end up in 1955 or 2155."

"We will be fine. I just need to run a few diagnostic checks, but everything is looking good," Nagle assured the CIA man.

"You looked pretty banged up. Aren't you concussed? Is your head clear enough to get us home?"

Nagle shifted his eyes and met Bedford's gaze. He winked and went back to work.

The CIA team prepared the pod for departure. They worked quickly to store the weapons, ammo, gear, and tech, including the items Nagle hid under the rocks before his capture. Tucker and Jackson took great care to store McNally's body. These men meant it when they said "No man left behind." Cole and Sanchez stayed outside and watched for anything that might delay their departure.

Sanchez was surveying the area with his binoculars when he saw it. "Damn it!"

Off to the west, about two hundred yards away, the GL6 forty-millimeter grenade launcher was laying in the dirt. It must have fallen out of the overloaded cart. Sanchez was pissed. However, this type of shoddy unprofessionalism was a tremendous rarity with his team. Despite the heartbreaking loss of McNally, the mission had been successful. They had eliminated all eight terrorists. Jesus was alive and safe, and except for a flashlight and thousands of shell casings, all the twenty-first-century technology was on the pod. The operation had been beyond taxing. Tucker and Cole were wounded, and they were all beaten up physically and emotionally. There would be time later to debrief and evaluate the workings of the team. But now, they had to get the grenade launcher back. Over the comms, Sanchez explained what he saw, where it was, and he was going to retrieve it.

A minute later, Sanchez had the launcher in his hands and was heading back to the pod. That was when he heard Cole over the comms.

"We got company coming from the south. Maybe three hundred yards out. Romans on horseback. Maybe ten or fifteen. They are coming on fast."

Lupercal saw it along with the other men on horseback. Out in the middle of a field was an odd-looking object. It was maybe ten paces long and looked sleek and smooth. It was in the shape of an oval. A man was standing next to it. As they got closer, Lupercal could see the man had pale skin and hair that was golden like the sun. It was the Wizard. Lupercal had heard about these strangers who had gained Cassius's confidence and about the weapons they possessed. Witnesses had told Lupercal how these weapons shot lightning bolts that killed men with tiny arrows. Now, Lupercal could see the Wizard was holding such a weapon. Ever the aggressor, Lupercal encouraged his mount to run faster, and the other cavalrymen followed suit and whipped their horses on. When the men were within two hundred paces of the object, lightning bolts erupted from the Wizard's weapon. Some horses stopped in their tracks while others kicked up in fear, almost throwing their riders to the ground.

"Papi, I'm going to fire warning shots over their heads to scare them off. But if they keep coming… I'm going to have to light 'em up," Cole explained over his mic.

"Copy that." Sanchez broke into a sprint toward the pod, his ride home.

Lupercal and the Romans regained control of their steeds. The general ordered his archers out of the wagon and to fire at the Wizard. In the distance, Lupercal saw one of the Wizard's men running across the open field. Lupercal thought, *I can surely take out one of his men.*

He ordered half of the archers to launch their arrows at the man running toward the object. He then commanded his cavalry to assault the Wizard and the object head-on. The Wizard, although powerful, would be put to the test when outnumbered by charging cavalry.

Arrows flew at Sanchez as he ran for the safety of the pod. The arrows were traveling at two hundred miles per hour, which made them impossible to duck or evade. Sanchez tried to make for a tough target and kept sprinting. He was thirty yards from the pod. Miguel was pumping his legs as if he were streaking down the sideline on his way to a forty-eight-yard touchdown run against Notre Dame. He did not get caught from behind that day on the gridiron, but he got caught by an arrow in his left calf. The pain was excruciating, and he tumbled forward. He scrambled to his knees. He briefly put the grenade launcher down and swung his M4 from his back to his shoulder in the blink of an eye.

The horses were closing fast and were now within fifty yards of the pod.

"Take out the horses!" Sanchez yelled. He and Cole fixed their sights on the charging broncos and opened fire. Bullets met animal flesh and bone, and the beasts dropped to the ground. Some of their riders flew off and escaped serious injury. Over one thousand pounds of animal crushed others as the barrage of bullets took their horses down. Lupercal was one man who eluded being pulverized by his steed. He was on his knees and searching for cover. He found it behind a dead horse. Cole continued his cover fire, and Sanchez limped as quickly as he could the last thirty yards to the pod. Arrows clanged against the pod as the last two CIA men dove to safety.

With everyone inside, Nagle hit the button to close the hatch. The door took the longest five seconds of Sanchez's life to shut. They could hear arrows and javelins striking the pod. Cole hustled to store away the last two rifles and the launcher.

"Get us out of here, Hal!" Sanchez barked.

"I need thirty more seconds. Is everybody secure? Remember, it's going to hurt like hell," was Nagle's retort.

Lupercal rallied his troops for one last push. The Wizard and his men were trapped inside this object. Eventually, they would have to come out. Lupercal ordered his men to surround the object with swords and bows at the ready. The Romans heard a slow, rumbling sound originating from the unknown object in front of them. The noise grew louder and louder. Several of the soldiers began backing away in fear. Soon, the sound was everywhere. It was in their heads. It seemed like the painful, thundering noise was inside every inch of their bodies. The pain knocked them to the ground. Lupercal held his hands over his ears and screamed as he fell to his knees. All around, the men were on the ground, writhing in torture as they thought their heads were about to explode.

Poof! The object was gone. The convulsion-causing sound was gone in an instant. Lupercal's head was clear, and he checked himself to make sure he was still alive. He was. His body was intact, and he was alive. The object had simply vanished. There was no sign it was ever there. The soldiers stood and rubbed their eyes and shook their heads at what had just occurred.

"General, what happened? Where is it?" asked a shaking soldier.

Lupercal tried to wrap his head around what had just happened. Things didn't do that. Things didn't just disappear. He looked around at his men. He saw scared and frightened faces. Faces that did not know what to do or what to think. He did not see the faces of fighting men, but fearful children.

Lupercal thrust his sword into the air in triumph and shouted, "We did it! We chased off the Wizard and his men! We have won!"

The Romans erupted in cheer and celebration. Another victory for Rome.

CHAPTER 37

The president and his same five advisors occupied the Oval Office. Bennett was informing the group about what he had discovered over the last two hours. Stories were now popping up online about archaeological digs in Judea that produced two-thousand-year-old shell casings. The artifacts looked like modern-day ammo. There were tales of a wizard who shot lightning, and they found more narratives online about angels fighting demons in Judea. Bennett surmised all this information was positive news.

Davidson's cell phone rang inside his jacket pocket. He checked the caller ID. It was his deputy, Ben Wakefield.

"Ben."

"Put it on speaker," demanded the president.

"Ben. You are on speaker now with the president, vice president, Director Evans, Special Advisor Scott, and Chief of Staff Mr. Bennett."

"Go ahead, Ben. What have you got for us?" said the president.

"They're back, sir. Mission complete. All threats have been eliminated. The child and mother are safe and healthy. Except for a flashlight and a thousand shell casings, all equipment is accounted for. We lost two men. Operations Officer Cam McNally was killed, and Father Patrick O'Connor decided to stay behind."

"To stay?" said the president.

"Apparently, yes, sir."

"God bless him."

EPILOGUE

Sanchez texted Beca and told her he was back. After medical treatment, a shower, a change of clothes, and an initial debrief, he was riding in an unmarked CIA sedan. He was being dropped off at St. Jerome's Church in Hyattsville, Maryland, just before the start of Mass.

Sanchez exited the company car in khakis, a black sweater, and with a limp that favored his right side. The brick structure looked like almost any other Catholic church on the inside. Marble floors, wooden pews, stained glass windows, and a crucifix above the altar made up the interior. An American flag proudly hung on the wall.

Sanchez was supposed to meet Beca in the vestibule. He saw her first through the crowd of people wanting to get inside the nave for Mass. Their eyes met, and he rushed to hold her. He embraced her like it was the first time they had hugged, and he held on to her like it would be their last. He kissed her full on the lips, and she blushed.

"Honey, we are in church. I'm happy to see you too," she whispered. She studied him as he finally let her go. "You look different to me. Are you okay?"

"I am good now. I'm just so happy to be back. Where's RJ?"

"He's in the back with the eighth-grade girls in the play. He's great. I must get back to him now. My parents saved you a seat up front. We will see you after Mass."

He wanted to hug her again, but she was gone. Miguel's in-laws had indeed saved him a seat with the perfect view of the nativity scene that would play out during Mass. However, the church was standing room only, and Sanchez gave his place on the pew to an older woman. Miguel could not think back to a time when he actually sat for Christmas or Easter Mass. Those Masses were constantly packed, and he had always given his seat up to an older person or a small child. The Mass started and moved along, just like every service he had attended. The pastor, Father Charlie, rose to read the gospel describing the birth of Christ.

"A reading from the holy Gospel according to Patrick."

Patrick? Patrick never wrote a gospel. Matthew, Mark, Luke, and John, but no Patrick. Sanchez thought to himself. Nobody in the congregation seemed to notice anything wrong about the author of the gospel. The gospel was read, and then the short Christmas play followed. From his spot along the wall, Sanchez was thrilled to see RJ. His six-month-old son did great during the show. He did not cry or fuss, and the girl playing Mary successfully held him for the full ten-minute performance. Both the gospel and the play included a part of the Christmas story that was new to Miguel. In between Jesus's birth in the manger but before the Wise Men arrived in Bethlehem to pay homage to the new king, a group of demons was defeated by a small band of angels. The demons had been sent to do harm to the baby and His family. Angels who hurled lightning bolts thwarted their attempt. The demons were defeated, and the angels returned to heaven. During the play, the grade-schoolers playing the roles of angels were having a grand time throwing lightning bolts made of foam at their schoolmates who were forced to play the roles of the fiends. Again, the parishioners took all this in stride.

After Mass, the family was standing in the pews, talking about the play and wishing people a merry Christmas as they passed them. Beca handed a sleeping RJ to her mother.

"Please take him. We will meet you at the car."

Sanchez watched his sleeping son and his in-laws leave the church. It was just Beca and him standing in the pew.

"Pretty interesting part of the play with the angels and demons battling it out, huh?" Miguel said with half of a laugh.

"No. Same as always, except the foam lightning bolts were new this year. Mrs. Fischer had them made special. They kind of looked like the NFL Chargers logo, don't you think?"

Beca always liked to pray for a few quiet moments before she left the church. Miguel knelt with her, and she grabbed him by the arm.

"Oh. Say a prayer for Father Patrick O'Connor and his family," she said.

A startled Miguel responded with a defensive "How do you know Father Patrick?"

"I don't," she said with a quizzical glance. "He is a priest who disappeared three nights ago. It is all over the local news. It is becoming a national story. In the middle of the night, he left the Dominican House of Studies in DC. No one has seen or heard from him since."

"Really?"

"Yes. It is so sad. Apparently, he is one of the brightest minds in the Catholic church. A brilliant scholar who speaks several languages. This may sound silly, but the media is saying he is a rising star in the church. He's young, articulate, and highly intelligent. I can't imagine what his poor family is going through...for someone to just disappear like that." She shuddered. "Pray with me. Be thankful for your safe return, for our son's first Christmas, and for Father Patrick coming home."

*****

RJ's first Christmas was a wonderful time. He received too many presents for a six-month-old. Beca's parents had brought their first grandchild enough gifts to cover three Christmases. Miguel was so overjoyed to be home. He felt peaceful, and Christmas suddenly meant a lot more to him now. He had been in touch with his men. They were relaxing, resting, and recovering. They, too, enjoyed a blissful Christmas. Miguel knew he had one more responsibility to fulfill. A request had been made of him, and he had a promise to keep.

A few days after Christmas, as the national news talked about the missing Catholic priest, Miguel explained to Beca he had to leave on a special trip. He had to do a favor for a friend. Miguel got in his car early in the morning. The gas tank was full, and he was ready for a long trip. He had a seven-hour drive ahead of him. Miguel was going to see Richard and Mary O'Connor in Worcester, Massachusetts.

ABOUT THE AUTHOR

PK Mags is a novelist inspired by Harry Turtledove, Mark Greaney, and Vince Flynn. PK is a graduate of Gettysburg College and lives in Pennsylvania with his wife and his two daughters.

Printed in the USA
CPSIA information can be obtained
at www.ICGtesting.com
LVHW091535171223
766490LV00059B/1271